THE EDGE
OF RECALL

www.kristenheitzmann.com

KRISTEN HEITZMANN

THE EDGE OF RECALL

BETHANYHOUSE
MINNEAPOLIS, MINNESOTA

Published by Bethany House Publishers
11400 Hampshire Avenue South
Bloomington, Minnesota 55438

Bethany House Publishers is a division of
Baker Publishing Group, Grand Rapids, Michigan.

Printed in the United States of America

Library of Congress Cataloging-in-Publication Data

Heitzmann, Kristen.
    The edge of recall / Kristen Heitzmann.
        p.   cm.
    ISBN 978-0-7642-2831-5 (pbk.)
    1. Women landscape architects—Fiction. 2. Labyrinths—Design and contruction—Fiction. 3. Labyrinths—Psychological aspects—Fiction. 4. Labyrinths—Fiction. I. Title.

    PS3558.E468E35   2008
    813'.54—dc22

                                                         2008014232

To Jessie,
who conceived it

CHAPTER

1

Houses smaller than her dollhouse, fields stretching out and away. A pond tossing sunrays as she leans against the window, nose pressed to the glass. The plane seat rumbles. She feels it in her fingertips, in her teeth.

Daddy points. "Look there."

And she sees it. Circle upon circle, living branches shaped like the inside of a seashell. Mesmerized, she follows the path with her eyes to the very center.

Daddy's voice holds all the mystery in the world. "It's a labyrinth."

"Miss Young?"

Tessa opened her heavy-lidded eyes to white light, beige walls. For a moment she'd thought she was in— But no, it was the emergency room. She rotated her wrist and winced. Her neck burned, and she could almost feel the grip there still. She drew a ragged breath.

The nurse put a hand between her shoulder blades. "Let me help you up."

"Thank you." Tessa slid her legs over the side of the exam bed and sat up, woozy, as the curtain slid open with a squeal of metal rings on rod. A man with a hawkish face and wiry hair entered. Dr. Brinkley. She'd spoken with him . . . how long ago?

"You've had some rest, Ms. Young?"

She pressed her fingers to her temples and realized that somewhere between arriving and now they had sedated her.

"Sheriff Thomas is back, if you're up to seeing him."

Her chest quaked as her mind replayed the knife flashing, Smith's stunned face. Would she have to identify him? Could she bear it? The sheriff entered, his pants and jacket shiny with rain.

"Is he . . . is he dead?"

"We went over the property, Ms. Young. There's nothing to indicate a homicide."

She had a moment of disconnect. What was he saying? "You didn't find Smith?" Her throat constricted. "That's impossible."

"The rain's ruined what trace of an altercation there might have been."

She jolted. "Someone attacked us. He stabbed Smith."

"Someone not quite human."

"I didn't say he wasn't human, just grotesque, misshapen—"

"Pale and malformed, rotten teeth and milky eyes. Wasn't that the description?"

The description conjured up his image. "Yes. That's what I saw."

The sheriff slid out the pad he'd jotted her words on before. "Yours was the only vehicle."

She nodded. "I don't know how he got there, but it isn't the first time. I thought I saw him weeks ago."

"You said your boss was six-one, one-eighty. How would this small, malformed person with no transportation—"

"He must have hidden Smith, buried . . . the body."

"We searched the field and surrounding woods." The sheriff

looked her over slowly. "I'll round up some dogs in the morning, but before I do, why don't you tell me what really happened?"

She stared. "What do you mean?"

"It appears you had a scuffle, but frankly, your story is . . ." He spread his hands. "Not plausible."

Her panic rose. "It's not a story. I barely got away. Someone attacked us. He—" She fought the grief that raised the pitch of her voice. "Have you talked to Smith Chandler? Can you tell me he's alive?"

The sheriff narrowed his eyes. "I'm going to give you a while to come to grips with things, rethink your statement. Go home now, and we'll talk in the morning."

Dazed, she got up and went out, shivering, to the dark, wet street. Go home? She was so far from home it made her head spin. Before driving her rental car back to the inn some miles out of town, she would try once more to make the sheriff listen. She huddled under the covered entrance and speed-dialed her phone, needing someone to vouch for her, someone with credibility, to make them realize she could never imagine something like this.

"Dr. Brenner? I'm sorry to call so late, but I need you to talk to someone."

"Hello, Tessa. Would that someone be Sheriff Thomas?"

Her jaw dropped. "You spoke to him?"

"You listed me as your emergency contact, and he was concerned. He said you were hysterical and incoherent."

She brushed her hair back with shaky fingers. "Did he tell you why?"

"He told me what you said."

"You mean what happened."

The pause said too much. "Tessa, this . . . experience. You do see the similarity to your dreams."

Her breath made a slow escape.

"All your classic elements—the maze, the fear of losing some-one, abandonment. Even a monster."

"It's not a maze—it's a labyrinth. And I can tell the difference between dreams and reality." Her voice broke. "I saw someone stab Smith."

"As his rejection stabbed you?"

"I . . . You can't think—"

"Listen to me, Tessa. It's possible the scenario you're describing is playing out like one of your dreams—or worse, that the real issues you've been dealing with have pushed you to a breaking point."

She started to shake. "Yes, I have dreams, terrible dreams. I also have a life. And I know the difference between what happens in my dreams and what happens in my life."

"To a soldier with PTSD, bombs landing on his home seem very real. The mind is a powerful thing."

She closed her eyes. "This is not in my mind."

"The condition can cause a person to overreact to a perceived threat or injury."

"What are you saying?"

"I want you to come back to Cedar Grove. Let me evaluate you . . . before you're charged with a crime you may not have been able to control."

"You can't believe I would hurt Smith."

"I think it more likely you've broken with reality."

"What about that I'm telling the truth?"

His silence stung. She hung up and clutched the phone to her throat. Fear and dread loomed like monsters, but this was real. She knew it. Only . . .

With trembling fingers, she dialed another number.

Wet and shivering, Tessa dragged herself up the inn stairs to her room. She locked the door and window, dragged the wing chair over to the door and propped it beneath the knob. Enfolded by the soft yellow walls and cozy furnishings, she surrendered to the grief. Smith was gone, and the hurt overwhelmed her. Hurt and fear. Every creak, every muffled noise set her heart pounding. She tried to close her eyes, but the pale face and eyes of his murderer were etched on the back of her eyelids. She had not dreamed or imagined him.

Perhaps she dozed, for she followed endless paths in endless circles until the cold morning light woke her. She opened her eyes and sat up. The sedative had left her brain filmy. Had Dr. Brenner authorized or even prescribed the medication? She had been hysterical, running for her life after seeing Smith fall.

Pain came, as hard and relentless as the rain outside. She wished she could believe nothing had happened, but Smith would have answered her call if he could. She checked her watch. Last night she had collapsed in her clothes, but she tore them off now and changed into clean khakis and a T-shirt. Her wrist throbbed as she ran a brush through her hair and pulled it into a ponytail, impatient with each minute that kept her from answers.

At the station, she found Sheriff Thomas conferring with a deputy. The sheriff finished his bite of bagel, took a swig of coffee, and cleared his throat. "Too much rain to go out there, Ms. Young. Dogs won't pick up a scent, and the ground's been ruined for footprints." He wiped his mouth. "So why don't we get the real story, now that you're settled down."

"Smith Chandler was stabbed in the labyrinth field, just past the old foundation. I saw him fall. I saw him lying in the rain."

"Where's the knife? What did you do with the body?"

Her chest constricted. The red sags under the sheriff's eyes and his drooping jowls gave him the look of a bloodhound, but he was on the wrong scent.

"We searched everything, Ms. Young, including your weird crop circles or whatever you're cutting out there." Sheriff Thomas cleared the gruff edge from his throat. "This will go down so much better if you just come clean."

"I told you what happened."

He shook his head. "I'm going to find out. Until then, it's probably best you don't leave the county."

Returning to the inn, she closed herself into the room, anger rising. Dr. Brenner had fed the sheriff's suspicion instead of giving her credibility. So what if this event had connections to her dreams? She was a specialist in labyrinths. Her work always overlapped the subconscious elements that haunted her sleep.

She went and stood at the rain-streaked window. Could anyone truly believe she'd killed Smith? The thought that she may have had a psychotic break and imagined it all shook her, but if there was no body and no evidence of murder, then Smith was alive, somewhere. Oh, please—let it have all been in her head.

CHAPTER

2

Five weeks before . . .

The pungent smell of roses permeated the air as the sun warmed the blooms. Tessa opened her eyes once more to the finished labyrinth bathed by the sun's honeyed glow. Leaning forward in the cherry-picker basket, she photographed the five-circuit classical labyrinth forming a single winding path to peace and wisdom—or, in this case, remembrance, as demonstrated by the rosebushes that formed the boundaries.

"There must be roses," Alicia Beauprez had said, her eyes misty. "On our first anniversary Roger gave me a single red bud. Our second anniversary, a red and a white, then red and white and yellow. Never a duplicate among them. Last year there were fifty-two varieties for fifty-two beautiful years."

Though she had never created a rose labyrinth, for several valid reasons, Tessa had not dissuaded her. It was Mrs. Beauprez's prayer walk, and she wanted roses to recall the love of her life along the way. So Tessa had interspersed hawthorn with forty multi-hued rosebushes to line the path, and a dozen black-cherry tree roses stood on three-foot stems around a bench at the center where Alicia could sit to enjoy them.

From her elevated position, Tessa photographed the entire landscape project. The labyrinth centered the property behind the house, giving the manicured lawns a focal point, and though it was her favorite element, it wasn't the whole story. She had terraced the difficult side yard with quince and hydrangeas and accented the patio areas with massive overflowing garden urns. The front fountain featured dual-height jets for a tiered effect in the brick-paved circular drive.

Satisfied, she signaled Jerome that she was finished shooting, and the cherry picker accordion-folded beneath her.

"All good?" Jerome raised his brows, knowing the delight she took in each completion, especially when the project included a labyrinth.

"Oh yes." She hopped to the ground. "I'll take Mrs. Beauprez for her final walkthrough, and then we'll pack things up. Nice work, as always." Her cell phone vibrated on her hip. Since it wasn't a number she recognized, she answered professionally. "Tessa Young speaking."

"Tessa, hello. This is Smith Chandler."

At that, her professionalism fled. The accent and timbre of his voice disarmed her as time warped and the past became achingly present.

"From Cornell."

She didn't need clarification. She was back there in her mind already, a little hopeful, a little lost. . . .

"Tessa, are you there?"

"I'm here."

"Is now a good time to talk? I've something I'd like to run by you."

Jerome and the crew were capable of loading the tools and equipment, but Mrs. Beauprez would be expecting her tour. Most of all, she could not talk to Smith without preparing herself. "Actually, it's not convenient. Can you call back in a couple of hours?" When she'd regained her equilibrium, if that was possible.

"Yes, all right. But, Tessa—it's important."

She closed the phone, took a deep breath, and went to find Mrs. Beauprez. Witnessing the joy in her clients' faces made all the hard work worth it. And this had been a dream project. After seeing photographs of previous work, Mrs. Beauprez had embraced her suggestion to make the formal garden into a contemplative path that led to the center and back. She would not let Smith's call interfere with the pleasure of leading her client down that rose-scented path.

The sun had dipped to half-mast by the time she returned to her hotel room. She untied and tugged off her Wolverine steel-toed work boots, changed into a fresh T-shirt, and splashed her face with cool water from the bathroom sink. The Beauprez landscape completed her current projects except for some consulting, design, and research, and she was eager to get home.

Five hours and forty-three minutes since Smith's call, he had still not called back. Typical, self-absorbed Smith. He knew it would drive her crazy not to know what he'd wanted—though not enough to call him. She tossed the phone onto the comforter and began to pack. As much as she enjoyed the different places she worked, going home grounded her.

She zipped up the suitcase, leaned back on her heels, and groaned as her thoughts circled back to Smith. He'd sounded excited. His plans and ideas had always enlivened him. She wished just hearing that eager tone in his voice hadn't conjured up the animated look in his gray-blue eyes, the motion of his hands as he described whatever it was. She should have heard him out and been done with it.

She turned and caught her reflection in the mirror. The enemies that had haunted her since childhood stared back. Doubt, uncertainty, fear. All her Pyrrhic victories amounting to nothing once more. How could she have anticipated a call from the friend she'd half fallen in love with a dozen times before catching herself?

Her phone rang, and for a second she considered not answering, but the anxiety of the last few hours dashed that thought. Better to know and be done with it than to keep wondering. She stepped over her suitcase. "Hello?"

"Tessa, it's Smith. I'm sorry it took so long to call back."

"Did it?" Sitting down on the edge of the bed, she pressed a hand to her face, waiting.

"Let me say, it's good to talk to you."

No way could she say the same, even if she wanted to.

"I saw your write-up in *Architectural Digest* and couldn't believe I knew the artist who'd created that labyrinth garden."

Her breath made a hard escape. That from the man who'd ridiculed her vision?

"You've made that crazy idea work."

"Maybe because it wasn't crazy." She lay back on the bed. That article had run two years ago. He could have picked up a phone and called her then if he was so impressed.

"So, anyway, I have a proposition I think you'll find intriguing."

She laid her arm across her forehead. "I'll just bet you do."

Smith leaned back in the squeaky desk chair and crossed his feet. Tessa sounded touchier than ever. The last thing he wanted was to irritate her, but was it humanly possible to avoid that? She would expect a complete explanation, and yet he couldn't violate the non-disclosure agreement.

She'd told him once that she loved lines, lines connecting one point to another—straight, curved, angled, as long as they served the purpose of continuity. She even liked lines at the store to keep people from trampling one another, lines into a movie on opening night to assure seating in the proper order.

He'd laughed, but she liked knowing one thing logically led to another. She didn't like surprises, just wanted to know which direction the line went and what connection it had to her. So straight to the end, without details? Best perhaps. "I want you to come to Maryland."

"For what?"

"I'm assembling a design team for a project that has something that will interest you greatly." That was as straight as he could put it. "I promise you won't be disappointed, Tessa, if you come and see for yourself."

"What makes you think that's possible? I have a very full schedule."

"I spoke with your secretary—"

"My assistant."

"Right. She said that you'd finished up a major landscape and had some downtime."

"I use downtime for design and research. I contribute to several publications and can't take off on a whim."

"Whim?" Smith ran a hand through his hair. "This is a serious offer. And you're so close, just a short trip north."

"How do you know where I am?"

"Again your sec—assistant, I'm afraid."

She sighed. "I haven't been home in two months. You can't call me up after six years and expect me to drop everything."

Smith looked at the contract he had laid out and ready. "You won't be disappointed."

"Oh no. You could never disappoint me."

Smith took the phone from his ear and stared, then replaced it. "Have I . . . missed something insulting in this offer?"

"Yes. It's insulting to think I'd run up there simply because you read about me in a magazine and think you can capitalize on it."

He rubbed his forehead. "It's not becau—"

"I suppose I'm flattered you now find my work useful to your project, but I actually remember you laughing with your friends. So no, I'm not really interested in working with you." The connection ended.

Smith stared at his phone. Laughing with his friends? Well, he had been angry and disappointed when she'd switched majors and gone a direction he'd seen no future in. He had felt compelled to dissuade her after all his mentoring. But that was ancient history. They had the chance now to combine their talents, yet she'd refused. Without even hearing him out.

She hadn't changed at all. Still an eggshell, cracking at every slight, imagining affronts where no affronts were intended. He hit his palm on his thigh. He had to get her on board. Aside from the fact that he truly did like and respect her, she was the perfect person for the project. Not because he meant to capitalize on her reputation—though he had yet to catch the notice she had—but because only Tessa could properly appreciate and take charge of what he'd found.

"Well?" Bair came into the office. "Got the labyrinth specialist?"

"Almost. We're talking again tomorrow." If she'd even take his call.

Gripping her shoulders with her hands, she presses into the thorny foliage, trying to be small, invisible. Lightning splits the sky. Thunder

cracks. She runs. Needles slide beneath her feet. She falls, sinking, sliding.
Her mouth forms a silent scream as she hears him coming. . . .

Tessa shot up, gasping in the darkness, her heart pounding the pulse in her neck. She held her face between her clammy hands, then, needing to see, fumbled for the lamp switch and searched the corners of the hotel room. Nothing lurking. She threw the comforter off and swung her feet to the solid, dry floor. She was safe.

She drew a deep breath to still the terror and dragged her briefcase onto the bed. She knew the drill. Doing something productive, something creative would take her mind off the dream. Don't search it for meaning. Get outside the emotions and stay there. She opened the briefcase. Her cell phone slipped out and lay on the comforter. Heart still pounding, she picked it up, tempted to call Dr. Brenner, who would talk her through this nightmare as he had so many others. No.

She had not disturbed him in the middle of the night for more than four years. Doing so now would indicate a deeper dependence than there was. Besides, if she called, what would she say, that Smith had caused a nightmare, reopened a wound? Dr. Brenner would tell her she was not a little girl anymore, that some monsters could be faced.

She could hear his placid voice as though he sat across the room from her. She couldn't confront her missing father or her dead mother for answers or explanations. But Smith's offer presented a chance to face someone who had hurt her. It might give her a way to make peace with the abandonment that drained her energy, her optimism, her faith.

Her stomach churned at the thought of confrontation, of holding someone accountable for wounding her. She had broken a cold sweat after disconnecting from Smith, after saying what had sprung to her lips before she could stop it. How could she face him now?

But if she didn't, she'd be the coward who'd had the chance and couldn't take it.

Hand shaking, she picked up the phone, leaned against the headboard, and punched the number. Her heart beat more wildly than in her dream. This shouldn't be so hard.

"Yes? Hello?" Smith's voice was thick and sluggish.

Her watch read just past two. She might have checked that first, but it was too late now. "Smith?"

"Tessa." He cleared his throat. "Is something wrong?"

She forced her voice through her swollen throat. "I need directions."

After hanging up, Smith consulted the time. Tessa had needed directions at two in the morning? He hoped that wasn't a harbinger of things to come.

"A'right?" Bair mumbled from the opposite bunk in the narrow trailer.

"I've snagged our landscape architect."

Bair's springs squeaked as he repositioned. "In the middle of the night?"

"Quite."

As Bair slipped back to sleep, Smith calculated the chances of not offending Tessa before he had her signature on a contract. Low probability and lower chance of quick resolution when it occurred. But the property owner, Rumer Gaston, had been impressed by the article in *Architectural Digest*. He wanted her on board.

And Smith did too. At least he thought he did. He sighed. Tomorrow was soon enough to face Tessa Young.

CHAPTER

3

Smith had not directed her to his office, as she would have expected. He was on-site already and wanted to meet there. His directions were clear, but the purpose vague. He had said only that he would explain when she got there.

Her chest quaked as she drove past pleasant marinas lined with sail and fishing boats, with gulls winging overhead and standing like pegs on the low wooden docks that stretched into the brackish water of bay and river joinings. She entered green leafy forests broken by brown fields of feed corn, low fields of soybeans and potatoes, then more forests with the occasional white-tailed deer peering out timidly.

Maybe she should have called Dr. Brenner. He would have helped her process the decision, but she was between appointments and didn't want to need more—*didn't* need more. It was only the imminence of seeing Smith that made her think it. Smith with his aristocratic confidence, his compelling personality and contagious smile.

She gripped the steering wheel and reminded herself this was her decision. Smith had made the offer, but she'd chosen to check it out. A professional reconnaissance and the chance for personal resolution. Both of them positive reasons to reenter his sphere. She could control her thoughts and emotions and would not be swept anywhere she did not intend to go.

She did wonder if he would look the same. She hadn't changed much—except in ways that would keep her from imagining in him what she hoped to find in everyone and never did. She had learned a lot since those days at Cornell when Smith's had been the strong hand guiding her through.

She'd appreciated his mentoring, but that didn't mean she had to become his clone. She had her own dreams and plans and realities. Why couldn't he understand that? Because Smith wanted what Smith wanted—and usually got.

His dynamic and friendly personality earned him his popularity. Who wouldn't like Smith Chandler? Who wouldn't want him near, imagine him caring, trust him and—

She stopped herself with a forceful recognition of reality. That was who she'd thought he was. He'd proved otherwise.

She arrived at a turnoff blocked by a gate marked No Trespassing. Very inviting. She parked and got out, but didn't see another car. If this was it, the least he could have done was be there to meet her. "Well . . ." She expelled a breath.

"Deep subject."

She spun, heart racing. He stepped out of the trees, tall and sinewy. His sandy hair, cropped short, was still bedeviled by the little cowlick in front where it swirled out. He peered at her through wire-rim glasses, his serious demeanor disguising a relentless wit and cunning humor.

Closure, she breathed. "So I'm here."

"So you are." Smith formed a wry smile as he approached the car.

Her ponytail holder had slipped loose, and she pulled it out and shook her silky, golden brown hair, pulling it back again with a motion he remembered so well, her hair always resisting whatever restraint she imposed.

"How was the drive?"

"Fine." She looked up with wide green eyes, a light sprinkling of freckles making her seem younger than she was. Or maybe it was the wary expression.

She smelled like fresh peaches, and he glimpsed the tube of lotion on the dash. She'd always gone for fruity scents in lotion and shampoo in place of more complicated perfumes. It was the one less complicated thing about her.

Her lightweight cargo pants and navy blue top flattered her figure. She had been willowy, hardly substantial, but now her muscles were toned, skin tanned; fit, yet feminine. She looked . . . really good. Pity she was so high maintenance, the sort of woman who required a manual, and signal lights to warn of impending detonation with no apparent cause.

He hadn't been happy with the way they'd fallen out but had cut his losses and moved on. Tessa, he recalled, tended to tote her injuries along. There'd been a very thin line between teasing and offending her. While he'd specialized in witty barbs, she had needed initiating into that sort of repartee. She didn't seem eager to be initiated into anything at the moment. But she would.

He unlocked the gate erected earlier that week for privacy and swung it wide. "May I ride with you?"

"Where?" The prospect seemingly unnerved her.

"About a hundred yards down, there's a trailer in the trees. We'll just step into the office before I show you the site."

She opened the car door, popped the locks, and he slipped into the seat beside her. It hadn't been asking that much. Why did she look like she'd rather jump out than jostle over the ruts in the field to the trailer.

"There's something here you'll want to see firsthand, but the owner insists that no one gain access without a non-disclosure agreement. Just a promise not to tell what we're doing here."

She turned off the engine. "Is it illegal?"

"Of course not." What kind of question was that? "But unless you've agreed not to reveal anything I show or tell you, I can't take you out there. Not even for a look-see."

Instead of the eagerness he'd hoped for, he saw frustration. "You had me drive up here—"

"You won't regret it."

"You said nothing about non-disclosures and secret projects. I can't imagine what something like that has to do with me."

"My clients value their privacy. That's all." Smith swung the door open and climbed out. "Look, Tessa, do you want to see it or don't you?"

She sighed. "I came to have a look, and if I have to sign something to do that, let's do it."

"Good." They weren't his rules, but he'd enforce what Gaston demanded. Even though their work would not be featured in any journal, the contacts they would make among a high echelon of potential clients was worth more than publicity. If that didn't matter to her, there was one thing that would. He'd threatened Bair with bludgeoning if he so much as mentioned that element.

They went inside, and Bair jumped up from his desk, scattering pencils, papers, and a stapler. Bair had known he'd be bringing in a specialist, but had not expected Tessa. Smith rather enjoyed Bair's reaction.

"Bair, this is Tessa Young, the landscape architect."

"Oh, uh, Tessa." He pumped her hand. "It's my pleasure."

Bair was a better show with a lovely woman than on a rugby

pitch—and he'd been an infamous crowd-pleaser out there. He'd had his nose broken three times in brawls, and his brawny arms hung like slabs of beef.

Tessa raised her brows. "Bear?"

"Nigel Bair. With an *a* and an *i*. Not the kind that climbs trees."

Smith grinned. "The kind that clobbers opponents on the rugby pitch."

"Never without provocation." Bair hid his scarred knuckles behind his back.

"Bair's in the final throes of internship and will come aboard my firm at this project's completion."

"It's nice to meet you, Nigel." Tessa's tone had warmed considerably.

Bair's freckled face flushed red. "Uh . . . Bair, please. No one calls me Nigel and lives to tell it."

Tessa laughed for the first time since arriving. "Okay, then. Bair."

Watching her loosen up as she hadn't before oddly annoyed him. Smith raised his chin. "The non-disclosure?"

"Yes, of course." Bair scattered more papers in his attempt to find it swiftly. "I'm chuffed you'll be working with us, Tessa."

"That's not decided yet." Smith caught sight of the form and pulled it out from beneath a folder. If she guessed how confidently he'd played her card with Bair, she'd refuse on principle. "Here you are."

She took the chair across from the desk. "Mind if I read it?"

"She'll want to see the contract as well, Bair. Try not to cause a landslide."

"Oh, I have that here." He took it from a file drawer behind him. "Your secretary gave me your fees, and Smith attached some bonusing as well."

She didn't correct his term for her assistant, merely took the form and looked it over. "Generous."

"Our client wants the best." Smith smiled. He wasn't laying it on; those were Gaston's words. Hopefully he hadn't talked Tessa up too much, in case she turned down the project. He didn't see that happening, though, not once she knew. If she could change the whole course of her life over the things, finding a real one had to be worth her time.

Tessa was not sure what to make of all the secrecy and hype, but the money being offered on the contract suggested Smith had not exaggerated. She signed the non-disclosure in order to learn more, but not the contract, not until she knew what he was up to.

"I left my Rover at the site," he said when they stepped outside. "I hope you don't mind walking in. We haven't cut a road yet, and the terrain would be rough on your sedan."

She shrugged. "I've been driving all morning—which, by the way, you owe me for. Extending my rental and gas."

"Expense it with Bair. He's handling the finances."

For some reason, that seemed funny. Bair's playing rugby—wholeheartedly, by the looks of his knuckles and physique—and crunching numbers. Prior to introductions, she would have thought him a construction foreman, but not all architects so completely looked the part as Smith.

"How do you know him?" In the interplay she'd seen, there seemed more than just a professional association between them.

"He was a couple years ahead, growing up in London. We'd chummed around, then lost touch for a while. After a few wasted years, he followed my lead into American architectural education, with the promise of a position in my firm."

"He seems nice."

"Don't let his bumbling boyishness fool you. Inside he's a . . . bear."

A bear who would provide a buffer between her and Smith. The breeze tossed strands of her hair and eased the muggy heat as they left the trees and entered a fallow field. Out of nowhere, a sense of foreboding caught her in the back of the throat. She slowed her steps.

Mistaking her hesitation, Smith said, "I should have driven up, but I heard your car and cut through to meet you."

"To sneak up on me."

He cocked his head. "You didn't provide much entertainment. Not even a proper startle."

After years of suppressing irrational fears, she had easily hidden the jolt he'd given her. "I don't have time for games."

"Ah yes, your busy *schedule*." He said the word without a *c*—as he'd used to in order to annoy her.

"Yes, my schedule, my plans, all of which you've interrupted."

"You're going to thank me."

"Hmm." If he thought they could pick up their old camaraderie, he'd be disappointed. She might be made a fool of once, but she absolutely always learned from her mistakes—especially those she had therapeutically discussed in more sessions than they deserved.

As they exited the woods and entered the meadow, he said, "We're standing on the grounds of the St. John chapel and monastery."

"You're building a church?"

"I should have said former grounds of a Jesuit plantation, built and destroyed by fire in the seventeenth century."

"Thoroughly, by the looks of it." She had not initially seen the outline of a foundation just visible in the sod. "I thought you didn't like historical reconstruction." Hadn't that been one of the reasons he'd trained in America instead of with the Royal Institute of British Architects?

"There's nothing left but that stone outline. I'm designing an estate home atop the footprint."

She didn't know why the idea troubled her. Creative reuse was a major part of architecture. Factories made into apartments, churches into restaurants. This was not even a preexisting structure.

"So why do you need me?"

"Because I found . . . Well, you tell me."

He led her past the foundation to a set of stone footers, probably from a sizeable gate, though there was no trace of a wall. She stepped in between the footers and caught her breath, recognizing the sod-covered, indented pattern of the circular path. She walked forward, then wove to the left, doubled back and kept moving even when the path disappeared beneath the viney overgrowth. She could have closed her eyes and walked it blind if the ground were not so uneven. Round and back, round and back she walked, hardly breathing, to the very center.

There she stopped and wrapped herself in her arms, overwhelmed by a sense of reverence and joy. Had Smith realized what this would mean? He couldn't know. No one really understood the depth of her fascination, its source or its solace. There in the center, she could almost—

Another feeling hit her. More than the foreboding, a feeling of danger that belonged only in her dreams.

Her breathing sharpened. Her heart raced. She'd experienced different things as she'd prayerfully walked many labyrinths, but she'd never felt repelled.

"Was I right?"

Smith's shout broke the feeling. Releasing her breath, she cut across to where he waited, poised on the balls of his feet. "Yes. It's a labyrinth."

"Aren't you glad now that you came?"

"I'm interested."

"Can you re-create it from what's there?"

The thought of anyone else doing so made her want to cry. "It must have a firm structure to have held its shape. What records do you have?"

"Some things the owner collected. There may be more in local archives." He turned. "Besides the maze—"

"It's a labyrinth."

"Besides that, there was a reflecting pond with a bit of a natural spring." He pointed to a sunken area, overgrown with reeds and grasses. She imagined it with clear water, shimmering in the stars, a fountain at one end, no jets, only trickling streams. With that marsh vegetation, she'd be willing to bet the spring was still there.

"Also a butterfly garden and beehives."

"No orchard?"

"Sorry?"

"A monastery of the time would have had fruit trees, don't you think? And why hasn't the forest reclaimed the meadow?"

"This is a natural clearing. According to the geologist's report, it sits atop a solid rock shelf with shallow soil, only two to four feet deep. I imagine that's why the landowner donated this portion to the church."

"That'll make planting challenging." She looked around at the hickory and oaks with a few loblolly pines surrounding them. All the elements intrigued her, but the labyrinth reached the place inside that nothing else touched.

She had built an intricate path in Malibu, another in Huntington Beach, and the one in Aspen that had been featured in *Architectural Digest*, plus dozens of smaller, less complicated designs. She'd created them in different shapes and sizes, planted, cut, or laid them with stone, crushed shells, or pebbles. But she had never resurrected an ancient preexisting path.

"I should have thought you'd bite your arm off for this, Tess."

"Yes, all right. I'm hooked." She should be thanking him profusely.

He flashed his charming smile. "Good. Want to catch a late lunch?"

"This is business, Smith."

"One professional to another. I'll even throw in Bair."

She weighed the stress of sitting with him in a sociable setting against the logistics they would need to go over and the fact that she hadn't eaten since an early breakfast of yogurt and berries. "All right."

She badly wanted to walk the labyrinth path again, but alone, completely alone.

CHAPTER

4

Tessa surveyed the verdant property through the window as Smith drove her back to the trailer in his Land Rover. It was more comfortable than looking at him, though his scent and energy entangled her anyway. Dr. Brenner called her perceptivity a hyperawareness of surroundings and individuals and believed it a result of stress or trauma. If he could measure the energy in the vehicle at that moment, he wouldn't say she exaggerated.

When Smith parked and went inside for Bair, she got out and popped the trunk of her rental car. She pulled a chilled bottle of fortified water from the cooler and took a long, cold drink. She twisted the lid back on, then glanced over her shoulder as the feeling of someone watching raised the hairs on the back of her neck. The woods spread around her with innocent vacancy, but still she shivered.

The projects she had done, especially lately, were in well-established and often guarded estate neighborhoods. She and her crew could easily work until dusk with no concerns. This property's isolation unsettled yet pleased her. But then, those emotions often warred inside. Dr. Brenner wondered why she obsessively pursued things that troubled her. She had yet to give him a satisfactory answer.

Smith and Bair came out of the trailer, jibing and laughing, the visible ease of their friendship reminiscent of what she had once shared with Smith, the last time she'd let anyone get that close.

She had acquired her assistant, Genie, in the same way as the cat she mostly called hers—a chance encounter and a mutual need. She appreciated her hardworking crews and knew they liked working for her. With the exception of one neighbor, the people in her small mountain community were all friendly with her, and yet the only person who knew the inner workings of her mind was Dr. Brenner. She wondered sometimes if she made more of his compassionate affection than actually existed.

While Bair climbed behind the wheel of the Rover, Smith joined her. "At this point in the day it probably makes sense to take both cars to the restaurant. We can fill you in over lunch, and then you can check into the inn for the night."

"Okay."

"Do you want me to ride along?"

"No thanks. I'll follow you."

He looked as though he might say more, then shrugged and climbed in beside Bair. Opening the car door, she released a slow breath. She could do this. With very clear boundaries, she could do this. She started the engine with a sense of purpose bolstered by a firm determination to stay focused on the project, which really was as exciting as Smith had said.

Maybe Smith's offer to ride along had less to do with accompanying her and more to do with Bair's driving. The moment they turned onto the two-lane highway, he took off through the woods, past slate blue inlets, fields, and scattered houses as though the country road were a Grand Prix course. That kind of aggression could come out in brawls, she supposed, though if Bair hadn't hidden his knuckles, she would have thought Smith exaggerated. Now she caught a glimpse of the bear.

He turned at a post office and mini-mart and parked a short distance up the side road in the narrow lot of a faded lavender Victorian house. The hand-painted sign out front read Ellie's Teashop. Not exactly the locale for a power lunch. At least Smith wasn't trying to impress.

He held open the door to the flowery foyer and acknowledged her wry glance with a tilt of his head. "Bair's got a thing for Ellie's granddaughter."

"I've not got a *thing*." Bair's face flushed as an aging woman approached.

"Well, who've you brought with you today?" Her peachy cheeks crinkled into her warm smile.

Smith returned the smile. "This is Tessa Young, Ellie. She's on my design team."

Though she had not signed the contract, Smith knew she would take the bait and swallow the hook whole. She wished she could be like the wise old bass in the bottom of the pond, but the shiny lure he dangled was too tempting.

"You're a builder too?"

"A landscape architect."

"Oh, I love gardening."

Tessa didn't say her profession required a great deal of technical expertise. It was enough that Ellie had called Smith a builder. They followed their hostess to a table tucked into a bay window, though they could have had their choice of empty seats.

The parlor room had a fussy, feminine charm. Sprigs of silk lilac graced the lacy tables set with china and silver. Even in that setting Smith managed to look appropriate. Bair looked like Babar the elephant in a dollhouse as he hunkered down at the finely set table. Smith pulled out her chair, reminding her how it was to be with a gentleman. She quickly recovered. No matter how courteous, he had ultimately failed in elemental chivalry.

"So." Smith lifted the menu. "The turkey croissant is excellent."

Not fair that he recalled her old standby or assumed she had not developed other tastes. He'd learn soon enough that she was not the girl who had seen in him all that she wanted to become. Instead she'd become herself, and while there might be areas she could improve, she didn't need Smith's hand to do it.

Bair's napkin slid off his lap and he bumped the table retrieving it. "My favorite is the pesto chicken on ciabatta."

Tessa glanced up. "You guys eat here often?"

Bair's ruddy cheeks deepened a shade. "We've only been on-site two weeks, but Ellie's, uh, reminds me of home."

"So, yes." Smith set down his menu. "Every lunch we've had out."

Tessa glanced at the choices, saw a grilled salmon on field greens salad, and set the menu aside. Smith was buying, after all, and she'd never seen him counting pennies. "Well, I suppose we should get down to business."

Before they could, a waitress came over with a pot of tea and filled their cups. Tessa would have preferred it iced, but the girl had merely brushed her with a glance that imitated contact without connecting. Her focus stayed firmly on the guys, making her priorities clear.

"Ready to order?" Her kinky red hair had been tortured into braids and wound tightly at her nape. Her eyes were the color of cornflowers, and the copper lashes provided an extraordinary complement in an otherwise unremarkable face.

The moment she'd approached the table, Bair had gone completely still. This was the granddaughter he liked?

Tessa ordered her salad and Smith toasted cheese with a tuna-stuffed tomato. Bair cleared his throat, the flush creeping up his neck like dye. Tessa had the urge to slap his back to clear the words that seemed literally caught in his throat.

The waitress waited, pencil to her pad, then looked up. "Your usual?"

He nodded. She jotted it down and left.

Smith laid his napkin across his lap. "Now that you've realized what an exceptional opportunity I've landed, I—"

"How did you land it anyway?" With his focus on commercial development, he didn't seem the likely choice. Unless that had changed.

"Through my father initially."

"The barrister?"

"He's a solicitor."

"Oh, that's right. A gown but no wig." He had explained the difference at length after she'd succumbed to giggles at the thought of an older Smith in a powdered wig.

"Just a suit now that he's practicing out of the New York office."

Smith's dual citizenship by descent from a British dad and an American mother, his American birth and London rearing, had been confusing enough. "Now your dad's an American too?"

"No. It's an international firm. He transferred several years ago when Mum had enough of London living."

"I see."

"Dad handled some legal affairs for the property owner, and when his client needed an architect he contacted me. The client liked what I did with the preliminary sketches, and here we are."

She understood referral. Most of her schedule she filled by word of mouth. And since Smith knew most of the world personally and had charmed at least half, he must have some pretty good word of mouth going for him. "I thought you were all about big professional complexes. Why this residential project?"

"It's an extensive residence. And impressing the owner here could lead to commercial opportunities."

"Who is the owner?" She lifted the teacup, breathing in the Earl Grey aroma that brought back the days when Smith's British customs had charmed her.

"A casino mogul and hotelier, Rumer Gaston."

"And Petra," Bair interjected. "Don't forget her."

His tone piqued her interest. "Petra?" She looked from one to the other.

Smith nodded. "Petra Sorenson. Gaston's fiancée."

"And a supermodel," Bair added.

"She must be beautiful."

"Stunning," Bair said.

"In an extreme sort of way." Smith shot him a glance. "Gaston's signing the checks, but Petra seems to be taking a personal interest." He frowned. "It could get messy."

"Shouldn't she be personally interested?"

"As long as they're in agreement." Smith sipped his tea. "Gaston envisioned this project before he met Petra, and we've already hammered out his concept."

"But then he got engaged."

"And I'm not sure Petra's taste runs along the same line."

"Better he find out now than build her a house she won't want to live in."

Smith opened his mouth to argue, but the young waitress arrived with their food. Bair looked as though he wanted to jump up and help her with the tray, but thankfully stayed put. Tessa breathed the aroma of tangy vinaigrette dressing and the savory salmon on her salad.

The girl set the toasted cheese before Smith and a sandwich

at Bair's place that was clearly pastrami with sauerkraut on rye. "Anything else?"

"Mustard with that?" Smith asked Bair brightly.

Bair nodded.

"Here you go." She produced a small jar of country style from her apron pocket.

Smith said, "Thank you, Katy," as she walked away.

Tessa frowned at Bair's plate. "I thought you liked the pesto chicken."

"I do." He lifted the top bread. "But she recommended this once, and well, I haven't the heart to disappoint her."

She caught the laugh before it came out. "You can't think she expects you to have it every time."

"No. But she always asks before I can say otherwise."

Tessa turned to Smith. "You should say it for him."

"Place his order?"

"No, but you could say something like 'Was it the pesto chicken you were going to try, Bair?' "

He looked at her with a blend of humor and condescension. "And miss the show?"

She narrowed her eyes. "What you find entertaining is frequently painful for someone else."

He turned. "Are you in pain, Bair?"

Bair looked from her to Smith and swallowed his oversized mouthful so quickly, she thought he'd choke. "Not pain, no. But I've never been overfond of pastrami."

Tessa stabbed a bite of salad and turned to Smith. "Tell me about your design."

"Well." Smith dabbed his mouth. "Mr. Gaston imagines it resembling the etchings he acquired."

"He wants to live in a monastery?" Somehow that didn't square with a casino mogul.

"A semblance, Tessa. Elements that suggest the monastic heritage of the property while remaining fresh and original."

"How are you doing that?" She just managed to keep the skeptical edge from her voice.

"I'll show you my conceptual drawings."

Her stomach clenched with the painful reminiscence of their heads together as he worked a concept, wholly caught up in the creative inspiration of his talent. Once he had it right, he did not like the plan to change. She pressed the memory down to where it didn't hurt. "What about the landscape?"

"He wants to keep the elements we discovered."

"So I'm doing historic landscape restoration?"

"Well, there is the landing pad. Gaston owns a jet, but I convinced him a runway would not be realistic given the woody terrain. He agreed to helicopter access and originally chose the labyrinth field—until we realized what was there."

She tensed. "Because he wants the labyrinth."

"Oh yes. When I told him I knew a specialist, he insisted I call you."

So that was it. Not even Smith's decision. Why was she not surprised?

"You'll need to determine an alternate location for the helipad."

She speared a baby spinach leaf, a mandarin orange, and a sliver of salmon. "What's the acreage?"

"Thirty-two. Much of it wooded. The entrance you design needs to make use of the trees as a screen."

That wouldn't be difficult. Even the trailer had been hidden from the road. She wasn't sure why a mogul and a model needed such secrecy. If they were in such demand, wouldn't they build their dream home in a more chichi area, not the backwoods of southern Maryland—lovely as they were?

Bair had nearly finished his pastrami—in spite of not caring for it—when Katy returned, hands on hips. "How was it?"

He managed, "Good. As always."

He'd tell Katy it was good even if he'd hated every bite. Katy took his plate with a self-satisfied smile, oblivious to his bluff.

Tessa handed over her empty plate. "He's in a rut, though. I made him promise to try the pesto chicken on ciabatta next time. Don't let him wiggle out."

Katy looked straight at her for the first time and shrugged. "Whatever."

Under Smith's amused appraisal, Tessa raised her teacup. "What's the timeline?"

"I haven't prepared the schedule, but I'm estimating four to five weeks for design, three to take bids, seven or eight months once we choose the contractor."

She sipped her tea. "How soon do you need my design?"

"There's some leeway on landscape. Why?"

"I'd like to start by uncovering what's left of the labyrinth."

Smith pressed the napkin to his mouth. "You'll bring in a crew right off?"

"Not immediately. I want to explore what's there myself first." Though usually she would bring in a crew to clean up and prep a property, she felt drawn to unearth some portion of the labyrinth herself. She wanted to grasp the mindset of the original creator, and how better than using her own hands to uncover his work?

At the appropriate time, she would bring in others to assist her in creating the gardens, pools, and . . . helipad. But the labyrinth would be different from anything she had done yet. "About this confidentiality agreement—"

"Not negotiable." Smith shook his head.

"You're all right with that? Even though we could publish—"

"You saw the fees for service, Tess. Gaston's paying for privacy."

"He's paying for secrecy." The money was way over anything she'd earned on a comparable project, but she would be re-creating an authentic seventeenth-century labyrinth. How could she keep that to herself? She knew from consulting on other historic sites that, even if it were declared a historic landmark, Rumer Gaston would have the right to deny public access. The vast majority of national landmarks were privately owned and partially or completely restricted to the public. He wasn't destroying, but rather restoring the site—for his private use.

While she couldn't fault him for that, the right attention could have her creating prayer walks across the country, the world. It would improve awareness and recognition of her specialization and all the possibilities therein. She imagined a photo shoot featuring Petra—though she'd never seen her—with the labyrinth as an exotic backdrop. Rumer Gaston might want privacy, but she'd bet Petra preferred celebrity. "Maybe I can change his mind."

Smith quirked a brow. "That I'd like to see."

He didn't have to sound so skeptical. She didn't pretend to be hard-nosed or irresistible, but she could be persuasive when she felt strongly enough. She had stood her ground on a wetland issue and won. If she could do it for something like that, how much more for this labyrinth and the ones that might come from it? So when Smith slid her the contract, she signed it. She was in this with them—for better or worse.

They drove from the restaurant to the inn where Bair had reserved her a room. The white historic house with a river view and formal gardens seemed a charming place to stay, and she thanked him for arranging it.

He blushed to the tips of his russet hair. "My pleasure."

Driving aside, she absolutely could not imagine him bludgeoning anyone.

"We'll see you tomorrow." Smith raised a hand in casual

farewell, the same gesture and tone he'd used so many times on campus, making her believe he'd be there just as he'd said.

The realization rushed in that closure was going to be painful. How would she accomplish it with months of working together? That seemed more like salt than balm. But he was right. She'd do anything for the chance to work on that labyrinth, even face him every day. She had plenty of experience facing things she'd rather not.

Her room was light and airy from a window with a priceless view of the river in one direction and in the other, the forest that she itched to capture on paper. Though she created her designs with software, she was never without a sketchbook. Meeting with clients, park officials, other architects, and consultants, she readily drew what they envisioned as they discussed it.

It was a professional skill but also a passion. She took the sketchbook out and drew the river scene as far as she could see. Then she drew the near shore. Using colored pencils, she drew one of the inn gardens abundant with autumn blooms. Though it had not been designed with the care she would have given, she captured it all as the sinking sun cast the sky with an apricot wash. Her tension eased.

She had been edgy since arriving. Smith had done and said nothing to indicate he realized the wreck he'd made of her six years ago. Granted, her emotional stability had been shaky before they met, but until he'd come into her life, she hadn't expected anything good. He had infected her with optimism and left her vulnerable to disappointment.

She shook herself. Personal healing was no longer her primary goal. If her guess proved accurate, the labyrinth pattern matched the four-quadrant, circular Chartres Cathedral floor labyrinth. Someone had carried its design across the ocean to duplicate it in living earth on a new continent. She imagined the faith and reverence with which that peace labyrinth had been formed, then the devastation that followed.

As the sun disappeared, casting the scene in pewter gray, Tessa turned from the window. She could dream all she wanted of restoring its original purpose, allowing its path to be a means to peace and growth. But if no one knew about it, what chance was there of that? As Smith had indicated, Gaston's pockets were deep enough to keep any secrets he wished.

Smith stretched out on the single bed in the trailer bedroom and released a long sigh.

"Now, that is what I don't get." Bair shifted in the covers of his bed across the room.

"What?"

"Why the sigh, when you've got a lovely woman from your past and months to make something of it?"

Smith squeezed the bridge of his nose. "First off, she's not a woman from my past in that sense."

"What sense?"

"The sense you mean."

"I don't mean any sense."

"Right." He'd expected Tessa to surprise Bair, but hadn't counted on his fixating.

"She's quite easy on the eyes. Brassed off with you, though."

Smith stared up at the ceiling. "That's nothing new."

"Still . . . I wouldn't be wasting this chance."

Smith gave his pillow a smart slap. "If you fancy her, Bair, see that it doesn't interfere with the project. Gaston's adamant about that maze."

"Fancy her! I'd think you'd be the one."

Smith settled back down. "You think I should chat up the

woman who thinks I'm a shade above Attila the Hun for reasons known only to her?"

"But that's just it. Who holds a grudge for six years against someone who doesn't matter?" He rose up on one elbow. "Didn't you see the way she looked at you?"

"Yes. One of those looks stuck six inches deep."

"I'm just saying . . ."

"I'm here to do a job, and Tessa's here to do the same. That's all."

"Fine, then. Do your job."

"And you do yours."

"Well, I don't know. If you're not interested—"

Smith rolled to his side. "Bair, Tessa's not . . . She's got issues."

"So've I."

"Hers are pervasive."

"I'm a great problem solver."

Smith frowned. "I thought you liked Katy."

"Katy's a nice girl. I'm just keeping my options open."

The irritation that came with the thought caught him by surprise. "Fine, then. And good luck."

"Just like that?"

Smith heaved a sigh. "Like what?"

"Nothing," Bair grumbled. "Go to sleep."

Smith tossed. When sleep hadn't come a full hour later, he rolled to his back and stared up at the darkness. He'd known this could get complicated; Tessa embodied complicated with her short fuse and oversensitivity. Bair had seen only the admittedly attractive surface. Scowling, he flopped over to his side and forced his eyes closed. Maybe it was best to let Bair have a go. No, best would be three professionals getting the job done without complication.

Not supposed to be there. Things should not be where they were not supposed to be. And the trailer had been there too long. It might be planning to stay. It should not, but might, because *they* had put it there.

And *they* had been all around and down and over the place they should not be. He smelled them when he came out, heard them when he was in. Their voices made him shake. Their eyes peering through the light with no pain at all.

He laid the metal spyglass on the ground near the trailer door. He would have liked to keep it, or smash it, but more than that, he wanted them to take everything and go. He stretched out his finger and ran it along the metal side of the trailer as he circled it in the moonlight. His finger jumped and dragged over the trim around the door, beneath the windows, the seams.

They were not supposed to be there. Not supposed to be. He needed them to go, but how could he make that happen? Fists clenched, he gave the trailer one last glare, then crept into the night.

CHAPTER

5

Silver gray light filtered through the giant oaks and loblolly pines as Tessa moved through the forest, her boots squelching in the mulchy ground, the scent of wet earth and leaves surrounding her. She'd left the car on the road so she wouldn't alert the men, since she really wanted to study the property alone. Smith had apparently sensed nothing yesterday at the labyrinth, and she didn't want him distracting her again.

Pausing at the tree line, she studied the meadow, adding its grassy fragrance to the heady organic perfume. She leaned against the ash gray trunk of a shagbark hickory and gazed up through the branches, studying the pinnate leaves hinting at the true gold they would soon flaunt. The green, leathery husks of the heavy nuts were turning brown and brittle. Soon they would fall, the husks splitting open around the hard nutshell that mallards and wood ducks, squirrels and raccoons could feast upon. It amazed her to think that the saplings she'd planted would one day be like this tree, old and storied.

She stepped into the meadow, absorbing the scene as the rising sun began to change everything around her, turning silvers to gold, grays to green and brown. A trio of white-tailed deer raised their heads, ears angling forward. Finches and orioles overlaid the morning with song as the deer sprang away. The dewy grass misted with the rising warmth. She crouched down and dug, cupping a handful of rich, pungent earth. Had it lain fallow for over two hundred years? She breathed its scent, always amazed at the complexities of the differing soils, and smiled to think she was a connoisseur of dirt.

She lowered herself to sit cross-legged and watched the transformation from dawn to day. She noted the slope of the land, possible drainage issues, natural vegetation. She observed the fall of sunlight at this time of day, and she would note it throughout the next hours.

All of this would impact her design. But what she wanted to do before anything else was unearth the labyrinth, learn what she could from its remains, read every clue the records might reveal, and lovingly restore it. Even though that was far from her typical job description, she didn't get hung up on titles and hierarchy. Her sense of purpose stirred. She was meant to do this.

There were so many things to consider, to discover. Had the monks followed the Chartres model of sacred geometry in placing the labyrinth to mirror an element in the church itself? The rose window in Chartres, if folded down, would perfectly overlay the pattern on the floor. She probably couldn't hope that Smith's design had taken any of that into consideration. He hadn't even been sure it *was* a labyrinth.

"Tessa?"

She turned as Bair reached the edge of the field and called, "Everything all right?"

She waved. "Yes, fine."

"I've got you set up in the office."

"Okay."

He seemed unsure whether to wait or go back without her. She sighed. "I'll be right up."

Bair rubbed his meaty hands as she joined him in the trailer. "That desk is for you. There's an outlet underneath."

"Thank you."

Smith's desk was against hers. It held a few stacked folders, a silver laptop, and a few preliminary sketches. Bair's held the fax, printer, phone, and heaps of folders. He turned and bumped his thigh, caught the landslide, and manhandled it back onto the surface.

"What is all that?"

"Detritus from old and possible projects I'm organizing until we're fully underway here."

Intern grunt work. "Why are you guys on-site, instead of Smith's office?"

"Gaston wants Smith on the premises, start to finish. A bit of a control thing. I'm here because Smith thinks this might prove an instructive experience."

"Oh."

He leaned close. "I don't think he liked the idea of staying out here alone. Lose your mind that way. Especially when you're as sociable as Smith."

She remembered that about him.

"It is out of the way, should something happen."

"What could happen?"

"You know . . . stuff."

"So you're watching his back?"

He shrugged. "Always have. He was a skinny kid, and smart. Not a good combination."

She smiled. "No?"

"Not when he let people know it. Plus he wore glasses. If I hadn't walked alongside, he'd have had more than his share of scrapes."

"What was in it for you?"

"Did I mention he was smart?"

"He did your homework."

"Not entirely." Bair flushed.

She didn't want to think of Smith as a boy, didn't want to think of him at all.

"There's tea brewed," Bair said. "And Smith bought some instant coffee, in case you prefer it."

"No one prefers instant coffee." Yet there was Smith, making assumptions. "I brought my own iced green, though it's in the car I left outside the gate, in case you guys were still sleeping."

"Let me have your keys; I'll drive it in for you."

"Thanks for the offer, Bair, but my name's on the rental, and I've seen you drive."

"I'll take it like a church mum. And I, um, transferred the rental to the company."

She canted him a skeptical glance, then surrendered her keys. "The tea's in a Nalgene bottle in the console. My briefcase is on the seat."

"Right."

As he exited, Smith came through the inside door in a blue button-down Oxford shirt and crisply pressed jeans. His hair was barely towel dried, his glasses slightly fogged, sleep softness still in his face.

"Didn't you sleep well?"

"It shows?"

She had not intended to notice or comment on anything personal, but he looked uncharacteristically rough around the edges. She nodded.

"I tossed all night. You'll laugh, but I think this property is haunted."

A frisson crawled her spine as she recalled her sensation of being watched. "By what?"

THE EDGE OF RECALL \ 49

"I've no idea. And don't tell Bair. I'd never hear the end of it."

He crossed the office toward the kitchen. "Hungry?"

"I ate." And she didn't want anything from him that wasn't directly job related.

Bair carried in her tea, briefcase, and a rather nice engineer's level that he held up to Smith. "Didn't we leave this set up yesterday?"

Smith nodded. "We did."

"What's it doing lying out by the door?"

Smith frowned. "I don't know. I left it covered on the rise beyond the foundation."

Tessa looked from one to the other, reading their perplexity and hoping it had nothing to do with the haunting Smith had just mentioned.

Smith rubbed his face. "One of us must've carried it back; I just don't remember doing it."

"I wouldn't have left it on the ground."

Smith wouldn't have left it either, Tessa knew. He'd never been careless with his tools or any of his belongings, not like other guys whose dorms looked like hazardous waste dumps. His natural orderliness stemmed from his highly organized mind. If he said he'd left it, he'd left it. But if neither had carried it back, who had?

She cleared her throat. "You mentioned monastery records?"

Smith made a move, but Bair beat him to it, rummaging behind his desk, then laying a large portfolio on her desk. "That's what we have so far. Gaston's collected them."

"Thanks." As the men moved to the kitchen for breakfast, she withdrew two matted etchings depicting front and back views of the original chapel and cells. Her breath caught when she saw a circular window that overlooked the green hand-inked labyrinth.

Excitement welled up, and even more so when she found a

handwritten document that described the prayer walk's dimen-
sions:

> Four steps in and turn to the left, twelve strides form the
> first curve. The pattern is regular yet intricate and interlaced,
> as are our lives.

Were these the words of the labyrinth's designer?

> The cross is the center, the path leading to the blood sacrifice
> that is our hope and our salvation.

Blood sacrifice referred, of course, to the crucifixion and death
of Christ, but had there been a physical cross at the center? Or was
it the symbolic destination of the pilgrimage?

Smith leaned his lanky frame in the kitchen doorway. "We're
completing the plot plan today, Tessa. If you want measurements
for the labyrinth—"

"Thanks, but I'll manage." She pointed to the back-view etch-
ing. "Just tell me that window is in your design."

When she'd finished organizing her workspace, Tessa gathered
her sketchbook and pencils. Being around Smith stirred up memories that muddied her mind like a jar of sand and water, though
Smith didn't seem fazed at all. Maybe he'd never felt as much as
she'd thought.

He had listened and cared when she'd opened up in ways she
hadn't before—outside of therapy. She could have sworn his compassion was real. But what did she know? She didn't have a mother
guiding and advising her, though she wondered what Mom could
have told her. I know how it is? I trusted the one I loved too?

She shouldn't have let her thoughts go there. Time was supposed to dull the memories, but the smell of the hospital room, the sad smiles of the nurses, the sounds of the machines still came back so vividly. Her mother's bald head, nestled against the hospital pillow, her brown eyes luminous in her pale face. Tessa could almost feel her mother's skeletal arms as she'd crawled onto the hospital bed beside her, an awkward teen and the woman she could not bear to lose.

She made her way through the sparser woods surrounding the trailer and forced her thoughts onto a more positive course. Her mother had instilled the strength to be alone and the ability to value life—however long it lasted and whatever trials it held. Vanessa Young had taught her that death could be peaceful for a wounded creature buried in the backyard or a person who had lived as fully as she could in the time given her.

But that didn't help the person left behind.

Her mother had delighted in the beauty of nature—delicate shells left behind when baby birds had flown, wild onions and herbs pulled straight from the earth. Tessa blinked back her tears. To block the painful connection to her mother, she had learned to create man-made structures: wood, steel, and concrete—Smith's delight, but never really hers. Once she'd switched to landscape architecture, the fractured pieces of her life had come together—as much as they could.

Her focus on labyrinths had concerned both Smith and Dr. Brenner for completely different reasons, but she knew there was something essentially healing in that for her. Never had she suspected Smith would react the way he had when she'd told him her plan, calling it a waste of her abilities. She'd had no way to explain how deeply she needed to reconnect with elements she might not understand, but that mattered nonetheless.

She remembered so clearly his earnestly dissuading her, their arguments, and finally, the day she had approached the classroom door and heard him laughing with his friends. She didn't have to hear to know the tone he'd used to express her vision, and the way they had looked away, clearing throats and waxing silent. She knew.

She shoved the hurt down as she approached Smith gazing through the level toward the rod Bair held. She drove the emotion from her voice. "Don't you already have a plot plan?" It was not ordinarily the architect's responsibility.

He drew back from the eyepiece. "Either this property had none, or the record's been lost."

"And you're not having a surveyor—"

"Gaston wants me to do it."

"Isn't that strange?"

"Unusual. But I'm qualified."

"I just wonder why it all has to be so secret."

Smith planted his hands on his hips. "Tessa . . ."

She raised a hand. "I know. They're paying for privacy." She looked across the field. "Will I be in your way if I walk the labyrinth?"

"Can you give me one day?" He marked something on his clipboard. "I need Bair to concentrate."

She folded her arms at his offhand compliment. As though she'd actually distract either one of them. "You have one day. And then the grounds are mine."

Smith watched her go. She had developed a confident façade he found heartbreaking. With her natural assets it should have come easily; instead she worked inordinately hard to create the illusion. What had happened to make her so brittle? Other people had lost loved ones and not shattered.

Bair cleared his throat, having left his post and come over. "Want to break for lunch?"

Smith shook his head. "I told her we'd finish this up today."

"Sure you don't want to . . ." He nodded his head the direction Tessa had gone.

"To what?"

"I don't know, smooth things over."

"There's nothing to smooth."

"And I've three eyes."

Smith frowned. "I allowed Tessa the last word and stroked her self-esteem. *That* was a successful exchange." He would not let Bair guilt him into thinking otherwise.

"Sooner or later you'll have to deal with it."

"With what?"

"Whatever the conflict is between you."

"There's no conflict."

"Right. You forget I've seen every form of denial. On some it's a goofy grin." He mimicked it. "Others the angry brow. Yours is a congenial neutrality."

Smith scowled. "What are you talking about?"

"I'm just saying I know a bluff when I see one."

Smith spread his hands. "What am I faking?"

"Your cool detachment."

Shaking his head, Smith planted his hands on his hips. "What business is it of yours?"

"None. Unless you consider the toxic fallout from the interpersonal interactions. Why don't you make your peace already?"

"We're working together, aren't we?"

"You're on the same project."

"I convinced her to come. I hired her. She is on my team. Now we have work to do, so if your counseling session is over . . ."

"Right." Bair threw down his hands and lumbered back to his position.

Smith noticed peripherally that Tessa had paused at the edge of the woods, where she moved among the trunks like a nymph, feeling the bark, even putting her nose to the wood and sniffing. She really was a nature hound. All right, then. Let her do the nature part.

He had a project to program and a manual to build out of all the information he had to sift through. Situating the house advantageously was his primary focus at the moment, but Tessa could rest assured that her labyrinth would find its match in his upstairs window. Form followed function, and that part was already in his design. Still, it pleased him to coordinate his efforts with hers. Bair did not know what he was talking about.

Deep in the recess, he held his head. They hadn't gone away. He had given back their spyglass, but they'd been out with it again. When he slept, he felt them there—walking, talking, doing things they should not be doing . . . there.

Another one had come. She walked differently, watching, listening, sniffing. Like him. But her eyes didn't hurt. The sun didn't send pain into her head, didn't scorch her skin until it flaked and oozed. She was one of them.

Why were they there? he asked, but he knew. They were taking it away. And he could not let them. Would not. They had everything else, the whole sunshiny world, but they wanted this too. His dark. His peace.

How he would stop them he didn't know. But he must. He would.

CHAPTER

6

Over the next two weeks, Smith spent his time acquiring and directing his team, spending hours communicating by phone, fax, and e-mail. Tessa had no trouble avoiding him, since Bair was able to tell her what she needed to know, where to find things, and how to get places.

From what she'd observed, Smith's leadership style was organized and competent, and he didn't shirk his own workload. His natural exuberance had matured into an industrious confidence, though she tried not to analyze him. He wasn't the reason she had stayed. Her energy went into preparing to re-create the labyrinth— and the rest of the landscape design that Smith had reminded her was equally important to the overall project.

For the most part, the engineer consultants were working remotely and connecting electronically, each discipline adding to Smith's base sheets their part of the design as the drawings neared completion. Smith would bring all the designs together under one set of plans and specifications that would eventually get the engineers', hers, and his own seal of approval. She felt the rising energy.

The design phase always excited her, and she would have to

guard the emotions stirred by observing people in a creative mode—especially Smith. Theoretically, she could create a landscape design remotely, as were the other consultants, working from the plot plan and the civil engineer's drawings. But she didn't work that way. She needed to watch the land perform before deciding how and where to develop it. And this time, of course, there was the labyrinth.

As she prepared to leave for the day, Bair leaned on the doorframe of her car. "You're welcome to join us, you know, for dinner."

She looked into his ruddy face with its flattened nose and blunt jaw, his hazel eyes, warm and guileless. He had no idea how hard she worked to keep her space. "Thanks, Bair, but no."

"Smith would ask . . . if he thought you'd like to come."

She pulled the car key from her purse. "He has no reason to."

"Right. I know." Bair shuffled. "It's just I hate to think of you eating alone."

She raised her face. "Gives me time to think." Brooding, Smith had called it. She called it contemplation. "Really."

"All right, then. Drive carefully."

She raised her brows. "Would you?"

"If I were you." He straightened up, grinning.

"See you tomorrow, Bair."

"Right." He stepped back but repeated his caution. "Be careful."

That second warning caused an uncomfortable sensation. "Has something else happened?"

Bair looked uneasy. "Like what?"

"Something I should know about."

He folded his muscular arms. "No, just . . . I'm sure it's nothing. That level is all. Weird."

"Maybe someone passing through thought you'd forgotten it."

"Passing through from where?"

She searched the woods, the hint of river through the trees. "No neighbors tucked in somewhere?"

"Not for quite a ways."

She hadn't realized that was still bothering them, and it made her uneasy.

"Well." He backed off and waved. "See you tomorrow."

Tomorrow and the next day and the next, for the number of months it took to work up the drainage, planting, and reclamation. Theoretically, she could have her design drawn in a matter of weeks, if she learned what she needed. Smith had said Gaston wanted the grounds close to the original, but while the building was accurately represented, the etchings gave only vague renderings of the landscape.

She pulled away from the trailer, thankful to escape talk of hauntings and weird happenings. In the two and a half weeks she'd been there, she had felt scrutinized more than once and repelled by something that was almost certainly not there. Now as she drove toward the gate in the deepening twilight, she thought she saw movement in the trees, something pale, ghostly. She shot a look over her shoulder. Nothing, of course, but she shivered.

She would tell the guys to keep their ghost stories to themselves. No, that would make her seem vulnerable. Dr. Brenner said everything had an explanation, but too often in her experience it was not forthcoming.

She stopped at the market, purchased a small French loaf and microwaved a pint of vegetable soup, and then drove two miles to the inn. She carried her food into her room and set it on the little desk, but before settling down to enjoy it, she checked the window latches and the door's lock and deadbolt. She turned the old-fashioned, T-shaped handle and watched the bolt slide into the socket. Locks were only effective against things that could not penetrate material boundaries. Monsters had laws of their own.

Returning to the desk, she peeled back the cardboard lid from the soup container and eased into the wooden chair. Maybe Bair was right about eating alone. It suddenly seemed pathetic. She dipped the bread and spooned the now-lukewarm soup into her mouth. Not great, but acceptable. She heard a creak outside the door and spun.

No other sound followed, only her edgy nerves overreacting. But now her mind persisted in pondering what might have bothered Smith and Bair. Noises? That sensation of watchfulness, of danger?

She swallowed another bite of soup and wished there had been more information about the property. She didn't need to know much more than the soil, the weather, and the pests to create her design. But for the labyrinth she wanted to get inside the head of its creator. That one small part of a document had whetted her appetite.

The footers at the entrance had clearly held a gate, unusual in labyrinths. She was sure she'd never seen a gated mouth before. Maybe it had been intended to provide the seeker the chance to walk it without anyone else entering until his circuit had been completed in solitude. Maybe they feared a hostile party would catch them unawares.

Labyrinth walls were predominantly pruned knee- or waist-high, like the one she'd made for Mrs. Beauprez. By the size of the entrance footers, however, she guessed the gate, and likely the foliage, in this one had been man-high, providing no view of the path beyond the next turn. The best vantage to see its layout would have been from the corresponding circular window of a loft or balcony within the chapel.

She finished her soup and jotted a reminder to pick up a shovel. Maybe it was crazy, but she did not want to share the project. Smith and Bair were occupied with the drawing and compiling of conceptual layouts. Her design would be part of that, but Smith had plotted the footprint and had rough locations for the other preexisting elements. He seemed content with her focus on the labyrinth. It was why he'd called her instead of someone he normally worked with.

She could tolerate the meetings where the consultants communicated on speaker phone and she and Bair and Smith sat together in the office. It was only when Smith shot her a smile or made a joke or referred to something she was trying not to think about that her composure slipped.

She twisted the wrapper closed around the remainder of the bread, tossed the empty soup container, and stood, thankful she'd followed her instincts and eaten alone. It was not pathetic after all. It was self-preservation.

Smith drove to a mediocre chain restaurant near the navy base, uneasy for more reasons than one. The business with the level still nagged. There was no doubt in his mind that he had left it in place. There were no properties near, no line of sight from the road. Was Bair drinking? Doing things he didn't recall? There'd been no sign of stupor, no fumes on his breath. He seemed better than he had in years. No way he could fake that.

If Bair hadn't moved it . . . what? Smith frowned. Maybe what he'd heard again last night was not the wind or forest creatures. He had taken a look when he could have sworn he'd heard the door rattling, but had seen nothing in the darkness. Still, they might not be as alone out there as they thought. Had they picked up a spy? Paparazzi hoping to make a spectacle of Petra? Not hard from what he'd heard.

Or Gaston might be a target himself. After the legal work Dad wouldn't discuss, his advice had been to use the opportunity but keep his nose clean. It had conveyed enough. Could a P.I. or someone with a grudge have traced their movements and be staking out the site, hoping Gaston or Petra would make an appearance?

Smith shook his head. Why would that person draw attention to himself? Leaving the level was more like a message being sent. A warning. Should he mention it to Gaston? He'd avoided anything of substance in his daily updates. They were tedious and silly, since developments at this stage were details Gaston neither needed to know nor probably understood, and he wanted the man to realize it. If he mentioned an issue, there'd be no end to the babysitting.

They ordered Cokes, and Smith said, "Stan Graburg is on board as EE. I wanted Malcolm for structural, but he won't be available in time. Bloke named Gordon Ellis is taking it."

Bair opened the menu. "You know him?"

"No. Malcolm says he's good, though. Big fella, good sense of humor. Should lighten up the team."

"You mean Tessa?"

He inclined his head. "She does good work, but she's—"

"Sensitive."

"Hypersensitive." Smith waited while the server brought their Cokes. He would have liked a Laughing Lab, but not if Bair was slipping. "Don't get me wrong. I'm extremely pleased to have her. I mean, she's treating the labyrinth like an archeological dig."

The waiter carried the other drinks on his tray to the next table and took that order.

Bair sipped his Coke. "Then what's with the sparks and barbs?"

"Are we back to that again?" When had Bair become a mother

hen? "For the last time, Bair, there are no sparks, and the barbs, well, that's just Tessa."

"I'm only saying —"

"Too much." He didn't need this getting messy. Too much rode on this project's success. In spite of what he had told Tessa, it surprised him that he'd received the contract. Gaston had to have architects in his pockets, yet he'd chosen him. He planned to show Rumer Gaston that he had chosen well. With an effort he shoved back the nagging doubt. He could do the job and do it well.

Like a fox on the prowl, he slipped from shadow to shadow. He'd gone out sooner than usual to see her as she left, risking the half-light before the darkness made him invisible. Risking her seeing him. But she hadn't. He'd been quick. Invisible. Silent as night.

He ran his tongue along the inside of his teeth, feeling the gaps, the soft gum between them as he loped along the road, keeping to the tree line. His joints loosened, his gait strengthened as the last of the light leached away.

Some nights he watched the ground for small prey. More frequently, he followed the line of the road to their place. So much there for the taking. If you were small. If you were clever. He drew the night air through his teeth in anticipation.

What would it be tonight, he let himself wonder. Something to eat, yes, but then what? He curled his fingers at his sides, anticipation tickling his palms. A chortle formed in his throat, the fear that had consumed him fading, fading. He would worry about them later. Tonight he was a ghost. A whisper. A half-forgotten dream. He would move through their world like a memory.

He pulled up the hood of his gray sweatshirt and scuttled on until the lights came into view—not so many, but more than he liked. A streetlight at the corner, porch lights sprinkled about. He had gone far and taken long enough that there were few headlights. He would wait until they slept, softly. Awareness fading.

He stayed in the trees all the way to the first houses. These gave cover, but he hadn't yet figured a way in. So he moved on to the one he knew. Waited. Watched. The dog lay like a black heap of fur. He crept close, closer. On hands and knees, he crawled.

The dog smelled him. He smelled the dog. Amber eyes opened, glowed red. He brought his face up against the short, tight, midnight fur, the floppy muzzle, moist nose. Warm, wet tongue, warm, dry breath. He rubbed his face on the dog's, shaking with joy.

The animal flopped to his side, surrendering his post, opening the way. Carefully, silently, he curled his shoulders in and pressed through the flapping door. He made his breath nothing in his ears, so only the sounds they made came in. One rumbly snore, one nasal whiffle.

He crawled across the floor, pulled up on the pantry door, and slipped inside the narrow-shelved space. He felt with his fingers, the packages, the cans, the flip tops that meant meat or soup or stew. He picked one, not knowing which it would be, and slipped out. Back through the little door, back past the dozing dog. But not to the woods. Not yet.

He pulled open the can and dug his fingers into hash. He licked his lips, licked his fingers, and when he found a trash bin, slipped the can inside. No trace. No trail. He worked his way past the dark backsides of a few more houses and buildings, skirting the ones with lights, squinting at the offense.

He moved past the sleeping church to a small brick building. His hands quivered. He moved around to the side, pressed between the scratchy shrubs and the rough wall. Gripping the grate, smaller even than the dog's door, he moved it aside. He almost had to dislocate his shoulders to squeeze through, but he made it and dropped to the floor with glee.

The pitch-black cellar smelled of dust and mildew. He breathed it like perfume, moving between the stacks without hesitation. He reached the stairs and climbed, went through the door, trying not to giggle. To the desk. The drawer. He felt for the metal cylinder, small and thin like a finger.

Bracing himself, he pressed one end, and a small, bluish light came out the point. The contents of the food cans could be a surprise, but not this. For this he needed just enough light to choose. He moved over to the first rack, the first floor-to-ceiling row of books. Heart racing, he let the light run over their titles, the numbers and categories on the white labels across their spines. He touched them, fingered them. What should he choose? What would he learn? This time.

CHAPTER

7

With a thrust of her boot, Tessa dug the spade's edge into the turf between the footers at the labyrinth's entrance. It felt as though she were disturbing something that had lain for a long time in peace and maybe wanted to stay that way. Then again, it was only dirt and grass and had no feelings one way or the other.

She had spent the last several days in meetings, poring over the plot plan, and generating her own drawings. She liked what she'd heard of the team members over the speaker phone, and the field engineer she'd met. But she had been there three weeks and was only now starting the actual recovery of the labyrinth.

Groaning when her phone rang, she stood the shovel in the ground. If it was Smith calling another meeting she'd scream, but it was her assistant. "Hi, Genie. What's up?"

"Two things. Wilmette Meyer called—and she *does* want the fountain after all."

"I already finished that job, and it wasn't in the bid since she insisted a fountain wouldn't look right."

"Now she thinks maybe you were right. She went back and looked at your original drawings and wants the fountain."

"I reworked the design to take it out. I'd have to undo things to get it back in."

"She said you could put it anywhere."

Well, if symmetry and aesthetics didn't matter . . . "Send me my designs, and I'll see what it would take. But I can't say when I'll get to it." Ordinarily she'd snatch it up, but what she would make on the labyrinth project easily covered all her winter expenses, and she didn't want the distraction. "Not till next spring. And make sure she understands this is a new bid."

"Will do."

"What's the other thing?"

"You missed your appointment with Dr. Brenner. He wants to know if you're all right."

Tessa made an exasperated noise. "I meant to call him, but I got wrapped up in things here. Can you ask him to suspend my appointments until I get back? I'll call to reschedule."

"Umm . . ."

"What?"

"He wanted to hear from you."

"Then why didn't he call my cell?"

"I don't know. He just said to have you call him."

She got it. He wanted to hear for himself what condition she was in, and he wanted her to initiate the call since she had missed the appointment. "I'll take care of it. How's the house?"

"A whole lot nicer than anything else I'd be in."

Having Genie move in had been a stroke of genius. It gave her a safe place to stay and kept the house, plants, and stray cat cared for.

"You haven't forgotten the plants?"

"Takes about three hours each time, but yeah, I'm watering them."

"Well, thanks for the messages. Take care." Tessa drew a breath and speed-dialed Dr. Brenner. His receptionist answered and Tessa identified herself.

"One moment."

Then Dr. Brenner came on the line. "Good morning, Tessa."

"Almost afternoon here."

"And where is that?"

"Southern Maryland."

"Aha. I thought you'd finished in Virginia and were coming back."

She thought warmly that it sounded like something a dad would say to an adult child who had changed plans. "I'm so sorry I forgot to cancel my appointment. I made a snap decision and got caught up in what I found."

"That's not like you."

"I'm sorry I didn't free up my slot."

"You know that isn't my concern."

"I know." The last time she'd missed without notifying him, she'd been in a bad place. "It's just when Smith called—"

"Smith Chandler?"

"He found a labyrinth, an actual historic labyrinth. I'm standing on it now. Or what's left of it." She looked over the ridged field. "Actually, if you didn't know what you were looking at, you'd miss it altogether."

The doctor's silence created a void she rushed to fill.

"I have the chance to re-create it. A Chartres-style labyrinth, eleven circuits in hedge. I've never seen that design done vertically. I'm . . . really excited."

"I can hear that."

"So I'll be here for a while."

"You think that's wise? Two stressors and no safety net?"

"I can call, right? I could have a session on the phone?"

"Yes, Tessa, you could. But will you?"

She ran a hand through her hair. "I thought you'd want me to face Smith. I thought you'd recommend it."

"I would. If it didn't involve a labyrinth."

"I didn't know until I got here. He was very mysterious. But I wouldn't miss this opportunity for anything. I know you understand."

"You know my concerns. I don't like your fascination with things that terrify you."

"Only in my dreams."

"Dreams that arise from an untapped trauma."

"Or the memory I've described again and again."

"A happy memory of flying over a labyrinth with your father would not account for the terror and despair of the nightmares."

They'd had this argument ad nauseam. "I'm fine."

"If you uncover that trauma while unearthing this labyrinth, and have no one there to help you process it . . ."

She didn't mention the sense of danger she'd experienced. While she appreciated his concern, she didn't want to intensify it. "I'll be fine."

"Let's discuss Smith and why you didn't tell me you were going to see him."

"I was between appointments when he called. I decided to see what he wanted."

"And then forgot your appointment altogether."

"Not intentionally. But this is a chance to deal with things, with . . . Smith. I want closure."

"Do you?"

"After I create this labyrinth."

Dr. Brenner sighed. "I'd like you to check in weekly by phone."

They hadn't talked every week for a long time, but with her

elevated stress level it might be a good idea, and with the money Gaston was paying she could afford to. "All right. But I'm fine."

"No nightmares?"

"None I can't handle."

"Hmm. I'm penciling you in at three o'clock your time Wednesday afternoons."

It would be good to fill him in on the progress, someone who understood. She kept her tone light so he wouldn't sense the tension he already suspected. He had helped process the hurt, and must guess how hard this was. For a brief moment she acknowledged the irrationality of keeping secrets from her therapist, then shrugged.

"Okay. Good-bye."

"Good-bye, Tessa."

She pocketed her phone, took hold of her spade, and stomped the blade into the ground. She lifted a chunk of sod and then another and another until the stone surface appeared. She got down on her knees and used the hand trowel to clear enough to get a look. The bordering walls rose about two feet, and though covered in sod, they had made the pattern visible to the knowing eye. She stood and applied the shovel once again.

It didn't matter that her skin prickled like a lightning storm if Smith got too close, or that she turned everything he said over and over, looking for innuendo and alternate meaning. It didn't matter that the feeling of being watched had not gone away. All that mattered was the labyrinth. Call her obsessive. She didn't care. She couldn't wait to see what lay beneath the centuries of sod.

Nothing would frighten her off, and she would not let her issues with Smith get in the way, when this could be the fulfillment of a longing that had been with her longer than any other.

Smith didn't know what to think of Tessa's working like a laborer. With her qualifications, she should never have to touch a shovel. Did she not understand delegation? Her part, like his, was to visualize, conceive, and direct others to bring those plans to fruition. Yet there she was, digging in the field all by herself.

She said she'd never recovered an ancient labyrinth before, but even if it were a dig, she could have workers uncover the site. He shook his head. Not his business. As long as she completed her design and executed it on schedule, she could do as she liked with the labyrinth—as it seemed she was.

Deeply focused, she appeared oblivious to his approach, though that could be intentional, he supposed. He stood four feet away when she finally noticed him with a sudden, searching gaze that made him want to run far and fast.

He cleared his throat. "Everything all right?" The question could have opened delicate areas better left alone, but thankfully she merely nodded.

He motioned to the spade. "You're really going to dig it out by hand?"

She brushed the hair back from her face. "I'm trying to see what's here. These side walls have held the troughlike shape of the path"—she dug in again—"for a long time. It looks like the stonework survived the fire."

"So it seems. The wooden structure burned readily enough."

"I wonder what started it."

"I'm guessing that would be *who*. According to Gaston's records, the religious feuds in this area got nasty."

She turned. "Didn't the Maryland colony pass a religious tolerance act—like a precursor to the First Amendment?"

"To start with. But others came in who disagreed. When they came into power, they destroyed churches and schools before religious tolerance was restored."

"So it wasn't an accidental fire."

"Records are sketchy on this exact one, but from what I've read generally, the odds are in favor of intent. Especially since it wasn't rebuilt. I'm not sure what you'll find digging around in there."

Her hand recoiled from the shovel. "You don't think people were in the labyrinth when the hedge burned."

"It wouldn't be the first time hatred in God's name had deadly results."

A shudder passed over her, but with only a slight hesitation, she repositioned the spade. "Thanks for the warning." She stomped it into the earth. It sank with a distinct metallic clang.

He tipped his head. "What was that?"

"Not a skeleton." She tossed the clod aside.

"Here, let me." He took the spade and maneuvered its blade close to her last cut. His also hit metal. She knelt and brushed the dirt away with her hands.

"There's something there."

He removed another chunk of sod, and another.

"Be careful of the stone walls." She shoved dirt off a discolored metal rod. "Here," she said. "Dig here." Off to the side of the path.

He obliged, and she cleared a metal curve and leaf. She looked up. "The gate?"

"Could be." He was not much for old things but had to admit this intrigued him, especially seeing how Tessa lit up.

She took back the spade and dug vigorously. When she appeared to tire, he took over, carefully removing the turf from the gate as she kept clearing the dirt. In a little more than half an hour, they lifted it from the ground where it had lain for possibly three hundred years. Tessa was breathless as she ran her hands over the vines and leaves.

"This *pax* symbol in the middle means *peace*. The labyrinth would have been used in that pursuit."

"Too bad it didn't work."

"Smith, this is—" She shook her head, speechless.

He pulled a smile. "Shall I consider myself thanked?"

She dragged out a grudging "Yes," but couldn't hide the excitement as she gripped an edge of the gate. "Can you help me move it onto the turf?"

They laid it flat and examined the design and condition. Six feet by three, he estimated, with a keyed lock.

Tessa brushed the surface with her hand. "I think it's bronze, oxidized, but it might still be saved."

"Think you'll use it?"

"If I could figure out why it was there in the first place. I've never seen a gated labyrinth. I was hoping the historical society might have something about the monastery, but so far I haven't found much."

"The college has archeological and historical information. They're currently rebuilding historic St. Mary's City. You might try there, but remember, Tess, you can't say anything about what we're doing. Not even to get information."

"It can't hurt to ask around."

He wasn't so sure. "Don't pique anyone's curiosity."

"I know how to be discreet, Smith. Better than some people I know."

"Meaning me, I suppose?"

"I didn't mean anything."

"I'm quite sure you did. You've been sinking those tiny barbs since you got here." He frowned. "What is it you think I betrayed?"

"Besides me?"

"You? How?"

"Never mind." She focused her attention on the gate. "Don't you have something to do?"

"I have loads to do, but I'm not leaving that statement—"

"Forget it, Smith." She rubbed furiously at the dirt caked on the leaves of the gate.

"Right." He wouldn't even try to parse her comment. If she thought he'd been anything but circumspect in their prior interaction . . . All right, he had told their classmates what he thought of her defection. And what he thought of her new plan. He sighed. She might have a point, but wasn't there a statute of limitations?

The last thing he needed was drama, when this opportunity could open doors to people and places he might otherwise bang on his entire career and never gain entrance. He'd have to trust Tessa to uphold the non-disclosure. Gaston was near maniacal on that. She might not like it—or him—but she'd better not violate the agreement just to pay back some real or imagined slight of years ago.

Gaston was not a man to cross. He would slap a lawsuit on them so fast. Couldn't she simply plant the labyrinth?

He blinked in the shadows that were not enough, squinting into the overcast light at her working in the field. He should be sleeping, but he couldn't resist looking. One more look at her on her knees, brushing the ground with her hands.

He could almost feel her hands. Stroking. How long since a person's hands had touched him? Humming softly, he slid his fingers down his arms, over his tender skin. In just the way she brushed the dirt. How easy it would be to creep up, creep up and see if she was soft, as soft as she looked.

But she would scream. Scream and shield herself. Run.

Better just to look. No! Better not to look. Not to want. She was one of them, not for him. No one for him. He clutched his head and slunk down, down low under the dark trees where the sun didn't reach. Needles and leaves crunched under his side, under his cheek. He wanted his place but couldn't get there, not with her where she was, where she shouldn't be, where she took the dirt off the place she should not be.

This one had been there so early he couldn't get back. A moan that was more like a growl deep in his throat made a chipmunk scurry, but he didn't snatch it. He curled up and let the moans come. What could he do, how could he make them leave? He knew so many things, but not that, never that, because he hadn't needed to.

Not since he'd been hidden, since she had made the screamers go away. But she was not there anymore. So long, so long since she had been there. And he was alone. And he had to make them go. And he didn't know how.

CHAPTER

8

Tessa had spent a good portion of every day over the month she'd been there on a different part of the property with her sketchbook and pencil, reading the land, watching what it told her about the play of light, the fall of shade, the flow of moisture. She sat down now, cross-legged, listening to the call of an oriole. Somewhere farther a squirrel chirped its way up a tree. Crickets and grasshoppers sang in the grasses as the fall sunshine warmed her head. With her design nearly complete, her excitement had grown, though nothing compared to her plans for the labyrinth.

She closed her eyes and drew a seed pattern of a Greek cross, four dots and two inverted half circles at the top, then two side-facing at the bottom. Eyes still closed, she added curving lines that yielded a seven-circuit design, not caring that some of the connections were off. The blind approximation calmed her racing thoughts and triggered creativity, while sharpening her analytical processes.

Feeling the cooling sweep of a shadow, she opened her eyes to Bair leaning over. "You drew that with your eyes closed."

She smiled. "It opens kinesthetic channels when sight is removed from the connection between thought and hand."

"Looks like a different pattern."

"It's the classic design. Not my personal favorite, but I've styled quite a few from turf, dwarf shrubs, and other ground covers. It lends itself well to landscape."

"What's this one?"

"I'm pretty sure it's the medieval design, like the floor of Chartres Cathedral. Possibly Roman, since both have four quadrants, but the Roman is traveled sequentially, and this path appears to run back and forth through the structure as a whole."

"You can tell all that from what's here?" He looked over the uneven ground.

"If you know what you're looking at."

She picked up her pencil and drew the design, then held it up for Bair to see.

He looked from the drawing to the field. "Yes, quite. Still, I'm surprised Smith recognized it."

She was too. Although she had drawn enough of them in his company. He had admired her doodling until she decided to make them reality.

"It's going to be big."

"Yeah." Translating the intricate and exact proportions to a topiary path would be her greatest challenge yet. If she intended the hedge to grow an assumed height of six feet, she would need a width of two feet for stability, path width two and a half. "Let's see. Twenty-two circuits, four and a half feet wide, plus the center, which equals one quarter of the total . . ." She did the math. "I'll be working with a diameter of a hundred thirty-two feet, or forty-four yards across."

"No small task."

Walking it, she'd been aware of its size, but now she consciously considered the job before her. "I'm pretty certain the original designer followed the straight-angled Chartres script without the decorative elements of the cathedral's floor labyrinth. I'll know more when I uncover enough of the path to see the first turns." Although now, with every cut of the spade, she wondered what she might unearth. "I wish I knew more about it."

"Have you read the documents?"

She nodded. "Mr. Gaston's documents contain the most information I've found. The etchings are fairly detailed for the structure"—a wooden colonial chapel with wings that would have held the priests' cells, kitchen, storage, education and workrooms— "but not so much for the labyrinth. I haven't found more than a passing mention of the monastery in records outside Mr. Gaston's."

"According to Smith, he privately acquired everything he could."

She raised her brows. Lots of people wanted to know the history of their land, but left it for the public as well. "St. John's didn't seem to have been around long enough to impact history before it got destroyed." She hoped with everything in her the priests' bones did not lie within the labyrinth.

"Hard to imagine that kind of violence."

"Is it?" She looked up, surprised. "With Islamic suicide bombers who want to kill us all as infidels?"

"But these were all Christians. They simply worshiped differently."

"True."

In spite of Smith's dire warnings, she had managed to learn a little about the local history without raising alarms. "Lord Baltimore envisioned a colony without an established religion, where all believers in Christ could worship in peace. The original act went so far as to punish with fines people who used terms like Puritan, heretic, Calvinist, Papist, or Lutheran in a 'reproachful manner.' Very forward thinking for the time, but naïve."

"What happened?"

"Puritans who had been forced out of Virginia and given refuge in Maryland wrested control, suspended the Toleration Act, and denied Quakers, Baptists, Catholics, and Anglicans religious liberty."

"That's a nice turnaround. So what happened?"

"Oliver Cromwell recognized the excessive persecution and restored the Toleration Act, but by then the monastery and its peace labyrinth had been burned to the ground."

"Makes you wonder what God thinks of it all."

"Yes, it does." She nodded. "Especially since the infighting between Christians hasn't stopped. It never took long whenever Mom and I tried a new church before one group or another was being criticized. I guess that's why some people choose a private relationship with God over any church at all." She had not meant to say so much, but learning the monastery's history had struck a chord with the nomadic search she and her mother had made for a place to rest away from petty quarrels and politics, and why she still sought God in the labyrinth's solitude.

"Well, um . . . I was wondering . . . when you might be finishing up."

"I don't know. Why?"

"No reason. Just . . . wondering."

"Is there something I need to do?"

"No, no." Bair shoved his hands into his pockets. "I'll just . . . head back in."

"Okay. See you later." At least in the field, she didn't have to shield herself from Smith, though, thankfully, they'd had little direct interaction since their last collision. As Bair trudged back to the trailer, she returned to her own business.

The stone path she had uncovered beneath the fallen gate appeared to be bedrock, a creamy white limestone bordered by walls of the same, with which the builder had created earth beds for the hedge. It all showed blackening from fire, and she imagined the flames sweeping over and engulfing it.

The house Smith designed might only hint at a monastic heritage, but she intended to restore in the labyrinth a place of peace, of seeking divine wisdom. This was more than landscaping, more than preserving a wetland or laying out a park. Nature had reclaimed the ground, but the path was there, and she would bring it all once again to life.

And then what? Turn it over to the people Smith and Bair had described? Gaston had chosen the property, established what he wanted there, and ordered Smith on-site. He didn't sound flexible enough to consider his fiancée's preferences. And Petra sounded petulant and spoiled. But that was all according to Smith, who was not the best judge of anyone. Certainly not people's motivations and dreams.

She hadn't met Mr. Gaston or Petra and would wait to draw her own conclusions. In the end it didn't matter who they were. This labyrinth, like the others she had built, belonged to someone else. She didn't make them for herself but so that others could have a path toward God.

She pushed up to her feet. It might not be hers, but as long as she had it, she would use it. She stepped onto the path. Her pilgrimages to the center and back helped her grow stronger and wiser from encountering the Creator who instilled nature with patterns and rhythms reflected in the stars, in the depths of the sea, the earth and creatures. An order to all created things that could not have happened by mistakes and mutations. Not random chaos, but balance and perfection—even if much of it had been disrupted.

A turn to the left, then an arc to the right. She had received her love of nature from her mother, along with the desire to both beautify and steward the earth. Landscape architecture gave her opportunities to do both. Her focus on labyrinths came from her dad, from that single memory, his parting gift.

As a child, she had imagined the labyrinth a riddle that when solved would break the enchantment that took her dad away. But whatever tale her mind conceived, it didn't take away the pain of abandonment. The loneliness. The regret. When she walked the paths he'd left her and encountered those companions, she drew them to the center for God to strip away and let her return unencumbered.

This time, they dragged themselves back with her. Instead of peaceful, she felt raw.

Smith drove toward the field, grimly wishing he'd come up with a better idea or just said no. He had successfully avoided Tessa since their last heated discussion, communicating when he had to in a manner that didn't ripple her pond. This, he was certain, would create a small tsunami.

Once again he ran the alternatives through his mind: leave Bair in the lurch, try to find a total stranger and be left with a sticky explanation of why he wasn't interested, or ask Tessa. If she didn't go ballistic, he might enjoy the third option. The odds of her not going ballistic made his hands sweat.

Bair was supposed to have asked himself, but hadn't. He said he thought it was better coming from him, but he had probably chickened out—Smith wanted to as well. The last thing he desired was to invade Tessa's territory after she had sniped at him for some betrayal from years ago, when he had been far less mature and considerate than he tried to be now.

It was thoughtfulness that had put him in this position. He and Bair had been friends long enough to cover each other's back. One date with Katy ought to cure Bair's infatuation, but he couldn't do it alone. Girding himself, Smith parked at the edge of the field and watched Tessa moving along the path she found so fascinating. It caused an uncomfortable sensation. With anyone else, he'd consider it attraction. With Tessa, it was more fatal attraction.

He could return to safe ground, but crippling shyness left Bair speechless with someone he liked romantically. Booze unlocked his tongue and his restraint, but once he started drinking there wasn't much that could stop him. Hence the wasted years and more than a few scars.

Smith sighed. He could do this much for a mate. It would be good to clear the air with Tessa anyway. He waited while she completed the circuit and joined him, her expression wary, and no wonder.

She brushed a strand of hair from her face. "Did you need something?"

"First, I wanted to apologize for the other day, suggesting you'd be anything but discreet." He hadn't intended to apologize, since he hadn't intended to insult her, but with Tessa it was always a good starting point.

Her eyes softened. "It's obviously a big deal."

"It is and I can't change that, but I know you understand even if you don't agree."

"And?"

He cleared his throat, remembering all the times Bair had been there for him. "Would you like to eat with us tonight?"

"No thanks."

"Bair's cooking. He's asked Katy, and it would be nice to have you there as well."

"Why?"

"He needs someone to make conversation. But we can't really have her out to the trailer with two men alone. Not socially. Unlike your being there professionally and not . . . romantically."

She shot him a look. "Why doesn't he take her out somewhere?"

"It's better in a controlled environment. And he's more comfortable on a double—"

"Date?"

"No. Well, yes. I mean if you want it to be."

She planted her hands on her hips. "But not because you want it to."

"I didn't think you'd want to, in that way."

She screwed up her face. "What do you expect after the last time?"

"What last time? You didn't think we were dating. . . ."

"I thought we were friends. I told you things, showed you more than—" She clenched her hands and looked away, blinking back tears.

He tried to think what to say while she composed herself, but nothing presented itself that wouldn't dig him deeper.

She squared her shoulders. "I'll do it so Bair can have his date with Katy. But don't think I wouldn't rather be anywhere else."

So there it was. "It wouldn't enter my mind."

"Good."

Not good. He'd made the request in good faith, and if she couldn't see that, it was her issue. But now they were back to the contention she'd arrived with, and the last thing he'd wanted was another row. "Tessa."

"Leave it alone, Smith. In fact, leave me alone. I'm working."

"Is that what you call it?" Her jaw slackened, a clear warning, but he'd worked up a head of steam. "Wandering around with your eyes closed? I mean, what's the point?"

"Have you walked the labyrinth?"

"No."

"Then you don't know what you're talking about. They've

done medical studies on the kinesthetic effects of walking the patterns found in labyrinths. But more than that, when people walk a labyrinth they connect to something greater than themselves. But I wonder, is there anything greater to you than you, Smith?" She turned and stalked away.

Right. He'd pulled that off brilliantly. Driving back to the trailer it occurred to him he'd set her up for a truly miserable evening. Well. It wouldn't exactly be ace for him.

"Well?" Bair said when he got back in.

"You'd better be grateful."

"She'll do it?"

If he didn't know better, he'd say Bair looked happier about that than Katy's coming. "Yeah, she will." He went straight through to the bedroom and slammed the door.

CHAPTER

9

Tessa went back to the inn and showered, then picked Katy up so Bair wouldn't have to drive with her alone. She had not realized the extent of his communication handicap, because she had conversed fairly easily with him on the job. She supposed if the thought ever entered Bair's head of something romantic between them, she'd never get another word from him.

Thankfully, he'd set his cap for Katy. The last thing she needed was more interpersonal stress. She should not have blown up at Smith, not shown the tumult that lingered barely deep enough for her to keep from lashing out every time he came near. If only she hadn't trusted him at such a fragile time. He'd been the first person she had opened up to outside of therapy. Why had he proved so unreliable?

As she and Katy headed back to the trailer, the girl plied her with questions. Bair hadn't supplied much in the way of personal history, so once Katy realized how little Tessa could tell her, she mostly chewed her gum and looked out the window. In her current mood, that was just fine.

Tessa chewed her lip. Why had she agreed to this? Bair had been kind, but she'd only known him a month. Dr. Brenner would blame it on her need to please even practical strangers. Okay, so, was that such a bad thing? Only when it put her in a difficult position. Like this. If Katy weren't there, she'd turn around. Had the guys guessed that? It suddenly felt like a huge setup.

She could have told Smith no; this was business. But colleagues dined together. She'd done it on other projects. It was only because he'd framed it as a date that it got sticky. Of course, he'd backed off that word like a scalded cat.

She sighed. She was merely a placeholder so Smith could support his friend. That was admirable, kind even. One night—no—evening—no—meal. She could do that. She wouldn't even be alone with Smith. As long as Bair was there—but Bair would be focused on Katy.

From the side of her eye, she glimpsed the girl who had no use for her if she couldn't spill any details. No matter. She'd make this night about Katy—Katy and Bair. She felt an immediate comfort in that thought. Kind of like group therapy, where you gave the speaker full attention and tried to enter their distress or excitement, even if it seemed so much less important than yours.

She had reams of experience doing that. The facilitators had called her empathy a gift. *"Don't know how you do it, sweetie, but you sure set people at ease. Wish you could attend every session."* And Dr. Brenner. *"Maybe if you gave yourself the same permission you gave others we'd get somewhere."* He kept thinking she held back, even when she told him there was nothing more to tell.

He wanted there to be a reason she was messed up. But there wasn't. She'd bared everything she thought and felt, answered every question that had an answer. If there were some other explanation for the dreams, the terrors, she would have told him.

She parked and Katy climbed out without a word. "You're welcome," Tessa murmured under her breath with no patience for thoughtless people.

Smith and Bair were in the kitchen when she followed Katy inside. Tessa avoided Smith's glance, as he did hers, but Bair beamed. She hoped this wouldn't be like that first month in Cedar Grove when she'd carried notes between two patients, believing they were communications of love—until she'd learned they'd been threatening things like setting the other's hair on fire. She'd never played matchmaker since.

Why people thought she had any kind of handle on anyone else's problems baffled her, yet repeatedly people like Genie came and curled up at her feet, wanting a saucer of milk and a soft pat. Thank goodness she rubbed Katy wrong. She wouldn't have to get involved.

The girl hung her hoody over her youthful shoulders and faced Bair. "Can I see what you're doing?"

He stared dumbly.

"You know, building."

"Well, um . . ."

Smith turned from the stove. "There's nothing to see."

There was the labyrinth with a dozen feet of pathway cleared. Nothing to Smith maybe, but not to her.

Katy nudged Bair's elbow with hers. "Come on. Walk me around."

Bair shot Smith a look, but Smith didn't object. He had indicated that anyone who approached the site without a non-disclosure agreement signed in blood would be shot at dawn. Maybe that only applied to her.

Katy stuffed her arms into her sleeves. "Let's go."

Sighing, Bair followed her out the door.

Tessa turned on Smith. "You don't mind Katy knowing?"

"She won't know anything. Bair can't get a word out."

"I thought the point was to save him from that."

Smith stirred a grayish gravy on the stove. "The point is to lend support, not wrench the date out of his hands. Somewhat emasculating, see, like placing his order."

"You couldn't tell her she wasn't allowed to see anything without a non-disclosure?"

"It would only pique her curiosity."

"Yet I couldn't see before—"

"I wanted you on board. For that you had to sign."

All right, so there was a difference.

He turned from the stove. "Taste this." He held out a spoonful of gravy.

She took the spoon and touched it to her tongue. "What am I tasting for?"

"Too peppery?"

She might have said too floury, but the pepper was all right. "It's fine." She set the spoon in the sink.

"Bair's cooked a roast and some potatoes."

Smith was making an attempt at surface civility. She could too. "Vegetables?"

"Carrots and peas. Frozen, I'm afraid."

"That's fine." But not the proximity to Smith, the clean scent of his soap and hint of cologne mingling with the beef roasting in the small oven. It could have been homey and nice in the kitchen together if all the things she'd wanted to say, all the hurt she'd stuffed inside, hadn't made a barrier in her larynx as effective as Bair's. She glanced up to find him watching her, a pensive expression on his face.

"You really would rather be anywhere else, wouldn't you."

She swallowed. "I shouldn't have said—"

"Yes, you should, Tess. I'm sorry I put you in this position. Bair's problem is Bair's problem. Sooner or later he's going to have to date by himself."

"You mean he hasn't?"

He sucked in his cheeks, considering, then said, "Not sober."

She shot him a puzzled look.

"He gets frustrated and feels awkward, and a drink or two takes that away. He's quite glib, actually, with enough drinks in him. But enough leads to too much, and too much leads to trouble."

"The brawls you mentioned?"

"That and other regrettable choices. Bair would tell you himself. He's done the meetings. It's just easier if he's not tempted."

"That's what you meant by a controlled environment? No bar?"

"No bar, no pressure, no audience beyond his personal support team." Smith spread his hands. "I know this isn't much of a date."

"This isn't a date. We're helping Bair."

"Still, I shouldn't have—"

"It's okay, Smith. I can get through a meal with you."

"Well, then." He stiffened. "This should be fun."

She hadn't meant to insult him. "I learn from my mistakes— that's all I meant."

"I'm your mistake?"

She didn't want to get into it. She was trying to be amicable. They ought to be able to manage amicability.

He braced his hands on his hips. "Suppose you tell me what precisely I did to hurt your feelings all those years ago."

"You didn't hurt my feelings. You didn't consider them at all."

He expelled his breath. "I can't open my mouth without considering them. At every juncture there's the risk I'll run right over them."

She folded her arms. "What is that supposed to mean?"

"It's like babysitting an egg, being with you. One wrong word, one mistaken assumption—"

"An *egg?*"

"A particularly thin-shelled one."

Angry tears burned her eyes.

"No, don't." He gripped the back of his head, looking pained.

"Don't what?"

"Don't cry."

She'd give anything not to. He caught her elbow as she turned away.

"Come here." He turned her around and locked her in his gaze. "This is exactly what I didn't want."

And she had?

"If you could ever stop taking things so personally—"

"Babysitting an egg?"

"Well, that was over the top." He frowned. "I know you've had a hard go, and I don't try to make things worse. If there was any chance, I'd make them better."

Any chance? He thought she'd never be happy, that she couldn't be. That wasn't true, not in the way he meant. "I don't expect you to. It's just that you made me want—"

"What?"

She lost the battle of the tears.

"Want what, Tess?"

No way. She was not— "You in my life," she rasped.

Brow furrowed, he drew a ragged breath. "I'm sorry for that."

She glared.

"No, I mean, that's not what I meant to say. It's just—everything I do is wrong!" He pulled her up by the elbows and kissed her.

An electric jolt coursed her nerves, fear and pleasure and jubilation and fury. She jerked back. "What was that?"

"Something incredibly stupid." He let her go and pressed his hands to his face. "Please tell me this won't jeopardize our working together."

Their work? Right. The thing she was actually there for. Not making Bair's life easier or Smith's life worse. "It won't. I'm a professional, and you might at least be able to fake it."

He laughed. "That's right. I'm the fraud here."

She narrowed her eyes. "Are you suggesting my field is—"

"Oh, give it a rest!" He forked both hands into his hair. "I'm sick to death of that refrain. I respect you, all right? I admire your work. I called you in, didn't I, instead of any number of landscape designers I could have used at less cost and irritation."

He appeared to be shaking. She'd never seen him rattled. Never. But if he thought—

"Er . . ." The door banged closed behind Bair. "All right?"

"Fine," they both said through clenched teeth.

Katy looked from one to the other. Bair's face took on panicked hues that he might end up alone with her after all. Or maybe he'd prefer it, given the sudden climate change.

Tessa drew herself up. "You should check the roast, Bair. The gravy's definitely done."

CHAPTER

10

Smith spun and grabbed the whisk, pushing it through the mud
that had simmered while he made a pass at her. Yes, she'd fantasized
years ago in her naïveté, taking everything he said and did for so
much more than it was. She had clarified that with Dr. Brenner.
Smith had never come on to her, even when she'd have liked him
to. Until now.

"Have a seat . . . Katy . . . and Tessa." Bair jerked out both
chairs at once.

Tessa pulled herself together and gave Katy a smile. "Strange
having Bair wait on you?"

Katy nodded. "Grandma wouldn't approve."

"You might be surprised." Tessa sat down. "My mom always
said to never refuse a grand gesture."

Katy shrugged. "I guess."

Then again, grand gestures could be totally wasted.

Tessa adjusted her seat while Bair pushed Katy in like a Viking
with a battering ram. What did he see in her that had him so mesmerized? Maybe it was her perceptions that were off. Smith had
looked dumbfounded at the notion she might have thought them
a couple once. It started to hurt. She'd known it would.

Bair set out a well-done roast, a bowl of potatoes, and another bowl of olive-toned peas and translucent carrots. Smith had none too successfully thinned the gravy and probably leached out what flavor it once had. The men took their seats.

Smith cleared his throat. "So I'll just bless this, and then we can eat."

Her swift glance showed Smith's head bowed. When had he begun to pray?

"Bless, O Lord, this food to our use and us to thy service, and keep us ever mindful of the needs of others. In the name of Jesus. Amen."

The sweetness of the old-fashioned prayer washed over her. Tension eased in her shoulders, and the hurt made only a small hollow in the pit of her stomach. While Bair cut the roast, the rest of them passed the starch and vegetable with stiff smiles and thank-yous.

Smith set the empty potato bowl behind him on the tiny counter and settled into his role. "How is Ellie? Her knee still aching?"

Katy shrugged. "Mostly when it rains."

"Swelling any better?"

Katy nodded, then turned. "So you make labyrinths?"

Tessa raised her brows. Bair must have said so, and she felt a surge of satisfaction that he'd broken the taboo Smith was so certain he wouldn't violate. "Yes."

"Why? I mean what's it for?"

"Architecturally or culturally?"

Katy shrugged.

"Well, some of the paths I build are simply decorative." Tessa set her fork down. "Other people desire a prayer walk or meditation tool. The labyrinth can be used as a pilgrimage or a metaphor for life's journey. A chance to search inside, to go deeper."

Katy blinked. "All that from a maze?"

"A maze is a puzzle to be solved, with twists and turns and dead ends. It requires logical, analytical thinking and usually has a different way out than the way in. The maze could be a metaphor of struggling through life, going one way and then another until the exit takes you by surprise."

"Or of learning from your mistakes and moving on." Smith cast her a pointed look.

She ignored him. "I build labyrinths."

"What's the difference?" Katy gamely chewed a bite of beef.

"The maze signifies entrapment, while the labyrinth, with its unicursal path leading into the center and out again the same way, provides enlightenment."

Bair frowned. "How is it enlightening to end up back where you began?"

"It's the process, the journey into your deepest self, your soul, the part where God abides. It's a passive path, a surrender even, to an order and design repeated throughout creation. A sacred geometry."

"Sacred geometry," Smith said. "The Fibonacci spiral and all that?"

"The fiba-what?" Katy frowned.

"Fibonacci spiral," he said. "It's a mathematical formula in which each interconnected area is the sum of the two preceding areas." Smith dabbed his mouth. "When you graph them, they form the golden spiral."

"There's also the golden ratio," Bair interjected, comfortable with the topic and talking more to Smith than Katy.

Poor Katy at a table of architects. Tessa almost felt sorry, but Katy had started it.

She wrinkled her nose. "Golden . . ."

Smith said, "The sum of two unequal quantities plus the larger of the two is the same as the ratio between the larger and the smaller. Architects proportion their works using the golden rectangle, in which the ratio of the space is divided roughly one to one-point-six-one-eight, etc."

"Clear as mud," Katy said, and spooned in peas and carrots.

Tessa bit back a laugh. Smith had always spewed math as though it were a second language, then looked baffled that others didn't speak it. She said, "Labyrinths imitate designs found in nature, in even the human form, that are too perfect to be accidental. So it points to a creator. You walk toward the center, toward the source of that order, releasing the chaos of daily life, seeking wisdom and wholeness. On the outward journey you return to the world—metaphorically—with the insights gained within."

Bair swabbed his mouth. "Sounds a little New Age mumbo jumbo."

Her eyes narrowed infinitesimally. "Hardly new, considering most cultures on the earth have had some form of labyrinth represented in their art and mythology."

"Not new, maybe, but all . . . Nirvana and one-with-the-universe stuff."

"Just because the tool has been used in alternative ways doesn't invalidate its concept. Satan quoted Scripture, but Jesus didn't toss it out." She cut into a stiff piece of roast beef. "And there are mysteries in the world, Bair, whether people want to see them or not." She hadn't meant to sound so defensive.

Smith warned Bair off with a look, and she could just imagine their conversation after she'd left. *Don't question Tessa's thing for labyrinths. She's irrational. Unstable.* The anger and hurt returned. She understood that people didn't get it. But why did they have to criticize someone who did? Katy hadn't understood Smith's mathematics, but she didn't call it mumbo jumbo or suggest it wasn't valid.

"So how come you can't talk about what you're building?" Katy washed a bite down her throat.

"The owner requested privacy." Smith's tone indicated end of subject.

"I bet I could guess."

The muscle in Smith's jaw quivered. "You could, but we wouldn't say. So what fun is that? Bair, can you pass the gravy?"

Tessa hadn't taken any, but now she wasn't sure she could swallow her meat without it. At least she knew she wasn't missing anything eating alone in her room.

"It's like a park or something with that maze."

Smith turned a stony face on Katy. Bair looked mortified.

Tessa forced the meat down her esophagus. "How long have you worked at Ellie's, Katy?"

"Too long." She jammed her fork into a chunk of beef. "I've done everything in this stupid county too long."

"Why don't you go somewhere else?" Tessa noted Smith's relief at her successful detour.

"How? Where? Opportunities aren't exactly growing in these woods."

Katy looked fierce, as though Tessa were personally responsible for her plight, then turned to Bair as though he could be her salvation. Tessa hoped that wasn't the whole story. "Have you gone to college?"

"No." Katy preferred the previous subject and plied Bair once more. "Are you building a theme park, outlet mall? Something to get me out of Grandma's teahouse?"

Bair cleared his throat. "We can't . . . say."

She pouted. "I won't tell."

Smith's face got stonier. Tessa knew that look. This time, she didn't come to his rescue. He'd roped them all into this—let him figure it out. To his credit, he didn't look to her for an escape. He'd avoided looking her way at all. The hurt grew.

She wished she were alone in her room to process the whole thing. Maybe call Dr. Brenner. It mattered that Smith had changed the equation. She hadn't foreseen this variable. Dr. Brenner would say he'd warned her.

"All right, Tess?"

She jumped. When had Smith turned to her? "Actually, I don't feel good." She pushed back from the table and stood up. "I need to go." Bair could deal with Katy. He wasn't helpless. She took her jacket and her keys and all but flew out the door.

"Tessa, wait." Smith followed.

She didn't want to wait, didn't want to argue, didn't want to cry.

He caught up at the car. "Please."

"I need to go, Smith." She suddenly found it hard to breathe. *No.* She would not let the panic into her consciousness. She backed against the car.

"What is it? What happened?" Furrows dug into his brow.

"Nothing."

He braced her between his outstretched arms. "If it's about before, I'm sorry."

"Sorry doesn't change anything." Her terror rose. The woods were closing in. She had to run, but she couldn't move. Dr. Brenner had feared an overlap. Here it was.

"Tess." Smith gripped her left elbow.

"Let me go."

"I can't do that."

She would not melt down in front of him. Her stomach churned. She bit her lip against the rising panic.

"I'll take you, if you need to go. I don't want you driving alone."

She couldn't speak.

"Is it asthma?"

She shook her head.

He took the keys from her hand. "We'll take your car. Bair can get Katy back and pick me up at the inn."

She'd stopped listening, her own panicked breath the loudest thing she heard.

He moved her around to the passenger side. This was wrong. She couldn't get in with him. She'd have no control. But she slid mutely into the seat, keeping the terror from her eyes. Never show fear. Monsters feed on fear.

"You're not afraid, are you?"

Her chest quaked, but she shook her head no.

"You won't say a word. Not one word."

Her head moved side to side. She would not be afraid. She would not talk.

She jolted. Where had that come from? The monsters in her dreams didn't talk. They only chased. She shut her eyes and barely kept from crying out when the engine started.

She gripped the seat. Smith reached across and strapped her in. She fought another scream. He'd either stopped talking or she couldn't hear him anymore. *Don't be afraid. Don't say a thing.* She opened her eyes after a while when she realized the car had stopped. He'd gone past the inn to the hospital in Leonardtown.

"I just want to make sure you're all right."

She wanted to tell him no, but she couldn't. It took everything in her to draw the humid night air into her lungs. He let her out and ushered her through the emergency entrance.

A moonfaced receptionist manned the check-in counter. "May I help you?"

Tessa shook her head.

"Just tell her what happened," Smith murmured.

The woman waited, then prompted, "Shortness of breath, pallor—maybe panic?"

"No." If she didn't recognize it, panic could not move from her nightmares into her life. She spent the sleeping half of her life afraid; she would not surrender the rest. She clutched the counter, feeling light-headed.

A few moments later a nurse coaxed her through the door to the cubicles. "Just come on back and we'll talk."

She didn't want to talk—not to this stranger, not to Smith, not to anyone who didn't get it. She did not want to hash it all out again. She was tired of trying to explain. "I don't need to be seen."

"Are you sure? You seem a little stressed."

"I'm fine." Her fists formed bone-white knuckles.

"Do you take medications? Anti-anxiety or . . ."

"I have a prescription for Xanax. I only use it when I can afford to be dopey."

The nurse made a note. "Did something set off an attack?"

Tessa tensed. "There's nothing wrong."

"Any other meds?"

"No." Not anymore.

"Why don't I get a BP." She removed the pressure cuff from the hook, but Tessa shook her head.

"I don't need treatment."

"Your friend seemed pretty concerned."

Her friend? If he'd taken her home, she'd be calm already. "I need to go."

"I'll just send the doctor in."

Tessa shook her head. "I don't need to see him."

"It's a woman tonight. Dr. Gail Adams."

Gender didn't matter. Tessa pushed aside the curtain and headed for the door. "I don't need to see her. Smith overreacted."

"I'd recommend—"

"I appreciate it, but all I need is sleep." Though she dreaded the thought. If she was no longer safe wide awake, what would the night bring?

The nurse sighed. "Come back if you change your mind."

Tessa swept through the automatic doors and out to the front. As Smith rose to his feet, she strode past him into the night. She'd walk to the inn. It couldn't be that far.

Outside he caught her arm. "Wait, will you."

"Where's the inn?"

"About three and a half miles."

How had they gotten so far past without her noticing? "Which way?"

"Get in the car, Tess. I'll take you."

The stubborn set of his mouth said he would not let her go off alone in the dark. Wanting this over, she buckled herself in and rode silently. She got out at the inn before he could think of getting her door. *Now leave*, she thought.

"Are you going to talk to me?" He'd reached the inn door.

"I'll see you tomorrow."

He rubbed a hand over his face, clearly agitated. "Tess, if I—"

"It's not about you." In a real sense that was true.

"I don't feel good leaving with no explanation."

He should try living without one. "I guess I'm not a good double date."

He held her gaze too long. She spun for the door. "I'll see you in the morning." If not for the labyrinth, she'd fly home and never see him again.

He didn't move until she'd closed the door and climbed the stairs. After that she didn't know because she didn't look back.

11

Bair had dropped Katy off when Smith got into the Rover. "All right?"

"Not really."

"She didn't seem ill earlier. But I guess things can just come on."

"She's not ill. She's upset."

"By what happened in the kitchen?"

"I kissed her."

Bair frowned. "I thought you weren't going there."

"I wasn't." He could not believe he'd acted so irresponsibly. "But . . . she was all shaking and teary-eyed. . . ."

"Tears." Bair nodded. "The brain scrambler."

"I know better. I *knew* better at twenty-two." He pressed his head between his hands.

"Maybe there's more to it than you think."

"There's not more to it. I like sane women."

"Sane didn't work out so well." Bair flicked him a glance.

Smith refused to add old anger to new angst. "I took her to emergency, thought maybe it was asthma or food poisoning."

Bair scowled.

"I mean allergic reaction, you know, since she couldn't breathe."

Bair hit the open road and took off. "What did they say?"

"She left before seeing the doctor. It was all I could do to get her to let me drive her home."

"All that over a kiss?"

Smith shook his head. "There has to be more to it. She told me something about nightmares once. Maybe they've become panic attacks. That's what it looked like."

"Would she want to be left alone, then?"

"If I'm the cause. Look, Bair, maybe you should liaison between us, so she won't have to deal with me."

"Bad idea."

"Why?"

"You might not see it, but she's got feelings for you."

"I see it. She despises me."

Bair shook his head. "Get to the bottom of the row you had and apologize."

"All I do is apologize. I'm not even sure I'm apologizing for myself anymore. It's as though I'm apologizing for everyone who's ever hurt, left, and betrayed her. If you acted as go-between—"

"Brilliant. When we're all cozied up in the office, you'll just talk past her and I'll repeat it back."

Smith released his breath. "No, obviously. I wish we weren't sharing the same space, though. It's being near her that's difficult."

"Why?"

Smith threw out his hands. "Chemistry, I guess." Except it wasn't only that. There was something deeper that tugged when she was near. It had since the first time he'd seen her crossing campus with a look on her face of equal parts utter delight and sheer terror.

It was the first time he'd experienced the pull and repulsion of her magnetism. He'd learned quickly how hazardous she could be, yet there'd been an excitement to it as well. But he'd been young and careless then. He should have learned something since.

Bair shook his head. "I've seen you when it's only chemistry. You've got stronger brakes than a 747."

Smith sighed. "I don't know what, then. Maybe I feel sorry for her."

"What did she do when you kissed her?"

"She . . ." He saw again the look in her eyes, a look that could swallow him whole, that had made him turn and run immediately. "It shouldn't have happened; that's all."

Bair shot him a pointed look. "Maybe it's time to dump your baggage."

"What baggage?"

"Danae."

"That's well done and over with."

"Then why not go for it?" Bair pulled through the open gate.

Smith hopped out and closed it, then got back in. "Listen, Bair. There's nothing personal between Tess and me. That would be insanity."

"Would it?" Bair pulled up at the trailer. "Because I think she's a nice girl, and maybe it wouldn't be so bad to have someone who wanted you as much as you wanted her."

Smith blew an exasperated breath as they climbed out. "This isn't about Danae. And Tessa's not— I told you. She's got issues. Serious issues that, believe it or not, don't involve me."

"You can't help her sort them out?"

"Not if—" Smith paused on the stoop and sniffed. "Do you smell that?"

"Urine."

"And not an animal's. That's human."

"How on earth would you know?"

"Hunting with Dad—and a few foul men's rooms." Smith stepped off the stoop. "It's still wet." He caught the glint in the moonlight and scraped the soles of his shoes in the dirt.

"Someone peed at our door?"

"Looks that way."

"But who? What for?"

Smith frowned. "I don't know. An insult. A prank. A warning."

"Warning?"

"In human culture, urinating on something is an insult. In nature it's a territorial challenge."

"You said it's not an animal."

"Doesn't mean he doesn't act like one." Smith searched the darkness around them. "The level was clearly not message enough. Yesterday it was a dead bird." He had disposed of it without alerting Bair or Tessa.

Bair stared. "What's he trying to say?"

"If I had to guess, he'd like to scare us off."

"But . . . it's almost childish, these pranks."

Childish . . . and sinister.

"Maybe it's a poltergeist." By his expression, Bair was only half teasing.

"Step over, won't you, and bring out the bleach."

Tessa shuddered. The panic had passed, but it left a residue of disgust. Why hadn't she simply dealt with the situation? She should not have disintegrated in front of Smith and Bair and Katy. There hadn't even been a reason—just an escalating physical response she couldn't tie to anything, directly.

Hands shaking, she made the call she'd been resisting. No point pretending she didn't need help. She would listen—to anything except giving up the labyrinth. The project had taken hold of her, and she would see it rebuilt, even if it meant facing Smith every day. She just had to get through the night, and she wasn't too proud to admit she couldn't do it alone.

Dr. Brenner's voice mail connected. "Dr. Brenner. If this is an emergency, press one. Or leave a message at the tone."

She pressed one. He'd want her to. Besides, it was earlier there.

"Hello?"

"It's me."

"What can I do for you, Tessa?"

She sat down on the bed. "I need you to relax me."

"All right. Tell me what's going on."

She swiped a tear from her eye. "I don't want to talk. Just the relaxation exercise."

He sighed. "Tessa. Have I ever put you in a vulnerable position without knowing the issue?"

"I think it was an anxiety attack."

"Brought on by what?"

Smith's kiss? His immediate rejection? She said, "I don't know. But I felt the woods closing in, the ground getting soft. It was my dream . . . only . . . I wasn't asleep." She shook just saying that much. His pause was so long she chewed her lip raw.

"This is fresh territory, then."

She recognized his probing tone. "It's been a little stressful, and I just need to relax."

"We can't ignore a change this portentous."

"It's not portentous." She clenched her free hand. She wouldn't let it be. "It was one high-anxiety moment. Now it's gone."

"You know better." He sounded disappointed.

"What do you want me to say?"

"Are you prepared to let out what's trying to break through?"

She rolled her eyes back. How many times were they going to have this discussion? "There's nothing trying to break through." Then what was the voice that had taken her by surprise? "Smith kissed me and I wasn't prepared for it. That's all. End of story."

He sighed. "Are you lying down?"

She lay back and adjusted her head on the pillow. "Yes."

"Close your eyes."

She did.

"I'm going to bring you to a safe place, but first tell me how it felt to be kissed."

She swallowed the lump that filled her throat. "I don't want to talk about it."

"If that caused the anxiety, we need to process the emotion."

She pulled her breath in through her nose. "It . . . felt nice."

"Nice how?"

Nice hadn't been the right word. It hadn't been nice; it had been shocking. "Powerful."

"Who had the power?"

She started to shake. "We . . . I . . . It was over too fast, and then . . . he . . ." Her voice broke. "Smith acted like it didn't happen. No, like it shouldn't have."

"Should it have?"

Her hand clawed the bedspread, tears escaping her closed eyelids. "I don't know."

"Sink back into that moment. Before he pushed away."

She felt Smith's lips on hers, his arms around her. She had felt his frustration, but something else, something tender. Something that might be the way a kiss was supposed to be. "I liked it."

"Stay there a moment."

"I can't."

"Why?"

A tear streamed down her temple. "Because he pulled away."

"How did that feel?"

"Like rejection. Desertion."

"Stay with that feeling."

That one was familiar. She let the hurt take over, let it morph with all the other hurts she knew. *Daddy? Daddy!*

She jolted up from the bed, eyes wide, gasping for breath, as though she'd run hard.

"Tessa."

"There's something . . . wrong. I think he's in trouble."

"Smith?"

"No. My dad."

The silence she expected. "Tell me what you saw."

"I didn't see anything. Just the feeling."

"Go back to that feeling."

"No." She started to shake. "Please."

"Lie down."

How had he known she'd sat up? Experience. Years of treating her. She sank back.

"We're going to your safe place."

"Yes." She closed her eyes. "Thank you."

"Relax your face." He led her through each part of her body until she'd released the tight muscles and the shakes had stopped. "How do you feel?"

She pictured a meadow filled with wild flowers so thick their delicate scents were pungent. "Peaceful."

"Good. Go to sleep. I'll talk to you tomorrow."

"Okay." She hung up. Tomorrow.

In the small trailer bedroom, Smith unbuttoned his shirt. "Maybe we've attracted a spy."

Bair's brow creased. "What for?"

"He could be looking for Petra or Gaston."

"Who knows this is their place?"

"Things have been filed in his name."

Bair considered that. "Maybe whoever it is wants us to report the strange activity. Petra's into the paranormal. You heard her talking about the unsettled energy of the property."

Smith nodded. "Petra likes anything sensational."

"In her defense, there is a feeling I get sometimes. I swear I'm being watched, yet when I look there's nothing there."

"I've felt it too. And heard things. Mostly at night. But there must be an explanation."

"Should we say something?"

"And have Gaston down here holding our hands?" Smith shook his head. "Keep our eyes and ears open."

"Still. Fouling the doorstep . . ."

Smith splashed his face with water and rubbed away the tension. "Very odd."

"Odd doesn't touch it. It's barmy."

Smith brushed his teeth and rinsed his brush, thankful whatever was out there had distracted Bair from Tessa. He didn't want to think about tonight. He just wanted to sleep. He got into bed and bunched his pillow into shape.

Bair took his turn in the bathroom, then sat on the edge of his bed. "Could be a nature reservist who doesn't want us to build. Maybe he thinks it's a mall or theme park as well."

Smith raised his head. "Did you get Katy off that?"

Bair sighed. "Persistent girl."

"No having her back."

"I suppose not—even if she wanted to."

"She'd want to."

Bair shrugged. "I had no chance to show my charming self."

"Girls don't want you charming. They want to bring you home and take care of you."

Bair scowled. "Katy's not like that."

True. She seemed more interested in taking care of herself. "I hope you're not simply her ticket out."

"Thank you very much."

"A charming ticket."

Bair heaved his pillow. "She wanted to know about you and Tessa."

"Nothing to know."

"She picked up on it that first lunch at Ellie's. Like sheet lightning arcing over the table."

"Ridiculous." Smith tossed Bair's pillow back.

"And then tonight. The very air singed."

Smith buried his head in his arms. "Enough already."

"Have you thought about the morning?"

He groaned.

"If Tessa comes back—"

"She'll be back." That much he knew. "Nothing will keep her from that labyrinth."

"But you do plan to . . ."

"Grovel?"

"Whatever it takes."

Smith sighed. "I'll protect this job, and that goes for Katy and Tessa and whoever's out there."

They lay in the darkness. Smith had just started to hope that was it when Bair murmured, "How was it? Kissing her."

"You really think I'm going to say?"

"I mean being back in the match."

"If you're asking whether the specter of Danae hung over me, then no."

"Good. That's good."

Smith released a slow breath. In the kitchen with Tessa, Danae had not entered his mind. He closed his eyes. What was he doing? He hadn't planned to reenter the match. He would let her know she didn't need to worry about a repeat performance. Her reaction had warned him off anything more personal than progress reports.

12

Tessa had hoped when she went to work that Smith would avoid her indefinitely, but he was waiting outside the office dressed in pressed jeans and a crisp Oxford shirt. In spite of meticulous grooming, he looked haggard, as though his night had not been restful. She'd slept after her therapy as if Dr. Brenner had ordered her mind to comply.

She sometimes believed he possessed that power. Like the old hypnotist movies. *You're getting sleeeepy.* Maybe that was why she'd resisted that particular therapy. No thanks. No spooky pendulums. But his voice did seem to convey her to whatever state she needed. Now she wished she'd stayed in bed.

She got out of the car and raised a hand to stem whatever Smith might say. "Let's just forget last night happened." She could deal with anything today if Smith left it alone—and if she didn't whiff his cologne and hear his voice and see the look he was giving her, his serious face, no hint of underlying humor, and more than a little concern.

"I need to know you're all right."

He'd called her an egg, but he would see how thick her shell was. No danger she'd break. "I'm fine."

"Sure?"

"I'm fine." She couldn't be more direct than that.

He drew himself up, cool and reserved again, professional. "So back to work?"

"Sure. I think I'll wander around with my eyes shut for a while."

He showed a flashing remorse for yesterday's comment, then inclined his head. "You're the expert."

She ducked into the office for her sketchbook and laptop, but before she could escape, Bair looked up.

"Feeling better?"

"Yes. Sorry about Katy."

Bair flushed, drowning out his freckles. "It was getting awkward anyway. With the non-disclosure and whatnot."

"Curious girl."

"I hope it didn't make you uncomfortable."

She almost laughed. Of all the things that had stressed her, Katy's curiosity came in a pitiable last. "No, Bair. It didn't."

"I know the meal . . . wasn't . . . great. . . ."

"It's the thought that counts. I'm sure Katy appreciated it." Though if anyone could be oblivious to Bair's effort, Katy fit the bill.

Bair looked as if he wanted to correct her misinterpretation, but Tessa grabbed the laptop before he could go on and escaped. Smith was busy with his palm device as she swept past, wanting nothing more than to immerse herself in her work and forget either of them existed.

She found a spot overlooking the labyrinth to finish constructing the preliminary CAD drawing she would submit to Smith. As she worked, the breeze stirred around her. A lazy bee droned by. Ordinarily she'd be at her desk, in the office. That Smith's presence made it impossible she considered a blessing.

After several hours of working in the sun, Tessa went back to her car for the cooler that held her lunch and fortified water. Her forehead and the back of her neck were damp with perspiration. She put the cool bottle to her cheek and closed her eyes until the sound of a car caught her attention—mainly the fact that it was being driven hard with the sonorous proof that it was built for it.

A high-performance roadster whizzed through the open gate and stopped a few yards away. The woman who stepped out could only be Petra Sorenson. Her legs alone appeared to be six feet long, with shin bones that looked as though they'd been pressed to a crease. Her features were gaunt, and her eyebrows angled out to a point. She wore her platinum white hair styled close to her head with a fan of black hair across the back of her neck. The effect was a little Cruella De Vil, but Petra made it stunning.

Tessa remained perched against the trunk of her rental car as the woman gave her the once-over and said, "Wife or girlfriend?"

She closed the lid of her bottle. "Tessa Young. Landscape architect. I'm in charge of your labyrinth."

The woman raised her brows. "The Neanderthals hired a female?"

"It's my specialty. Smith had no choice." And probably regretted it now.

Petra's mouth pulled, and the overweening smile really worked on her. Tessa watched her enter the trailer without knocking and wished she could have seen the effect.

A moment later, Bair ducked his head out. "Er, Tessa, would you . . . join us, please?" He held the door as she closed up the cooler and went inside.

Smith slanted her a glance. "Petra wants to share some ideas."

Bair brought his desk chair around and awkwardly bumped it into the back of Petra's legs. Anyone else would have toppled, but she managed a controlled descent. Her slick short skirt left more than enough leg to hold both men's attention.

Petra folded her fingers around her knee. "I'd like to see the blueprints."

"They're still in process," Smith told her. "I have the preliminary design." He reached for his portfolio. "Dictated by what Mr. Gaston described and elements of the etchings he provided."

Tessa recognized Smith's exacting hand in the drawings he handed over.

Petra looked from one sketch to the next. "What's this?"

"The master suite."

Tessa saw the round window figuring prominently in the design. Somehow she hadn't thought of it in Petra's bedroom.

"Where's the Roman bath?"

"I . . . hadn't heard about a Roman bath. Mr. Gaston spec'd an Italian marble soaking tub there." He pointed.

Petra raised an eyebrow. "Marble's fine. I want it sunken. Five steps at least and much bigger." She studied the drawing, then pressed her finger. "Here?"

Tessa startled when Petra directed the question to her. "Smith would have to—"

"Maybe circular? Beneath the window?"

Tessa imagined Petra bathing beneath the window that overlooked the innermost sanctum of the labyrinth. So much for sacred geometry.

Smith straightened. "It's not possible to put a sunken bath in an upper level. It would have to be raised."

"Why?"

"Because . . . there's a ceiling underneath."

Tessa caught the hint of condescension he struggled to conceal.

Petra thrust out her lower lip. "Move it to the first floor, then."

"The bath?"

"The master suite."

Smith did a slow blink. "Mr. Gaston located it in that upper central position."

"Then find a way to sink the tub. Now, I'll need a runway from the closet. Mirrored. I have to see how an outfit performs." She glanced over, probably realized Tessa didn't share that need, and turned back to the plan. She touched the closet section of the sketch. "Longer through here. Mirror both walls. I'll need at least six strides."

Smith tried for a smile. "Maybe the three of us should sit down, you and Rumer together, before I proceed."

"I want to surprise him."

Smith leaned back. "These are major change orders. I'll have to make sure we're all on the same page."

"Rumer wants me happy."

Bair covered a snort with a cough.

"I'm sure," Smith said ingenuously. "But something as monumental as relocating the master suite—"

"Monumental?"

"Mr. Gaston was firm on its placement. He wants to look out from there, over the maze and gardens."

"Oh, that old maze." She turned. "Do we need it?"

Tessa hid her alarm. "The labyrinth will be the centerpiece of the whole property. Unique and chic. The window in the upstairs room mirrors its center in perfect symmetry. Really good stuff."

Petra frowned. "Make it a gallery or something, then. I've loads of photos and covers."

With all those pictures of herself, would she ever think to look out the window?

Petra counted off on her impossibly long fingers. "The Roman bath, the runway, oh, and the massage room."

Smith saw his escape. "We could locate your Roman bath and massage room in the solarium." He flipped the page back to the main level. "Here."

"Solarium." She rolled her eyes. "That's so last century."

"Mr. Gaston envisions it a cigar room. But we could incorporate a sunken tub, massage table, and even a sauna, without doing violence to the plan."

Petra skewered him with a look. "Se-ve-riously. Why would I open my pores in his cigar room?"

Smith conceded the point. "I could relocate the humidor. Maybe to the library, here." He pointed.

"Library? Where would you put the retro discothèque?"

Smith's mouth parted, but it was a long moment before his reply came. "When would be a good time for the three of us to meet?"

Petra's eyes narrowed, and Tessa saw a crack in her façade. "You want Rumer to overrule me."

"Ms. Sorenson, I want this house to be everything you both want it to be. You have innovative ideas I'd gladly incorporate. But they're not blending with the vision Mr. Gaston and I discussed before your engagement. I'm only suggesting—"

"Wipe it out."

"What?"

"All the starchy library stuff, the cigar room, the—"

Tessa interrupted before she could ax the labyrinth. "Maybe the four of us could sit down. Then you won't be outnumbered."

Smith's gray eyes concealed his reaction to that. If it seemed she had aligned against him, she couldn't help it. Petra was apparently unsure of Rumer Gaston's flexibility, and had hoped to inveigle Smith into working behind her fiancé's back. She must not realize the tight fist Gaston had on this project, or the fact that Smith would relay any such changes to the owner, in any event.

Petra studied her intently, then, assuming she had an ally, said, "All right. The four of us. Rumer's lapdog will call with his schedule." She arose from the chair like Cleopatra from her throne. How did someone learn to move like that?

Bair stared after her until the engine roared to life.

Smith leaned back in his chair, his jaw out of joint as Petra drove away. "Guess that puts the skids on."

Bair nodded. "Think she was serious, or just jerking our chains?"

"She's serious," Tessa interjected. She had no doubt.

Smith pushed up from the chair. "I hope they can come together on something before we end up with a his-and-hers monstrosity. Let's go get lunch."

Bair looked at her. "Tessa?"

"I brought my own." She faked a smile. Smith hadn't intended her inclusion, but Bair didn't know that.

"Welcome to join us," Smith said without looking.

"No thanks." She headed for the door, knowing her exit would be nothing like Petra's. She didn't care. If Smith couldn't look at her when offering an invitation, then she wanted no part of it. She wasn't hungry anyway. The sandwich she had brought would only turn in her stomach.

CHAPTER

13

Tessa heard the Land Rover leave as she stalked back to the labyrinth. Having the whole place to herself, she drew a deep breath, and it felt like the first time she'd breathed since arriving. Last night's panic had fled, and the sunbathed field welcomed her.

She had told herself she was fine forgetting last night, but she wasn't fine. It stung that Smith was. She jammed the shovel into the ground, heaved the dirt, and jammed in the shovel again.

She wasn't crazy enough to think she could uncover the entire pathway herself. She simply wanted to discover all she could of its original construction, to sense, if she could, something more than she'd been able to learn about its creator. She closed her eyes and drained the animosity from her mind so she wouldn't taint with anger a path that had been laid in reverence to God.

The only way she would maintain that focus was to press Smith out of her thoughts completely. She imagined the path restored, rebuilt where needed, new plants taking root, the gate repaired, rehung. The silence that would permeate the space where pilgrims walked—no, where Petra walked—if she ever bothered with "that old maze."

Tessa sighed. It might feel like more, but it was still a job.

This was her living, Petra the client. Maybe she could gear the labyrinth to the supermodel as she'd modified the last for Alicia Beauprez. A little retro discothèque in the center. She groaned at the sacrilegious thought.

Mazes were frequently built for fun and entertainment, but not the Cathedral labyrinth intended as a symbolic pilgrimage to the Holy Land. How could she reconcile that with these owners? Line the hedge with mirrors?

She needed to calm down and do her job. Just relax and . . . That reminded her she had not checked in with Dr. Brenner as she'd promised. It was always harder the day after a crisis, partly because she had to face the fact that she wasn't able to cope alone, and partly the embarrassment of having been so transparent. She closed her eyes. Just get it over with.

He returned her message within ten minutes. "Hello, Tessa." His unvaried greeting revealed little of his frame of mind.

"Calling to let you know I'm all right. And thanks."

"Have you interacted with Smith today?"

"Successfully. We're putting it behind us."

"Explain that."

She rolled her eyes. "I asked him to forget it happened, and he's done so."

"Amazing. You two should patent that. There'd be less heartbreak in the world if everyone could simply erase a difficult interlude."

"It's not erased." Far from it, and talking made it worse. "We're simply choosing to maintain a professional distance."

"And how will that bring the closure you're after?"

"That will come when I'm finished with this labyrinth." She brushed the wispy bangs back from her face.

"Ah yes, the labyrinth."

"I met the property owner—well, one of them. I'm attempting to adapt the labyrinth to her personality."

"Master of the safe segue." He gave a soft laugh. "My appointment's here anyway. Ciao."

His sign-off gave a much better clue than his greeting as to his mood and the degree of satisfaction he felt regarding their communication. Both must be fairly good to rate "Ciao."

While she was at it, she called Genie and checked in. The cat was gone, but Tessa assured her he'd be back. "He has to leave once in a while to prove his independence. Otherwise his life is very nearly that of a domesticated animal."

"Can't have that, I guess." Genie laughed. "Though he's content with square meals and sun spots the rest of the time."

Tessa enjoyed the way they'd begun communicating as friends since Genie had moved in to house-sit. Surrounded by herbs and suncatchers with which Tessa and her mother had filled the rooms, Genie couldn't help but feel part of them. Maybe Tessa should stop waiting for her to take off.

"All right, then. Talk soon."

With no more immediate distractions, Tessa slid the phone into her pocket, left the spade where it lay, and stepped onto the path. She needed to settle her spirit, sink into the place she hoped to find answers and peace.

She closed her eyes and drew a deep breath, then studied the path a moment before moving in, counting her strides as a rhythmic measurement to later plug into the mathematical calculations. The rhythm of the labyrinth worked on a subconscious level, like a sacred dance, especially when traveled with meditational intention. She always strove to make the journey as fruitful as possible.

As she neared the center, she slowed, finding a block inside her. She searched it intuitively, but it didn't take much self-realization to attribute it to her resentment toward Smith. To progress past, she would have to forgive the fresh wound he'd caused and surrender her anger. Her steps halted. A true block, then. Would she have to turn back without the fulfillment of reaching the center?

She needed divine insight, needed divine comfort. Was the anger worth losing that? Yes, if it protected her from the hurt! She clenched her hands. No. It wasn't. Anger would debilitate. If she allowed a block now, how would she find the purity to re-create what had been laid in reverence?

She probed the block, realized with some surprise that it stemmed more from the fact that she had enjoyed and desired the kiss than from Smith's action alone. That was enough, she decided with relief, to break through the block. She would share the blame and, in seeking forgiveness, forgive.

Tears prickled, tears of gratitude and awe. She had done what she needed in order to complete the path into the center. But as she stood there in silence, only a hollow opened inside her. She sighed and lowered her chin. There was no point forcing it.

She'd learned long ago that the only constant in her life was disappointment. Maybe she'd accomplished all she needed on the path to the center, and what she'd bring out was the insight she'd gained at the point of blockage. She'd forgiven Smith for last night, forgiven herself for wanting it to be real. Maybe God had no part in something so insignificant.

She drew herself up and scrutinized the vines clogging the center, vines she recognized with dismay. Maybe it was time to bring in a Bobcat and do a little earthmoving. With a phone call, she arranged for that, then walked the path out, striving at least to leave the disappointment where she'd found it.

At the exit, she crouched down and lifted the end of the heavy gate. With the Land Rover, she could deliver it to a metal repair shop. The sooner she got it out of the elements the better. But Bair and Smith had taken the Rover.

Getting a firm grip, she lifted and carried it a few steps, then set the corner down. It was too heavy. The corrosion smeared her hands and thighs. Though the morning had started cool, the muggy air clung to her skin. She rubbed an arm over her forehead and saw Smith coming her way.

Lunch hadn't lasted long, or else she'd wrestled with the block longer even than it had seemed. The knot that found her stomach suggested she had maybe not accomplished as much as she'd thought. She laid the gate back down on the ground and braced herself. "I thought you were getting food."

"I was. But Rumer phoned. He wants to fly us to Nevada to meet with him and Petra."

"Us?"

"She's insisting on the foursome you suggested."

She had offered to meet, not fly across the country with Smith. "Why Nevada?"

"He's opening a new casino in Laughlin."

"Can't the discussion wait until he can come here?"

Smith looked away. "He's been here, seen it, described what he wants. He expects us to convince Petra she wants it too."

"What?"

He turned back, his gaze probing hers. "He wants no division in the ranks."

"So it's three against one?"

Smith spread his hands. "He hopes I . . . we . . . can describe and illustrate the project's entirety in a manner that will intrigue Petra and help her let go of some ideas that don't fit."

"It will be her house too, Smith."

"I know. As I told her, I wouldn't mind incorporating things she wants, but she and Gaston need to come together on this."

She shook her head. "He doesn't want to come together. He

wants us to do a hard sell on his fiancée. No wonder she tried to schmooze you instead."

"Thank you. I'm obviously a pushover."

She rubbed the tarnish on her hands. "I didn't say that. I just understand now why she came out here by herself with her ideas. She's marrying a manse lord."

Smith frowned. "God forbid a man should have a say in his property."

"What about Petra's say?"

"He's flying us out for Petra's say."

"So we can shoot her down."

Smith sighed. "I don't like it any more than you do. But he's signing the checks."

"That's all it comes down to?"

He faced her full on. "Do you have any idea how important it is to impress him here? He's building all over the world. First-class hotels. I'd have the chance to do cutting-edge designs."

She didn't believe it was only the money. Smith wanted a patron for his art. "I suppose she deserves it for marrying someone like that."

"Age-old story, Tessa. He's rich; she's beautiful. It's mutually beneficial."

She looked back at the labyrinth. "I don't want to be part of it."

"You made yourself part of it."

"I only thought—"

"Listen. Neither of us likes this. Maybe we can work up a design that really will please and impress Petra while retaining the elements Gaston insists on."

Tessa raised her brows. "We?"

"Why not? You had good ideas once. You think like a woman.

You heard her requests. If Gaston and Petra can't come together on this, maybe we can."

That was the last thing she wanted. "Why don't you ask Bair?"

"He's not the creative force you are."

"I don't want to—"

"Work with me?"

It would be too close to what they'd had. "I don't know your software or the codes or—"

"All I want is your input and ideas so that what we present pleases both parties."

"I'm not qualified." Or prepared mentally or emotionally to work that intensely with him. She started for the office.

"Is it that or is it me? Because I promise I won't cross the line between business and personal."

"I can't make that promise." It was out before she could shoot it in its tracks. It didn't matter if it was work, it would feel personal.

His eyebrows arched ironically over his eyeglasses. "I promise I'll bear it if you find yourself losing control."

She planted her hands on her hips. "Why did you kiss me last night?"

"Because I wanted to."

"I don't believe you."

He spread his hands. "I had no ulterior motive. I certainly didn't premeditate it."

"Because the thought would be dreadful?"

"Because my last relationship didn't end well."

Her mouth froze around her planned retort and left her with, "Oh."

He sent his narrowed gaze off to the side. "That's not the point here."

"Maybe not. But it helps."

"How?"

"To know it's not just that I'm unstable."

He hung his head. "You're not unstable, Tess. Just high maintenance."

She glared. "Petra's high maintenance."

"Petra's above my price range. You're . . ."

"What?"

"Nothing." He started for the office, trying to make his escape.

"I'm what, Smith?" She stayed right behind him.

"Why do you make me say things that will only cause trouble?"

"You started saying it. Now finish."

He turned on his heel, and she ran into him. He caught her elbows. "You need more than any man can give."

She opened her mouth. "You have no idea what I need."

"I think I do. It's in your eyes, your—everything about you."

"Then let's be clear. Whatever you think I need, I don't need it from you."

"That's good. Because I don't . . ." He let go. "I don't have much to offer."

Not at all what she'd expected him to say. How could he even think it? "That's not true."

He started walking.

"It's not true, Smith. You might not want to waste it on me, but—"

"Tess." He turned with hurt in his eyes. "Nothing's wasted on you."

"It's all right. I don't actually expect things to work out. They never do." She got moving before the pity reached his eyes. She didn't want to see it and wasn't trying for it. "I guess you can show me what you want to do."

She held the hurt at bay while he opened the program and brought up his concept. She could see why Rumer Gaston didn't want to relinquish the design. Smith had played off the monastic elements, but with fresh, clean lines and creative space. She saw what she'd already guessed, that he had a natural talent waiting to be recognized. No wonder he wanted this so badly. But Gaston wasn't the only one involved.

"All right." She settled into the chair she'd pulled over from her desk. "This is what I heard. As you said, Petra's part of the equation is her beauty. She wants the house, especially the bedroom, to remind Rumer why he has her. She'd rather he watch her bathe than look out the window over his property. If he must look out, she'll surround him with her image. She'll walk the runway for him when she dresses, because that's where she shines. Though difficult to believe, I think she's insecure in the relationship."

Smith had turned and was staring through his glasses as though she were a fascinating specimen. "How did you get all that?"

"Lots of therapy." She didn't want him looking at her with such intensity. "The thing that really works for her is motion. You saw how she moved; Bair couldn't keep his eyes off. A disco—lights, music, and motion—would give her a place, once again, to display her assets. If you can't include it, we need to figure out what else might do that."

"So the key is to create elements that give Petra security. What's Gaston after?"

"Power. He wants to be king."

"So in essence we're balancing their egos."

"His ego with her insecurity."

Bair brought them cups of tea and tried not to look worried. Did he think they'd tear each other apart the minute his back was turned?

He shifted. "Mr. Gaston wants to send a jet to Baltimore in the morning. Will that . . . timing work?"

Subtext: Had she agreed to go and could they possibly be ready?

When she didn't answer, Smith shrugged. "He doesn't know we're attempting this consolidation. He thinks I'll be rehashing what we already decided."

Tessa studied his face. "Are you willing to risk it?"

"Let's see how successful we are."

They worked through dinner and into the night. Bair made roast beef sandwiches from the leftover beef and kept them supplied with tea. He had slumped down in the only comfortable chair in the corner of the office and drew long, snuffling breaths through his half-open mouth, insisting when they addressed him that he did not need to go to bed.

"Well," Smith said, jamming his fingers into his hair when the night had slipped to morning and crept toward dawn. "It's not complete by any stretch, but we have a concept." His eye and her gut instincts had brought it together.

"I think it could work." She yawned, suddenly aware of the fatigue.

Smith rolled his chair back. "I'll drive you in."

She shook her head. "I'm okay."

"We'll be taking your car to the airport in the morning anyway."

"In the morning?" She raised her brows sardonically.

He looked at his watch. "In a few hours. I'll drop you off now and pick you up on the way. No point your driving out here for me."

She guessed he was rationalizing to support his position, but she was tired enough to accept.

Smith shook Bair's shoulder. "Go to bed, Bair. We're finished."

He opened his eyes. "Mmm . . . wide awake."

"I'm taking Tessa back. Get some sleep."

Bair pushed himself up. "Right, then."

While working, their discord had disappeared. Now, alone in the car with him, her defenses collapsed. It had been so wonderful pooling their ideas, playing off each other, sparking fresh concepts. They had integrated gardens with the architectural motifs to strengthen Gaston's vision and relocated the master suite to meet Petra's needs. With cleverly mirrored angles—not unlike labyrinthine elements—they had created an inner space that would reflect her like the facets of a diamond. To Tessa's half-trained eye, they'd created a masterpiece of cooperative adaptation.

Smith at last pulled up to the inn. They hadn't spoken a word, both inhabiting their own thoughts through the entire drive. But now Smith parked and turned. She met his fatigued gaze with her own and allowed the smile that spread between them. It was all she could do not to reach over and smooth the hair he'd left standing.

"So, I'll come for you nine-ish?"

She nodded. "I'll throw together an overnight bag and something to meet in."

His smile turned drowsy. "Don't outshine Petra."

"No worry there." She reached for the door handle, but Smith touched her arm.

"Let me." He got out and opened her door.

She climbed out on shaky legs.

He took her elbow and walked her to the door, stood a moment and said, "So, thank you."

She shrugged. "You did the hard work."

He shook his head. "It was both of us absolutely, and . . ." He looked away. "I better let you get some sleep." He opened the inn door.

She slipped inside. "Good night."

"Pleasant dreams."

He didn't know what a thoughtful wish that was.

CHAPTER

14

Smith drove back to the office, overwhelmed by what he and Tessa had accomplished. It was what he'd imagined years ago—only better, so much better. He had technical skill, innovation, and creativity, but her insight was remarkable. She brought an intuition that gave the structure exactly the personality they'd been striving for.

They were an awesome team. And he didn't want to think it because it wouldn't last. When would their paths logically cross again over a labyrinth? And more than that, they might have called a truce to accomplish this thing, this incredible thing, but once the afterglow faded they'd be who they were before and nothing would be right and . . .

He sighed. He needed sleep, but he reached the trailer more invigorated by their interaction than fatigued. In the dawn light, he moved toward the door and jammed his foot against something. What . . . ? He bent and stared. The gate. Tessa's gate lay beside the stoop, when they'd left it lying in the labyrinth field. He straightened and searched the woods around him. Whoever was there liked playing games. Or was he restricting them to the trailer, removing anything they left elsewhere?

Determined not to give the intruder any satisfaction, Smith

moved past the gate and went into the trailer. Bair's guess at some-one who didn't want them to build might be the closest of all. Should he mention it to Gaston? What if it escalated to sabotage when they started building? He crept into the bedroom and removed his shoes, shirt, and jeans while Bair slept undisturbed. He had a responsibility to apprise the owner, even if it sounded crazy.

He tried to rest, but his thoughts would not still. It seemed like just minutes later he was driving back to get Tessa, fortified only by strong tea. She opened the inn door as he drove up, tossed her carry-on into the backseat beside his, and got in. He couldn't stop the smile.

"What?"

"You look like you did all those mornings you wanted to cram." Tousled and soft-faced and adorable.

"And you wouldn't help me."

"You didn't need help." It was even more evident now. Not as technically proficient, perhaps, she nonetheless worked out of a reser-voir of something inside her that no head knowledge could trump.

"Whatever you say." She settled in as he started for the airport, and after a while said, "Do you think Bair might haul that gate somewhere to be repaired? I was hoping to borrow the Land Rover and take care of that."

Strange how she picked thoughts right out of his head. "Bair's heading up to the main office while we're gone, but he can drop the gate somewhere on his way."

"Does he know where to find it?"

Smith turned. "Actually, yes. It was lying beside the stoop."

"What?" She frowned. "What's going on?"

He shrugged. "Bair thinks a poltergeist, but that gate would be an awful lot of material matter for a ghost to relocate, so I'm leaning toward human mischief. So far the pranks have been harmless." He refrained from mentioning the odorous activity on the doorstep.

"But . . . it's just weird."

"Quite."

She sank back in her seat and rubbed her eyelids.

"Did you sleep?"

She nodded. "Like a rock for two hours."

"Good for you."

"Didn't you?"

He sent her a sideways glance. "Just that nasty surface sleep where your mind keeps whizzing over everything. Lines and patterns and measurements." Her sitting beside him, challenging him as he'd never been before.

"Do you want me to drive?"

He shook his head. "I'll sleep on the flight."

Silence settled, pregnant with unsaid words. Finally she murmured, "Do you think they'll like it? What we did?"

"I've learned not to anticipate anything either way. Sometimes people can't envision it, even with the 3-D model in front of them. Sometimes clients think they know what they want, but when you give it to them on paper, it's all wrong. Sometimes they catch the magic. You just never know."

"Catch the magic." She smiled. "It was, wasn't it."

His throat tightened. "Yes."

"You said last night you don't bounce ideas off Bair. How come?"

"Bair thinks very concretely. He's going to handle commercial structures that emphasize utility over design. He's quite good with cost control."

"Then you've never done what we did last night, pooled creative energy and funneled it into conceptual design?"

"Not like that, no." He stared ahead at the road until his voice would convey no more than he intended. "I sometimes shared concepts with Danae." In a business sense, Tessa had no need to know about her. After last night, he wasn't sure they were firmly business only.

"Did she work with you? Another architect?"

"No. She didn't know anything technical. I simply wanted her opinion on everything." He watched that sink in. Way more than he'd wanted to reveal.

"She must have loved your drawings."

"Not everyone is fascinated with lines."

She turned, slightly agape. "You remember that?"

"Why wouldn't I?"

"Because . . ." Her throat worked. "I didn't think anything I said had much of an impact."

"You're wrong."

She looked out the window, hurt rising from her in waves.

"Tess?"

"It was easier to think you hadn't really gotten me than that you'd turn on me, knowing . . . how I was."

"It was six years ago. I was full of myself and my plans. I assumed everyone wanted a piece of what I had to offer. When you changed direction, it was as though I'd failed somehow."

She turned back, eyes glazed with tears. "You'd failed? You never failed in anything."

He pulled a crooked smile. "That shows what you know."

She turned back to the window.

He sighed. "I suppose it confirmed your philosophy that nothing works out."

"It went a long way. That and never trusting anyone who has the power to hurt me."

He swallowed the ache in his throat. "I'm sorry, Tess. Really." When she merely shrugged, he said, "You've got to give me more than that. Tell me you forgive me." The pain that washed over her face confused him. "Or not. If you don't want to."

She stared down at her hands. "I do want to. It's what I came for. To find closure."

"That sounds final."

"I thought it would be." She bit her lip. "Last night was . . . really great. The way we clicked, the energy. I'm thankful for that."

"So am I." He didn't want it to end there. "I'd envisioned it, you know, working like that with you. That was why I tried so hard to dissuade you from changing course."

"It was? You didn't say that."

"Yes, well, that would've been begging. I had far too much head for that."

"I don't know what to say. All this time I thought . . ." Her hands fell open on her lap.

"It's quite obvious what you thought all this time." He formed a grim smile.

"It might have helped to talk."

"A little like stepping on a land mine."

She glared. "You didn't even try."

"Would it have changed your mind?"

She shook her head.

"Then I'd have been limbless for nothing."

"But I'd have understood your motivation."

"Would you have even heard me? Once you'd shut me out?" Her gaze fell to her hands. "I don't know."

They drove in silence until she picked up the previous thread. "So who was Danae, if not a colleague?"

"An event planner." Probably not exactly what she was asking. "On a big scale. Openings and whatnot."

"How did you meet?"

He really didn't want to go into it. "One of my parents' gatherings."

"In London?"

"New York." Why had he started this?

"Did they introduce you?"

"A friend of the family."

"What does she look like?"

He shot her an exasperated look, but he'd opened the door; he couldn't blame her coming through. "Tall. Straight brown hair. She wore it twisted up in back to look professional, rarely let it down, literally or figuratively."

"What attracted you?"

"She was very sure of herself." The opposite of Tessa, he realized, and while it had attracted, it had also troubled him. "I'm not sure I would have attempted anything if she hadn't taken the lead."

"How long were you together?"

"A little over two years."

"Why didn't you marry her?"

"Honestly, Tess!" He regripped the wheel and composed himself. "She wanted my silver spoon more than she wanted me. Unfortunately it wasn't all she imagined, and when she found someone with a shinier spoon, she took it."

Tessa stared at him so hard he scowled.

"It happens."

"I'm sorry."

"No need."

She chewed her nail. "What did you do?"

"Moved on. Focused on what really matters."

"What really matters?"

He turned. "Were you always this talkative?"

She nodded.

He dropped his head back against the headrest. "Success."

"You mean money?"

"I mean success in all areas, faith, friendship, and yes, finances."

"You really want this project to work."

"I do."

"You could have spent yesterday creating exactly what Rumer Gaston wanted."

"I already had." He glanced at her. "But you wouldn't have supported it."

"It didn't feel right."

"That's where all your decisions come from, don't they? Your feelings."

She frowned. "I've been known to think."

"Really, though, it's as if you attach some emotion to everything, even words. The way you sensed what Petra was feeling underneath the demands."

"I'm only guessing."

"I think you hit it dead on. But I would never have deduced as much."

"You were distracted."

He slid her a glance. "Not as much as you might think. That kind of beauty is riveting, but it's not real. Not to reach out and touch her. Not like you."

Tessa laughed out loud. "You're saying if Petra and I were lined up and someone told you to take your pick, you'd reach for me?"

"I did, didn't I?"

"And regretted it within seconds."

"Yes, well, there's regret and there's regret, if you know what I mean."

"I've no idea."

"Picking Petra would be like gorging on sweets."

"And I'm like eating your vegetables?"

He rolled his eyes. "You can make this an insult if you want. In point of fact, I like vegetables, as long as they don't start out frozen and end up boiled within an inch of their lives."

She folded her arms. "So I'm good for you."

"That can't be right."

"You know, Smith"—she skewered him with a glance—"you could just let a compliment stand."

"What fun would that be?"

"This is fun?"

He cocked his head. "Shockingly, yes."

She faced forward with an odd expression.

He said, "What?"

"It's almost like we're friends."

"We are friends, Tess. I know I didn't pass with flying colors the last time. I'm not sure I'm much better now, but the thought appeals to me."

Her hands made little fists on her knees. "I just keep—"

"Dredging up the past. You could drain the pond, you know."

"Could I?" The eyes she turned to him were swollen with uncertainty.

"Starting with not despising me."

"I don't." She almost sounded convinced.

"We could pretend we've just met, and I admire your work, and you think I'm spectacular."

She shook her head. "*I* admire *your* work, and you think I'm spectacular."

"We're mutual admirers, and I do think you're spectacular. You were last night."

She put her hands over her face. "I don't know what to do with that."

"It's called letting a compliment stand."

A smile peeked out behind her palms. "So that's what it's like."

He smiled back, amazed by how good it felt. "That's what it's like."

CHAPTER

15

Tessa boarded the private jet, trying not to ogle the opulent furnishings, leather seats that looked softer than any chair in her
home, polished wood trim that shone like glass, flat-screen TV and
surround-sound speakers. She had worked with affluent clients, but
none had sent a jet like this for her to meet them for a chat. Smith
seemed at ease with it, so she kept her remarks to herself.

A pilot and copilot greeted them from the open cockpit, and an
attractive middle-aged attendant offered them the first two of eight
seats. The only thing resembling all the other flights she'd taken
was the seat belt and the roaring rush and thrust of the takeoff.

When they were in the air, Smith turned to her. "So I think
it only fair you tell me your status."

"My status?"

"Are you seeing someone?"

"Besides Dr. Brenner?"

"I thought that was—"

She grinned. "Oh, you mean personally."

"Did you just tease me?"

"I guess so."

Smith pressed a hand to his heart. "I'm honored."

She wrinkled her brow. "To be the victim?"

"Quite. Now answer the question."

"I'm not seeing anyone." She squished deeper into the seat. "I haven't been with someone for two years like you—or even one. I haven't dated all that much."

"I can't believe that, Tess."

"Why not? You think I'm not worth the trouble."

He crossed his arms. "That's not exactly what I said. Besides, I saw you turn heads. I heard guys talking. Until they realize what a handful you are, I'd think there'd be plenty of interest." He said the last with a glint, only half kidding.

She shrugged. "When someone asks me out, I think, he seems nice enough. How long before he proves me wrong?"

"Doomed from the start, hmm?"

"Pretty much."

"So if I wanted to date you—"

Her heart hit her ribs.

"Say, take you out to dinner, you'd click your stopwatch and wait for me to disappoint you?"

"Dr. Brenner calls it 'deserted child syndrome,' when a primary relationship ending in betrayal makes it hard to trust."

"Ever?"

She shrugged. The attendant came by with coffee and Danish pastries. Tessa accepted a cup, though she should try to sleep instead of caffeinating. Two hours wasn't enough to stay sharp, and she had no idea what to expect from this meeting. If she spoke up for Petra, Rumer Gaston could decide he wanted someone else handling the landscape. Would Smith fight for or fire her?

He chose a cheese Danish and asked for tea instead of coffee, then turned. "What else does Dr. Brenner say?"

"That I shouldn't be dealing with you and a labyrinth at once. He called it two stressors and no safety net."

"He knows about me?" Smith looked genuinely stunned. "That's disconcerting."

"You're a faceless stressor. He's more concerned about the labyrinth."

"Why?" His brow furrowed.

"When my dad left, I started having nightmares. Mom and Dr. Brenner helped me deal with them until she died. But my running, screaming, into the woods didn't work for my aunt Estelle, who got charge of me, so she asked Dr. Brenner to let me stay in a nice facility until it was safe to let me out."

"How old were you?"

"Fourteen."

Smith frowned. "What has that to do with labyrinths?"

"They're an element in the nightmares, usually complete with a monster."

"I thought you liked the things! You build them, Tess." He no longer looked sleepy at all.

She must be past caring to tell him all this. "My last memory of my dad included a labyrinth we saw from his airplane. The image stayed with me so powerfully I studied everything I could find about them. And I love creating them, walking them. Just not in my sleep."

He studied her a long moment. "Are you looking for him when you walk the path?"

"For Dad?" Her chest squeezed. "Only in the dreams. I can't ever find him, but I keep trying and trying."

Smith's face softened. "Is it ever time to stop trying?"

Tears stung her eyes. "My mind doesn't think so. Dr. Brenner believes there's something we haven't uncovered." Smith would never think of dating her again.

"Something about your dad?"

"I have no idea."

"That's hard."

She lowered her chin. "I guess it is, but it's been so long, it's just life."

He reached over and took her hand in his warm, smooth palm, his strong fingers. "I'm glad you told me. It explains a lot."

Smith felt the tension in her fine-boned, freshly calloused hand and let go.

She slid it into her lap and looked away. "Any chance we can forget this conversation?"

"Not if forgetting the kiss is any measure."

She turned. "I thought you wiped that whole night out."

"It doesn't work that way, Tess. Refusing to address something doesn't mean it goes away." Then something occurred to him. "Was that part of it? The panic?"

Her jaw tensed. "I don't know what that was. It hasn't happened before."

"I've never gotten that response from a kiss."

She huffed. "It wasn't that."

"I wouldn't mind leaving you breathless, but not gasping. Definitely not the shaking, voiceless pallor."

She glared. "It was not the kiss. That left me—"

"What."

"Nothing."

"You started saying it, now finish." It delighted him to turn it back on her.

She shook her head.

"Shall I tell you how it left me?"

"I know how." Her words snapped like crackers on New Year's Day.

He tipped his head. "You know what I said, not what I felt."

"You turned and ran like Hermes with his feet on fire."

"Because I didn't expect it to be so . . . good."

Her eyes narrowed. "What did you expect?"

"Nothing. I acted without premeditation, on instinct if you will. I'd made you cry and I hadn't meant to and it seemed the thing to do."

"Kiss and make it better?"

"Yes, to put it foolishly." He shoved his fingers into his hair. "I meant to comfort, but then it wasn't that at all. It was . . . brilliant, and I'd like to do it again. I'd like to do it a lot. All the time. And *that* is why I ran like Hermes with his feet afire."

She stared, speechless.

"Tessa." He moved the breakfast tray to the floor beside their seats and rotated his to face her. "Can I try to show you I'm not a monster?"

"I know you're not."

He untangled her hands and held them firmly in his own. "You don't believe it, but I've cared for you from the start." He saw the skepticism fill her eyes. "The thought terrified me when I was too callow to handle what I saw. It doesn't anymore."

She searched his face. "I just told you I spent time in a mental hospital. I have incurable nightmares and don't trust anyone."

"You trust Dr. Brenner."

"I'm not in love with him."

Smith raised his brows.

"I mean . . . I don't mean I am with you. It's just . . . not the same thing."

"I certainly hope not. Sharing puts me in a rotten temper, and I tend to say things like, 'Bog off and good riddance.' "

A smile tugged at her mouth.

"As Bair says, a sane, safe woman didn't make me happy, so why not take a walk on the wild side? Feel free to chip in here anytime, before I go completely over."

She shook her head. "You seriously need to sleep."

"Without a doubt." He couldn't believe he'd said half of what he'd said, but for the first time in too long he felt unfettered. "I need sleep, and I will, but you have to tell me if I'm off course. Otherwise I plan to court you in a manner that leaves no doubt as to my intentions."

She drew a jagged breath. "I don't know what that means."

"It means that I let you slip out of my life once, but I won't again unless you tell me—"

"To bog off and good riddance?"

"That does make the point." His chest tightened. "Is it what you want?"

She shook her head.

"I told you friendship appeals to me, but I have to say I don't think it will for long. I'm letting you know up front so you're not shocked when the game changes." Her concern was palpable, but she hadn't run screaming. Probably because they were thousands of feet above the earth. "I'm going to get some rest now."

"Okay."

"Haricot verts crisply steamed and tossed with crushed shallots and kosher salt."

"What?"

"One of the vegetables I especially like." He raised her hand and kissed her knuckles. A smile broke over her face that shot a piercing pang through his chest. He'd never felt protective around Danae—defensive, but not protective. Now he believed he'd do everything in his power to keep from hurting Tess again. He released her hand. "Get some rest."

Absolutely impossible with her heart trying to break through her rib cage. She dropped her head back against the seat and breathed with difficulty, not gasping terror, but a reckless joy. Trusting Smith with her emotions was like letting the boggy ground suck her in until she could no longer fight, only let it take her deeper and deeper. He'd rejected her once. He'd do it again. And she'd be years getting over it.

But until then . . .

She touched the knuckles he'd kissed. He'd never done anything so intimate. Not even his spontaneous kiss the night before last. He'd said that was instinctive. This had been intentional. Her eyes closed. She loved how they'd spent the night, sharing ideas and feeding each other's creative enthusiasm, though it had left her vulnerable.

Even if it only lasted a little while . . .

He'd been attracted to Danae's self-assurance. He wouldn't find it in her. She knew her business and did it well. But it scarcely masked the personal doubts that lurked inside. So what was it he thought he saw?

She closed her eyes. Smith's breathing had slowed and deepened, drawn thickly into his throat. She'd never heard him sleep, but the sound of it now made her drowsier still. A hungry, lapping drowsiness.

Woods spreading before her. No path. No hedge. Silver trees and darkness. Her feet make no impression. Branches snag her nightgown, tear the silky edge of the blanket she rubs with her fingers. She weaves between the trunks, faster and faster. She runs, her face wet with tears.

"Daddy!"

The darkness comes together and looms over her. "You're not afraid, are you?"

She hides it, hides it down deep and shakes her head.

"And you won't say a word. Not one word."

She woke with a jolt to find Smith watching her. "Did I scream?"

"Not yet."

She'd been working up to it; she could tell by the dampness of her chest, the pumping in her temples. He had caught her hand in his and ran his thumb slowly back and forth along her index finger.

"It was either wake you or give our flight attendant a scare. Bad dream?"

She swallowed. "I don't actually have them all the time."

"Often enough, it seems."

She frowned. "The weird thing is, there was a monster but no labyrinth. And he spoke."

"What did he say?"

Her throat closed around the words. "I don't know."

The attendant brought smoked turkey on foccacia, rose-cut radishes, chocolate-dipped wafer cookies, and sweet, fresh grapes. Definitely not typical airline fare. Smith brought the trays up between their recliners to form a joint surface, and once again she was sharing a meal with him.

He said, "Would you like me to bless this?"

Her faith was private, accessed meditatively, experientially. She and Mom had attended many churches, no one denomination offering everything they looked for. Mom had said once under a sky of stars that it was more church to her than any building, but Tessa nodded. Smith's quaint prayers warmed her.

He thanked God for the food and the opportunity before them. Not just success with Rumer Gaston, but for their friendship and maybe more. The thought caused a shiver down her spine. She looked at him. Something subtle had changed, a softening in the tightness around his eyes and mouth.

"Still shaky?" His voice was barely louder than her thoughts.

"Just processing."

"The nightmare?"

"I don't know why it's changed."

"Is it always the same?"

She shook her head. "No, but it's always a labyrinth, and the monster chases or blocks me. It doesn't talk and it doesn't happen when I'm awake." She gripped her hands. "Dr. Brenner called the panic attack new ground."

"Is that good?"

"It doesn't feel like it. He thinks I'm blocking something, and any breakthrough is good—except I shouldn't be doing it without him."

"Maybe he's the block and I should have a shot."

She jolted.

"Why not? I won't even charge." One side of his mouth pulled up. "Tell me the rest. Now the monster speaks instead of herding you."

She wasn't at all sure she could do this. It was one thing to pour out every detail to her therapist. Was she out of her mind telling Smith these things?

He prodded. "It talks, but you can't understand what it's saying."

"No, I understand. It sa—" The block was like a blow. *"You won't say a word. Not one word."*

"Tess?"

She dropped the sandwich onto the plate and buried her shaking hands in her lap.

"Maybe the monster's changing because you're not alone anymore. Maybe this monster, whatever it is, wants you to feel isolated."

His insight shook her. Deep in the fear was the belief that

she could tell no one, that she was alone in the awful knowledge that . . . that what?

"I haven't been alone. Dr. Brenner has talked me through it every time. The bad ones anyway."

"But you don't love him."

"He's as old as my dad."

"Who left you."

Her heart pounded. Was it possible she didn't trust Dr. Brenner? Or maybe she thought if she let go, she'd lose him too. He'd never been unprofessional, but she depended on him as she would her own . . . dad.

"Maybe I can tell the monster to leave you alone."

She shook her head. "Dr. Brenner's tried everything to make the nightmares stop."

"Not everything." He set their dishes on the floor and lowered the trays. "Now then. The other night when I kissed you—"

"I am not making out on this airplane to trigger a panic attack."

"Just enough to make it talk."

"That's not funny, Smith."

"I'm not teasing, Tess. If you knew what it was saying—"

"I know what—"

"Then tell me."

It felt as though a hand gripped her throat. *Not a word.*

"I can't. Not like this, not now." She got up and went to the bathroom, more to distance herself from him than from any real need.

He stood as she returned, then retook his seat. "I'm sorry. I thought it might help."

She sighed. "I understand. I wish I could fix me too."

CHAPTER

16

Smith took Tessa's cue and kept the conversation light, telling her about Bair's wild rugger days. "He got so aggressive in the matches he'd behave badly, so drunk afterwards he behaved worse. The crowds loved him, but he didn't think much of himself. When I offered him the chance to complete his education in the States and join me, he jumped at it."

"I can't picture him violent."

"It wasn't pretty."

"But he's so . . . gentle."

Smith laughed. "Not on the pitch."

"Was he good?"

"You mean to make a career of it?" He shrugged. "Good entertainment."

"I wonder if he misses playing."

"I'm sure to some degree." He looked over. "Do you still play tennis?"

"I'd be very rusty."

"Maybe we could hit around a little when we land. If the resort has a court."

"I seem to recall you making me run a lot more than necessary."

He smiled. "I'm rusty too."

"Love-thirty handicap."

"All right." He fought another smile because he did remember making her run. "I'd like to loosen up before meeting with our clients, and the slots aren't really my thing."

"But if you did continue working for Mr. Gaston, wouldn't you be designing casinos?"

"Or other resorts. Or vacation homes. Some possibilities for labyrinths there too, you know."

"Somehow I'm not seeing it."

He laughed. He'd forgotten what an easy conversationalist she was, naturally open, whereas Danae had made him pry out what little she ever surrendered of her inner thoughts. He'd wanted to know so much more.

Tessa picked up on his frown. "Are you worried?"

"Yes. You?"

She shook her head. "Your design is perfect."

"Our design."

"All I did was talk."

"You found the heart of it."

"Well." She leaned back. "That's a big part of what I do. Gleaning from the different clients the specific purpose they intend for their paths."

"Is it ever dark?"

"Dark?"

This could get touchy, he realized, but went on anyway. "You know, like the nightmares. There is a bit of paganism involved in the whole labyrinth thing."

"There's paganism in Christmas trees and Easter eggs and days of the week and wedding rings."

"Wedding rings?"

She nodded. "All of them, things Christianity has sanctified."

"I just wondered if you'd built any, knowing they would be used for occult purposes."

"I wouldn't do that, Smith. Not for something satanic."

He searched her face. "So your labyrinths draw people to God."

"Not all. The one I just completed is more of a memorial for an old woman to remember her husband. I imagine her steps will take her through thoughts and reflections of their years together."

"I see. Nothing frightening in that."

"Depends"—Tessa shrugged—"on how ornery he was."

Smith's mouth pulled up. "Quite."

Hot and loose-jointed from their tennis match, Tessa climbed into the shower. The exercise had been good, but now it was time to prepare for their meeting with Petra Sorenson and Rumer Gaston. She hadn't been entirely honest about not being nervous. Had she read Petra correctly? Would Mr. Gaston accept the changes, appreciate the beauty of Smith's design? What if her resistance to Gaston's original plan cost Smith the contract?

She turned around in the water and let it rush over her face. She had to believe they'd both "catch the magic." Some tweaking was possible, but by and large it was all there, a cohesive blend of their needs.

She met Smith in the lounge on the twelfth floor that Mr. Gaston had chosen for their rendezvous. She had put on the only semi-dressy outfit she had with her, a navy layered skirt with a matching off-the-shoulder top. She had pulled up her hair, since Smith thought that looked professional, and threaded her earlobes with a dangle of freshwater pearls. She had a bracelet of the same, but only the gold cross necklace her mother had given her lay in the hollow of her throat.

Still, Smith's expression when she walked in was gratifying. His gray suit and blue shirt played off the hues in his eyes as he watched her approach. He stood with elegant ease and held the high stool at the round table. She climbed up, and he murmured in her ear, "Petra watch out."

"This old thing?" She smoothed her skirt. "Why, I only wear it when I don't care how I look." She'd always wanted to use that old movie line.

"Well, it's bewitching. You're bewitching." He reached over and took her hands. "How am I supposed to concentrate?"

She allowed a tiny smile.

"Tess, you're beautiful."

"Don't sound so surprised."

"It's just that . . . why do you mask it?"

She raised her brows. "I don't. I just don't flaunt myself."

He brought the knuckles of both her hands to his lips. "I'm smitten."

"That didn't stop you destroying me on the tennis court."

The tease was back in his eyes. "I'd have to play blindfolded not to."

She narrowed her eyes dangerously, but before she could adequately insult him back, the dazzling duo entered the room. Or rather Petra dazzled in a slinky silver shift and Mr. Gaston rode her wake—a full six inches shorter, but every bit as commanding. His broad brow spread between deep-set eyes and a coifed hairline. His lips pulled thinly over perfectly capped teeth, yet the thickened bridge of his nose and a pale scar near one ear gave the impression of a thug who'd come into money.

He thrust out his hand, squeezing just a little too hard as he welcomed her, eyebrows raised in a way that had more to do with seeing what she thought of him than anything he thought of her. "So this is our maze specialist. You held back on me, Chandler, not mentioning your 'expert' was so charming. What are you drinking, Ms. Young?"

"Nothing yet. I just—"

"Champagne." Gaston turned to the server who had material-ized at his elbow. "Perrier Jouet Belle Epoque '96." Then to Petra. "Martini?"

She nodded with an aside to Tessa. "No bubbles."

Tessa smiled. She was not fond of champagne herself but hadn't been offered a choice.

"So." Rumer Gaston rubbed his palms and eyed Smith con-spiratorially. "What have you got for me?"

No small talk, then. Tessa glanced at Petra, whose mouth had firmed. Did she assume, like her fiancé, that they had ignored her requests?

The table surface would not have been adequate for blueprints, but Smith opened his laptop and accessed the CAD design that he had rendered in 3-D for this presentation. The sommelier appeared with a silver wine chiller and the champagne wrapped in white cloths. With practiced ease he kept the cork from launching, then poured the flutes to the exact height and set them around. Didn't champagne signify completion and satisfaction? In celebrating up front, Gaston showed reckless confidence that they had done his bidding.

The server brought Petra's martini, and even in that she'd been singled out. Tessa chose to believe Mr. Gaston merely knew her preferences, but it sent a visual message of solidarity in the rest of them. Maybe that was why he hadn't asked hers or Smith's opinion before ordering. It was all so subtle.

Smith gave a brief explanation of how they had created what he was about to show them. Tessa felt a prickle up her neck as Rumer

Gaston realized his original expectations had been modified and Petra's ideas given credence. At first, he simmered, but then as he grasped more and more of the plan, his mood shifted. He looked at Smith with a penetration that made her glad his focus wasn't directed at her. When it had all been laid out, Smith stopped explaining and waited.

Petra touched Rumer Gaston's arm and excused herself. With a motion of her head, she beckoned, and Tessa slipped off her stool, thinking her timing couldn't be worse. This was the time to have her say, to let Rumer Gaston know what she thought.

Inside the black and copper ladies' room, Petra situated herself before the mirror to speak as one reflection to another. She arched an eyebrow. "How did you do it?"

"Do . . . ?"

"That wasn't Smith Chandler's original design."

"We thought about what you wanted and melded it with Mr. Gaston's ideas."

"But how did you make him change it? I could have *yarked* for days, and he wouldn't have heard me."

"He heard you." Tessa tucked a wisp of hair back into her clip. "He asked me to collaborate on a design that would work for both of you."

Petra frowned. "How well does he know Rumer Gaston?"

Tessa shrugged. "Only through this, I think."

"Rumer expects to get what he wants, the way he wants it."

"If you had told him your ideas, he might have brought the changes to Smith himself." Had they done Petra and Rumer a disservice by working the plan without them?

"You don't understand." Petra touched a gloss wand to the center of her lower lip. "I came in here on the chance he might change his mind—if I'm not there to see it happen."

Tessa had no idea how to respond, but Petra read her thoughts.

"Why do I put up with that? Because Rumer is riding his star, and it's rising fast."

"But you could—"

"Have anyone I want?" She drove the wand into the bottle. "I'm twenty-three. How much runway do you think I have left?"

Wasn't twenty-three incredibly young to feel washed up? "He's your fiancé. He must want to know what you like."

Petra flicked her fingers through the white front of her hair. "Whatev. I got what I wanted. That's what counts." She turned from the mirror, all sharp cheekbones and smooth skin.

It was like talking to a shell, a beautifully polished shell the real creature had left behind.

The pulse pumped in Gaston's temple. "This is not what we discussed."

Smith held the laser beam of Gaston's gaze with difficulty and resisted making excuses. He wished Tessa hadn't left the table. She might have explained their reasoning—her reasoning—better than he could. "We felt it a good blend of the elements we'd been given. Yours and Petra's."

"I'm surprised you made that choice. It shows confidence, willingness to take a risk."

Smith shrugged. "Designs get modified."

"Mine don't."

Again he held his tongue. Tessa had said Gaston wanted to be king. It was in his bearing, his tone, in his command of the room, his casino, his castle. Tess had never met him, had heard only Petra's side, yet she'd hit it dead on. Probably fifteen years more experienced and immeasurably more voracious, Gaston pinned him with a stare that could shrivel.

Smith didn't let it. The afterglow of what they'd accomplished had resettled while showing the design, and he would not betray their effort by apologizing. Either Gaston agreed or he didn't. They could tweak or revamp or throw the whole thing out and start over. But he would not apologize.

Gaston's eyes narrowed. "Petra show some leg? Promise to play nice?"

Smith stiffened. "Actually it was Tessa. She thought it important you both enjoy your new home. Petra's ideas at first seemed incongruous, but after hashing it out, we found creative ways to blend the visions—as I imagine you and your fiancée would have done."

"You imagine wrong. I decide what makes Petra happy. And I give it to her. Anything I want her to have."

Smith bit hard on the responses that came to mind.

"Lucky for you"—again that penetrating stare—"I like what you've drawn. You have some talent."

"Thank you."

"And your little maze specialist. Will she deliver?" He intentionally left that ambiguous.

Smith knew his type, always keeping people uncomfortable, on edge. "She's the best in her field." He pictured her in the literal field she found so fascinating. "You won't be disappointed."

"Who could find her disappointing?"

He refused to be sucked in and deftly changed the subject. "There's something else you should be aware of. Some odd happenings." He described the events, letting Gaston draw his own conclusions. If someone was making a point by moving their things, marking their doorstep, Gaston might already know why.

But he looked blank. "What's it about?"

"I thought you might know."

Gaston scowled. "I told you I wanted privacy."

"I don't think word's gotten around. This business started

as soon as we got there, so I thought maybe someone had issues with our building there. I don't know the recent history of the property."

"You don't have to."

"Unless it escalates to vandalism and sabotage. Is there anything you know that could have upset someone?"

"Of course not. Have you seen the miscreant?"

Smith shook his head. "He's eerily invisible."

As Petra and Tessa reentered the lounge, Gaston hissed, "Don't tell Petra. She'll make something supernatural of it."

Smith nodded. "I'm sure there's a reasonable explanation."

"Figure it out and deal with it."

Smith stood as the women joined them, seated Tessa, and noted that Petra seated herself, albeit gracefully. What was Gaston's game? Decked out in his designer suit, his chunky gold ring and Rolex, was he above courtesy? Gaston honed in on Tessa, and the talk turned to landscape and labyrinths.

She explained, "Your labyrinth is a replica of the Chartres Cathedral design, originally laid as a symbolic pilgrimage to the Holy Land. The floor labyrinth in Chartres has over eight hundred feet of paths contained within a tiled circle. Some penitents walk it on their knees."

"Ow." Petra grimaced.

"But I believe the St. John labyrinth stood about six feet high in hedge, with a diameter of forty-four yards. It's going to be quite outstanding once the new hedge has matured and is properly trimmed."

"Will you be trimming it?" Petra flicked a speck from the table.

Tessa shook her head. "I've started uncovering the stone path. I'll restore that, then plant a new hedge. It will take some time to mature before it can be trimmed. You and Rumer will need a topiary professional to maintain the path, but it could easily be quite a famous garden. I'm certain any number of publications would feature it."

Petra lit up. "You mean like *Lifestyles of the Rich and Famous?*"

Gaston iced Petra with a glare. "That's not happening."

Tessa must have missed the chill in his expression, since she pressed her point. "It could be completely anonymous. The publications would not reveal the owners or address. But it could be quite an impressive feature."

Petra pouted. "Why have it, if no one knows?"

"Do you see all this, all these people?" Gaston's eyelid twitched. "Who here doesn't know me? Who doesn't want something from me?" He swept his arm around the lounge, crowded with partiers who seemed more interested in themselves or possibly Petra. But Gaston's face had reddened. "You haven't been in enough magazines, you have to put our house on display too? You think I want to live in a circus?"

Petra blanched. "No. It was stupid. Forget it."

"Forget it; forget it." His lip curled. "I don't forget. But maybe you forgot who you're marrying. Maybe it's all air inside that sugar coating." He gripped her chin and wagged her head.

Petra cringed like a scolded dog, far from the vixen who had swept into the office insisting Rumer wanted her happiness.

Tessa straightened. "That's not—"

Smith gripped her knee. "I'm sure Petra understands that Tessa meant the finished property will equal anything you've seen in those types of publications. We're all in agreement regarding the nondisclosure. Your privacy and Ms. Sorenson's will be protected."

Gaston backed off. "Petra has lived a very public life. There isn't much of her people haven't seen."

Smith flushed at the insult, but calling him on it would enflame

Gaston once more. Though Petra's eyes glittered, she said nothing. He followed her cue. His priority was to save the project and make sure Tessa didn't voice the outrage in her face. "If there's nothing more, do you mind if Tessa and I tour the casino? I'd like to see what you've done." What someone had done for him, but he knew where to place the credit.

Released by a curt nod, Smith slipped his laptop into his briefcase. He took Tessa's elbow and helped her down from the high stool. With a hand to the small of her back, he moved her purposefully away from the table. Indignation rose from her in waves. He moved her out of the lounge before she could vent it.

"I won't do it."

He kept her moving toward the elevator.

"I won't build a cathedral labyrinth for that man."

He'd never seen her so furious.

Her eyes snapped. "He'll desecrate the path."

They slipped into the emptied elevator and thankfully had it to themselves. "I understand, Tessa. But we're under contract. You're under contract."

She crossed her arms like blades across her chest. "You saw how he treated Petra. She's scared to death of him."

"She's engaged to marry him."

She shuddered. "He's a monster, Smith."

Her extreme reaction should not surprise him. The man was odious, but that didn't mean they couldn't build his house. After tonight he'd minimize any contact Gaston might have with Tessa. He'd guard her if he had to, but he could not afford to give it up. "Do you trust me? Even a little?"

Her throat worked. "This isn't about you."

"Gaston and Petra's relationship is their problem. Our business is to complete a project we can be proud of. Think about what we did, how we did it. There's value in the work no matter who it's for."

She started to shake. "I can't make a labyrinth for that monster."

He had to change her mind. Had to overcome Gaston's oafish behavior. He turned as the elevator slowed, held her gaze with his, and took a chance. "Then make it for me."

CHAPTER

17

Dismayed, Tessa allowed Smith to guide her out of the elevator into the lobby. He led her straight through to the outside terrace along the Colorado River. The dark water was shot with colorful streaks of light from the casinos that dimmed the stars and illuminated the far bank. The desert night sweltered, the surrounding land was arid, making the river look oddly out of place.

Exactly the way she felt. She didn't want to be there, didn't want anything to do with Rumer Gaston. Imagining him lurking in a labyrinth of her creation twisted her stomach and chilled her spine. She would not, could not do it.

Smith touched her arm. "Tess."

She turned. "Please don't make this personal. I can't build the labyrinth for you if Gaston owns it."

"We're only completing a contract."

She clenched her hands. "He's evil."

Frustration and a hint of desperation filled Smith's face. How could she make him understand?

"There's a fine line between what I do and what I dream. If I build a labyrinth for a real monster, what will keep . . ." She shuddered.

"Come here." He enclosed her in a strong embrace that felt so good—even if it was so that he could make his next point.

He eased her back. "Don't take what I'm going to say wrong, but could you be exaggerating this just a bit? Gaston possesses a loathsome self-importance and is markedly discourteous, but evil?"

She searched his face. "How would you describe his humiliating Petra?"

"Wretched. But, Tessa, she could have walked away. She could have thrown her drink. Or slapped him."

Maybe. But Petra wouldn't do it because Gaston had control of her thoughts and emotions. It frustrated her that Smith didn't get it. "You still want to work for him? You see yourself completing his home, then moving on to resorts and casinos around the world?"

"I want to deliver what we've promised, Tess. I wouldn't be much of a professional if I quit on every client I didn't like."

He was right, but it terrified her to bring the nightmare to life, to meld her worlds.

Smith softened. "Think about it. Sleep on it. We need to see our way through with integrity."

"I know." She dropped her chin. "And I know you think I'm overreacting. But the first time I stepped onto the path, I sensed that maybe this labyrinth should be left alone."

"What do you mean?"

"I felt a danger, like . . . I don't know."

He took her hands. "I won't let anything hurt you."

She shook her head. "You can't promise that."

"You're not afraid." But she was! Her chest squeezed. Her legs jellied. She turned and gripped the rail. She would not melt down in front of Smith again. She needed Dr. Brenner, needed to tell him the monster spoke.

"You won't say a word. Not one word."

Her throat closed up.

"If you do, I'll find you."

She clutched the rail.

"Just the way I did tonight."

She sensed more than felt Smith supporting her, his words lost behind the evil whisper. She had nowhere to hide now that the monster had escaped her dreams and entered her consciousness, unless . . . She hardly dared think it. Maybe she had to build the labyrinth to trap him back inside. Maybe that was why it had a gate.

"Tessa, talk to me."

She made herself turn. Smith clutched her elbows as though she might fall, but her legs had solidified. She knew what she had to do.

Smith drove his gaze into hers. "Are you all right?"

She nodded.

"Can you breathe?"

She realized she'd been sucking air through fear-clogged passages. "I can breathe."

"You've no idea how that scares me."

"Me too." Her eyes teared.

He framed her face with his hands. "Was it the monster?"

She nodded.

"What did he say?"

"That if I said anything, he'd find me." Her whole body shook.

"Who is it, Tess?"

"I don't know."

He stroked the tears from her cheeks with his thumbs. "What doesn't he want you to tell?"

"I don't know."

"Don't know or won't say?"

"I don't know, Smith."

He expelled a breath. "Something happened, and it's thrown your whole world askew. It's infuriating."

"I'm sorry."

"Don't. Don't ever apologize for that. It's not your fault."

She expelled her breath. "I don't know what it is, or was, or if it's real at all. Maybe something's just wrong in my brain."

"Did Dr. Brenner tell you that?"

"No. He insists there's not."

"Good, because I don't think you're responsible."

"I don't know what to think anymore."

"Well, maybe you shouldn't try so hard. Let it go for now."

She dragged her gaze to his eyes, saw concern but also warmth.

He ran his thumb over the corner of her mouth. "Let it go, because right now I want to kiss you."

"Why?"

"I think we could use it."

"A therapeutic kiss?"

"Exactly." He raised her chin and leaned in.

"I need to warn you—"

"No, you don't."

"I might be falling in love."

"Then be warned yourself. You're not the only one." He reached around and pulled the clip from her hair, and buried his fingers into the fall of it. He kissed her lips, her cheek, her temple.

She clung to him. "I'm an egg."

"I won't let you break."

"I need more than anyone can give."

"It's true."

"I'm afraid it'll hurt too much."

He cupped her face with his hands. "I'm not saying you won't get disappointed. I know you will. And I'll be at my wit's end. But it could just be worth it."

Not if it ended badly again. He'd called her high maintenance, but he was high voltage, and every sign said keep away. She sniffled.

He snatched her a cocktail napkin from the nearest table, and she
dried her face and blew her nose, not wanting to think how she
looked now. "You'll get tired of me disintegrating."

"I intend to stop it."

"It doesn't work that way."

"I think it might."

She huffed a laugh. "We never have agreed."

"We did last night."

"That was work."

"That was pleasure."

She slanted him a hard look. "You only want someone to spark
your creativity."

"That isn't all you spark, or all I want." His gaze intensified.

"Smith . . . I . . ."

He turned her away to face the river and encircled her in his
arms. "It shouldn't surprise you that I'm attracted, but don't worry.
I've learned restraint and I practice it. My return to faith has given
me that much."

She wanted to know what had caused the change, but felt
vulnerable asking.

He pressed his cheek to the side of her head. "Relax, Tess."

She leaned against him, wanting his strength and sureness, even
though the closeness alarmed her. "I know you've had—"

"Please don't bring up Danae."

She looked up over her shoulder. "You were together two years.
You must have loved her."

He frowned. "I don't want—"

"Do you still?"

"I'm not trying to fill her slot. This is wholly new, wholly
unexpected. I just want you to believe I won't act on what I feel
in any way that harms you."

Surprisingly, she did. She leaned her head back against his chest and closed her eyes. "I've never had a champion."

He rubbed his face in her hair. "I'd like to try."

"When the youths taken as tribute were forced into the labyrinth to be devoured by Minotaur, the hero Theseus went with them. He tied a ball of yarn, a clew, to an olive tree so he'd be able to lead them out after he had battled the monster to the death."

Smith pressed his cheek to her head. "I won't let you face this alone. We will battle it to the death. And I'll bring you back again."

Dr. Brenner had been wrong. Smith was not a stressor. He was the first hope she'd had in so long.

Though he left her at her room with a light kiss, when the tap came a few minutes later, she wondered whether he'd thrown restraint to the wind. Shaking, she opened the door—to Petra.

"I want to show you something." Her silver sheath shimmered as she walked.

They rode the elevator to the keyed penthouse level. Tessa couldn't help but stare as Petra crossed the room, illuminating the sumptuous space as she went. She used a remote to open the drapes over the wall of floor-to-ceiling windows. The lights of the other casinos glittered like a jeweled shawl draped over the shoulders of the dark desert. Tessa joined her at the window, staring silently out.

"This is what I want." Petra turned and swept her hand across the room. "No one else in this casino can even access this floor."

Tessa nodded, unsure why Petra was telling her. "It's spectacular."

"One snap of my fingers and people jump to bring me French croquettes, Russian caviar."

"Do you like caviar?"

The corners of Petra's mouth pulled. "I don't have to. I can have anything I want."

"And it's worth it?"

"Yes." She laid her elegant fingers against her throat. "Don't mess this up for me. Okay?"

Tessa frowned. "How?"

"By challenging Rumer."

Tessa folded her arms. "I didn't challenge him."

"You would have. I saw it in your face. If Smith hadn't taken you away."

"I don't like how he treats you."

"He treats me like a queen."

"A puppet queen."

"Is there any other kind?" Her eyes glittered. "I know what I have."

Tessa swallowed her arguments. She couldn't help it if Petra wouldn't see the monster with her eyes wide open.

He crept up to the trailer. No cars. No lights. He heard nothing inside. The gate was gone. Were they? Was she? His fingers itched as he reached out and pressed his palm to the trailer door. He tried the knob, but it was locked. He turned, scanned it in the darkness, and paused at the air-conditioner in the window.

Slowly, softly, he crept. He reached, pulled himself up against the siding, and nudged the window up. A giggle filled his throat. He pushed it another inch and another. It squeaked the rest of the way up and bumped at the top. He took hold of the machine and eased it inward, using its weight to pull him up as he climbed with his feet. Dangling by his waist on the windowsill, he set it down and scrambled the rest of the way inside.

Blood rushed to his head as he straightened. He'd invaded

their place the way they'd invaded his. The silver light of moon and stars drifted in and rested on desks and tables. A green light winked on a computer at one desk. He had experimented with one they'd left on in the library, but it hurt his eyes, and anyway, he didn't like it as much as the books that talked about it. He liked manuals, manuals that told how things worked, even things he didn't have, like cell phones and TVs and computers.

He turned to the next desk. It held drawings. He crept close, examining the lines with his fingers. He lowered his face and sniffed the paper. The drawings were hers.

He left that room and moved to the one at the end with beds and a bathroom. He used the bathroom as he always did when presented the chance. He pocketed a tube of toothpaste and moved back through the bedroom, through the desks to the kitchen. He opened one cabinet after another. The only flip can was sardines. He tucked that and a package of crackers into his jacket.

The refrigerator light speared his eyes before he could unscrew it, then darkness reigned again. He drank from the carton of milk, felt an apple in one drawer and slipped it into a pocket. Normally he'd stop, but he didn't care if they knew he'd been there. He took a package of thin meat and devoured it, resealed the package and put it in with the apple.

Then he went back to her drawings. The intricate trees and leaves and flowers delighted him. The circle drawings with all the winding lines shot him with excitement. He slipped them carefully inside his jacket against his side and chest. Then he saw the book, a horticulture manual.

A shiver crawled up his spine. He ached to look inside, but wouldn't. Not yet. He went to the window, replaced the air-conditioner, and closed the window against it. He took the book, opened the door, pushed the lock, and closed the door behind him.

CHAPTER

18

Smith did not include Tessa the next morning when he went down to meet with Gaston. He hoped she had slept well after he'd seen her to her room, but it wouldn't surprise him if she'd taken everything he'd said and reworked it into something else. Before he could deal with that, there was Rumer Gaston.

The man breakfasted alone, and Smith approached the table, wondering if their conflict last night was past, or whether it had passed over like the angel of death and he would now realize his firstborn had died. Gaston looked up, giving him no hint of smile. "Can't spare the jet this morning. I'm waiting on some calls and"— he waved a hand—"things have come up."

"All right." Smith nodded. "I'll make other arrangements."

"No, no. Make yourselves at home. Enjoy the amenities." His eyes turned sly. "If you haven't already." He laughed low in his throat. "Where is your little specialist? I'd like to give her a private tour."

Smith held his anger in check. "Sorry. She's not available."

Gaston laughed more than his little joke deserved.

"Oh, you Brits need to lighten up. Told your father the same thing."

"I'm sure he appreciated the advice."

Gaston appraised him. "I like you. You know why? You surprise me. You look so innocuous, then show some vigor after all."

Smith didn't know how to answer that.

Gaston raised his cup and sipped his coffee. "I'll let you know when you can leave. In the meantime, make the best of things. As my guests."

Smith didn't argue. If Gaston really had a conflict, they'd need to be patient until he worked it out. If this was a power game, he'd only feed into it by protesting. "Will you contact me when the jet is available?"

"Sure, sure. Just let people know you're here courtesy of Rumer Gaston." The smile turned ugly. "And try not to be so stiff. People come from all over to enjoy what I offer. People more talented and appreciative than you."

Smith's jaw clenched. "Right."

Gaston's eyes narrowed. "You may go."

It finally came clear that he hadn't been hired for his design. He'd been acquired as a puppet. Gaston's demanding his on-site presence, his daily reports, all fed the megalomania. Tessa had not exaggerated. "Right, then. I'll wait to hear." He turned, seething, as much from the insult as the thought of relating the delay to Tessa.

She opened her room door at his tap. "We're ready to go?"

"Uh, no. May I?" He'd rather discuss it behind her closed door than anywhere Gaston's closed-circuit cameras might capture her reaction.

She let him in. "What's the matter?"

"There's a delay with the jet."

"Something mechanical?"

"Uncertain availability. Would you like to get some breakfast? We're Mr. Gaston's guests."

She pulled her purse onto her shoulder. "I don't want anything from him, but I wouldn't mind a walk along the river, and maybe a croissant or something."

"Sounds lovely." And getting her out of the casino was probably prudent. He checked to make sure his ringer was on, but even when they had traveled a length of the river, finished rolls and tea, and returned to the casino, Gaston had not called. Tessa grew increasingly agitated.

When they returned to her room, she stalked to the window. "He's playing with us."

"Thank you, dear. I've gathered as much."

"He's an oaf."

"A total prat."

"What are we going to do?"

"Wait, I suppose. Fancy rummy?"

She punched his shoulder. "I want to go back."

"Does that mean you've decided to continue?"

She opened her mouth, but his phone rang. He answered. "Yes, Mr. Gaston. We'll be right down." He pocketed the phone. "I know you're a professional, Tessa—"

"But?"

"But I feel I must beg you not to antagonize him further."

"No problem." She planted her hands on her hips. "I'll wait up here."

"I very much wish you could. But he's summoned us both." He reached for her hand. "If you don't mind, I'd like to play it more intimately between us."

"Why?"

"For your protection."

"From . . ."

"Innuendo, coarse comments, or worse."

She narrowed her eyes. "He wouldn't dare."

"Trust me, he would. He thrives on discomfort. He has us—me—in a pinch. If we're a couple, it may inhibit his game."

She scowled. "I hate this."

"It's not such a terrible thought, is it? Being a couple?"

"That's not what I meant. People shouldn't manipulate through fear and . . . and . . ."

"They shouldn't, but some do. I'm sorry."

"For once, it's not your fault." She drew back her shoulders and flung open the door. "Let's get this over with."

But Gaston didn't want it over with. He insisted they lunch with him, though the thought killed any appetite she had.

"Is Petra joining us?" Tessa barely kept a civil tone as his smirk set her teeth on edge.

"She's being pampered in the spa."

Out of range of any potential insurrection. That seemed to be all he wanted to say about his fiancée, though he proceeded to sing his own praises. Throughout the meal, Smith gave subtle indications of relationship. At one point he wrapped his arm over her shoulders. While done for Gaston's benefit, it still felt nice and bolstered her.

Maybe she was overreacting, but there was something unsettling in Gaston's eyes, some element common to bullies that searched for cracks in others. She didn't claim to be a pillar of strength, but most people didn't set off alarms in her head. Could his have been the repellent force she sensed in the labyrinth? Was the ground crying out against him?

Smith maintained his dynamic and professional manner as they discussed not only the current project, but other ideas they both had. His eyes had a luminescence when describing what he saw with his inner eye, what he would translate first to paper, then structure. If Rumer Gaston wasn't impressed, he ought to have been.

The strain of maintaining a marginal deference lodged in her neck. She had to admire Smith's ability to rise above. He could have been a diplomat—or a con artist.

When they had finished eating, Mr. Gaston once again equivocated about their flight. He gave Smith a few noncommittal assurances, then casually spread his hand. "I'll let you know when it's convenient for you to leave."

She had a keen impression of a cat letting the mice emerge just far enough from their hole before he pounced. It made her more angry than afraid, and Smith finally seemed to have had enough.

He straightened. "Maybe we should secure a commercial flight."

Her heart leapt. She would fly cargo to get out of there.

Smith's tone was eminently reasonable. "We both have work to do, and—"

"You work for me." Gaston eased back in his chair. "On my schedule."

Smith looked momentarily nonplussed, but recovered. "I can expense the tickets, and—"

"There's no need for that. Petra and I are flying into Denver in an hour. You can go with us. After we land there, you and Ms. Young can continue on to D.C."

They were flying in an hour and he hadn't said so? Maybe he'd been waiting for Smith to challenge him. He looked satisfied with the frustration that had flashed in Smith's face.

Although the thought of flying with them was thoroughly unpalatable, Smith accepted. They worked out the details of timing and transportation to the jet. Smith's aplomb impressed and annoyed her. If he could kowtow so convincingly, how real were any of his signals?

While professionally appropriate for the owner to communicate directly with the architect heading the project, Rumer Gaston so utterly excluded her from the discussion she felt like furniture. Gaston made no attempt at the smarmy charm he'd faked last night. Had Petra told him about their conversations? Did he consider her a threat?

Dismissed at long last, Smith ushered her to her room and retreated to his own. Though she could not wait to get out of the casino, the thought of being trapped in the jet with Rumer Gaston twisted her stomach. She didn't mind flying in the least, and it was quite possible she'd flown with people far worse and never known. But there was something about him that made her hands sweat. She sat down on the bed and called Dr. Brenner, but he was away at a conference.

"No, it's not an emergency," she told his receptionist. It wasn't. She knew that. Watching Rumer Gaston shut Petra down had keyed into something inside that she couldn't access or process alone, but it wasn't an emergency.

At the knock, she opened the door. "Smith, I can't fly with him. I'd rather pay for my own ticket."

"I know." His gaze went over her. "But he's the owner. Uncomfortable as this may be, we need to remember that."

She shook her head. "He doesn't own *us*."

"He does, however, have final say over who completes the contract. An insult now would be unwise."

The truth made it no less frustrating.

"Don't blur the lines, Tess. This is business."

And she would act accordingly, but her stomach churned. Things that needed to stay separate were already blurring. She took her bag from the bed and preceded him out the door.

On the jet, Rumer Gaston continued his churlish refusal to acknowledge her. He chatted with Smith about his casinos and plans to expand his empire worldwide. He seemed to like the sound of his voice better than anything else. While he and Smith were engaged in that discussion, much of which was a repetition of the morning's, Petra sent her several tense looks, obviously not wanting it known that she had sought her out the night before. She aggressively perused one magazine after another, commenting on each model's flaws and strengths. The flaws took the day.

Tessa made it through the flight in almost complete silence, even after Petra and Gaston disembarked at DIA for a limo trip to his casino in Black Hawk. Exhausted, she pondered the idea of shutting Rumor Gaston in the labyrinth. Obviously not reality, yet he had merged in her mind with the monster of her nightmares. That was the one she had to silence. The one she had to escape.

Smith parked by the Land Rover outside the trailer. No surprise Bair had returned from the main office ahead of them. He had expected to be back long before this. Smith glanced at Tessa, concerned by her silence. If she expected to go back to their strictly business interface, he'd have a difficult time of it. He hadn't said and done anything lightly, though now it seemed perhaps rashly.

She got out and started for the trunk, but he caught her hand. "Tess."

"We should unload before we lose the light."

"It's been a rotten, trying couple of days. One more delay won't matter."

"We've had nothing but delays. Rumer Gaston is a manipulative control freak."

"A petty, domineering prat."

"An egomaniac."

"All mouth and no trousers."

She cracked a smile, and he held out his arms. "Come here." He drew her in and lowered his face.

"Bair's—"

"Irrelevant." He kissed her softly.

"I don't want to make him uncomfortable."

"He'll think it's brilliant. He's been lobbying for us since you arrived."

"I'm just . . ."

He brushed her lips with his thumb. "Afraid?"

"I have to do this labyrinth, Smith. I can't have two stressors."

"You still consider me that?"

"No, I . . . I don't know."

"Frankly, I've had one wreck of a relationship, and a rocky record with you so far. If anyone should be afraid, it's me."

"Are you?"

"Shockingly, no." He felt more peaceful with the direction things had gone than he had with Danae. For the first time he wondered if he had really wanted her, or if she'd only made him believe that. Had he been an accidental accomplice to his own mistreatment?

That would not happen again. Tessa might be unpredictable, but he could not imagine her being untrue. Her doubts were not insurmountable. "I want to take care of you." An unprecedented sensation.

"You can't."

"I think I can." He covered her fingers with his. "I think God's planned it this way."

Her brow creased. "I don't know how to take your new faith."

"Not new. I was raised in church."

"Yes, but—"

"I admit I became my own god for a while in college and thereafter, but I've reevaluated, and I'm not actually as brilliant as I believed."

She raised her brows. "No kidding."

"I now find things I had considered unnecessary quite applicable. Things like prayer and supplication."

"What does that have to do with me?"

"Nothing, unless you meant the things you said last night. In which case my prayers for guidance are relevant to you as well. I want to do things right, not . . ." He shook his head. "Not blunder along as I have before."

"But how do you know what's right? I don't mean morally, but, just, personally?"

"That's where you have to trust. I don't pretend to have the answers. But if I submit myself to God, I believe He will guide me, guide . . . us."

Her eyes pooled. He lowered his face and kissed her surprised mouth with tenderness, confidence, and desire. He knew her so much better, cared so much more than he'd realized. He wanted her to—

The door sprang open. "There you—oh."

Smith released Tessa and turned to Bair, frustrated that their first deep connection had been so abruptly interrupted. "Don't stand there gobsmacked, help us unload."

"Right." Bair stepped off the stoop.

Leaving Tessa looking dazed, Smith opened the trunk. They'd been loaded down with wood and marble and fabric samples Petra had collected. Gaston hadn't objected to their taking the whole lot back with them, though it remained to be seen if any would pass his final say.

They carried it all in. Tessa put her laptop down and looked around her desk with a frown. "Where are my drawings? And the horticulture manual?"

Bair lowered a heap of samples to the floor in the corner. "Haven't touched anything over there."

"I left them right here, on my desk."

Smith swept the room with his gaze. "Could you have brought them to your room? You were hazy when we left."

"I don't think so." She pressed her hands to her lower back. "But I'll look when I get back."

"So?" Bair queried, expectantly.

Smith turned. "Gaston approved the design, but moaned like billy-o over flying us back."

"What for?"

"Maybe to punish my impudence in changing the plan, or to reestablish his control. Or simply because he's arrogant."

Tessa turned. "He's not simply arrogant. You're arrogant, and I've never thought you evil."

Bair barked a laugh.

Smith frowned. "I'm not arrogant; I'm confident."

She raised her brows. "I'm confident. You're arrogant."

"Arrogance suggests an overinflated ego. Mine is appropriately inflated." Did she really see herself as confident? Maybe professionally. And if she thought him arrogant, their moment outside may not have been as deep for her as for him. She turned to Bair. "But he recognized the genius of the design, so that's what matters."

Genius? He did not take full credit for what they'd created, but still, no one had ever called his work genius.

"Mr. Gaston's ego is dangerous."

"At any rate, the sooner we're done with this the better." Tessa shivered.

Bair frowned. "You all right?"

She wasn't. Something subtle had shifted, as though he'd looked away at the wrong moment.

"I'm fine." She expelled her breath. "I'll see you guys in the morning."

Smith walked her out. "What is it, Tess?"

"Nothing."

"If you're worried about Rumer Gaston, there's no need for you to interact again." He was the architect, Gaston the client. He would maintain a private and singular communication from now on, no need for any contact between Gaston and any member of his team. Whatever games Rumer Gaston played would be played with him directly.

"I know."

"If it's me . . ."

She looked away. "I'm just tired."

They both were. "All right, then. We'll talk in the morning." He handed her the keys. "Drive carefully."

"You sound like Bair."

"Careful driving's not in his nature."

"It is for me, apparently." She freed her hair from the ponytail and worked her fingernails over her scalp. "He says it almost every time I leave."

"He's been seeing you off?"

"You didn't notice."

"Should I have?" In trying hard to maintain their distance, had he missed something important?

She drew a weary breath. "I need to go."

He wanted to pursue it, but her signals were all "back off," and ignoring Tessa's signals had proved hazardous. "All right. Good night."

CHAPTER

19

Smith sighed as he pulled the door closed behind him. "You may as well get it out before you burst."

Bair folded his arms. "I knew it. I didn't have to see you snogging to know just how it was."

"I told you the problem was having her near."

"How near did you have her?"

Smith scowled. "What do you think?"

"A fancy casino. A stunning woman. A night together." Bair shrugged. "A bloke might succumb to less. Especially when you've been gutted before."

"I wasn't gutted. Disappointed, angry, but—"

"Devastated," Bair shot back. "I saw you."

"All right. Excuse me if I don't bounce off women as easily as you."

"Easily?" Bair's brow lowered. "You think paying for a son I never see is easy?"

"I don't mean that."

"I hardly knew her name until she came requesting DNA, but that doesn't make any of it easy."

"I know that, Bair."

"Good, because that wasn't me. It was the booze. And since then, nothing's been easy."

"I shouldn't have said that. I just—" Smith forked his fingers into his hair. "Look, we're both frazzled. What you saw out there was . . . Tessa's already talking herself out of it."

"Why would she?"

Maybe he'd moved too fast, or come on too strong. "Because she doesn't trust people. Some . . . deserted child syndrome. She's telling herself all the ways I could disappoint her." He walked through the bedroom to the bath. "By tomorrow, there could be complete animosity again." She'd seemed so open, so hopeful. She'd admitted serious feelings for him, and he'd felt it—until the final chill when she said good-bye.

"That's a bleak view."

Bleaker than he'd let on. Her mood shift concerned and disappointed him. He had done his best in a difficult situation, and if she blamed him for Gaston's behavior and everything else out of his control, then it would not be a matter of whether, or how badly, but how soon he let her down. "Have you seen the toothpaste?"

"I assumed you took it."

Smith turned. "I have a travel size in my dop."

Bair shook his head. "I didn't find it earlier."

"That was a new tube."

"Guess we misplaced it."

As Tessa had misplaced her drawings? Her book? He cocked his jaw. "Anything else missing?"

Bair caught the drift. "Don't know. Let's have a look."

They walked through, checking the closets, the desks. Bair shook his head. "Who would take toothpaste and leave a computer?"

"It could be here. Nothing's actually been nicked to this point. Only moved."

Bair frowned. "We seemed a little short of food, though I don't remember exactly what we had."

"Food and toothpaste would be more useful than a computer to someone staked out somewhere."

Bair turned. "You think he was in here?"

"Possibly."

"Door was locked when I came in."

"So he locked it behind him."

Bair went over, opened the door, and observed the lock. "Think he picked it?"

Smith searched the room and paused at the window. "Or came through there."

"Small opening. And how would he maneuver?"

"I don't know. But it was unlatched." He went over and pushed the window up, then lifted the air-conditioner down. "Look here. These scrapes." Bare wood showed through the fresh paint peels.

"And here again." Bair pointed to another scrape at the base of the wall. "He must have lowered it down from the window to climb through. Awkward, wouldn't you say?"

"But not impossible."

"Don't think I'd fit."

Smith nodded. "It would be a squeeze."

"So someone small."

"A kid?" Smith wondered aloud. Bair had called him childish. "A runaway?"

"I'd think he'd steal anything he could pawn."

Smith nodded. "Quite. Well, we're not going to solve it tonight."

"Should we talk to the police?"

"And tell them our toothpaste is missing?"

"Right." Bair laughed sheepishly.

"I mentioned the occurrences to Gaston, but he told us to handle it."

"I wouldn't mind, if I knew how."

Smith nodded. Unless it escalated, the best plan seemed to be to wait. Gaston already thought him stiff and unappreciative. He didn't want to look foolish and reactionary as well.

～

She was back, and it filled him with unparalleled glee. He had watched for her, wanted her. He knew her now, knew her by her drawings, her beautiful drawings. So exact and perfect. And the lines. The lines in the circle mesmerizing. He wanted to ask about the circle.

It was what she did in the field. She walked the lines. He wanted to see her walking it again. He had hoped she would come out alone and walk it. But she hadn't. She had stayed with them. Especially the tall one, who devoured her like a fox with a rabbit. His heart galloped. His head hurt. He had almost revealed himself, almost rushed at them to make him stop. Only by strength and cunning did he restrain himself.

He had waited for the darkness. In the shadows she belonged to him, like the plants in her horticulture manual that bloomed at the sun's passing, at the coming of dew. Jasmine. Moonflower. Angel's-trumpet. Sweet scenting the night.

In the moonless night he loped. He had read her book, imagining her hands hollowing and planting and pressing in the plants that scented the night. No gaudy day bloomers, no sun soakers. He'd learned more than he'd known before from its pages, not just about the plants detailed in the text, but about her too. The pages she had marked, the notes penciled into the margins, but most of all the receipt tucked into the flap for the inn where she stayed, where she now slept, or prepared to sleep.

It was far, but now he knew. He knew where she went when she left, and in the silence of the night he drew near to her. To where she slept, where she dreamed. He wanted to see her dream, and so he passed through the night, loping, loping, risked the light that spilled yellow onto the ground, risked the spaces until he could hug the walls of the inn searching for entrance.

His hands found the coal chute, but the grate was firmly attached. He huddled, regarding the grate half shrouded by shrubs. He moved his fingers to the chute itself, pulled the iron handle, felt it give. Infinitely patient, he pulled again, imposing a constant force to counter its resistance.

With a groaning squawk the cover slid open to a dark and narrow cavity. Small. Very, very small. Could he make himself that small? Already on his knees, he extended one arm into the hole. Pressing his head against his shoulder, he eased himself into the maw, letting it swallow him like a snake, squeezing, undulating, its crushing muscles drawing him deeper into the darkness.

His other shoulder loosened in the socket, slipping down his side as he drew it into the throat. His front elbow pressed against the inside wall. He slid inch by painful inch, pushing with his knees, releasing the air in his lungs. Farther, deeper.

His arm came free of the metal grip. He seized the inside of the grate and twisted, clinging with both hands as he bent his waist and pulled his legs inside, giggling. He'd gotten smaller than ever before. He dropped to the cement floor, rolling his shoulders to set them back into their sockets. He spread his arms and fingers, cracking the knuckles, straightened the painful slump of his spine with more insistent crackles, then turned, scouring the darkness.

A cellar. He liked cellars. Dark, cool, musty cellars. Since this one was new to him, he crept around, feeling the pipes, hearing their hiss and gurgle. At last he found the door. But it was too soon. He'd wait, wait in the darkness until everyone slept, everyone dreamed. Then he'd find the place where *she* dreamed.

⌒

Gasping, Tessa clutched the sheet and bolted up in her bed. Something pale and gray moved in the darkness around the door. A draft of rank air touched her. The scream lodged in her throat. She was not asleep. She had come very much awake, though her racing heart matched her primal nightmare fright.

As she reached, her hand shook so badly she dropped her cell phone with a clatter to the floor. She wanted to call Dr. Brenner, but for the first time, she doubted he could help. He might not even believe her. How could anyone believe a nightmare had entered her room?

She stared into the darkness where it had disappeared, unable to catch even a glimpse. Did it stare back at her? She pressed her eyes shut as the whisper chilled her heart. *"I'll find you. Just the way I did tonight."*

She gulped. "I haven't said a word." Her voice wavered. "Not a word."

She had told Smith about the warning, but she didn't know what she was supposed to keep secret. She strained toward the dark hole around the door. Was it there, waiting? Would it leap if she illuminated the darkness?

Her mouth went dry as powder. She groped for the wall switch. Light poured over her and spilled into the narrow doorway beside the bathroom. The door was closed, the space before it empty.

She slipped from the bed and went to it. With trembling fingers, she felt the knob: locked. The deadbolt was not. She frowned. Had she forgotten to turn it? She'd been dead on her feet from the strain of Gaston and the trip back, emotionally wrung out from the turn of events with Smith.

She lowered her forehead to the door and whiffed the scent she had caught before. The monster's essence? Her knees almost collapsed as a different smell, an olfactory memory, invaded her consciousness, the smell of antiseptic breath. *"You're not afraid, are you?"*

She pressed her palms to the door. If the monster was real enough to breathe . . . She moaned. "Leave me alone. I haven't done anything wrong."

Fear spiraled up her spine. *Daddy!* The monster's breath gagged her, stifling her cries, choking them back into her throat with the words she couldn't say. She staggered back from the door and fell to her knees beside the bed, groping for her cell phone.

She had meant to call Dr. Brenner, but it was Smith who answered in a half whisper, "Tessa?" She must have hit the wrong speed dial, or had chosen it subconsciously.

"He was here . . . the monster . . . in my room." She heard him changing position, or maybe getting up and moving into the office so he didn't disturb Bair.

"Did you see him?"

"He said he would find me and he did."

"I thought Gaston was the monster," he said gently.

"He . . . is one. But this was . . . this one came out of my dream. I know how that sounds, but I can't explain it any other way. I opened my eyes and he was there."

"And then what?"

"I turned on the light and he was gone." She knew what he thought. Who wouldn't?

"Do you want me to come over?"

Her shaking had stopped, her heartbeat normalized. "I just wanted you to know." She must have, or the intuitive part of her had, the part she accessed through the labyrinth, the part she trusted more than the rest of her mind.

"I'd feel better doing something."

"You already have." He'd listened without contradicting her, without saying it was only her imagination.

He sighed. "You're all right? You can breathe?"

Amazingly. "I guess I needed to tell someone." *"Not a word."* She sank into her pillows. Was the command losing its power to control her? "He's gone now. I'm okay."

"Sure?"

"I'm sure." She threaded her fingers through her hair, loving the sound of his voice in her ear as she switched the light off.

"Will you sleep now?"

"I think I will."

His warmth and tenderness filled the space between them. "Then I'll see you in the morning."

She suddenly felt bad. He wasn't paid to take emergency calls in the middle of the night. What had she been thinking? "I'm sorry I woke you."

"I'm not." He added softly, "I thought you'd spend the night pushing me away."

She closed her eyes with a sigh. "The night's not over."

"Don't you dare."

"Good night, Smith."

"Peaceful dreams, Tess. I mean it."

She clicked off the phone and let her hand fall. If only.

CHAPTER

20

After searching her room unsuccessfully for the drawings and horticultural manual, Tessa headed for the property in the brisk autumn morning. She arrived at the same time as the flatbed truck delivering the Bobcat, which saved her from discussing the night before with Smith. In the light of day, the monster in her room seemed strange and ridiculous, and even though Smith had taken her seriously, she didn't want to discuss it.

The driver jumped down. "You ordered the Bobcat?"

She nodded.

"You have an operator?"

"I'm using it." When Smith chose a contractor, she would bring in a team. Until then, she wanted control of what happened with the labyrinth. She knew how to operate the mini skid loader and would take the care necessary for this delicate job.

She signed the agreement, assured the guy one more time that she knew what she was doing, that it was indeed a flat landscape she'd be clearing, and she understood how the narrow wheelbase made the vehicle unstable on hilly grades. If she used the rope hook, she would look out for springy rebound. Finally convinced, the driver moved the lumbering truck back out to the street.

She climbed aboard, took hold of the levers that independently controlled the left and right skids, and headed for the labyrinth field. The agile Bobcat had as much power as she'd need, and the ability to rotate around its center for complete maneuverability. If the labyrinth wasn't such serious business, it would be playtime.

Though God may not have spoken to her in words, he'd shown her what had to be done. Physically, symbolically, or psychologically, she had to lock the monster back where he belonged, where he could not hurt her or anyone she loved. It was no accident that the labyrinth on this property was of the cathedral design. No other script had such sacred intention.

She believed—had to believe—that in this place, in this way, she would bring an end to the fear. Here, once and for all, God would deliver her. And if Smith was part of that, how much better it would be. The danger she had felt would not overcome her purpose or the satisfaction of participating in her own liberation. Soon the monster would be helpless, and she would be free.

Starting near the mouth she had cleared by hand, she carefully tore away the sod with each thrust of the Bobcat's blade. Near the center, a new growth of kudzu had sprung up, but she wouldn't tackle that yet. Instead, she worked to clear the circumference and get a look at the size and condition of the labyrinth. The scent of earth and bruised grass filled her senses, until the sound of her name broke through her concentration.

Catching sight of Bair, she stopped the Bobcat and cut the engine. The exhaust cloyed, then wafted away as he reached her.

"Thought you might be ready for a break."

She took the snack of apples and cheese and the icy bottle of green tea she'd stashed in their refrigerator, even though she hadn't intended to break yet. "Thanks."

Bair planted his beefy hands on his hips. "Didn't really see you as the bulldozer type."

She wiped the damp hair from her forehead with the back of her hand. "Landscape architects get to play in the dirt. You should ditch Smith and come have some real fun."

He flushed. "You've, um, made some . . . progress."

She looked over her shoulder at the exposed ground, then tapped the lever. "Goes a little quicker like this than with a shovel."

"Easier on the back."

True, but the vibrations had all but numbed her forearms.

Bair swallowed. "Looks more like a, uh, trough than a path."

"The base is bedrock. They dug down to it, then raised the sides to form the beds for the hedge."

"Oh, I see. Is that how it's usually done?"

"I've never worked this design with a vertical element. Only flat, or nearly so."

"A path with no walls?"

"You're still thinking of a maze. Most labyrinths are stone tiles or turf. With hedge walls this will be a completely different experience."

"Different how?"

She pressed her hands to the small of her back. "In a turf or floor labyrinth, you watch the ground to stay on track, but the whole way is laid out in plain view. In this one, with walls as tall as the walker, you can't see the entire path, only the part before you."

"Then it will be like a maze."

"Without dead ends, but yes. You won't know what's around the corner." Or who. She shuddered, imagining Rumer Gaston, or last night's creepy specter. Or the monster trying to break through her subconscious. "Anyway, it's going to take a lot of work to re-create."

"Then it's good I brought fortification."

For his sake, she crunched an apple slice. "Thanks again, but why exactly are we having this picnic?"

Bair cleared his throat. "Smith's, uh, taking a call."

"Not Petra changing things."

"Not Petra, no."

She searched his reddened face, his discomfort triggering hers.

"It's, um, Danae. I don't know if he told—"

"He told me."

"Right. Well, I came out to give him some privacy."

Privacy? "I didn't know he still talked to her."

He shifted from foot to foot. "Odd timing, actually. She hasn't called in over a month."

One whole month? "I thought she left him for someone else."

He nodded. "She did, but he's . . . loyal, you know?"

No, she didn't know. He'd cut and run the moment she didn't fit his parameters. They hadn't talked once since their relationship blew up, not until he'd called her for this job—at Rumer Gaston's urging. Her mind flew back to the day she'd heard him laughing with his friends and confronted him.

"*You told them I'm switching paths? You think it's funny?*"

"*I don't think it's funny. I think it's a tragedy.*"

"*Tragedy, Smith?*"

"*And a waste.*"

"*Because I prefer landscape to structures?*"

"*Because you think you can make something out of your ridiculous labyrinth fixation. Nobody cares, Tessa. They're an obsolete oddity.*"

She shook, remembering. They hadn't spoken again, and their

paths had scarcely crossed, yet he spoke regularly with Danae, who had obviously made an indelible mark. "What's she like?"

"Well, she's nicely put together. Long legs, long hair. That's Smith's downfall. He can't resist a soft sweep of hair."

Why was he telling her this? "So, she's pretty."

"Not so much pretty as attractive. Commands the eye, if you get my meaning."

Oh, she got it. "What did she call about?" She deliberately chewed her way through the apples and sharp cheddar chunks.

Bair shrugged. "I don't know."

Maybe he did; maybe he didn't. The reason was less important than Smith's response.

"Has he asked her to stop?"

Bair kicked the dirt. "He doesn't like to give up on people."

She could offer a different opinion. "He still has feelings for her."

"He'd, uh, have to say."

"But you're warning me."

He squinted up at her. "I only know what I saw."

"And that was?"

"She hurt him."

Her throat squeezed. "Didn't he tell her to bog off and good riddance?"

Bair frowned. "Is that what he said?"

"It isn't true?" She clenched the tea bottle.

"I'm sure he wanted to. And . . . maybe he thinks he did. Guys remember stuff the way they wish it had been."

"But in reality?"

Bair shrugged. "I think he told her he'd be there when she realized her mistake."

She trembled.

"Don't cry to me when you realize your mistake."

"You're the last person I'd cry to, Smith."

"Good."

She drew a ragged breath. He'd said he wasn't filling Danae's slot. But if he thought he could slip her in next to Danae's hallowed ground, he'd better think again.

Bair cleared his throat. "Are you all right?"

"Not really." She drew herself up. "But I will be."

"I didn't mean to upset you."

"What did you mean?"

"I don't want you getting hurt."

Again. She knew what Smith was capable of. Bair must also. "Thank you." She smiled, though tears crawled up her throat and invaded her eyes. "For caring."

He reached for the empty baggie and bottle. She didn't remember eating or drinking any of it.

Bair scrutinized her. "He wouldn't intend to. I'm just not sure he's let her go."

She started the engine. "I should get back to work." She was there to build a labyrinth. And she would. Nothing had changed—except the joy was gone.

Smith spent the day taking over for light-hearted Gordon Ellis, who'd suffered a coronary and was convalescing. He could draw the specs for the structural engineering himself, and may as well, since they were on schedule with the base drawings and on-site with no other projects and only Danae's phone call interfering.

Why would she tell him she was breaking off with Edward unless she considered reconciliation possible? He had left the door open in more ways than one, but things had grown a great deal more complicated. He had not only his own feelings to think about, but also Tessa's. They were just starting off, but it was no light thing to disengage, even at this point.

Did he want to? He had just wondered whether he'd ever cared for Danae, and now this call had made him—*Stop*. He dropped his head back and rubbed his neck.

At least Tessa had been out in the field. He wouldn't know how to explain—if he even could—without her overreacting. No, without her being hurt.

Eventually, it registered that Bair had exercised extreme self-control, and that raised a flag. Smith turned in his chair.

Bair looked up. "What?"

"Nothing you want to say?"

"What would I say?"

"Let's see . . . 'How long are you going to let her jerk your chain?' or 'Tell her to stuff a sock in it!' or 'Who does she think you are—her nanny?' " All things he'd never held back before.

"Doesn't do any good." Bair looked back at his work, but a flush had crept into his ears, where his anger showed.

"What am I supposed to do—refuse her calls?"

"I wouldn't know."

He'd known every other time. "What's up?"

Bair raised only his eyes. "I don't know what you mean."

"Right." Smith headed for the door. The call had obviously chafed Bair's sore spot. He didn't need to deal with that on top of the rest.

Smith followed the drone of the Bobcat to the labyrinth field. Tessa had made good progress, not having come in since the equipment arrived. She kept working as he approached, kept working as he stood there. After her reaching out last night, he'd expected acknowledgment at least.

She finally pulled to a stop. "What do you need?"

"I wanted to see how you were."

"I'm fine."

"Want to take a break?"

She shook her head. "I'm working, Smith."

Her mood seemed to match Bair's. And then it struck him. "Climb out a minute, Tessa. I want to talk to you."

"There's no need."

"There is." He crossed the raw dirt to her and reached out. "Give me your hand."

"I don't need help." She got out without touching him.

"I don't know what Bair told you, but you've obviously taken it wrong."

"I don't think so." She wiped her palms on her pants. "And it doesn't matter anyway."

"Because I was bound to disappoint you, and now it's come sooner rather than later?"

She looked into his face. "I don't want to get caught in the middle."

"There's no middle to get caught in."

"I've seen your back before, Smith. If you're not done with Danae, I don't need this."

He would strangle Bair. Slowly. Why had he ratted him out? "It was a phone call, Tess. She does it sometimes. I don't know why."

"Because you're loyal."

"Is that what Bair said?"

"He said you're not over her, and I appreciate that, because you didn't say so. Maybe you thought the egg would break, but I prefer truth to lies."

"You're saying I lied to you?" His temper flared. "You've judged and condemned me before even hearing me out?"

"You didn't exactly run out here to discuss it."

"No, but Bair certainly did."

She raised her chin. "He didn't want me hurt. He sounded as though he'd seen it before."

"Are you talking about his cousin?"

"What about her?"

"He set me up. I told him I wasn't ready. He let her believe a little mending of a broken heart would put me right. It took months to be rid of her intensive care."

"And now here we are."

"Because I want to be."

"And yet you took her call."

He folded his arms across his chest. "As I took yours. In the middle of the night, no less."

Blood flushed from her neck into her face. "You said you wanted to make the monster go away. You let me believe it wasn't stupid to you. That you took me seriously."

"I did, and I do."

She drew a jagged breath. "Did you tell her about it?"

"What?"

"Danae. Did you tell her about the egg you're babysitting?"

"No."

"Because you don't want her to know there's anyone else in your life?"

"It's not her business to know!" It felt wickedly good to see her flinch.

"As it wasn't mine to know she'd called? That's right. I'm in a different slot. The wholly new one."

"Blast it, Tess. This isn't fair." He flung out his arms and stalked away from her before he said something he would really regret. He'd been right at the start. He should not have taken things the direction he had. Tessa was too reactionary. And Bair was going to pay.

He heard them shouting, a different noise from the other noise that had disturbed his sleep and filled him with dread. He hugged himself now, sick at heart over what she was doing. The tractor, tearing up the ground. He had trusted her. Now this. How could she? Because she didn't know. Didn't, but would. Soon. Too soon. He had to stop them, stop her. Had to, but how?

The shouting stopped, but maybe she was angry. Maybe she would go. Their fight might make her go away, make her leave it alone, leave it all alone, leave him . . . alone. He grabbed himself in his arms. He would lose her, yes, but that was better, better than losing it all. Oh, let her go away before something bad happened.

His stomach twisted. He should not have watched her sleeping. It had been so easy, finding her room. She and the old couple were the only guests. The heating vent gave him access from the room next door that wasn't locked, and oh, he'd come out under her bed and heard her breathing.

He'd waited, simply listening for so long. Only when the breathing changed, when it grew strained, did he come out to see, to know what troubled her. He hadn't made a sound, but she'd known he was there. She'd opened her eyes, and he was already to the door, already turning the locks and letting himself out.

He had slipped like a shadow into the next room, but she never opened the door. She must have thought she'd imagined him. He liked that idea, liked being in her imagination. Even if it frightened her. That made it seem real. His heart raced in his chest. He hadn't wanted to frighten her, but now the thought caused a certain excitement.

What use was it to think of her as unafraid? What chance was there of that? But thinking of her the way she'd looked, springing up with a cry, staring in fear . . . Should he like it? He was like a snake holding her with a stare, watching her tremble, too paralyzed to move. He liked that. And she deserved it for what she was doing. He clenched his hands and ground his teeth as the noise started once more.

CHAPTER

21

Tessa put the engine on idle and snapped her phone open. "What."

"Hello to you too."

She drew a deep breath. "I'm sorry, Genie. Hi."

"Bad day?"

"Um . . ." Genie didn't usually ask personal questions. Why was everyone suddenly concerned about her day, her feelings? No one actually wanted answers, so why bother asking the questions? "No, I . . . well, yeah, kind of. What's up?"

"Lyle Donner."

Tessa gritted her teeth. "What's the issue this time?"

"Pine needles."

Shaking her head in growing annoyance, Tessa listened to the current complaints from her cantankerous neighbor. "Okay, I'll handle it, Genie. Thank you." She made the next call, carefully separating the anger she felt toward Smith from the anger she would direct at Lyle if he so much as interrupted her.

"First," she told him, "I'm not responsible for the direction water flows. Your property is downstream from mine. On a mountainside. You might have considered that when you moved in."

"My yard is choked with your pine needles. I hate pine needles."

"I know. That's why you cut all the beautiful trees around your house. I could complain about the ugly view of your backside."

"I'll show you my backside if you don't watch it, missy. Get down here and clear up your mess."

"I'm working in Maryland. And even if I were there, I'm not responsible for what nature deposits in your yard." How could pine needles be worse than the dog doo from his two rusty curs that occasionally wafted its scent up the hillside? "Furthermore, I don't want you harassing my house sitter. She's taking care of every reasonable thing she can. I'll notify the marshal if you bother her again."

She didn't think Genie had anything serious to worry about. He was too obese to pose a physical threat, so he preferred annoying people to death. She was in no mood for it today.

"You'll call the marshal? I'm calling the marshal."

Tessa jammed her fingers into her hair. "You know what? Call. Make your complaint. I'm sure he has nothing better to deal with than pine needles." She hung up and started to cry. How stupid was that?

She pocketed her phone and swiped a hand across her eyes, but the tears kept coming. She hadn't wanted to hope, hadn't wanted to care. Why had Smith made it personal? To get back at Danae? She lowered her face to her hands as the tears became sobs. She should know by now that people she loved always let her down. Could it never just be good?

She stepped down from the Bobcat and started for the woods. The wind had kicked up and it would likely rain, but she didn't care. She wouldn't melt. Even if she cried all the tears inside her.

What if Smith had come out instead of Bair? What if he'd said, "Danae called, and I didn't want to talk to her, but I did because it was the right thing." Instead, he'd let enough of the day pass until she couldn't hear anything he might have wanted to say.

And what could he say, anyway? He wasn't ready to move on. He'd admitted as much. She didn't blame him for that. It was hard letting go in the face of rejection. She ought to know. But it hurt so much that he had made something happen between them that she had tried so hard to avoid. All she'd wanted was closure.

She pressed through the trees as the rain began. The rest of her soon matched her face. At least it would not be obvious she'd been crying. The last thing she needed was Smith's pity. Or Bair's, for that matter.

Lightning flashed with quick thunderous applause. She squinted up. The sky had blackened like twilight, roiling clouds releasing a weight of rain on her and soaking the woods. She should make her way back to her car, but she'd taken off in the other direction and didn't want to become a lightning rod crossing the field.

Instead she searched for a hollow or bank where she could ride out the storm. She shivered. The next crack of thunder brought a blast of rain. She could not use the base of a tree for shelter with lightning all around. She needed a place in the ground. She half ran in search of anything that would surround and shield her.

Suddenly it was like that piece of a dream Smith had awakened her from, the woods, the dark sky. The storm. Leaves instead of needles, but the ground growing soft and precarious. She shivered. At last she reached the broad river's edge. The ground banked steeply down toward the swollen, slate-gray water pocked with raindrops. She pressed into a curve in the upper portion, where roots and forest floor overhung enough to keep off the worst of the downpour.

She wrapped her knees and breathed the ozone scent of rain, rotten leaves, and wet earth, forcing each breath deeper, slower. There'd be no panic this time. She was in control. She'd be fine.

She pressed her chin to her knees. She could climb back onto the forest floor above, if she had to, but the rain came so hard she didn't want to try to see her way anywhere. It was too easy to get lost.

Her heart hammered at the thought of being lost in the woods, running and groping as darkness settled and monsters awakened. She squeezed her knees to her chest and moaned. Why was she out there? Even if Smith was there, she should have run for the trailer instead. What stupid urge had driven her away from safe shelter?

Fear spiraled up. She needed Dr. Brenner. And now she realized she had missed calling when she should have. He would be angry or at least disappointed.

She pressed deeper into the ground and speed-dialed his number. Tucking the phone under her soaking hair, she waited for the chance to tell his machine she was sorry and beg him to call. But he picked up and said, "Hello, Tessa."

"I'm so sorry I missed my appointment time." Thunder cracked directly overhead, leaving a long line of static.

"Is it storming there?"

"Yes, actually I'm caught in it. Out in the woods."

"What are you doing out there?"

"Waiting for it to stop." Rivulets of rainwater rushed down around her to join the swelling river. "Can we talk?"

"I have forty minutes free on a cancellation. Start with why you're in the woods."

She told him about Smith. He made her stay with the feelings, exploring the anger to the hurt beneath. Without the terror of the storm, she might have resisted experiencing the pain. At the moment, she preferred it to the fear.

She rubbed her nose and face with her wet hands. Smith hadn't meant to hurt her. It was inevitable. No one could give her what she needed. She expressed that to Dr. Brenner and let the calm cadence of his response soothe her further. Though the rain fell in sheets, it had softened in intensity. Lightning darted around the clouds, but the thunder only rumbled.

Next she told him about Rumer Gaston, and then about the pale form she'd seen in her room that had vanished into the shadows at her door. "I know what I have to do. I'm building a gated labyrinth and closing all the monsters inside."

"What if there's a reason he's coming out, Tessa? What if it's time to name it?"

She rubbed a streak of mud off her shin, wishing he hadn't honed in on the one monster he wanted unveiled. She was glad now that she hadn't told him it had started to speak. "He can stay forever nameless. I just want to be done with it all."

"So no more labyrinths?"

She hadn't thought in those terms. Would this labyrinth be her last? Could that be the cost of freedom? "Maybe."

"I'm glad to hear you consider it. Cutting them out of your consciousness might eliminate them from your subconscious once and for all."

He'd been saying that for years, but she hadn't been ready to let go. Maybe now she could.

"Is it still storming?"

"Not quite as hard." The sky overhead hung bruised and weeping, but it no longer struck out. Her skin was clammy. Her hair dripped down her face and back and reminded her of Danae's long hair that Smith couldn't resist. She pushed the pang away. "I guess I could make my way back now."

"Probably a good idea. I'll talk to you next week."

"All right. Thanks."

"Take care."

The moment he was gone, the phone rang again. "Tessa!" Smith all but shouted.

"What do you want?"

"Where are you? I've been trying and trying to get through."

"Why?"

"Because I'm out in the rain looking for you."

She closed her eyes against the emotions that evoked. "You don't need to." She stood up and climbed out to the top of the gully. Her battery warning started to beep.

"I saw your empty Bobcat and couldn't imagine where you'd gone."

"It doesn't matter, Smith." She started in the direction she thought the field lay. She had approached the river at a slight angle and approximated it now in the opposite direction. "Go get out of the rain. I'm fine."

As she slipped her phone into a pocket she caught sight of him some distance ahead. He saw her at almost the same time. They moved together inevitably.

The storm had overtaken his face, and thunder infused his voice. "Do you have any idea how worried I've been? What were you doing?"

"Nothing. I just got caught in the storm."

He gaped. "Help me understand. You have nightmares of being lost in the woods, but actually getting lost in a torrential storm in a forest you don't know doesn't matter?"

"I wasn't lost. Just because you couldn't find me doesn't mean I was lost."

"Who were you talking to?"

"Dr. Brenner. I missed my appointment, and since I wasn't going anywhere soon, I used the time productively." Could she ever spin it.

Rain ran down his face and hair. His features formed grim planes, his mouth a tight line. "I thought something happened."

"I'm not your responsibility."

"Tessa . . ."

She held up a hand. "Please don't. I've dealt with it, and I don't want to go into it again." She increased her pace. "We made an error in judgment. Thankfully errors can be corrected."

"Is that your opinion or Dr. Brenner's?"

"He doesn't tell me what to think, only helps me clarify."

"And now that you're clear, I'm a mistake again, an error in judgment."

She spread her hands. "Not you personally, Smith. Just . . . all of it."

"You're determined to hurt me as thoroughly as you believe I've hurt you."

She stopped walking. "I don't want to hurt you."

"Yet one phone call that I did not initiate is enough to cast me to the seventh level of hell."

She jolted. Dante's seventh circle of hell was introduced by the labyrinthine monster, Minotaur. Smith could not have meant anything more than a figure of speech, and yet . . .

Her voice shook. "I'm trying to accept where you are and—"

"You have no idea where I am. You say you're not lost, but you are. You don't see the forest for the trees."

She lowered her face as the rain ran down the neck of her shirt. It was soaked already and made no difference. He used that moment to close the gap. His warm grip burned the storm-chilled flesh of her bare arms.

"Look at me."

She looked up.

"I don't want anything to happen to you. I don't want you hurt. I don't want to hurt you."

"I know. But it happens anyway. I get that." She pulled away and started walking. "I'm not looking for pity. I just need to do what doesn't hurt."

"And that is?" He caught up.

She didn't have an easy answer. Closing him out would hurt. Not doing that would hurt more. She gripped herself in her arms. A moment later Smith's jacket came around her shoulders. She said, "You'll get soaked."

"Do you think I care?"

"I don't know, Smith. That's the problem." He'd meant it differently, but the words were out and she meant them, so she let them stay.

"I care, Tess. I don't know how else to tell you." He wiped the rain from the back of his neck. It was hardly more than a drizzle now. "I gave Bair the blazes for making you believe otherwise."

"He didn't make me believe anything."

"Just dropped seeds of doubt into your verdant expectations of disappointment. Really, Tess, what chance do I have?"

She raised her eyes from the ground. "What chance do you want?"

"I'm open to possibilities. Are you?"

She searched his face. "Were you really worried?"

"What do you think? Besides the violent thunderstorm and the dense woods, our prankster is still out here. And I don't know what his game is."

She shivered. She hadn't thought of that, hadn't thought at all, just reacted. At some point, she would have to stop reacting and make conscious choices. She only hoped she could make the right ones.

CHAPTER

22

"I'm driving you back." Smith left no room for argument, though Tessa didn't mount much resistance.

"You're overreacting."

"So what if I am?" He set his jaw.

Her teeth chattered as he wrapped her in a thick blanket and tucked her into the passenger seat, not unlike the times he'd rescued Bair from equally unwise decisions. Tess maintained the position that she hadn't required rescue. She had merely run for the woods in a lightning storm instead of joining them in the trailer. If she was that skittish, how could he make any of this work?

He got in and started the car, as annoyed with himself as with her. He had complicated an already tenuous situation, mixing business and personal matters, and had quite possibly compromised the project. Moreover, he'd endangered a consultant by creating a hostile environment she had avoided by exposing herself to hazardous weather conditions—a litigator's dream. But that wasn't the crux. The crux of it was letting down the people he cared about.

Smith gripped the wheel and backed out. Danae had temporarily derailed him, his lapse upsetting both Bair and Tessa. He couldn't help that Bair couldn't stand Danae, but now Tessa thought she would have to play second fiddle. Maybe it was still too soon to move on—except the feelings he had expressed to Tessa were real.

That was what he wanted her to know. His heart had nearly stopped when he'd seen the Bobcat standing empty in the field with lightning striking all around and rain pummeling the ground. He'd thought all kinds of awful things and nearly gone out of his head when her line kept going directly to message. Only by grace had he found her. And maybe that grace would help him now.

He believed, so help him, that they'd been brought together again for a reason, that it was bigger than either of their personal desires. He wanted her to know she mattered to him. But she had processed the emotions with someone else and returned to her dim view that nothing could ever be good and worthwhile. Why did Dr. Brenner allow her that dismal default position? To keep her dependent on him?

Smith scowled. He'd never done battle with someone's psychiatrist, but he would if it came to it. He wanted Tessa to believe, to accept the possibility of happiness. Even if he wasn't the one to give her that, he wanted her to know it was possible.

When they reached the inn, he said, "I'll wait in the foyer while you shower and change. Then we can talk."

"You're as wet as I am."

"But not muddy."

She went up, unaware perhaps of the bedraggled state that made her look more vulnerable than ever. Foolishly, he imagined washing the mud from her hair, feeling the water stream through the tresses, the scented lather, his fingers stroking her scalp. He tried not to imagine the rest of her, clean and wet, and forcefully dragged his mind to the issues between them.

After a while, she came back downstairs fresh and dry, her hair temporarily and disappointingly controlled by a clip. She held out a bulky, faded sweatshirt.

"No offense, Tess, but I don't think your clothes will fit me."

"It's my dad's."

"Your . . . dad's."

She shrugged one shoulder. "I keep it with me. And wear it sometimes."

At a loss for words, he took the sweatshirt. His shirt had mostly dried as he'd waited, but he pulled on her father's sweatshirt, soft and wooly inside from years of washing. "Thank you. Are you sure?"

She studied him. "It fits."

"And it's warm." The gesture touched him because their relationship so far had been his reaching out and her reluctantly accepting. This was the first time she'd made an overture, and it exceeded expectation.

"I know it's weird."

"It's not weird."

She slanted him a look.

"Well, a slight degree on the weird scale. But more poignant. Touching, actually."

She huffed a soft laugh. "Pretty soon you'll be patting my head like a puppy."

"I try to resist the vicinity of your head. Your hair has a deleterious effect on my self-control."

"Bair said you have—"

"Do you think we might forget whatever Bair told you and let me speak for myself?"

"I suppose." She folded her arms. "Could we do it over food?"

"Definitely." He pressed open and held the door. "Anything in particular?"

"Crab cakes?"

"Brilliant. I know just the place." He drove past small strings of homes, a couple churches and businesses and lots of woods to a whitewashed cinderblock building. The crumbling parking lot failed at the dock that reached out into the brackish waters where the Potomac joined Chesapeake Bay.

Tessa scrutinized the dubious edifice with neon beer signs in the windows and not one car in the lot. On this wet, stormy night, it hardly looked open. But it served the best crab cakes, fried soft-shell, and broiled flounder he and Bair had found—before Bair's fixation with Katy had locked them into Ellie's.

"Come on." He ushered her toward the door. "The owner's a waterman. What his wife cooks tonight, he caught in his nets this morning."

Inside, a white-haired, ruddy-faced man in a ball cap cast them a blue-eyed stare as they took a place at one of the red cloth–covered tables. After a while he ambled over with menus, but Smith told him they'd have crab cakes and fries.

He nodded. "I like this date better than the last." The owner headed for the kitchen with their orders.

Smith shot a glance across the table. "He means Bair."

She nodded. "I assumed so."

Would they ever reach a point where damage control wasn't foremost in his mind? Only if she reached the point where disappointment wasn't foremost in hers.

"Do you have other things of your dad's?"

"Yes. Mom and I never got around to disposing of them."

"Because he might come back?"

"We just liked having them."

"And your mom's things?"

She shrugged. "I only carry a piece or two when I'm going to be away awhile."

Her vulnerability found the sensitive spot between his chest and abdomen. "They're a comfort, then."

"And a reminder. I like to think of her. Of them both. Even though Dad left."

"You're not bitter."

"Mom made sure. She never showed me her anger. We worked through the hurt together. I guess I kept the disappointment, though."

As with their conversation on the jet, she divulged personal matters with a self-effacing honesty that amazed and refreshed him. He reached over and took her hand. "I've never known anyone so transparent."

"As a jellyfish." She looked up. "And like jellyfish, I sting."

"In self-defense. But you don't have to protect yourself from me."

She started to pull away, but he tightened his hold.

"I need you to know that even if Danae showed up on the doorstep, begging"—which she never would—"I wouldn't want that relationship. Not any—"

The owner brought their plates to the table—golden crab cakes, shoestring fries, slaw, and a dinner roll so flaky it looked as though it might take wing. "Anything else?" He fixed his gaze on Tessa.

She met it with a smile. "This looks great."

Smith thought so, too, but the man didn't seek his opinion. With his attention firmly on Tessa, he waxed talkative. He'd been written up in a book about notable people in Maryland. Like his father and grandfather, he net-fished the waters off his pier, and his daily recordings of things caught and things seen had garnered the interest of the Smithsonian Institute.

Smith waited for the fisherman to finish his anecdote and walk away, then bowed his head. "For what we are about to receive, Lord, make us grateful. In communication, make us humble. In affection, generous. Amen." He looked up to find tears in Tessa's eyes and remarkably recognized them as good tears. "In two years, I never saw Danae cry."

"Never made her cry?"

"That either—incredibly."

A little pinch formed between her brows. "You must think I'm a faucet."

"I prefer a leaky tap—unless I'm the cause. I like that things touch you and you're not afraid to show when something matters. In all the time we were together, Danae only showed what she wanted me to see."

"You must have liked what you saw."

"As far as it went," he conceded. "Then I hoped to see the real Danae, but maybe I had. Maybe she was all striving and surpassing."

"What am I?"

He cocked his head. "There is a lot of reacting and retreating. But your self-knowledge and revelation intrigue me."

She dug her fork into the crispy, golden crab cake, shooting steam up like a geyser.

In just that way words erupted from him. "I like seeing your delight, your excitement, even your distress, written across your face. Danae was a literary tome of hidden meaning."

"And I'm crib notes?"

He looked into her face. "You're the pulp novel I can't put down even when I have to prop my eyelids open."

Joy flashed in the corners of her eyes where the lashes came together and laugh lines would one day reveal these moments. He thought of her growing older and said, "I want to spend time with you, Tess. Lots of time. I can see spending my life with you." He might be out of his mind, but this was the sanest he'd felt in a long time. "I know that sounds premature, but I won't date anyone again that I can't imagine growing old with."

The worry returned to her brow. "Even if you mean that, it won't last."

"I'd like to show you it could." Or shake her until she saw in herself what was so readily apparent to him. She might seem fragile and reactionary, but there was something solid and achingly real inside her. Maybe that was what he'd really been afraid of, but he wasn't anymore.

He leaned in. "I'm so thankful you called last night, that you trusted me."

She sipped her iced tea and set down the glass, but didn't let go. "I'm trying to."

"That's all I ask."

"Don't you see how frustrated you'll be? Look how angry you got today."

"It's true. I don't remember the last time I shouted at someone. It was quite purgative actually."

Amusement touched a finger to her mouth.

He spread his hand. "Maybe I need airing now and then. You'll be good for me."

"Someone to holler at?"

"It's not my preferred mode." He took a hearty bite of crispy, tender crab, savoring the buttery, aromatic flavor. "I regretted it almost immediately. Especially when I saw you'd disappeared." Finding her soaked in the woods had torn him up. He couldn't imagine *not* finding her. "Next time we fight, could you not go so far?"

"Next time?"

"Or in such inclement weather? Maybe we should only holler on clear days."

"Fair-weather fighters?" She laced her hands and rested her chin.

"Quite. And I'd appreciate you talking to me before you call your shrink."

"He hates that term."

"As well he should. But head-shrinking in this instance seems appropriate. He wants to keep you in his box."

"That's not true."

He thought it could be, but didn't argue. "From now on, beat your fists on my chest."

"You walked away."

"I won't do that again, no matter how irrational you become."

She licked the salt from her lips, putting thoughts into his head. Well, why not? They had the place to themselves. He leaned across and kissed her. Salty and crabby and sweet. "I think, impossibly, I love you already."

After an amicable evening together, Smith escorted her to the inn door. "If you don't mind my taking the car, I'll fetch you in the morning."

She nodded, reluctant to go inside and spend another night where the monster had found her. "That's fine."

He cocked his head. "Are you all right?"

"Yes." She made it show in her face since he read her like a paperback.

"Well, then. See you in the morning." He leaned in for a soft kiss that deepened only enough to express a desire to linger.

Lingering worked for her. She had loved him already, loved him for a long time, or it would not have hurt to lose him. She had told herself back then that they were only friends, but something had fed the smoldering betrayal like wood chips, and that something licked up now and threatened to burn when his mouth returned to hers.

Love hurt, the song said, but it wasn't love that wounded, it was loss. Loss could engulf and consume her, reduce her to ashes, and yet she drew his kiss inside her like red-hot coals.

He drew back and smiled. "Tell me to go."

Don't go, the something inside her whispered, but it must not have made it to her face, because he kissed her forehead and backed off the porch, step by step. He stopped when he reached the ground. "If I don't show you my back at this point, I'll run into the car."

Her eyes widened; her smile spread. He'd heard and understood. Had six years, or his own rejection, or the faith he credited changed him so much? "Good night, Smith." She reached for the door and went in, less concerned about the night to come—but only until she started to climb the stairs. She changed course for the end of the foyer, where the innkeeper busied herself behind the tall podium desk.

Nan Duncat smelled of lilac and furniture wax and tried to look as though she hadn't watched through the glass door panels. "Oh, hello."

"Nan." Tessa stepped up to the desk. "Could someone have gotten into my room last night while I was sleeping?"

Nan looked surprised but didn't issue an instant denial. "Why do you ask?"

"I thought I saw someone. Or some . . . thing. It looked thin and pale, but I only saw it for a moment and then it was gone." She sounded stupid, and Nan would surely laugh.

Only she didn't. "You've seen our ghost? In your room?"

Tessa searched her face. Surely she hadn't said ghost.

"Oh good." Nan clasped her hands. "Now that he's found us, I can put the inn on the haunted register."

"What are you talking about?"

Nan leaned forward. "The lost soul who walks this county, unable to find his way to the other side."

Tessa stared at her. "People have seen this . . . ghost?"

Nan nodded. "Honey, this county has loads of ghosts. They've got Moll Dyer and her praying stone up in Leonardtown"—she said it like Lennittown—"and all those confederate prisoners at Point Lookout. I'm just tickled this one's found the inn."

"It's not very comfortable to wake up to."

"Oh, he's harmless. In all these years he hasn't so much as

said boo." She raised a finger. "He's a clever one, though. He can move things."

Her heart thumped. Things like gates and tools?

"He borrows them. Some people think he got cheated in life, and he's trying to find justice. Others say he was a thief that keeps trying to get caught, so he can pay his due."

Should she tell Smith it was a ghost who had messed with them? Was that what she'd glimpsed that day when she'd been driving out? "I may have seen him before. Out where we're working."

"Oh my." Nan touched her cheeks. "Maybe that's why he's found the inn. Maybe he followed you here."

"That's not . . ." A shiver found her spine. "A great thought. Besides, I'm not even from here. Why would he follow me?"

"Well, I've done some reading on ghosts. And it seems they attach to sensitive people who might help them find their way."

No. That couldn't be right.

Nan rested her hands on the desk. "I know the Good Book tells us not to conjure them up, but I can't see any reason, if he's already here, not to make him comfortable."

Tessa stood dumbfounded. She had no intention of comforting ghosts. She had enough trouble with monsters. She looked up the stairs. "So no one else could have gotten in?"

"Did you lock your door?"

"And the window." She hadn't unlocked it since making sure it had been secured.

Nan shrugged. "There's no other way in. I think it's safe to say you've seen the ghost." Though she might not be the best judge of any alternative explanation.

"Well." Tessa released her breath. "Better than a monster, I guess."

"Oh, honey. Don't bring them here."

Not *monsters don't exist*, just *don't bring them here*. "I won't."
Not intentionally.

She went upstairs and looked out the window. A few random
swaths of lightning still brightened the sky, but the rain had stopped
while she'd been gone with Smith. Now that night had fallen, she
could hardly believe she had waited out the storm in the woods.
What if it hadn't stopped? What if she was out there still?

She wished she hadn't given up her dad's sweatshirt. She'd
have slipped it over her now. But it warmed her in a different way
to think of Smith in it. Why had she revealed that strange quirk
of carrying her lost father's and dead mother's things around? She
jolted. Was that why a ghost had found her?

That was crazy. Ghosts were not real. And monsters were? In
her nightmares he was, and just yesterday she had believed the
line between dreams and reality had blurred, that the monster
had escaped.

She gripped her head. She needed the peace inside that only
paring herself down and standing before God could bring. If it
were not dark, she'd walk the labyrinth right now. She collapsed
onto the bed.

Why couldn't Nan have said, "Of course no one was in your
room." Wasn't that an innkeeper's responsibility? Maybe Nan
thought people who saw ghosts wanted to see ghosts.

Tessa closed her eyes. She'd be happy to see nothing other-
worldly ever again. How was she going to sleep? She'd be all hollow-
eyed and ragged when Smith came for her tomorrow. She hadn't
worried how she looked before. Now she thought about it all the
time. She reached back and freed the hair that had a deleterious
effect on his self-control. The thought made her smile, but then her
stomach clenched in fear. Why was she risking the hurt? Again.

He should not see her. Would not. She was not like him. She had made him hope, with her beautiful drawings, with the way she moved through the field, through the trees, with her face to the sky sniffing the scents, sensing the air.

But now he knew. She had dug up the ground, would keep digging it. She was where she did not belong, and he would stop her. She had to be stopped, and she would be, but he wanted to see her now. When she was gone he'd never see her again, and this was the time, this was the chance, and he wanted it. He'd worked himself into a run, panting with his tongue out.

No moon shone through the purpled sky. No stars reflecting from the pools splashing under his feet. He wanted food and so he went. In season, he ate from the planted fields, corn and soybeans and vegetable gardens. Sometimes he caught fish, but mostly it took too long. On bad nights he ate the pet food from bowls on porches and lawns. Only if no pantry could be pilfered.

He could not take from the same ones often enough to be noticed, so he always looked for new ways in. Now he had found entrance to the inn. A new pantry. That was why he wanted in there. For the new pantry. He would not go up to her, would not creep in beneath her bed, not hear her breathe or look at her face. She had betrayed him.

Because she didn't know! If she knew, she wouldn't take it away. She would leave him alone and make them go. Make them go away. If he could only tell her, only show her.

But she would scream. She had almost screamed the night before. Almost screamed when she saw him. What would it sound like, her scream?

He reached the inn, creeping softly through the wet, dark night. It hurt to squeeze through the coal chute. But it would be worth it. His stomach growled. A mouse scuttled. He let it go. A new pantry full of food, and she slept upstairs. He could just . . . look.

CHAPTER

23

"Bair." Smith whispered across the darkness.

"Mmm."

"I want to apologize."

Bair rolled with a slow groan. "Now?"

"You were justified in your concern."

"About what?"

"Tessa." He turned. "The truth is, I fell for her pretty hard in college, though I'm not sure I admitted it to myself. I didn't want to be strapped with someone so needy."

Bair grunted.

"It's still a challenge, but there it is. I can't help but love her."

Bair lurched onto one elbow. "You're in love?"

Smith startled. He hadn't expected an explosion. "I think it's possible."

"You spent the night with her and insisted it wasn't a big deal."

"What?"

"In Gaston's casino."

"I didn't spend the night with her. We had separate rooms and kept it that way. I told you—"

"What you say isn't always what you mean." Bair's eyes glinted in the moonlight through the window.

"That's absolutely not true."

"You told me at the start to have a go if I liked."

"With Tess?"

"You said don't let it interfere with the project."

"That was . . ."

Bair rolled up to sit. "I've done nothing more with Katy because it's been so easy being with Tessa, no trouble at all talking to her. She listens and knows what I mean, and opens up, and—you've set me up."

Smith sat up, flabbergasted. "I never meant to."

"You lied from the beginning."

"I didn't think I was. I'd been so wretched over Danae, and the last thing I intended—"

"Don't even start with Danae. I heard the way you talked to her, so conciliating, so understanding. Do you think you can keep them both dangling?"

"Of course not. Bair, I had no idea you'd developed feelings for Tessa." He truly hadn't realized. Was that arrogance, self-absorption?

"If a mate clears the road, he ought to stay off it."

"You're right. I changed horses in midstream."

Bair rubbed his face. "You haven't told me how she feels."

His pause conveyed enough.

"Right, then." Bair flopped back down. "I'll head back to the office tomorrow. You have things well in hand here."

Smith almost said there was no need for that, but in Bair's mind there might be. "Is that what you want?"

"I won't witness another Anna."

Smith frowned. "You're half responsible for Anna."

"Because I didn't listen to what you said?"

"Exactly."

"Well, this time I did."

Smith expelled a slow, pained breath. "You're right. I see that."

Bair clenched his hands in the shadows. "You ran Tessa off into the woods."

"I don't deny I'm lousy. I have no idea why she's held on, but she has. I'm sorry."

"Will you stop that? I could see how it was from the start, from her side at least. She didn't hide it."

And he'd taken the chance anyway. Smith refrained from apologizing again. Bair lay down and rolled to his other side. There wasn't anything more to say.

Surprisingly rested, Tessa sat up in the fluffy bed. No nightmares had wrenched her from sleep. She'd seen nothing in the dark. But now she whiffed the same strange scent she'd noticed the night before. Had someone been in her room? She crept from the bed and checked the door. Even the deadbolt was engaged.

She washed and dressed with the thought that Smith was coming for her, but the exhilaration of that didn't overcome the sense that she hadn't been alone last night. She flung open the window to drive the last vestige of the odor away, then locked it again before going downstairs.

At the desk, she asked Nan, "Could there be a leak or something that might have caused an odor in my room?"

Nan looked up. "You smelled something strange?"

"The same thing I smelled the night before. Could it be a gas leak or—"

"It's the ghost. Other people have mentioned a damp, rotten scent. One person called it the smell of the grave."

Tessa shuddered.

"They have some booklets about him at the library, people who've seen our ghost and written about it."

"So this isn't new?"

"There's been talk for . . . ten years, maybe."

Then it couldn't be the monster from her dreams. But it could be whatever was hassling Smith and Bair.

"I'm heading to the mini-mart if you'd like a lift. It's just a short walk from there to the library."

"Which library do you mean?" She didn't recall one in that vicinity.

"The old Baldwin private collection. It was donated to the Methodist church down the way and fills the old rectory. Volunteers have catalogued and made the books available to the locals. Locals have added to the collection over the years. And some have added the books to theirs. Like I said, I'll give you a ride."

Nan had obviously noted her car absent from the lot. And of course she'd seen Smith leave last night, and the manner in which he'd taken his leave. In no time the mini-mart clerk would know she had a thing with that handsome architect. But she might learn something useful.

"All right. Thanks." She'd grab some yogurt at the mini-mart and go do a little research. As they drove she called and asked Smith to wait an hour or so before picking her up.

"Yes, all right, Tess." He seemed abrupt, but then, she could be reading into it. Maybe she'd interrupted him, or Bair was nearby. Bair, who thought Smith wasn't over Danae, whose cousin had tried to heal his broken heart, who had looked truly concerned when he'd seen them kissing.

Smith had not picked up on that, but she'd seen the expression on Bair's face. She'd talk to him today, let him know she and Smith were all right and he didn't have to worry. Funny what a sweet friend he'd become. She was no longer outside their circle. They'd invited her in.

But Smith's tone had not been inviting. He might regret opening up the way he had. That was hard for lots of guys. They'd come into the group and become human clams for the rest of them to peck at. For some, it was about wresting control from the facilitator. For others, a last defense.

Smith had said he could see spending his life with her. He didn't know how pervasive her issues were, how much of her reality had been shaped by her therapy. Her peers had been people who couldn't cope—like her. Dr. Brenner said she wouldn't have a successful relationship until she'd figured herself out. She didn't seem to have the facility.

Smith didn't like her talking about him to the psychiatrist. She got that. But thinking Dr. Brenner could be holding her back, keeping her dependent—that was wrong. He wanted to help; she knew it. He cared about her.

Nan brought her to the mini-mart and, while Tessa chose a peach yogurt from the cooler case, convinced the clerk her guest could be a ghost whisperer. Tessa adamantly denied it, which seemed to only confirm the sort of humility that could draw a wandering soul. Nan had been the one to turn her questions to the supernatural, and she seemed determined to believe it.

Tessa resisted it still, though she had thought she'd seen something. Smith had been the first to mention hauntings; Bair called it a poltergeist. None of them had found a camp or lodging anywhere near the property, yet someone had moved the level and the gate.

That reminded her she needed to find out where Bair had taken it for repair. As Nan and the clerk continued their discussion, Tessa slipped out her phone and called the office number. Smith answered, "Chandler Architecture."

"Oh, I called this number looking for Bair."

"Sorry, Tess. He's gone back to the main office in D.C."

"Again?"

"He's going to handle things there for a while."

"Oh. Well, let me have his cell. I want to know where he took the gate."

"I'll find out for you."

"That's okay. Just give me the number." Did she imagine the reluctance with which he complied? She jotted it on her palm, then stepped out of the mini-mart and phoned Bair. "Good morning, Bair. I'm looking for my—" She halted at the sight of the Land Rover outside of Ellie's. "I thought you were back at the office."

"I'm on my way. I stopped for, um, breakfast before leaving."

"Then I'll just duck in and ask you." She crossed the distance between Ellie's and the mini-mart.

"Ask me what?"

As she hung up and pulled open the door to Ellie's, Bair almost barreled into her in the foyer, with Katy held fast by the wrist.

Tessa stepped back. "Where's the fire?"

Bair flushed. "We were . . . leaving."

"Katy's going with you?" Her surprised remark earned a glare from the mutinous redhead.

Bair pushed his keys into Katy's hand. "Go ahead. I'll . . . um . . . be just a moment."

When the door slapped shut behind Katy, Tessa turned back. "What's wrong? Why are you guys flying out of here like—"

"Ellie's going to be a bit shorthanded, that's all."

"But I thought you couldn't be alone with Katy."

His face heated with anger. "Did Smith say that?"

"I must have misunderstood. How long will you be gone?"

"Some time, I'd say."

"Are you all right?"

"Chuffed." He looked anything but pleased. "Well . . . I have Katy waiting." He pushed through the doors. "Don't say I didn't warn you."

Warn her . . . What had he—about Smith? Had they fallen out over yesterday? She pushed through the door as Bair hit the gas and backed out in one fell swoop, then tore away with tires ablaze. She stood with hands to her hips and watched them go.

She realized she hadn't found out about the gate, but she wasn't going to call him now. She'd deal with that later, or let Smith. Smith. She wrung her hands. Bair had been the anchor, the friend she'd counted on to buffer her and Smith. With no third party, their relationship would have to stand on its own.

No longer hungry, she slipped the yogurt cup into her purse and walked along the side road toward the red brick neoclassical church and rectory. Pigeons strolled the ridges of the steep gray roofs. She crossed the dewy lawn and rang the bell at the side door as Nan had instructed on their drive over.

The soft-faced woman who opened the door hardly came to Tessa's chin. "Yes?"

"Hi, I'm Tessa Young."

"Oh, the architect. Nan Duncat called. I'm Joliet." She looked like someone's ebony-skinned fairy godmother.

"Hi. Nan sent me over to read the local ghost stories, especially the newest one."

"Our night prowler."

"Prowler. Then he's not a ghost." Of course he wasn't. She knew that.

Joliet shrugged. "I don't know how he gets through locked and alarmed doors. Seems a little more substantial to me, though."

"You've seen him?"

"Only the books he's borrowed."

"He checks books out from the library?"

The little woman cast her a wry look. "He hasn't signed his name or checked anything back in." She led the way to a back section and drew several booklets from the shelf. "Maybe he is a ghost. You can draw your own conclusions."

Tessa thanked her, and then a thought struck her. "While I look at these, could you see whether you have anything related to a Jesuit plantation monastery called St. John's?"

Without hesitation, she said, "We did have. But those documents were purchased."

"Really. By whom?"

"He remained anonymous, but paid enough to replace our roof and more."

"I see." So that was how Rumer Gaston had come to possess the only documents she'd found so far. "Do you know what happened to the residents after the monastery burned?"

"No. But it wasn't a good time for priests. You haven't dug up any skeletons, have you?"

"No, of course not."

"Don't be so sure you won't. Up in Annapolis they discovered a poor indentured servant in William Fuller's cellar. I saw it on a history show. At first they thought it might be one of the prisoners his bunch were executing in the streets during the Battle of the Severn. But it turned out to be an ill, overworked youth, thrown down there with the garbage." She shook her head sadly. "If you're seeing ghosts, it might be that more perished in the fire than the monastery."

Tessa couldn't resist a shudder. "I haven't seen any ghosts."

"I don't believe in them myself." Joliet touched the booklets. "But there are plenty who do. Especially this particular one."

"Well, thanks." Tessa took the ghost booklets written by several county citizens over to a small table near the window.

Her throat squeezed when the first one chronicled sightings of a pale form moving through the darkness as if searching for some-thing or someone. She couldn't say she had actually *seen* a pale form in her room. She could have dreamed or imagined it. The writer claimed to have glimpsed it more than once in the twilit woods around their farm, but had never gotten close enough for a more thorough examination.

Her pulse quickened when the next booklet described the odor the author had noticed when the ghost had been in her kitchen. She went on to say that apparitions were frequently accompanied by the smell of sulfur or smoke, but that this one left more of a moldy body odor behind. She had asked Nan if it could be a gas leak, but moldy body odor better described the rank aroma.

The most absurd account mentioned an affinity for animals and the ability to move and behave like one, especially loping with the gait of a wolf, though it ran erect. He too mentioned an odor, described it as gamey, and found it most remarkable that dogs didn't bark or raise their hackles as with other supernatural sightings. That writer believed the creature a wolf man, though there was no evidence of fur.

Tessa shut the booklet. This was ridiculous. Plus it distracted her from the real monster she needed to contain—even if he existed only in her head. She slid the items back into the shelf and thanked Joliet, then slipped out her phone and dialed Smith.

A short while later, he pulled up. "I thought you might be up for breakfast. Since Bair took the company car, we'll have to stick together."

"What happened with you two?"

"Why do you ask?" His smooth composure didn't fool her.

"Bair looked like fury as he dragged Katy off."

Smith jerked his head. "Bair took Katy?"

"I don't think Ellie was happy."

He released a hard breath. "Mind if we eat there?"

"As long as you tell me what's going on."

Smith pulled up to Ellie's. "Bair's brassed off because . . . well . . . he doesn't like the way I . . ." He rubbed his hands down his face.

"Shave?"

Smith slanted her a glare. "He thinks I lied about our relationship and allowed him to grow fonder of you than he would have."

"Me?" She almost yelped it.

"Yes, you."

"Then why did he snatch Katy?"

"I don't know, but I've got to go inside and do damage control."

Her head reeled. Bair had feelings for her? "I don't believe it. You must be mistaken."

"Tessa, today I could be a complete mug. But it's out of his own mouth."

And words didn't come lightly from Bair's mouth. She followed Smith into Ellie's, feeling responsible in a whole new way.

Ellie greeted them in the foyer, more flushed and flustered than angry, it seemed.

Smith apologized for Bair. "I didn't realize they'd be leaving together. I sincerely hope he'll treat your granddaughter respectfully."

Respectful didn't exactly describe what she'd seen. On either of them.

Ellie sighed. "I'm more concerned about Katy's behavior. That girl's been looking at this county over her shoulder for years." Ellie arched a brow. "Your friend might find himself canoodled."

Gauging by her expression that morning, Katy would not let anything interfere with her plans. And if Bair was smarting, he'd be more susceptible than ever. Tessa glanced at Smith, then back to Ellie. "How old is she?"

"Nineteen. And off to regions hither and yon." Ellie spread out her hands.

Legal age, thank God. Katy's determination to get out of town probably trumped any true affection for Bair, but he wasn't robbing the cradle. Katy only seemed like an adolescent. Tessa pictured him eating pastrami day after day because he didn't want to say he didn't like it. Her heart ached.

Smith repeated his apology, and it struck her how much responsibility he bore for others. Warmth seeped past her angst. The feelings were coming fast and strong.

"It's Katy's own doing." Ellie showed them to a table and shook her head. "Since she dropped her shift, I'll take your order. Do you know what you want?"

Smith ordered the vegetarian omelet.

"Just the fruit plate, please." She wasn't sure she could eat even that.

"I'll have to put a help sign in the window." Ellie walked away, sighing.

Tessa leaned in. "Smith, this is bad."

He nodded grimly. "I should have seen it coming."

"How could you?"

He shot his gaze across to her. "I know the effect you have on me. Why should I think him immune?"

She groaned. "I feel terrible. How could we not realize?"

"Bair's not exactly demonstrative." He pressed his hands to his eyes. "And I was too busy figuring myself out."

"Have you?"

He released a sigh. "Not quite. You?"

"Not even close. But there's a chance I'm not seeing things, at least things that aren't there."

"Such as?"

She flicked him a glance. "The monster in my room."

"Did it happen again?"

"I slept through it last night. But this morning I smelled him."

"You . . . what?"

She folded her hands. "It seems he leaves an unusual odor. Have you noticed it?"

"If you mean the prankster, the only odor I noticed was when he marked our doorstep as his territory. But what was he doing in your room? And how did he get there?"

"Since he's a ghost, he obviously came through the walls."

"Be serious, Tessa."

"I am. There are at least six accounts in the library of a pale night prowler that smells like the grave. Nan's delighted the ghost finally found her inn. She's hoping he'll haunt it regularly."

Smith frowned. "Tell me you're joking."

"I wish I were."

"Our prankster is known as some sort of ghoul?"

"Well, one called him a wolf man." She thanked Ellie for the tea that poured steaming into her cup and the plate of fresh-cut fruit.

"This looks wonderful." Smith's smile brought a hint of pink to Ellie's cheeks, but he sobered again when she left. "Wolf man?"

"The point is, people have seen him. And a while back I saw something in the woods that matched their descriptions."

"You never told me."

"You thought I was crazy enough."

"I don't think you're crazy, Tess. I think there's an explanation for everything."

"I'll ask next time he appears. Nan thinks he's following me."

Smith frowned. "I don't like that."

"Neither do I. I have enough monsters in my life already."

"I don't like that either."

"It's unanimous."

After breakfast, they drove out to the site. She could not help glancing over to the spot where something had seemed to watch her. Shady woods and nothing more. Smith held the office door open, but she shook her head. "I'm going back to work. There's a gnarly vine out there I want to get up."

"Gnarly?"

"Gnarly."

His grin faded. "Tess. Be careful."

She nodded. "I always am."

But she hadn't been. The thought that Bair had become attached and she hadn't guessed distressed her more than she had wanted Smith to see. Why had she not realized that Bair's attention was more than friendly? Because he'd been interested in Katy—speechless over her. He hadn't been speechless at all in their interaction. Should that have told her something?

She pressed her hands to her face. If he started drinking again, would it be her fault? Dr. Brenner was very firm that each person had responsibility over his or her own issues. Maybe it was better she hadn't known. If she had, things would have been unbearably awkward, even more than being alone with Smith, the pressure of which already had her in a heightened state of anxiety.

CHAPTER

24

Alone in the office, Smith debated calling Bair and demanding he return Katy. In this tight-knit county, they could not afford enemies. But Ellie thought her granddaughter the instigator, and maybe there was something to that. Bair had acted in anger, but Katy had been making her move since she'd first laid eyes on them.

They were two adults capable of their own decisions. Maybe it was even a good thing. By going off alone with her, Bair had overcome an obstacle—unless he turned back to drink in order to communicate. Smith sighed. Bair had said himself when he'd come out of rehab, "You can't be responsible for me, Smith. I have to do it myself." He'd helped where he could, but ultimately it was up to Bair. Like the rest of them, he'd stand or fall by his own choices.

Smith opened his CAD software and sent the base sheets Bair had completed to the electrical and civil engineers. He produced a schedule for their return drawings, complete with specs, and looked over the budget—well within the dollars already allocated. Then he pulled up materials and suppliers he had tentatively selected for the first concept and went over each item for suitability in the new adaptation.

After several hours, Tessa came in for a drink. As she started back out the door he stood up and stretched. "How is the gnarly vine coming?"

"I'm going to tackle it as soon as I've cleared the outer perimeter. I want to see the labyrinth in its entirety."

"Still planning to do it yourself?"

"As much as I can. It feels personal, Smith, like a mandate."

He'd thought it a job. An important one, a great opportunity, but a mandate?

"Possibly a swan song. Dr. Brenner wants it to be the last labyrinth I build."

"Really." Would she let her therapist decide her career direction when it had been so crucial to her? He wondered again what kind of power the man wielded.

"He always says that. But now, I wonder. If I can trap the monster once and for all . . ." She sighed. "I see what you're thinking."

He had not shown a thing, he was sure. "How can you trap a nightmare into a hedge? It's too . . . mystical."

"I know."

"And the monster, Tess—I admit I'm confused. There's Gaston, the ghost, and the monster in your dreams." He hadn't realized labyrinths were so tied in to her psyche. Would he have called her if he'd known the emotional landscape she'd be tearing up with each drag of sod?

"I can't explain it. I just know I have to build this labyrinth, that it matters, somehow, more than any other."

That was better than the refusal she'd voiced in Laughlin, but he worried. "I've just about completed what I had for today. Would you like some help?"

She narrowed her eyes. "You want to get your hands dirty?"

He'd once boasted that he would never do a single day of physical labor. He was the idea, the concept, the conceiver. Others were out there to labor. There was no doubt in his mind she remembered his words. "Why should you have all the fun?"

She scrutinized him, then shrugged. "Okay. If you're serious. Bring gloves. I might have some cutting for you."

"My favorite." He smiled. "Especially gnarly vines."

"It's kudzu."

"The bane of the south? Is that even destructible?"

"Over miles of countryside, no. But in my labyrinth? Absolutely. I'll just have to be thorough. Not leave any remnant of crown or seed. If it reestablishes, it could cover the hedge and deprive it of sunshine."

"Can't have a kudzu labyrinth?"

She shot him a glare.

"Then it's death to the kudzu. I'll wrap up some things and join you."

"All right." She shook her hair loose before recapturing it in an unconscious gesture that made him wonder whether anything he had to do was even close to important. He exhaled deeply. He did have calls to make, a fax to send. After she had gone, he successfully shifted focus, but before he'd finished, she came back.

He looked up. "Something wrong?"

"I thought I left the key in the Bobcat, but I must have brought it in." She went into the kitchen, where she had filled a bottle with the green tea she kept in the refrigerator. Puzzled, she came in and searched around his desk.

"Bathroom?" he suggested.

She rejoined him, shaking her head.

He rose. "Could you have dropped it on the way here?"

"I guess, but I can't imagine."

"I'll help you look. Just let me grab those gloves." They went around the back of the trailer to the small portable shed. He got a pair of work gloves. "Need anything else?"

She took down the narrow pruning saw she had brought in days ago. "This'll do, if you're serious about helping."

"I wouldn't have offered otherwise." A gust of moist wind caught them as they started across the field, searching the ground as they went.

"I just don't think I dropped it." She shielded her eyes and stared out toward the site. "I'd have put it in my pocket if I took it, but I remember turning the engine off and leaving the key in the ignition."

"Could it have fallen out?"

"I searched all over the Bobcat."

They reached the field and scoured the ground around the vehicle. No key. He straightened and looked into the woods. "Our prankster could be at it again."

"The ghost?"

"Tell me once more what you read."

"It seems there's a prowler who goes through locked doors and helps himself to things."

"Why do they think he's a ghost and not a burglar?"

"He gets into impossible places and he's perfectly silent."

"No wailing or clanking of chains?"

She shot him a glare. "People described a thin, pale figure moving through the woods, loping like a wolf, only erect. He goes through walls and smells like the grave." She shuddered again. "I smelled him, Smith. The night I called you and again last night."

"If he's corporeal enough to stink, I would guess he's not a ghost."

"Then how did he get into my room?"

"I don't know and I don't like it."

She looked up at him. "You thought I was dreaming that night, didn't you?"

"Didn't *you*?" He met the challenge.

"I don't know what to think anymore. When it's happening, it's so real."

He looked around the field. "It is real. Someone is messing with us. The question is why."

"I'm not imagining it?"

"No. And you're not the only one he's disturbing. While we were in Laughlin, he got into the trailer and nicked our toothpaste."

"Did you report it?"

He slanted her a look.

She frowned. "How did he get in?"

"Through the window with the air-conditioner."

"That's a small window."

"Quite." He scanned the woods around them, unable to shake the feeling that they were being watched. Or at least that someone was aware of them, but who, and from where?

She sighed. "I'll have to call for a replacement key. In the meantime we can see what we're up against with this." She kicked at the woody vine. "I'm not giving up. He'll have to do worse than take away my toys."

"You think it's you he's trying to stop?"

"All I know is what I've felt. Like someone—or something—wants me gone."

They'd all felt it, then, that resentful watching. Smith's discomfort increased.

She raised the pruning saw. "Sorry, but that's not going to happen. I have a labyrinth to build." She gripped the vine and cut a rooted part of the kudzu. "This is a young vine, recently established. Left to itself it'll spread to the woods and take over, but it hasn't had time to get vast and vigorous enough that I can't remove it."

He looked over at the trees surrounding the field, the rest of the meadow itself. "I don't see any more. I wonder where it came from."

"Probably a seed, blown or carried and deposited." She straightened. "Whoever takes over as topiary gardener will have to watch for residual growth, but I intend to do my best to see that there's nothing left of it."

"Have you decided what to plant?"

"I saw some hawthorn in the woods that could have been seeded from the original. The monks would have valued its berries as an antispasmodic and cardio tonic. But the thorns make it a better choice as a deterrent hedge to keep trespassers out than a path intended to draw pilgrims in."

"So no hawthorn."

"Bay laurel, myrtle, and privet are all possible, but I was leaning toward yew."

"Me?"

"*Taxus baccata 'Fastigiata.'* Irish yew." She looked across the labyrinth field with a narrowed gaze as though picturing it there already. "It's a densely growing conifer perfect for topiary. Thrushes and waxwing and other birds eat the seed cones, though the rest is famously poisonous."

"Famously?"

"Rulers are recorded as having chosen its poison over surrender to Caesar and other conquerors."

"You're not thinking . . ."

"Of poisoning Rumer Gaston?" The look in her eyes had disquieting elements. "Of course not."

"I mean you'd warn him," he pressed.

"Not to eat the bark and leaves or boil up any tinctures?"

"Stop teasing, Tessa."

The corners of her mouth deepened. "I've actually settled on boxwood."

"Glad to hear it. What other herb lore do you know?"

"All kinds. Dandelions aid liver function. Sarsaparilla increases blood circulation and stimulates breathing. Combined with sassafras and burdock root, it cures syphilis. Thyme is effective against Staphylococcus, E. coli, and tuberculosis. And quite useful in killing hookworms."

He grimaced. "You learned that where?"

"From my mom."

"The earth mother."

"Don't knock it." She scowled.

"I'm not. Truly." But he couldn't keep the grin from his face. "You're a wealth of . . . unusual knowledge. Labyrinths, ghosts, herbs. I'm fascinated just thinking what else you might know."

She shot him a dubious look.

"I'm serious."

"I'm sure you know plenty of odd things yourself."

"Ogee arch, quatrefoil, voussoir."

"I don't mean weird terms and definitions." She swiped the windblown hair from her face. "I mean stuff."

"I think I've lived a very ordinary life with a very ordinary body of . . . stuff."

"I don't know what fork to use for oysters."

"It's a rather small, three-pronged affair shaped like Neptune's trident."

She laughed. "There you go." She stooped and took hold of the vine. "Anyway, before I can think of planting, I have to be rid of this vine." She tugged, then looked closer. "Huh. These leaves have been torn off. The property must have been recently and regularly grazed."

"Do deer eat kudzu?"

"Seasonally, I think, when there's nothing they like better. Goats especially like it. Even people. Ever had kudzu jelly?"

"Can't say that I have. Am I missing out?"

"Tastes like bubblegum."

"Not quite the thing for toast, then."

She smiled. "It decreases the desire for alcohol."

He raised his brows. "So this weed people want to annihilate could cure alcoholism?"

"I'm not claiming that. And even if it cures cancer, this particular vine cannot remain in the middle of my labyrinth. I wanted to use the skid loader to clear the matted surface and sever as many root crowns as possible. The roots themselves don't regenerate. Once I've cleared all remaining crowns by hand and painted the stalks with glyphosate, I'll only need to watch out for seeds."

"And since we haven't the Bobcat?"

She frowned. "We'll have to cut it by hand."

He looked at the mess of vines. "Let's search the field. The key might've been tossed, not taken." Futile without a metal detector, but he didn't mention that.

"We'll never see it in there. It's too thick."

"Too thick, as well, to attack by hand." No sense at all in that. He caught her hands and pulled her over. "And there are so many better things to do." He'd intended to be professional during the working day, and pursue their relationship after hours, but that didn't ever really work.

She raised her chin. "Are you giving up already?"

"Only suggesting alternatives." Her mouth tasted of moist air and pollen.

"I thought you came to help, not distract me."

Liking her throaty breathiness, he sank his hands into her hair, making the band slip down. "I thought this was helping."

"No, it's . . . well, it isn't helping. You said you wanted to get your hands—"

"My hands are exactly where I wanted to get them." He made the band slide the rest of the way off her silky, silky hair.

"Smith," she rasped. "I have to do this."

"Wait until you have the equipment you need."

"I can't let him stop me." Her gaze drifted someplace far that he couldn't see, a place of nightmares and monsters. She thought she had a mission, a mandate, some assignment she hadn't received from him, the architect, but from . . . God? Her therapist? Her own mind?

"You can go back." She rested her palm on his chest. "I know you have things to do."

She expected him to fail her, even in this small thing. Her stopwatch ticked away toward disappointment. He didn't want to disappoint her, yet it made no sense to attack the weed by hand when she would have the machine running soon enough.

"Go on." She smiled. "I'll be fine."

He shook his head. "I don't think you should work out here alone. He's been toying with us, but that's not to say it won't escalate." It wasn't his place to tell a consulting architect what she should be doing or not. What about someone he cared about, might possibly love, and certainly wanted to protect?

"I have pepper spray in my purse."

"And your purse is . . ."

"In the trailer."

He cocked his head. "Not exactly within reach."

"I'll keep the spray with me after this. But Nan says he's harmless. Never even says boo."

His phone signaled a text message, and he released her. Checking the ID, he stiffened. "I need to deal with this, but I don't want you out here alone."

"I'll walk back with you for the pepper spray."

Probably the best he would get. He responded to the text as

they walked. *Not now. Not here.* Relieved when no response came, he clipped his phone back onto his belt.

The wind caught tendrils of Tessa's hair across her forehead and around her face as they walked. He wanted to lock her into the trailer and make her stay, because being out there had given him a bad feeling, but that was ridiculous. He didn't succumb to feelings.

They reached the trailer and went inside. While Tessa located her purse and the defensive spray inside, he texted: *Call you tonight.* He did not want to be put into an awkward position. More than that he didn't want to put Tessa—

A knock rattled the door. It opened. "Smith?"

In sync with Tessa, he turned. His heart raced; his spirit sank. "Danae."

Nearly as tall as he, she wore fitted slacks and a knit shell that draped her effectively. Pearls graced her ears and throat. Her hair hung shining to her waist.

His throat constricted. "Danae, this is Tessa. Tessa, Danae."

Tessa pocketed the pepper spray and shook his ex's hand. "Hi."

"Hello." Danae flashed a smile. He noticed once more how pronounced her features were, the peaked arch of her eyebrows, the shelf of her cheekbones, the Roman arch of her nose. An arresting face, made dynamic by her keen gaze. There was nothing airy about Danae.

Tessa slipped past them to the door. "I'm going back to work."

He wanted to argue but said instead, "Be careful."

As the door closed behind her, one thought rose above the others; why had he not told Danae he was in a new relationship?

CHAPTER

25

Tessa pocketed the pepper spray and called the machinery rental shop for a replacement key. They had closed for the day. Tension spiraled up her spine, and now she would not be able to release it with the levers of the Bobcat. She fetched the shovel from the shed. That and the pruning saw would have to do.

Her grip tightened on the shovel. Danae was not beautiful. She was striking and impressive. And she wore her hair down.

Why hadn't Smith told her Danae was coming? If that was what he'd needed to deal with, he could have warned her. Unless he didn't want her to know. Then why ask her to come back to the trailer?

She shook her head. All she'd asked from him was the truth. All she'd wanted was candor. And loyalty. And love. She would have liked him to mean what he'd said. And maybe he had, at the time, in a way. Maybe he'd thought he meant it. She could understand that. People couldn't know when things would change. They just did.

She brushed a tear away. The problem was things didn't change for everyone at the same time. Someone was always left behind.

Dragging the shovel and carrying the saw, she strode through the quickening wind that pushed and bunched the looming clouds.

After facing the last storm in the woods, she should go back inside. But the trailer was occupied. She would get in the car and go back to the inn, but Smith had the keys. She kept walking.

She had a duty, a mission. A monster to trap. Dr. Brenner didn't want the monster locked away. He wanted it brought to light. That was not happening. She would do war one kudzu crown at a time, if she had to, before she would give that monster the light of day.

Especially now that she was vulnerable. Dr. Brenner had been right that she should not have two stressors. Smith didn't want to hear about it, but he had no idea how hard it was not to question every word, doubt every action. Being with him was like looking at the sun. She wouldn't realize she'd been burned until her eyes went dark. Then all she'd have would be memories to tuck into the cache of cherished people who had mattered enough to risk loving, even though the loss was excruciating.

A gust of wind propelled her toward the labyrinth field. She had arrived embittered and resentful, reacting to everything like a raw nerve. Then she'd found joy, though joy implied carefree, and this joy was wary; this joy's edges were sharp and they cut when she least expected it—a glance, a brush of Smith's fingers, the tug of them in her hair—each of those glances, every touch would now be glass in her heart.

Smith was in the trailer with the woman he'd loved, maybe still loved, and there was nothing she could do, because she didn't ask God to answer prayers like mail-order requests. She sought him in the labyrinth, gained what divine insight she could find, used the meditation to go deeper, grow wiser, transform herself again and again into what she had to be to survive.

After her long drive, Danae had headed straight for the bathroom, and from the length of time spent in there, she must be freshening her hair and makeup. He didn't want to think why. She came out and flashed her close-the-deal smile. He braced himself for questions about Tessa, but Danae started more subtly.

"You're surprised, I guess." She slid the glossy brunette strands behind one ear.

"Well, yes. How did you know where to find me?"

"I went to your office first. Bair gave me directions."

Of course he did. "It's a long way down. You could have called."

"I wanted to see you. I'm sorry if it isn't a good time. I was looking so closely for the gate I missed your replies."

"It's all right." If she was already that close, he'd have let her come anyway.

"If you're too busy . . ."

"No, I'm not." He thought of Tessa out in the field. "Would you like some tea?"

"Oh yes. Do you have it iced?"

"Um." He moved toward the kitchen. "Some chilled green, I think. Tessa won't mind sharing."

"She must be the landscape architect."

"That's right."

"Bair told me."

"Told you . . ."

"She does labyrinths."

He poured Danae a glass of tea.

"You don't mind that I came, do you?"

"Of course not, but I'm not really set up for company." He brought a chair around for her, turned his to face it. "This isn't the most comfortable office. I'm sorry."

"You've worked from a trailer before."

"I'm on-site for the duration." Far enough that resuming their relationship would be difficult except by phone, if he even wanted to.

He needed to tell her, but couldn't find the words to explain his relationship with Tessa. For the first time he understood Bair's disability. "So . . . how are you?"

"Well, I'm getting some influential clients, planning some amazing governmental events. Mostly through Edward's contacts, I admit. He's in the House now. Did you know? Representative from Pennsylvania."

"I didn't know."

"My weekends are scheduled three years out, except for slots I keep open for VIP accounts. Ed is constantly amazed and, I don't mean to sound boastful, but really impressed by how much I accomplish. Things move so slowly in his bureaucratic world."

"Yes, I imagine."

"I'm excited at the way it's all taking off. No White House events yet, but it's possible, Smith. It's not just a pipe dream. People know who I am, what I can do."

"That's wonderful."

"It is. I have all these ideas and contacts—oh, Smith, you should see my contact list. People are practically begging to be considered. Florists, caterers, entertainers, security. Even go-fers."

"Then what's the matter?"

"The matter?" Her smile was just a little too bright.

"Yes, Danae. The matter."

She deflated. "Edward."

"I'm not comfortable—"

"I know. You don't want to say anything against him. You're so considerate."

Not really, when it came to the man who'd had no qualms about disrupting a relationship in progress.

"I don't know if we're happy or just successful. Sometimes I think back to before . . . and miss what we had."

What he'd had wasn't enough. "He can give you so much more."

"It's not just about that. I know you think it is. But it didn't seem as though we were getting anywhere. I felt—" She stood up and paced. "Stalled. In neutral." Her hair swayed as she walked.

"And now you're getting somewhere."

"I am. But . . ."

"It's not making you happy?"

She sighed. "I don't know. Put it in perspective for me, Smith, with that logical mind of yours. Make sense of it."

"You don't need me for that. You've always known exactly what you wanted."

She sank into her chair. "Everything is going right, just the way I planned it, and yet . . . there's a nagging thought that won't go away." She speared him with a stare. "Ed is, well, we fit together in so many ways, yet . . . I don't know that I can trust him."

"In what?"

"I can't really say. It's a feeling sometimes. Maybe he's too good a politician, always having a ready answer."

"Is he cheating on you?" It was in his bag of tricks. And hers. They'd gone behind his back at least two months before she'd broken off.

"Of course not. No, I didn't mean that. I don't know what I meant. Sometimes success is scary, I think."

"Be careful what you wish for."

Her smile had more sadness in it than it should have. "I'm so glad there's no rancor between us."

He swallowed. "What would be the point?"

"Exactly. You're so level, Smith."

What did that mean? No drive, no upward momentum?

"Just seeing you, talking like this. It's really nice." She reached over and squeezed his hand. "And it sounds like you're doing well too. This big project and potentially more for the same client."

"Potentially."

"I'm happy for you. Finally someone recognizes your talent. I knew it would come."

"Did you."

"And bringing Bair along. After everything. So thoughtful."

"He'll make a good architect and benefit the firm."

"You always think the best of people."

Not always. Sometimes he thought the opposite. Sometimes he was right.

"Oh, Smith, it's so nice to see you. You look wonderful."

His chest tightened. "So do you."

She looked at her watch. "Do you want to have dinner? I have so many stories to tell you."

"I'm sorry, I can't." He stood up.

"It's so last minute, I know. Maybe another time, with advance notice. I'd love to catch up."

He needed to see that Tessa was all right, though odds were next to none for that. There'd be damage control to be done.

"Let's not let it go so long next time."

Reaching for the door, he smiled. "Brace yourself. The wind's kicked up. It's getting ready to rain."

She chucked his chin. "Always looking out for me." Her hand settled on his shoulder. "I'm glad you're in my life."

That was his cue to lean in and kiss her. He would have, too, if not for Tessa. He couldn't stop himself from thinking it, but he could resist acting on it. Danae, it seemed, could not. She kissed his mouth. He'd given her no reason not to, except for the reason she'd given herself—Edward.

There might be grim satisfaction in doing unto Edward as he had done unto him, but Smith would regret it. He stepped back.

"I'm sorry." She smiled limply. "Old habits die hard."

They did. He held her upturned gaze. "I hope you beat the storm."

"I like driving in the rain, remember?"

He nodded.

"I've been remembering the smallest things, like the way you hold your pencil." She laughed.

"What's wrong with how I hold my pencil?"

"Nothing. It's just . . . a funny thing to remember, don't you think?"

If there was a message there, he missed it. She had not asked about Tessa, nor explained why she would drive all the way down for no clear purpose. Just more of what had frustrated him before. He was no doubt expected to read between the lines, but once again she had baffled him.

He opened the door, and she went through. Though he'd be heading out to find Tessa, he didn't step out with Danae. Walking her to the car would only prolong the leave-taking, and the longer he took now, the more explaining he'd have later.

She caught her hair at the nape as she walked through the wind to her Lexus. He had always previously gotten her door, but it would offer another chance to kiss, and some old habits had to die, hard or otherwise. He waved and closed the door, waited until he heard her drive away, then prepared himself for the trial to come.

CHAPTER

26

After severing multiple root crowns along the lengths of vine, Tessa put down the tools. Work was not going to stop the disappointment. The longer Smith stayed in the trailer with Danae, the worse it got. She didn't blame him for being loyal, as Bair had said. He might even still be in love with her.

How often did the chance come to have someone you'd lost back again? If Danae wanted to try, would he? Her diaphragm contracted. She had overreacted to the phone call, but this—what woman drove hours to see her ex-boyfriend? One who still cared, still loved him. She should be happy for them. Why should she be surprised? After six years, the sound of his voice had brought her to his side.

Tessa stood up and stretched her back. She needed to calm down before Smith joined her. They would still have to work together, and she did not want him to feel bad or worry about her. She could call Dr. Brenner, have him talk her through the emotions, but Smith had asked her not to use that as a first course.

Instead she crossed to the labyrinth's entrance. She stepped onto the bedrock traveled long ago by sandaled feet, buried in burnt hedge and broken promises, and considered those who had come in good faith, served willingly, and lost everything—maybe even their lives. She would not die of this hurt, but how many more people must she lose? Tears stung.

She took a step and imagined a gate closing behind her, hedges rising up on either side. Spreading her hands as though to touch their dense foliage, she walked the short length of the mouth, turned left in the first shallow curve, and doubled back. She moved straight toward the center and curved halfway around its perimeter. Twice the path skirted the center and then wended away to complete all the other circuits before actually entering in.

It was like a dance where the petitioner courted God, drawing near, then away, around and back before daring to enter the presence. She'd never thought of it that way before, but Smith demonstrated a faith she struggled to comprehend, praying with intimacy, as though the Divine delighted in fulfilling his desires. And wasn't he getting what he wanted?

She pushed away the pain and cleared her mind of distractions. Forcing ghosts and monsters and Petra and Gaston, Bair, and even Smith from her mind, she opened to God's touch—another new thought, that God could or would touch her life. A yearning clutched her so powerfully she dropped to one knee.

Her hand landed on the grass and vines and stony earth. Staggered by the need, she felt completely alone, empty, hollowed out like a husk. What could ever fill such emptiness?

Her breath caught on a sob. Smith had been hurt by his breakup, but he focused on what mattered and moved on. He didn't crack open and find nothing inside. No wonder they'd all left her. She needed more than anyone could give because she was a gaping black hole.

Pressed to the trunk of the massive shagbark, breath held tight inside his chest . . . enraptured . . . he watched. Though she was close, perilously close, she did not know it was his place she wept upon.

Above them, clouds bunched together like suckling pups vying for a teat. He smelled the coming rain, heard the skittering of creatures taking shelter in the forest floor. Another storm, lightning bolts of pain to sear his eyes. He could not get back without her seeing.

But he wanted her to see. Wanted and dreaded it. Wanted her tearful eyes to rest on him, and if she screamed her fear would have to satisfy him. Hunger twisted, but not his stomach's hunger. Hunger for a glance. One glance from her. He wanted and feared it, aching as her tears soaked the ground before the coming rain.

He would make her look, make her see him. He squinted through the stormy half light into the field where she hunched. He would go to her, soothe and comfort her. He wanted to. Wanted and he would.

But before he could, the other one did. No, no, no. Rage rose up, rage he hadn't felt in so long, rage he couldn't control, rage that could hurt, that could . . .

"Tessa." Smith crouched beside her. He should not have left her alone. He should have told Danae to leave, should have told her he cared about someone else. He should have realized Tessa would take it to the extreme. "Tess, I'm sorry."

"It isn't you." She sat back on her heels. "It's me. I keep trying and trying to find what's missing, but I can't. I don't know where else to look."

Stunned by her distress and its apparent lack of connection

to him, he sat back on his heels. "Tess, you're searching for some mysterious God when what you need is the Father who loves you."

She jerked her face up. "The Father who loves me?"

"God's not a cosmic force. He's a true being who wants you to know and love him, as he knows and loves you."

"You don't understand." Her breath had jagged edges. "Fathers disappear and never come back. Fathers leave their children to the monsters."

He shook his head. "God isn't like that. He vanquishes monsters. And he wants to give you everything you need."

"I needed my daddy, Smith. I wanted my mother to live. I want to sleep without fear, to live without a psychiatrist on speed dial. But none of that is going to happen. If God is a father"—she gripped the vine and yanked—"then he's run off too."

"God is faithful, even when we're not."

"How am I not?" Her eyes flashed.

"I don't mean you. I didn't mean it personally, only that—"

"Never mind, Smith. It doesn't matter. "

"It matters."

She shook her head. Fury rose from her like heat as she jerked and tugged the vine, then staggered back.

Thunder rumbled overhead, but neither looked up from the filigreed metal disk just visible beneath the tangle.

"What's that?" He bent over.

"I don't know." She knelt and shoved away the leafy vines that had covered but not rooted over the disk. "The Chartres labyrinth had a disk in the center that was surrendered in the revolution. Maybe this is a copy." She and Smith ripped back more vines. Approximately three feet in diameter, the disk appeared to be bronze like the gate.

"Something used to be attached." He pointed to brackets in the center.

"A cross, maybe. In your documents the labyrinth's creator mentioned a cross at the center. I thought it might be symbolic, but it could be here." She pulled at the vine once more.

Smith straightened and searched the lowering sky. "We'll have to come back to it."

"I want to look."

Lightning split the sky. "Tess, really." Thunder rumbled. Smith caught her arm. "If it's under there, it'll be there tomorrow—and the next day."

Wind tossed her hair. "What if he takes it?"

"Who?"

"The monster. What if he finds it?"

"He'll likely leave it on the doorstep and save us hauling it."

Lightning flashed again.

"Come on. I don't want to be barbecued where we stand."

She scowled up at the sky as rain rushed upon them like water tipped from a garden pitcher.

Smith held out his hands with a wry look. "Satisfied?"

She lurched up and screamed, "Smith!"

He spun. The creature was no ghost. Lightning flashed on the blade he held, the blade he plunged.

The scream had scarcely left her throat when the monster reared up from Smith and grabbed at her, his gruesome face a twisted mask. Teeth bared. Eyes pale. She stumbled on the uprooted vines and fell back with a cry, prying at the hands that squeezed her throat. *Smith!*

He hadn't moved. As she fought, he lay motionless in the rain with the knife in his chest. Groaning, she heaved the monster off, groped toward Smith, shook him. No response.

The monster seized her wrist. She landed a kick, but he didn't let go. Shoving her free hand into her pocket, she seized the canister. There was no distance between them, and it might not work in the rain, but it was all she had. She twisted the lock and raised it to the monster's face. Holding her breath, she depressed the nozzle.

He screamed and collapsed to the ground, clawing his eyes and choking. She staggered back, coughing and crying as well. Smith lay still as death, eyes closed as rain pooled in the sockets. With a moan, she turned and ran. She could hardly see, hardly breathe. She stumbled and fell, pushed herself up and ran.

Her heart pumped; her lungs burned. Gasping, she fell into the trailer, grabbed her purse, and found her phone. She staggered back out the door, eyes blinking against the burning spray. She pulled open the car door and slid inside, dialing 9-1-1 as she started the ignition. He hadn't followed. But he would. Monsters always did.

He rolled in agony. Nothing had ever hurt so much. Choking, crying, gagging, he dragged himself to the body and pulled out his knife. They would come. They would search. He couldn't let them see what he had done. No, no, no. No one could know.

He pawed the man's chest where the knife had gone in. There should be more blood. His heart should have gushed, yet this wound hardly bled. He couldn't think about that now. He blinked through streaming eyes and dragged himself to the disk.

Gripping the center bracket, he pushed the heavy metal aside.

His throat burned. His nose streamed. His eyes screamed. Crawling back to the body, he got to his feet and dragged. No one could find it. No one could know. He rolled the body into the hole, then followed as lightning seared the sky.

CHAPTER

27

Tessa had poured out the story in detail, told Sheriff Thomas what had happened and watched him grow more and more skeptical. How could he not believe her? How could he think she had killed Smith? Everything had spun out of control.

Had she truly lost her mind? Dr. Brenner believed her delusional. She wished, oh, she wished she were.

But she had seen Smith stabbed, fought off his killer. Unless . . .

Could she have imagined that very first call, conjured up the whole job? How likely was it that her old college crush had found an ancient labyrinth and wanted her to build it? Maybe he'd been "on-site" because she'd imagined him there, given him a companion to round out the scene, a whole cast of characters with whom he interacted in the fabric of her mind.

How real were Rumer Gaston and Petra Sorenson? Katy and Ellie. She swallowed the lump of dread in her throat. The day she'd arrived Smith had appeared out of nowhere in the woods, shown her the trailer. Was it some deserted hulk she had holed up in to live out her delusion? Maybe the nightmares weren't breaking through; maybe her whole reality was a nightmare.

She moved her head in a slow rejection of that thought. This was real, terrible in its reality, but real. Smith had come between her and the monster. Theseus had defeated Minotaur, but Smith had not been prepared to fight. She curled up on the bed, hurting worse than she could bear. Guilt crushed her, and inside the guilt, the monster's words reverberated.

"You won't say a word, will you. Not a word."

But she had.

"I'll find you. Just the way I did tonight."

She had told Smith, and the monster had killed him. No tears could wash away the awful truth. They could not ease the pain. Smith was gone. Dr. Brenner had betrayed her. She had no one, nowhere to turn.

"God wants to give you what you need." Smith's words penetrated, but they weren't true.

"God vanquishes monsters."

No. She shook her head. Smith had trusted God and died. She had tried to tell him fathers could not be trusted. He'd been so sure she was wrong.

Now there was no escape. No help anywhere. She closed her eyes, sick to death of running, of hiding. No matter what she did, the monster would find her. For so long she had struggled to survive. Now she welcomed an end to it.

In her mind, she lay down beside Smith on the soaked and streaming ground. Why had she left him? Why had she run? She wrapped her arms around him as the monster charged, flames blowing from his nostrils, bearing down on her, but before he reached her, he became the creature in the field—pale eyes, pale skin like death, knife flashing.

Her breath came in shallow gasps as the monster changed again—now neither the monster from her dreams nor the creature she'd fought in the field.

His broad man's face came close, protruding eyes beneath dense brows, fleshy, deeply indented upper lip, square bluish jaw. His breath smelled sharp, metallic. Sweat pearled his forehead, sheening his cheeks. He squatted, shining the light into her face.

"I see you."

Her throat cleaved.

"You're not afraid, are you?"

Her head made slow arcs side to side.

"Did you see something you shouldn't have?"

She shook her head, even though she'd seen it all. Sobs climbed her chest.

"You won't say a word, will you? Not a word."

She couldn't if she tried.

"Because I'll find you, just the way I did tonight."

He would. She knew it. The monster would find her.

Her phone rang and she jolted up. "Hello?"

"Tessa. Bair here. Sorry, but I haven't been able to reach Smith, and—"

She collapsed on the bed, sobbing.

"Tessa? What's the matter!"

"He's dead, Bair. The monster killed him."

"What!"

"He attacked us and stabbed Smith, but no one believes me and they can't find him."

His stunned silence silenced her too. Then he rasped, "Who can't they find?"

"Smith. Or the monster. They don't believe me, Bair. You have to help me find him." She started crying harder.

"Calm down, Tessa. Let me . . . how did . . ." His heavy breaths came across the line. "Where are you?"

"The inn. The sheriff won't let me leave the area, even though he doesn't believe me. It's raining and he won't look for Smith and I never should have left him."

"All right. Hold on. I'm coming."

The thought brought a flicker of relief. Bair should be part of this. His friendship with Smith had spanned years, and their falling out was nothing compared to the companionship she'd seen.

When he knocked some time later, she let him in, feeling grateful and relieved and miserable at once.

He stared hard into her face. "You were serious."

She gulped back tears.

His features twisted. "Driving down here, I told myself you'd said it so I'd bring Katy back where she belonged. I thought that if I returned her, I'd find Smith all right."

"I'm sorry."

"I . . ." Bair dropped to the wing chair. "I can't believe it."

"No one else does either."

"I don't mean— I just can't take it in." He clenched his hands on his thighs. The rims of his eyes reddened. "I should've . . . told him I was happy for you."

She sat down and put her arms around his big shoulders. He was real; he was solid, and that made everything else real. She pressed her face to his sleeve. "It hurts so much."

They grieved together, hardly speaking. Finally she said, "We can't leave him out there."

Bair nodded. "They're not even looking? What's wrong with them?"

"They won't take me seriously. My therapist told them I'm having a psychotic break."

"Are you?"

She didn't begrudge his hopeful tone. "I wish I were. But look." She held up her purpled arm, the grip marks clearly visible. She had only started to feel it.

"How did they explain that?" He ran his fingers over the bruise.

"They didn't, just sedated me and said I need help."

He heaved a sigh. "Let's go have a look."

She shook as she rode beside Bair to the scene she'd escaped—was it only last night? If Bair were not there, strong and solid, she might convince herself Smith had never called, never come back into her life, never made something happen between them she hadn't dared hope for. She wasn't sure she could have imagined the last part, but she wanted to believe it so badly.

Grimly, Bair drove up to the gate, plodded over to open it, then drove to the trailer and parked. He got out and stared, unable, it seemed, to take a step into the empty office. She touched his arm, and he unlocked the door and walked the trailer from end to end. "Were you attacked in here?"

"In the meadow. At the center of the labyrinth."

He turned and plodded to the door. She ached at the stoop in his shoulders, the way his freckles spread starkly over his skin. He didn't want this to be true, maybe blamed himself for not being there. "Where exactly?" He stepped out into the lingering drizzle.

"Out past the Bobcat. I'll show you."

Her feet squelched in the wet grass and old leaves as they walked back to the place where Smith had fallen. Were they inviting the monster to strike again? Smith had stood between her and whatever he was, a person—but with so many things wrong that when she had tried to describe him the sheriff thought she was lying.

She pressed closer to Bair, aware for the first time that he must be as tall as Smith, though his broad build disguised it. As they neared the meadow, her breath caught on a sob. Bair squeezed her shoulder. "We'll find him."

But after scouring the field and forest edges and returning to the place they'd started, Bair dropped his hands to his sides. "I don't know where else to look. No way we can cover the woods, just the two of us."

Tessa clutched her soaked sweater, drizzle running down the back of her neck. "We can't give up. This is right where he fell. That's the vine I pulled. That's the disk we found. Smith has to be here."

Bair's face showed more than frustration. It showed doubt and distrust.

"Where else would he be, Bair? If what I'm saying isn't true, where is he? Why won't he answer when I—or you—call?"

Bair looked around. "Maybe he wasn't killed. Maybe he crawled off somewhere."

Her chest constricted. Had she left Smith wounded and dying? "Wouldn't he call for help?"

"He might have lost his phone. It could be anywhere in this vine."

She gripped his arm. "Call it."

Bair speed-dialed Smith.

Tessa tensed. "Did you hear it?"

Bair searched the ground. "I don't know. It was faint if . . ."

"Call again." She couldn't say for sure that she'd heard anything more than her own wishing. The second time neither of them heard anything. She wrapped herself in her arms, aching from lost hope. "What are we going to do?"

"I'm going to see the sheriff." Bair turned back, moving purposefully now.

She hurried beside him back toward the trailer, afraid to hope he would succeed where she had failed. Would anything in Bair's personal history disqualify him? He had issues with alcohol and aggression, but as far as she knew, no psychiatrist calling him crazy. They'd have to listen.

She followed him into the trailer. She had never seen him

so grim, so self-contained. He pulled the air-conditioner out of the window and locked it, then turned. "I want you to stay here, Tessa. Keep the door locked and stay out of sight unless you hear Smith."

She nodded, tears springing to her eyes. Bair couldn't believe him dead. He hadn't seen the knife in his chest, hadn't seen him lying unmoving in the rain.

"I'll bring the sheriff back, but it might take a while to organize a search. You have to be here in case Smith gets this far, especially if he's in bad shape."

She gulped. "Okay." He didn't say it, but they both knew it would be better for Bair to see the sheriff without her.

"If you need a weapon, use whatever you can find to protect yourself—whatever it takes. Do you understand?"

She nodded. "I will."

"You have my number."

"Go, Bair."

He looked at her hard, then grabbed her into a clutch and released her.

She sniffed. "Don't let him say no."

"I won't."

Then he was gone, and she had to face her deep and terrible failure alone. If she hadn't been so messed up, would the sheriff have believed her? Would Smith already be found? She should have been calm, coherent, convincing. But she'd fallen apart. She'd been as worthless to Smith as she'd been to her daddy. *What?* She gripped the chair back.

Images pushed in, though she couldn't tell if they were real or not. It had started in her room at the inn, the man's face, the bulk of him squatting before her, his calm, evil words. *"Did you see something you shouldn't have?"*

Yes! A wail pierced her control. She pressed her hands to her temples, seeing a shadowed violence she did not want clarified. With everything in her, she locked up the vision like a monster in her mind's maze, but it lurked there, on the edge of recall, terrifying and tormenting her.

She sank to the floor, clutching the sweatshirt her dad had worn in the mornings, and unlocked a good memory instead. Daddy stoking the wood-burning stove, catching sight of her over his shoulder. "Come here, kitten. Come get warm." And she'd run to him and piled onto his back like a cub. He'd stood up so tall and trotted around the room, bouncing her until her laughter brought Mom to the doorway, an amused smile on her lips.

And another one of him standing, hands on hips, as Mom led the brown horse that felt like a mountain beneath her, Daddy shaking his head. "Not sure horses are her thing, Vanessa."

"I'd rather ride Daddy's back." She'd slipped off, knowing he'd catch her before she hit the ground.

Those were all she could find, but she soaked the sweatshirt with tears, laughing and crying. It was more than she'd had in so long.

CHAPTER

28

It shouldn't be there, but it was. He pressed his head again to the wrong side of the chest and heard the rhythm of a heart. He'd heard it when he grabbed the body, heard it beating where it wasn't supposed to be. The knife had not stopped it, and now the rage was gone and there was only fear—deep, terrible fear.

What was he going to do? He held his head and rocked. Fear coursed through him. They'd find him and hurt him. Nursey had said so. He remembered the blows. If he was seen, if he was seen again . . .

How could this be happening? Why had they come? They should have left him alone, left his place alone. He looked across at the man who shouldn't be there. Should not be there. This was his place, his place, his place. Why hadn't he finished him?

The stranger stirred, pain pulling his face. His breath came out in a soft moan. Any minute he would wake up and it would be too late. He should finish it now, finish him now. He should; he had to.

He stared at the man he'd stabbed without thinking. He wanted to strike again, but the rage didn't come. The rage didn't come because the man she'd called Smith opened his eyes. He recoiled, but he didn't scream and he didn't look away.

Smith hurt. His hip, his shoulder, his head, most of all his chest where the knife had plunged. Muffled voices hollering had drawn him from his faint. He had heard his phone, or thought he had, though everything seemed surreal.

Someone had clamped a hand over his mouth, pressing his bruised head to a surface as hard as stone. That someone sat across from him now in a state of distress. Smith shifted just enough to ease the pressure in his chest. His wrists and ankles were tied, although he doubted he could put up much resistance regardless. Not seeing Tessa, he prayed she had gotten away.

The man who attacked them held his knees and rocked. "It's not where it should be."

"What's not—" Smith winced.

"Your heart. Your heart! I heard it pumping there. I heard it. It should be here."

He pressed a hand to his own chest. If he felt his heart there, more was wrong than the protruding mandible, sloping shoulders, and obvious scoliosis. His eyes and skin were pale, his hair sparse. Nature had not been kind. And yet he must be strong to have moved someone half again his size.

Smith fought for breath. "Who . . . are you?"

He stopped rocking but didn't answer.

Smith drew a painful breath. His chest felt like sludge. His skin like cold luncheon loaf. Every time he spoke it felt like the knife jabbed him again, but he needed to create a bond. The guy might not be a natural killer, as there'd been opportunity to finish the job and he hadn't. "I'm . . . Smith."

"Donny." The guy pressed his hands to his mouth, too late to catch the word that came out.

Smith nodded and closed his eyes. "Donny." He ached. A weight settled in his limbs. By the tacky feel of his shirt, he'd lost a lot of blood, and he felt weaker than he could ever recall.

Donny lowered himself onto his haunches, smelling very much like the grave. This was the person who had invaded Tessa's room. Had to be.

Smith slumped. Fatigue snuck in beside the pain, weighting his eyelids that descended against all resistance like the slow creep of glacial ice. If he gave in, would he be killed in his sleep—now that Donny had located his heart?

It was quiet, but were they gone, or did they only pretend so they could catch him, trick him, trap him. Like the fox trotting past the nest as though he didn't see, but seeing and circling and coming back when no one expected.

The hollers had stopped when he'd silenced the ringing phone, and he hadn't heard them again. Maybe they were gone. He got up and walked, circling while Smith watched. Around and around the cistern, walking, watching, walking, watching. He stopped sharply. "Stop staring. Why are you staring at me?"

"I want to know . . ." Smith's face screwed up in pain. "What . . . now?"

"I don't know, I don't know, I don't know!" He'd been out of his head. Scared. So scared and angry. Angry, yes, but not to kill. Smith had scared him and he'd stabbed, stabbed before the tall man could catch him and hurt him. Now, what now?

"Let me . . . go."

"No." He shook his head. "Cannot let you go." He wasn't stupid. He knew.

"Help me."

"No, no, no, no, no." He would not be fooled. He knew what had to be done, but couldn't, couldn't do it. "I know what happens when bad things happen."

Smith lowered his head to the floor.

Donny stared at him. They had found his place, and the rage had come, and not just the rage but the fear, the awful, awful fear, and he would have nowhere, and people would stare and scream and hurt *him*, and he'd be shut up, nowhere to run, nowhere to find things, to learn things, no night stars, no rain.

But he looked at the man lying there. Had he meant to hurt him? Maybe. Stop him? Yes. Stop her? He had to. But not hurt her. "Not her." He clenched his hands. "I never meant to hurt her."

"Tessa?" Smith rasped.

Tessa. Tessa. Donny moved the name through his mind. "Tessa. Yes, Tessa. I didn't want to hurt Tessa."

Smith's face twisted. "Did you?"

"No." He pressed his hands to his face. "She hurt me. She sprayed my face."

His eyes still burned. His nose ran. His throat felt like fire. But he understood. Skunks and weasels and other things stung or shot noxious fluids when they were attacked. He circled.

Smith's voice got rough. "Let me . . . go."

"I can't." Donny circled the other direction. "It's done and it can't be undone. No one can know, no one. No one but . . . no one but her." The thought took hold. "Yes. Yes. If anyone is going to know, it's her, Tessa. Tessa can know. Call her. Tell her to come. Tell her to come alone. Only alone."

Smith rasped, "No."

Donny blinked. "Tell her to come, or I'll push you in the well." He saw Smith's fear of going into the water without hands free, without legs free to kick. Donny shuddered. He didn't want to do it, but she had to come. All he wanted was her to come. "Tell her."

Smith winced. "No."

Donny circled the well, pacing the stone cistern that was his place, his hollow, his burrow. His home! Why had they tried to take it? "I want to talk to her. I want to make her see. She will understand. She won't take it. She won't take it away."

"Take . . . what?"

"My place."

Smith laid his head back and closed his eyes. His breath got thick and heavy. Playing possum? Donny crept over and shook him. Smith screamed in pain. His wound bled again. Donny pressed the phone into his hand. "Tell her."

It had been almost two hours since Bair left. Tessa wanted to call, to know where they were, when they were coming, but she couldn't remind them she was part of this. She hoped Bair hadn't mentioned her at all, just told them Smith was missing and shouldn't be. That something must have happened.

Snuggled into her father's sweatshirt, sleeves rolled at the wrists, she paced the office. She had to do something. She was supposed to wait, but she couldn't stand it much longer. She'd seen the knife in Smith's chest, shaken his unresponsive body, but the thought that he could be out there, not dead but dying . . .

She was not waiting any longer. As she looked for a pen to leave Bair a note, her phone rang. Her breath caught as she flipped it open. "Smith!"

He rasped, "Come to the field."

A cry caught in her throat. She wrenched the door open, flew out, and sprinted for the meadow. The sky had broken into sullen patches of gray and washed-out blue. Her feet squelched the wet grass and threw water up the backs of her legs. Her jeans clung to her ankles, but her daddy's sweatshirt kept her warm.

She neared the field and didn't see Smith. If he had collapsed in the longer grasses, she might not see him until she was upon him. "Smith?" The Bobcat stood empty and still undrivable. She scanned the field as she crossed the fresh-cut labyrinth's perimeter. "Smith!"

She shrieked as someone jumped from behind the Bobcat and grabbed her. The smell of him cloyed as his hand clamped her mouth and nose. She fought to free the arm he'd trapped against her side, to claw his hand from her face, to breathe. Her knees buckled, and she tried to use her fall to break his hold.

Her lungs burned, crying for air. She tried to bite, but he'd pressed her face to the ground, his hand like a surgeon's mask, cutting off her air. She felt herself softening, her eyes darkening. The hoarse whisper on Smith's phone must not have been Smith's voice. Her mind grew fuzzy. She couldn't . . . fight. . . .

⌒

She was beautiful and soft, and he didn't want to hurt her. If she'd been a rabbit, he could have snapped her neck, but he didn't want her dead, didn't want her hurt. He wanted her there, wanted her to know, to hear, to see. She would understand, had to understand.

Any minute she would open her eyes. He hadn't held on any longer than necessary to make her stop fighting. He didn't want to tie her, but he'd had to. She was smaller, weaker than Smith, but he couldn't let her fight, couldn't let her run. She had to understand.

But what if she didn't? He'd have to stop them, stop them both, but how could he? They'd seen. They would take it all. They shouldn't be there but they were. He looked at her soft face, reddened where he'd gripped her, closing off her breath, but only until she stopped fighting. Could he stop it for good?

Moaning, he rocked on his haunches, knees beside his ears. He had watched her dream, wanting her to see him, but now she would open her eyes, she would look and she would scream. She would scream and maybe the rage would come and he would hurt her, hurt her before they hurt him. He didn't want to—didn't, but he had to. What else could he do?

CHAPTER

29

Smith? She opened her eyes to his face, all gray hues and haggard hollows. Her chest seized. She couldn't touch him, couldn't feel if his flesh was warm or chilled, because her hands were bound behind her. Inching closer, she heard his labored breathing. *Smith!*

She searched the dim space and located the light source, a camp-style lantern turned very low, barely illuminating a circular pit lined with stacks of . . . books? Borrowed from the private library, and other places, no doubt, books and gadgets were packed and piled like a strange nest.

She didn't see the monster, but she smelled him. The whole place reeked of him—or he of it—damp and musky. She turned and he was there, sitting like a gargoyle, watching her.

She swallowed the lump of fear in her throat and pushed up to sit, inwardly recoiling at his protruding jaw crowded with teeth, his pale eyes staring, but not with malevolence, with dread. He was not a monster. He was a young man, malformed, angry and pathetic, but real. Looking at him, she was less afraid than angry herself. "Who are you? Why are you doing this?"

"Not me. *You* did it." He jammed a finger at Smith. "He did it. And the other one."

"We've done nothing to you."

"You tried to take it."

Smith stirred but didn't wake up. She pressed back against him, just to feel him there, living and breathing. "Take what?"

"My place. You dug it up and it's not yours. It's mine."

Dug it up? The labyrinth. She looked up and saw the underside of the disk. She was beneath the labyrinth. "It isn't ours or yours. The property belongs to someone named Rumer Gaston. We're only building his house and gardens."

"No! You can't. It's mine." His face twisted. "Mine."

She didn't want to pity the beast who'd stabbed Smith and suffocated her. But he seemed terrified. What if he had no one and nowhere else to be? She looked around. Smith had said the meadow sat on a stone shelf. How had they missed this? "What is this?"

"A natural cistern. The well used to fill it with water, but now it doesn't come up by itself."

She turned. "Is that the well?"

"Are you thirsty?" He got up more swiftly than she would have guessed he could, given the curvature of his spine and gangly limbs.

She nodded, more to keep the connection with him than from any real thirst. He went to the hole, drew water, and poured it into a cup. He brought it to her mouth. She sipped. If it were contaminated, then he'd be sick, wouldn't he? "Thank you."

"It's a pure artesian spring. Like the water in bottles."

It startled her that he knew about bottled water.

"How do you know that?"

"I know lots of things. I read lots of books." He raised the cup and drank from it. "Mmm." He moved his tongue over his jumbled and protruding teeth. "My water, my books. My place."

"How did you get here?"

"Nursey brought me."

"When? How long have you been here?"

"Nine years." He acted as though that were no big thing.

Hard to tell his age with the deformities, but he couldn't have been more than a boy. "How old were you?"

"Eleven."

"She took care of you?"

"She brought me things. Food and books. Then she didn't come anymore. I get my own things."

"How?"

"I find them."

Tessa shook her head. "Why are you living here, in a well, in the dark?"

"It's a cistern. I like it dark." He squinted.

"Light hurts your eyes?"

He glowered. "You hurt my eyes."

"You hurt Smith." She raised her chin. "And me."

His breath came rapidly. "Why didn't you scream? When you woke up and saw me, why didn't you scream?" He circled the well. "Why don't you shudder? Why don't you scream when you look at me?" He stopped in front of her.

She met his eyes. "I've lived with monsters. I would know if you were one."

He grabbed himself in his arms and circled. "You shouldn't have come. You don't belong here."

"You have to let us go. Smith needs help." She half turned to look at him lying there. "Listen to how he's breathing. He needs a hospital."

"His heart's on the wrong side."

She frowned. "What do you mean?"

"Feel it. Feel it."

"My hands are tied."

He stopped and stared at her. "If I untie them, you'll hurt me. Spray me."

"I don't have any more pepper spray. Check my pockets if you don't believe me."

"You'll get away."

"I'm not leaving Smith."

He circled again like a lion in a cage, pacing, pacing, as in its mind it ran the savannah plains. "If you try anything, I'll drown you in the well."

"I won't." She had to help Smith, but she didn't want to wound the pathetic person before her. When he'd attacked, she had fought back with everything she had. Now she'd glimpsed his reality. She bent forward so he could reach her hands.

He cut her free with the bloody knife he'd plunged into Smith's chest. "Feel it. Feel his heart."

She put her hand to Smith's chest, her breath catching on a sob as she felt its beat.

"Why did you touch him there?"

She frowned. "That's where the heart is." She stiffened as he squatted before her, his chest heaving with choppy breaths.

"Feel it. Feel mine."

She extended her hand, but he grabbed her wrist and moved it to the other side.

"There. That's where the heart is."

She felt the rapid pump on the right side of his sternum and realization sank in like Donny's blade. "You meant to kill Smith."

He jerked back. "I didn't want to. I . . . I had to stop him. I needed you to understand and he got in the way. He got there before I . . . I didn't want to."

"But you would have. If you hadn't been wrong about hearts." Her sympathy vanished.

He gripped himself, shuddering. "He would have seen. He would have taken it. You won't take it away from me."

"It's not my decision."

Once again fear filled his face, fear and confusion. Once again her anger faded. Did he even know the trouble he was in?

"What's your name?" She held his pale amber eyes, their thick, lashless lids blinking slowly.

"Donny."

"Donny, I have a friend who can help. He works with people who haven't been treated well. He'll help us know what to do."

He shook his head. "They'll put me in a cage. She told me. She told me what happens when bad things happen."

"You mean when people do bad things?" At the least she'd make him own his actions.

"Yes. Yes, but I didn't want to. I wanted you, and he . . . he should not have been there." He gripped his frizzled hair. "No, no, no."

"We won't press charges." In case he didn't know what that meant, she said, "We won't let them put you in a cage. Dr. Brenner can help. He'll take responsibility." She believed that, but truthfully she'd say anything to get Smith medical care. Immediately.

She turned and felt the pulse in Smith's neck. "He needs a hospital, Donny. If he dies, I can't help you."

Donny grabbed himself in his arms, stood up, and circled. "No, no, no, no, no. He can't go. They'll find me. This is my place."

"They're going to take it. Rumer Gaston has already taken it. It's only a matter of time."

His hands clenched. The tendons in his neck stood out like ropes. He circled faster.

"They won't be nice, Donny. Let me call Dr. Brenner. He'll work with the authorities and do everything he can for you." She knew he would. He'd be fascinated by this case. Donny's physical deformities might earn him the protection of advocacy groups. Working together, they might help Donny out of this pit.

"No. You're trying to trick me, trap me, fool me."

"Talk to him yourself. You decide."

He slowed, eyeing her over his shoulder, then came to a halting stop. They studied each other in silence while Smith labored to breathe. Then Donny's shoulders slumped even farther, his spine curling. "Only talk."

She took out her phone, speed-dialed Dr. Brenner, who thought she was having a psychotic break with reality. This should shake his world a little. She got his answering machine. "Dr. Brenner, it's Tessa. I need you to call—"

"Tessa, this is Marianne. Please hold a moment."

He must have instructed his assistant to interrupt if the crazy woman called.

"Hello, Tessa."

"Dr. Brenner, I need your help."

"I'm so glad you've—"

"Not for me, though." She looked across at Donny. "It's for the person I told you about, the one who stabbed Smith."

His silence irritated her so much she didn't wait for his measured response. She explained what had happened and where she was. "Smith needs a hospital. But Donny needs an advocate. I told him you would be that person." She might possibly have shocked him speechless at last. "I'll let him tell you himself."

She stood up and put the phone to Donny's ear, put his hand up to hold it there.

Gripping his patchy pale hair, he said, "You can't trick me." But then he listened. They talked back and forth as Dr. Brenner must have found words at last.

Tears rose in her throat as she dropped down to Smith, touched his clammy face, then reached around and untied his hands and feet. She choked back her sobs as she eased him upright against the wall of books. "Smith."

His eyelids flickered, then opened. He rasped, "Chin up, Tess. I'm alive."

Smith groaned in pain and frustration. Somehow Donny had lured her into the pit. Now they were both caught, except he realized his hands and feet had been untied and she didn't seem frightened, although her concern for him was thick enough to spread on toast.

He looked up and saw Donny on the phone. "Who?"

"Dr. Brenner."

"Your . . . shrink?" He'd have laughed, but his wound hurt like blazes. He wanted nothing more than a bracing dose of pain meds. And to get out of there, to get Tessa out. How could she not be terrified?

"He's coming," Donny half whispered.

"Good." Tessa took her phone back. "He'll know what to do. He's helped me for a long time." She turned. "Now, help me get Smith out of here."

Donny gulped twice. "You won't let them in. You won't let them see."

"No one will see."

Smith couldn't believe it when Donny moved to obey. Tessa had tamed the monster. Admiration flooded him. She wasn't weak at all; she was the most amazing person he knew. Their eyes met, and she clearly saw everything he felt—including the pain when he tried to move.

"Lean on me." She slid her arms around him.

He had no choice. Pain screamed in his chest and fresh blood streamed when they took his arms and moved him to the base of the log-and-branch ladder. Eight rungs. He had to climb them all. Tessa went first and removed the lid, then lay on her stomach on the ground outside, reaching down.

Sweat beaded his forehead, but he would only grow weaker if he waited. He dug deep for the strength and pulled himself up the rungs while Donny pushed from behind. He couldn't help hollering with each of the last three rungs. He rolled onto the ground and almost blacked out. Tessa dragged his legs free as Donny slid the disk back into place, disappearing inside. Tessa tugged the vines over the disk, then knelt beside him in the mud. Thankfully, the rain had stopped.

"Honey, can you walk?" she murmured in his ear as she might encourage a child or wounded pet. He must have looked dreadful to earn that tone. But he'd do anything she wanted. Anything but climb. Or throw the discus.

He struggled to his feet, leaning so hard she might collapse beneath him. It took everything he had not to cry out with every jar, but she kept him going until he gasped, "Need to . . . rest." Without her arm firmly around his waist, he would have sunk to the ground, and he was not sure he'd get up again.

She took the moment and dialed 9-1-1, but before she connected, the wail of sirens reached them. She looked up. "Bair must have gotten through. They're coming."

His relief approached euphoria.

"Smith, you can't say anything about Donny. Not until Dr. Brenner gets here."

"What?" He pressed a hand to his bloody chest.

"They know you were stabbed. Just don't mention Donny or where he is until Dr. Brenner can speak for him."

"Tessa."

"I promised they wouldn't put him in a cage."

"Brilliant."

"How else could I get you out of there? And he's . . . oh, Smith, he's so pathetic."

She'd made a deal with the devil, but he was too knackered to argue. Blessedly, the emergency team met them where they were with a stretcher. Tessa squeezed his hand in reminder as they carried him away. Prone, his chest was too swamped for speech anyway.

Standing with Bair, the sheriff, and a handful of searchers, she couldn't stop the tears as they carried Smith away. He'd lost so much blood and lain on that damp stone all night. If Sheriff Thomas had listened—but Donny would have kept Smith hidden or been discovered himself when searchers crawled over the property. Maybe for Donny's sake this was how it was meant to be. Smith might say God had intended it. She recognized a divine symmetry, Donny's line crossing theirs at the exact point it needed to for them to be tools of his deliverance.

And if God had his hand in that, might he have it over Smith as well? She had given up begging when her mother died, and just yesterday doubted God's very existence, but now, with Smith alive, she dared to reconsider.

Bair turned to her. "What happened, Tessa? When I saw the trailer empty, the door hanging open, I thought the worst."

"I couldn't wait any longer. I went to look again."

The sheriff planted his hands on his hips. "And just happened to find Mr. Chandler wandering around?"

His tone unnerved her. Now that they'd found Smith, did he still not believe her? "He called me to meet him at the field, and I . . ."

"Well, which is it?" The sheriff narrowed his eyes. "He called, or you couldn't wait?"

She'd already changed her story. Why did he rattle her so much? "He called and I ran to find him."

"What time was that?"

"I don't know. I didn't think about it, I just—"

"Show me the phone, please."

She gulped. How would she account for the time they'd been in the pit without revealing Donny's hideaway? She handed over her phone.

"Almost two hours from when he said to meet him before you called for help?"

"I was . . . looking."

The sheriff perused the field. "You searched this field for two hours and he never called out or so much as raised a hand?"

Her stomach dropped. No wonder he doubted her if that was the best she could do.

"Were you expecting his call?"

She shook her head. "Of course not. I thought he'd been killed."

"So it surprised you."

"Yes."

"You thought you'd finished him off?"

"What?" She and Bair said it simultaneously.

"Proved a little hardier than you expected?"

Stunned speechless, she looked from him to Bair.

Bair stuttered. "Don't be ridiculous. She's in love with the man."

She flushed. "I'm not—"

"Making it more likely, not less." Sheriff Thomas crossed his arms over his chest. "Did you have a falling-out? Lovers' spat?" He turned to Bair. "How would you describe their relationship? Rocky? Tempestuous?"

Bair groped for words.

Tessa sucked in her breath. "I did not hurt Smith."

"I understand he got a call from his ex-girlfriend. And you were angry enough to stay out in a thunderstorm."

"How did you—" She turned to Bair.

Bair sputtered. "He asked why I left." He turned to the sheriff. "That doesn't mean she—"

"Did she call again, come visit?"

She shook her head. "I mean, yes, but—"

Back to Bair he said, "Didn't you say this young woman has harbored a grudge for years?"

"Don't . . . twist my words. I . . . I said—"

Sheriff Thomas turned. "Tessa Young, I'm bringing you in for questioning in the attempted murder of Smith Chandler."

She gaped.

Bair drew himself up. "What reasonable cause do you have?"

"Her doctor's diagnosis of a psychotic condition."

Psychotic? He was the one out of touch with reality. But she kept quiet. She could not defend herself without betraying Donny. She had promised he wouldn't be put in a cage. Fine. She could handle a cell. How different would it be from Cedar Grove?

CHAPTER

30

Smith opened his eyes in a metal-barred bed. A plastic oxygen tube was snugged into his nose, feeding him a brisk stream of air. Something had numbed the pain in his chest, but a sack of cement lay across his sternum. He turned and saw Bair crammed into the chair beside him. "What are you doing here?"

Bair raised his eyes. "Where else would I be?"

"Off with Katy."

"Now, don't rub that in."

Smith managed a smile, then touched the bandages on his chest.

"Your surgery went brilliantly. The pneumonia not so much."

So that was the weight on his chest. "Where's Tessa?"

Bair's face reddened. "The sheriff took her in for, um, questioning. He kept her overnight."

"He arrested her?"

Bair looked miserable. "Her story didn't match up, and she'd been so volatile."

Smith dropped his head back, grimacing. "Let me talk to him."

"She said for me to tell you not to break her promise. Whatever that means."

Smith groaned. "She can't be serious."

"Anyway, you'll have to wait until morning. The sheriff's gone home for the night."

But not Tessa, who sat in a cell somewhere because she wouldn't tell what had really happened. Wasn't she the one who wanted monsters locked up?

Bair hunched forward. "Are you going to tell me what happened?"

Smith didn't know where to start without exposing Donny. He hadn't seen, couldn't remember? Both lies, and Bair would see through him anyway.

Bair frowned. "Sheriff Thomas thinks Tessa went bonkers and attacked you, then tried to make out like you'd both been jumped."

Smith scowled. "That's ridiculous."

"Her psychiatrist told him she might be having a psychotic break."

"Why would he say that?" Tessa depended on him overly much, but that was Dr. Brenner's fault and certainly didn't make her unstable. She'd shown remarkable courage and sense.

Bair shrugged. "She was hysterical the night it happened, something about a monster coming out of nowhere. And there's a lot of time unaccounted for today." He clenched his hands. "Did she try to kill you, Smith? Are you protecting her?"

If he were, he'd be rousting everyone out of bed and demanding she be set free. Instead he was protecting the miscreant who'd stabbed him. "She's telling the truth."

"She can't be. Not the whole truth."

No, but that was the promise she'd made, and he'd agreed, tacitly if not audibly.

Bair loomed over him. "You know who did this. And you're not saying."

"Not tonight."

Bair threw out his hands. "I drive down here, thinking you're dead, spend hours searching for your body in the soaking rain, hours getting grilled by the sheriff, and you won't say where you were and what happened?"

Smith sagged into the pillows. "Just don't go back to the trailer."

Bair stared. "He's out there, is he? The one we never reported?"

"It's complicated."

Bair scowled. "He's out there free and you're lying here with a hole in your chest."

"Tomorrow, Bair." Smith cracked his eyelids open. "Where's Katy?"

"Back where she belongs. And don't worry, nothing happened."

A smile pulled Smith's mouth as he surrendered to the drowsiness. He'd almost been killed and Tessa was in jail, but the strongest thing he felt was gratitude and a sense that things were in better hands than his.

Tessa lay on the steel bed with a blanket in the holding cell, replaying the twists that had put her there. Yesterday she'd been upset that Danae had come to see Smith. She'd been distraught that God had let her down like everyone else. Somehow finding the cross had seemed terribly important, but then Donny had attacked, and . . .

She couldn't think of him that way, springing up behind Smith, teeth bared, knife flashing. Even in that moment she saw his fear, but that didn't change the fact that he had plunged a knife into Smith's chest. If Donny's anatomy had not been wrong, Smith might be dead. How could she feel compassion?

She'd spent formative time with misfits and people like herself whose issues overwhelmed their capacity to cope. She'd seen the difference between patients with true pathologies, and those who'd been broken by life. She didn't know Donny, but she had responded empathetically to his plight. Having seen her emptiness, she could ache for his. Maybe God had not been silent after all. Maybe he'd heard and answered in a way she could not have imagined.

"God is not a cosmic force. He's a true being who wants you to know and love him, as he knows and loves you."

When she'd heard Smith pray, it had sounded like a communication of true connection, not something she'd allowed herself when so many pleas had gone unanswered. He was right that she'd kept God in the labyrinths, a mystery, a divine source of wisdom like Superman's kryptonite-crystal-encased ancestors. It was always her decision to enter—and hers to walk away. She had thought she opened herself, and maybe she had, but on her terms, seeking knowledge, growth—not relationship.

Smith's words had startled and disturbed her. *"You're searching for some cosmic force of a God when what you need is the Father who loves you."*

She shifted on the hard bed. It still disturbed her. If she allowed a relational God, a Father, how could she know she wouldn't lose him too?

"God is faithful, even when we're not."

Why had that bothered her so much? Smith had said he didn't mean her specifically, but as he'd said it, she had felt a stab of faithlessness, something she couldn't identify. Had she failed God—or someone else, someone Smith's words illuminated? Her daddy?

Panic seized without warning. Tears choked her. How could she have failed him when she hardly remembered him? Her mother had told her time and again that she was not to blame for his leaving, yet the feeling persisted stronger than before. If she had failed her own daddy, how could she stand before a Father God?

Tears burned her eyes. Maybe she couldn't. Maybe she wasn't expected to.

"God wants to give you what you need."

Smith had said she needed more than any man could give. But God? Could God fill the emptiness, the wretchedness she'd seen inside herself? The aching hunger, the crushing guilt. The abandonment. Was that the real monster she feared?

"God vanquishes monsters."

She had no path to walk, no meditational prayer, no thoughts or feelings to examine. She lay in the darkness, afraid to sleep, afraid to surrender. When she thought Smith had died, she had almost surrendered to despair. Could she submit to hope?

Smith rode a slow spiral to wakefulness. He felt worse than the last time he'd opened his eyes and wouldn't have opened them now but for the persistent voice calling his name. He woke to a man in a gray dress shirt and pale yellow tie, a tidy mustache and goatee, intense brown eyes that seemed to know him, even though they'd never met.

"I'm sorry to wake you, Smith, but some idiot has locked Tessa in a cell."

Smith blinked in the morning light coming through the slatted window blind.

"Dr. Brenner." The man extended his hand.

Smith didn't take it. "You told that idiot she was psychotic."

"Given her hysteria, I thought it possible."

"Who were you to make that call without even seeing her?"

"She's been in my care a long time. With her history . . ." He spread his hands. "Anyway, she refuses to clear herself until you tell me where to find our friend."

Smith dragged air into his lungs, scrutinizing the person Tessa put so much faith in. "Seven point eight miles past the Brockhurst Inn, you'll come to a gate. I don't know if it's locked, but there's a key in my jeans pocket." He motioned to the closet and the doctor found the keys.

"You'll have to walk from the office trailer to the meadow just visible through the woods." Again it took moments to catch his breath. "Past the Bobcat you'll see a mess of vines. Beneath that, a bronze disk. The disk covers a cistern and he's inside."

"All right."

"He's dangerous."

"Yes, I gathered that." Dr. Brenner clasped his hands before him. "Tessa said he has your phone, so I can let him know I'm there before I open the hatch."

She had thought it through. Smith swallowed. If Tessa had called the doctor in to help, she must still trust him. "She promised they wouldn't lock him up."

"I'll do my best to keep that promise." He headed out the door.

Smith lay back. He hadn't overestimated the man's hubris, and it irked him the way he'd dismissed Tessa's truthfulness beneath her issues. More irritating still was the sense of possessiveness he'd given the word *care*.

The phone rang in his hand, but if he answered it, everything would change. Donny gripped his head. He hadn't slept; he hadn't eaten. He hadn't read one book. He was losing it, losing it all, and he didn't know how he'd let that happen.

But the phone rang and vibrated in his hand, and he pushed the button that said Talk and listened. "Donny, this is Dr. Brenner. I'm outside and I'd like to come in. Or you come out if you prefer."

He didn't want anyone else in his place. It was his no matter what they said. His chest tightened as he looked at the space he'd filled with things that mattered and pleased him, things he'd collected. His throat ached when his glance landed on one thing, the thing he prized most of all. He bent and picked up Tessa's drawings, slipped them into his shirt, then told the doctor he was coming out.

What choice did he have? It was over. He was found. They might hurt him, but he had to go out. Tessa said he'd already lost his place. Only a matter of time. She had not stopped it. As though he carried a sack of books, he climbed the ladder and pushed aside the disk.

Bright. It was too bright. Even the crack around the disk. The sun would hurt his eyes, hurt his skin. He wanted to crawl back down, but then the light dimmed with a yellowish hue.

"I'm holding a hooded poncho over you," Tessa's friend said. "And I have dark glasses for your eyes."

His heart swelled. She had thought of that! Thought and made it better. He crawled out of the cistern beneath the poncho and the man there slipped it over him. Then he pulled on the dark glasses and looked out. It was bearable, but he still shrank from looking at Dr. Brenner. At last, however, he had to.

The man held out his hand. "I'm Dr. Brenner."

Donny looked at the hand, then put his out too.

Dr. Brenner clasped it. "We have our work cut out for us, but I think I can be of help to you."

CHAPTER

31

Waiting in the daylight was worse than the preceding night. Trapped in there alone, she felt more keenly Donny's plight. Tessa wrung her hands, longing to hear that Dr. Brenner had taken charge of Donny and confirmed her story with the authorities. She wanted to get to the hospital, to know how Smith was, to see for herself that he'd made it through surgery as she'd been told.

When finally someone unlocked the cell door, she sprang up. She had not been officially arrested, only held, so it took little for her to be released. Sheriff Thomas was not there to offer his apologies—like that would ever happen—but she didn't care. The deputy told her that Dr. Brenner and Donny had gone. Since Cedar Grove was a lockdown facility, he must have received custody, at least for now, and they were on their way to safety.

She had spoken briefly with Dr. Brenner and directed him to Smith so that Donny's location would not be overheard by anyone at the jail. She was not trying to circumvent justice, only give Donny a chance to be heard where he had a chance of being understood.

Dr. Brenner would assess Donny's mental, emotional, and physical health and make a determination as to his immediate care.

He would not live like a rat in a drain anymore. There might be little help for his appearance, but he would receive what medical attention he might need, and he would not be punished for his fear of being seen. She didn't know who had screamed and hurt him, but those emotional scars had certainly contributed to his attacking them.

She stepped into the sunshine and breathed the fresh air. Freedom truly carried a scent unlike any other. The ground was drying, the sun absorbing the excess. It no longer mattered what evidence had washed away. Smith was found, Donny rescued, and no one thought her a killer or a lunatic.

With no other transportation from the station, she walked to the hospital. Smith rolled his head to the side when she entered, looking far from hale but a good deal better than the last time she'd seen him. "You're all right!"

"More or less."

She rushed in and gripped his hand. "Does it hurt?"

"Not if I stay in front of it."

"Oh, Smith, I'm so sorry."

"For what?"

"Staying out there in the rain. Not warning you soon enough. Running away when I thought you were dead." Her elation fled as she recalled the rain pooling in his eyes.

"You came back."

She squeezed his hand harder. "I wouldn't have gone if I'd known. I was just so scared."

"I don't believe you."

"What?"

"Nothing scares you."

"How can you say that?"

He fumbled with the sidebar, then seemingly exhausted, he frowned. "Put it down, will you?"

She maneuvered the bar to its below-the-mattress position. "Come sit."

She climbed onto the bed, concerned. "Bair told me you were doing better."

"Bair told me you were in jail."

"The sheriff thought I tried to kill you."

"That comes from not telling the truth."

"He wouldn't listen when I did tell the truth. And then he thought I got mad about Danae and stabbed you."

Smith frowned. "Were you upset Danae came?"

Did he really wonder? "Not enough to kill you."

Smith took her hand between his. "Tess . . . I don't want to deceive you."

Her defenses went on high alert, her heart pounding as she prepared herself to hear *Sorry, but we're getting back together.* That expectation had led to her cracking open and seeing herself as she was. Smith had seen it long before that. He must have been so frustrated, coming out to the field to tell her his decision and finding her in an emotional-spiritual crisis. No wonder he'd wanted to go inside where she wouldn't run off in another storm. What a case he must think her.

"Danae kissed me, Tess. I should have stopped her, but I didn't."

Her thoughts stalled, then caught back up. "Didn't . . . want to?"

"I think I wanted her to *want* to kiss me. I should have stepped back, but my bruised ego took it as . . . as affirmation."

She searched his face, unsure where this was going.

"Don't ask me why I needed any sort of affirmation from her; I can't tell you."

Now she was confused. "Because you love her?"

He sank back. "It's not like that." He didn't say what it was like, or that he didn't love her. His throat worked. "Please believe it has nothing to do with you."

That she could easily believe. What was unbelievable was that he'd expressed feelings for her in the first place. "I understand."

"I'm fairly certain you don't." He closed his eyes and gathered himself. "I know I'm risking my chance with you, but I didn't want this between us."

"The kiss, or your feelings for Danae?"

"I don't have feelings for her." He drew a boggy breath. "I have . . . residue."

She understood residue. Hers had become sediment.

"It's not as much about her as it is about me."

"I get it. Bair said you weren't ready. I know how hard it is to let go, believe me. I've had—"

"Tess. Don't jump to conclusions." He closed his eyes, clearly worn out by their exchange. "I don't want this to change what we have."

"What do we have?"

He opened his eyes with an effort. "A chance to try again."

Tears stung. Maybe he meant that, but could she risk it? He had wounded her before, with less between them than now. Bair's warning might be the truest thing she'd heard. "You need to sleep."

"Will you be here when I wake?"

She swallowed the lump invading her throat. "I don't know."

Pain washed over his features as she turned and went out, but it could have been the medication wearing off. There was no medication for hers. She met Bair in the hall, toting a clear package of scones and a thermos that probably contained tea.

He startled. "You're out."

Had he thought she'd be locked up for good?

"On bail or . . ."

"They didn't arrest me."

Bair looked from her to Smith's door.

"He's asleep," she said.

"Oh. Would you, um, like one?"

In spite of the hurt descending like fog, she was hungry. "Yes. Thanks."

"Want to step outside?"

"Sure." She needed to get out, away from the turmoil, away from Smith.

They perched on a bench in the sunshine. Bair handed her a scone, then the thermos cup filled with tea.

"Thanks."

He readjusted his position. "I, um, hope you don't blame me too much."

"I don't blame you at all. Sheriff Thomas wanted a scapegoat. I fit the model."

"I should've . . . kept quiet about . . . you and Smith."

"Really, Bair. It didn't make much difference. He'd made up his mind when I first went to him. In his opinion I had more motive than some malformed stranger who might not even exist."

"So . . . you're all right?"

She shrugged. "Sure."

"He didn't hurt you."

"Smith?"

Bair's eyes took on a knowing look. "I meant the one who stabbed Smith."

"Oh. Some bruises and sore muscles. He didn't want to hurt me. I believe that."

"What happened out there, Tessa?"

She swallowed a bite of scone and washed it down with a sip of tea. "There's a cistern under the labyrinth. We found the disk that covers its mouth. He'd been living there since he was only a boy."

"He?"

"Donny."

"The bloke who stabbed Smith."

She nodded. "But it was self-defense. He's . . . It's hard to describe how awful he looks. He thought if people saw him they'd hurt him. It's happened before."

"So now you're free, and he's in custody?"

"He's with Dr. Brenner. For evaluation. I don't think he'll find him dangerous."

"In spite of the fact he tried to kill Smith."

Frowning, she brushed a crumb from her leg. "He didn't intend to kill Smith. He struck in fear. I understand that."

"Does Smith?"

"I think so."

"I'm not sure that makes it right."

She turned. "It isn't right, Bair. Lots of things aren't. What matters is how we move forward." Donny was not the monster. As much as she dreaded it, she still had to find out who was.

"And you and Smith?"

She lowered her gaze. "You were right. He isn't over Danae."

Bair flushed. "Would you . . . consider someone else?"

"I'm sorry, Bair." Tears glazed her eyes. "I'm not over him."

With the hood of the poncho pulled low over his face, Donny hunched in the seat beside the airplane window and stared out, fascinated by the world far beneath him and reluctant to view the world close around him. Dr. Brenner had the next seat, and they were joined at the wrist by handcuffs. He had agreed because the sheriff would not let them leave without them, and Dr. Brenner said it was necessary. He had no choice, no choice, and if he thought about it, fear came up inside him like the well before it stopped rising.

"Would you like a drink, Donny? Juice or soda?" Dr. Brenner talked in a soft, slow voice, the kind of voice you'd use to make a rabbit come closer, closer until you snatched and broke its neck. Donny stayed still and stared out the window. It was all white now, clouds, clouds, clouds. Only clouds, and it made him dizzy not to see the ground, even though it was so far away.

"Would you like to read?"

Donny perked up. "Read what?"

"There are magazines in the pouch beside your chair, or I have a journal about some behavioral studies being conducted on dolphins. Those are—"

"I know what they are. I know all about dolphins."

"I'm interested in what you know."

Donny didn't turn. "Dolphins sleep with half their brain at a time. They hunt and navigate with echolocation and communicate with very high-pitched squeals and whistles and whines. They form bonds that last their whole lives and carry their sick or dying pod members. But some strong dolphins bully weaker ones."

"Why do you think that is?"

Donny stared into the white, endless white, outside his window. "I'll have the journal now." When he didn't turn from the window, Dr. Brenner slipped the book into his lap. Donny covered it with his free hand and propped it between himself and the window. Reading calmed him enough that he stopped thinking about his place, his place and Tessa and his things, for whole pieces of time.

Smith sighed. He shouldn't have told her. He was trying so hard to build their relationship with honesty and integrity that he didn't know when to keep quiet about things that would hurt. How had he thought she would understand when he didn't?

He regretted that kiss and wanted Tessa to know, yet he couldn't put the blame on Danae. He had tried to describe his confusion, his reluctance to make the same mistakes. That had been his intention, but he knew what she'd heard. Rejection.

He'd wanted her to know he didn't take it lightly that Danae still had a hold on him. He cared enough to tell the truth, trusting her to bear with him. Who was he fooling? Even an optimistic woman would have trouble with that.

Tessa had proven herself courageous and resourceful, strong and capable in a terrifying situation. But this was a matter of the heart, and she guarded hers ferociously. What small impact he'd made was surely compromised.

He sank into the weariness with a weight that had less to do with his injury than hers. Why had he thought honesty the best policy? They'd been through an ordeal, and he could have used it to sweep Danae's kiss clean away. Instead he had followed the nudge of his conscience with Tess after he'd ignored it altogether with Danae. Wasn't that the difference between who he'd been before and the man he was trying to be now? Making Tessa see that was something else altogether.

Sleep overcame him until he heard hushed voices.

"Sheriff Thomas kept making everything I said sound like . . . something else."

"It's all right, Bair."

"Except you spent a night in jail."

"It wasn't that bad."

Smith should let them know he was awake, but he couldn't open his eyes. Would every waking be worse than the last?

"Having shared the experience, I'd have to disagree."

Bair didn't reveal that to very many.

"You were in jail?"

"Assault and battery. Not proud of it. Not proud of a lot of things."

Then why the confessional?

"Like the matter of my son."

"Your . . . Really, Bair? You have a son?"

"Three years old next month."

Was he trying to win her sympathy? Maybe not purposely. Something about Tessa invited full disclosure whether you intended it or not. Still, Bair was normally reticent when sober.

"Do you get to see him?"

"I suppose I could, since I send support. But I didn't know his mum. It was one of those . . . bad decisions that seemed brilliant to me and Johnnie Walker."

Tessa made a sympathetic sound. "I was afraid you'd start drinking again so you could talk to Katy."

"No, she pretty much did the talking. Everything she expected, only she phrased it prettier. 'Wouldn't you love to do this; why don't we have that.' " Bair's voice leapt to a falsetto and Tessa laughed. Tessa laughing was a good thing. But laughing with Bair?

"Tell the truth. Aren't you glad she's home?"

"I suppose it's best."

"I don't think she appreciated you."

"Now, when you say things like that . . ."

Smith opened his eyes and coughed hard and violently. The pain was like being stabbed again, with a knife to both lungs. Tessa and Bair jumped to his side. He hated being ill and injured and not knowing where he stood. It hurt more than his pride to see them side by side, yet he'd done it to himself. Gripping the bedrails, he left off coughing and wheezed.

"Do you need the nurse?" Bair reached for the call button.

Smith rocked his head side to side on the pillow. It took too much energy to lift it—a fact that annoyed him to no end.

"Smith?" Tessa's eyes held true concern. "Are you in pain?"

"Only when I cough." Or breathe. Or think. He wanted to touch her but didn't.

Bair cocked his head. "You look knackered."

He was. Completely worn out, though he'd done little besides sleep.

Tessa touched the side of his face with the back of her fingers. "You're burning up."

He pressed his head against her hand, wanting her to keep it there.

"Call the nurse, Bair."

He hadn't thought of Tessa as nurturing, only needing. How many other things had he missed that he might now have no opportunity to learn? She hadn't deserted him yet, wouldn't bail on the project, but he might be the one watching her bond with Bair. Not the best thought he'd had in a while.

When no nurse came immediately, Bair said, "I'll go find someone."

As the door closed, Smith drew a labored breath. "Tess."

"Don't." She shook her head. "You shouldn't strain."

Was it that, or did she not want to hear what he might say?

"I need to—"

The nurse preceded Bair into the room. Tessa moved aside as the efficient blonde inserted the thermometer into his ear, drew it out at the beep, and disposed of the black, conical tip.

"Spiking, are we?" She smiled at Smith, then turned to Tessa. "Can you keep some cool cloths on his head while I page the physician?"

"Sure." Tessa went to the bathroom and wet a washcloth. Smith jolted when it touched his skin, half expecting it to sizzle. She settled him with a gentle hand to his chest. "Lie still. You need to stay calm."

He looked into her face, wanting to take back everything he'd said. How had he thought he wasn't ready to love her?

"So, I've some things to work on," Bair told Smith. "I'll leave you in good hands."

"Thanks, Bair. Can you catch up on my mail, as well?"

"Sure thing." He went out.

Smith refocused on Tessa. "I want to tell—"

"I'm leaving if you keep forcing it. Whatever you have to say can wait. I have something to tell you too."

He groaned. "What?"

She shook her head. "Not now."

He gripped her hand. "Tell me."

She slid her hand free and flipped the cloth on his forehead. It was almost imperceptibly cooler on the new side, but he didn't want her to go even as far as the bathroom to refresh it. "Tell me, Tess."

"I need to go home."

"What?" His fears materialized.

"I'm starting to remember something."

"I promised to be there." How had things gotten so far from that night in Laughlin? He dragged air into his boggy lungs. "It's just too soon."

"Smith—"

"I'll take you, but I need some time."

"I'm not asking you to. You've been stabbed. You have pneumonia. You're not going anywhere."

"Give me a day to get out of here." His vision blurred.

"Gaston wants you on-site."

"Gaston can get stuffed." He didn't care about the job or the owner. All he knew was that Tessa should not face this thing alone. "Please."

"Things aren't the same, Smith. You said that before Danae—before you got the chance—"

"That's not the chance I want."

"I'm not sure you know what you want."

"I know I don't want you to go back alone."

"It's not your problem."

"Tess." He pressed a hand to his face.

She sighed. "We'll talk about it tomorrow."

As the nurse came in to remediate his fever, Tessa slipped out behind her. What were the odds she'd be back?

CHAPTER

32

Tessa stared out the window while Bair drove her back to the inn. He had also taken a room there, reluctant to return to the trailer, even though Donny was gone. Maybe he wanted to be closer to Smith. Or to her. She would have to be careful not to encourage his feelings.

Bair held the door open. As they stepped inside, Nan clasped her soft white chins between her soft white hands. "Is it true? You caught the ghost?"

Tessa tensed. "I don't think you can catch ghosts."

"Insufficient matter," Bair said, and she wanted to hug him.

"Oh, I know that." Nan waved a hand. "I mean the creature people thought was a ghost. Was he arrested? Is he in jail?"

Time to set the rumor record straight. "He was taken to a secure care facility for psychological assessment."

"What's wrong with him? Heard tell he's all, you know, deformed."

"He has some physical issues." It had taken a great effort not to show her revulsion at first sight, but it had diminished when she recognized his suffering. "I really don't know anything else."

With Bair flanking her, Tessa mounted the stairs. At the station, she'd overheard talk about other complaints against someone matching Donny's description. The stories must be flying if it had reached Nan already.

Bair stopped at her doorway. "I'm going to pick up some dinner. Would you, um, would you like me to bring you something?"

"I don't know, Bair. I'm not really hungry."

"You've been shaken up."

"Mostly I just need to think." Or, more accurately, keep herself from thinking, remembering. Donny's attack had caused ripples in her mind that lapped at dark shores. Smith's interlude with Danae had cast her adrift toward those shores. He thought he could still help her, but a champion's heart could not be divided.

"I'll drop something by and leave you to your thinking."

"Thanks."

A while later, Bair knocked on her door, bearing a fish sandwich and coleslaw. He dropped the napkins and bumped her head when they both went down to pick them up, sputtering an apology while she assured him she was fine—although she wasn't. Already the night pressed in, and she did not trust her subconscious to hold its secret.

The nightmare in the cell the night before and the memories that kept forcing her to the point of recall conspired to keep her eyes open until the sun rose on another clear day. She took a path to the bank of the river just beyond the cultivated gardens. It had no rhythmic pattern, no ordered steps, no intrinsic mystery. She did not practice any of the exercises she often used to unclutter her mind and open her soul on a labyrinthine prayer walk. Instead, as she stood on the river's shore, she attempted Smith's style of communication with a personal God. "Father . . ." It took moments to get past that word alone. "I can't do this myself."

She'd intended to say more, but the whole idea of God as father overwhelmed her. She was unprepared to probe that relationship, emotionally or spiritually. Dr. Brenner would tell her to explore that feeling. What makes you uncomfortable? And she'd tell him guilt, an overwhelming, crushing sense of guilt.

She drove herself to the hospital and entered as the doctor attended Smith. She waited until he'd finished listening to Smith breathe, checking and rebandaging the incision, expressing optimism and caution—coughing stressed the wound, but was required to clear the lungs and so on. She took the doctor's place when he left. Smith cast her a look that tugged the ropes of her heart into a knot.

Smith reached for her hand. "I'm glad you're here. I wasn't sure you would be."

"I'm not sure I can stay."

"I'd like you to." His eyes said more than his words.

Shying from what she saw there, she said, "The doctor sounded encouraging. Your fever's down."

"I don't want to talk about me. I want to know about your memory."

She could at least tell him that. "It started at the inn after the sheriff ordered me not to leave and Dr. Brenner thought I'd gone over to the dark side. When I thought you were dead." Her throat constricted. "I kept seeing you lying in the rain, and I just couldn't take it anymore. In my mind I lay down beside you, and the monster charged." She knew it sounded bizarre. "First it was like the minotaur. Then it was Donny. Then I saw the man in my dream who said I couldn't tell."

Smith searched her face. "And what doesn't he want you to tell?"

"What I saw." She looked away.

"What was it, Tess?"

Tears pooled in her eyes. "I think something happened to my dad."

Smith tightened his grip. "What happened?"

She couldn't answer.

"How old were you when he disappeared?"

"Not quite six."

"That's pretty young to remember anything with certainty."

"I know. But I have to try."

Smith drew a swampy breath. "Whatever you need to do—" he wheezed—"I want to be with you."

"I can't wait, Smith."

"One more day. Please."

She looked away. "I think some distance would be good."

"It won't. I need to be there for you."

"I have no idea how you mean that."

"In every way you can think of, I mean it."

"You're hankering for veggies?"

His laugh started a cough that lasted agonizingly long. He laid his head back and fought for breath, then rasped, "You're what I want and what I need."

"We'll talk about that when I don't wince every time you say something."

"Promise you'll wait."

"Smith—"

"Promise or I'll sic Bair on you."

"Bair's on my side."

He dropped his head back, eyes closed. "I dreamed about you. I never dream."

"Everybody dreams. It's how the mind processes the junk of real life."

"I never dreamed about Danae."

"She's a custard, too smooth and creamy to cause psychological indigestion."

He pulled a wry smile. "I love your amazingly odd remarks."

"You introduced the food metaphors."

He turned his head to look at her. "I'm asking . . . with every-thing in me . . . for you to wait."

If that wasn't sincere, she would never know it when she saw it. He had been honest in sharing his struggle to let go of Danae. She appreciated that he didn't love lightly, but she'd never felt so vulnerable. She nodded. "Okay."

Relief softened the fatigue etched into his face. "Would you do one more thing?"

"What?"

"Show me how we were in your mind."

She had a moment of confusion, then realized what he was asking, that she put herself physically beside him as she'd been in that moment of despair.

He caught her hand. "I want to hold you."

Warmth jellied her legs and made her chest quake. No one had ever said that to her without serious ulterior motives. She could not for the life of her guess Smith's. "It's not exactly private."

"That's a good thing." He pulled a sideways smile.

She swallowed the churning emotions. Would she have hesi-tated if he hadn't told her about Danae? If she appreciated his honesty, she shouldn't hold it against him. But it wasn't resent-ment that held her back. She didn't want to close her eyes and see *him* again.

"The last time I climbed into a hospital bed my mother died."

"I'm not dying."

But he could have. She freed her hand and put the bedrail down, climbed in next to him, and laid her head against his chest, hearing the rattle of his slow exhalation. His arm came around her. Hope and hurt pressed in. She drew a breath almost as ragged as his and realized she was not willing to let him go.

With Tessa nestled against him, Smith prayed. He had made a hash of things, but he knew what God expected of him. It had nothing to do with their relationship or their future, or his desires or hers. She had said her mandate was the labyrinth, and maybe all that had happened was part of that, but his was to shield and protect her from a wholly different monster.

Not Gaston, not Donny, not a figment of her imagination or nightmares, but a real person and quite possibly a real event no child should have witnessed. She had been young enough that maybe she had misinterpreted what she saw and her father was alive somewhere. But the degree of trauma that had persisted suggested otherwise.

He stroked her arm lying along his chest. At first she had felt stiff and awkward beside him. Within moments she had relaxed, and now he sensed her slipping into sleep. The ordeal had been physically taxing on them both, but was also an emotional and perhaps spiritual battle for Tessa. One night in jail and another in fearful recollection. Had she even slept? Her deepening breaths suggested not.

Holding her broke through restraints he'd established after allowing Danae to drive the pace and direction of their relationship, a flimsy defense for his choices. He did not lay the blame on Danae. He had willingly followed her lead and, in consequence, left behind some element of himself that could not be recovered. He regretted that.

Like the prodigal, he had repented and returned, and the Father had received him with open arms. Now it remained for him to walk once again with integrity. The love he felt, holding Tessa, seemed a purer, less self-serving love. He wanted to protect and honor her, yet there was no denying his desire for her. Somehow he had to keep a balance.

He put a finger to his lips some time later when Bair came in, though Tessa slept so soundly he doubted a fire alarm could wake her. He had dozed a little, but mostly basked, premature as that may be. "I don't think she's slept much," he whispered.

Bair agreed, then told him, "Gaston's been calling. The office line forwarded to me and I told him what happened. He offered his condolences for your injury and wanted an update."

Smith rolled his eyes.

"I told him you weren't able to talk."

"Good."

"But he's insistent. He wants to be kept in the loop."

"There are some things he doesn't need to know." Smith shifted and winced. "One is that Tessa needs to go home. I think she witnessed something as a child and it's surfacing now." A coughing jag caught him, but he quelled it. "I'm going with her."

"Sure you are."

"As soon as I'm out."

"Not holding your breath, are you?"

"Funny." He wheezed.

"While you're gone, should I put the project out for bid?"

Smith considered that. "Until the business with Donny is ironed out, I'm not sure we can begin construction. Tell Gaston we're clearing some obstacles before proceeding."

He would revise the schedule when they were through this. Surprising how the project that had seemed so vital had lost significance. He hoped he'd be able to rekindle the earlier enthusiasm, though a little matter of life and death had put it in perspective.

Bair tipped his head. "How are you?"

"Up and down."

"Tessa?"

"Fragile. Yet strangely resilient."

"Not as resilient as you might think."

"I know, Bair. Believe me."

Moments after Bair left, Tessa opened her eyes. Her disorientation was adorable. "It's all right," he said, but she pushed up to sit.

"I cannot believe I fell asleep."

"That's what happens when you haven't had any rest."

"How long was I out?"

"A while."

She rubbed her eyes, then let her hands fall to her lap. "At least no one saw me."

"That's not . . . exactly true."

She turned, dismayed. "Who?"

"Only a nurse or two, and Bair."

She groaned. "Why didn't you wake me?"

"And spoil the first good sleep you've had in how long?" He took her hand. "If it's any consolation, the last five hours did more for my healing than anything since you pulled me out of that hole."

She slanted him a look. "Tell me you didn't say five hours."

"I slept for half of them."

She expelled a long, slow breath. "I outslept the patient?"

"I had somewhat of a head start, a few days' worth."

She slipped off the bed. "I should have known better than to lie down. Although the last thing I thought I could do was sleep."

"I told you I'd take care of you." The look she gave him pierced his heart. Was that so hard for her to believe?

Two long days later, Tessa met Bair outside Smith's door. "How is he?"

"Impatient. He's never been hurt before. No broken bones,

no teeth knocked loose. He thought he'd be walking out long before this."

"Have they said when?" She tried not to sound as anxious as she felt, but the wait was draining her.

"Probably tomorrow. The important thing is for him to realize he's not a hundred percent. But Smith, you know, he always thinks he's a hundred and ten."

She did know. She touched Bair's arm in passing and went inside. Smith's color had improved; his breathing seemed less strained, but his hair stood out around the cowlick and he looked irritable.

She smiled. "Hi."

He reached for her hand. "Tell me you've brought my release papers."

"I wish I could."

"I know you're tired of waiting, but there's a conspiracy to keep me bedridden." He dropped his head back, exasperated.

"You're not helping by stressing everyone out."

"Stressing them? I'm the one being told to breathe into this, cough into that. Rest and relax while we poke and bleed you."

"Hmm." She untangled his call button. "I would have guessed you a stoic patient."

"I don't know what more they want from me. I walk, I talk, I eliminate." He winced as he shifted position. "Besides, I thought you wanted to go."

"I need to."

He reached over and took her hand. "Come here."

She moved closer.

"All the way."

She shook her head. She had not climbed into the bed since that first time. Lying next to Smith had all but eliminated her

320 \ KRISTEN HEITZMANN

defenses against the feelings she had for him, and the shell that
was left could crumble without warning.

His tone softened. "Are you all right?"

She shrugged. "I need to deal with it." She had kept the nightmares at bay by hardly sleeping more than an hour or two at night.
She could not go on indefinitely.

He said, "I'd leave now if they'd let me out."

"Then stop spiking a fever so they do." And so she wouldn't
keep worrying that maybe they'd missed something, maybe this
wasn't over, maybe a million other things could go wrong.

"I can't stand doing nothing." Smith rubbed his eyes under the
spare pair of rimless glasses Bair had brought in.

She hadn't noticed his other pair missing until she saw him
straining to read the pocket New Testament Bair had brought
him early on. He must have lost his glasses in the attack, because
the rain had pooled in his eye sockets. That image might never
fade.

"Do you want your laptop?"

"Bair brought it."

"Phone?"

"Your friend Donny pinched it."

"It's probably in the cistern." She wrinkled her brow. "Unless
they've cleared it out. Did the sheriff tell you?"

"No. Since I didn't press charges, and Dr. Brenner took away
his suspect, he seems to have washed his hands of it."

"I wonder how he is."

"The sheriff?"

"No. Donny."

"Please don't expect me to commiserate."

She didn't. How could he? "What do you think they'll do with
the books and things he collected?"

"Give them back to their rightful owners."

"It was his whole world."

"Except for all the places he nicked the things."

"But the cistern meant everything to him. That's why he had to defend it."

Smith sighed. "All right, I pity the culprit."

"Who's also a victim."

Smith took her hand. "But still capable of choices."

"He could have killed us and no one would have known about his secret place."

"If you weren't so compassionate, we would not have made it out."

"He didn't want to hurt us, Smith."

"You, he didn't want to hurt. He had no qualms about dunking me in the well."

She smiled. "I've wanted to dunk you a few times myself."

"That goes without saying." He tugged her by the arm until their faces were inches apart. "There's one medicine I'm missing."

Her heart thumped. "The therapeutic kiss?"

"Quite."

"You haven't charmed it out of the nurses?"

"Very few sources are curative."

"Did you learn that in school?"

"From my mother, the originator of the therapeutic kiss. However, I've outgrown that variety."

The last person who had kissed him was Danae, and she had no doubt it was the adult version.

He saw her hesitation and guessed its source. "Can we put that business behind us?"

"I'm trying to."

"Some therapies work both ways."

"I'm not sure I can take that medicine."

"We could start with a small dose and work our way up."

322 \ KRISTEN HEITZMANN

She shook her head. "There's no small dose."

He sobered. "I know that, Tess." His fingers brushed her cheek, slid down, and raised her chin. "I'm willing to take it like a man, if you are."

She drew a ragged breath. "I don't have that capacity."

"Then you should take it like a woman, because I can't wait one minute more."

She leaned in and touched his lips with hers. Then it was certain overdose, but she didn't care because she was not willing to lose him to Danae or anyone else. She had to stand firm and fight, not run a—

She staggered back, gripping the rail.

"Tess?"

Panting and crying, she ran through the woods, no labyrinth path to lead her, only moonlit pines and fear. She slipped and rolled into the hollow of a large stone. Gasping, she pressed herself into the hole too little to hold her. Hide me. Hide me.

"Tessa, what's wrong?"

She blinked back her tears. "It keeps coming when I don't expect it."

He pulled her back. "Tell me."

"I'm running away, trying to hide, but he finds me, Smith. I know it."

Smith sat up in the bed and brought her head to his chest. "It's in the past. You only need to acknowledge it."

"I can't."

He threaded her fingers with his. "Do you find it odd that intimacy triggers it?"

She looked away. "It was thinking I would fight for you that triggered it."

"It was?"

"I didn't fight the other time. I ran away."

"You were a tiny little girl."

"I loved my dad."

"But there was nothing you could do."

"What if there was, Smith? What if that's why I won't remember?"

CHAPTER

33

With room to spare, Smith stretched out. The only seats available on a flight without multiple connections and significant hassle had been first class. Tessa had balked when he procured them, until Bair said, "It's no hardship for him, Tessa. Let it go." It wasn't a hardship, and cramming his long legs into coach would have been. Nevertheless, he was glad when the flight ended.

Though a painful hitch still warned him when he'd moved too suddenly, he felt fairly strong as they deplaned in Colorado Springs. No convincing anyone else of that, however. Bair shouldered both carry-on bags, moving through the crowd like a lineman. Tessa had suggested he come along instead of waiting by himself, and Smith could think of no reason to say otherwise.

He hoped she didn't still feel the need for a buffer, though she'd been distant and ragged since they'd kissed. She looked exhausted as well. He could only hope once everything came to light, she could let it go. *Please, God, let her find answers.*

They stopped at the luggage carousel, where Bair moved forward to snag Tessa's suitcases as they tumbled down and circled. Since she was going home, she had brought all the clothing she'd had with her from the previous project to replace it with more seasonally appropriate things. He hoped that was the only reason she'd brought everything back home.

While they waited, a woman came toward them with a loose-hipped stride. Her multiple bracelets and India cotton pants matched her black mane of hair, olive-toned skin, and almond eyes. She and Tessa hugged briefly; then Tessa turned. "Genie, this is Smith Chandler, the architect on our project. And his intern, Bair."

"I finally meet the infamous Bair?" Genie cocked a dark eyebrow.

Bair lost the capacity for speech and gave her a sheepish grin.

"Bair," Tessa said with more affection than necessary, "this is my assistant, Genie."

They piled into the aged but rugged Jeep Wagoneer that Genie had parked in the short-term lot and headed across the city to the mountain pass that would take them to Tessa's home in Green Mountain Falls. The red granite slopes cloaked with dark pointed pines were splendid, but from his seat in the back, Smith watched Tessa stare silently out the windscreen while Genie drove.

As the Jeep climbed the mountain, ragged white clouds overtook the peaks and spit slivers of snow.

"It is October, isn't it?" Bair mumbled.

"October in the mountains," Genie said over her shoulder. "But it's not supposed to do much until the weekend."

They followed a dirt road to one of the higher properties tucked a quarter of the way up the mountainside. Genie parked and they all climbed out. Natural stone chimneys flanked the sizeable cabin with a broad front porch situated for gazing across the valley. The log walls blended with the pines surrounding it. The green shingled roof across the front rose to a second or loft level farther back. Neat, compact, with warmth and character in the hewn logs and shutters with pine-tree cutouts.

A small animal pen at one side stood empty, but a large orange cat waited on the porch to be let in out of the weather. "I see Ros-coe's returned." Tessa scratched the cat's outstretched neck.

Genie nodded. "The day you said he would."

Smith joined Bair at the Jeep's hatch, but Tessa turned. "Leave the bags, Smith. We'll get them."

Another cheery reminder of his less-than-fit condition. Admit-tedly the travel had taken more out of him than it should have. He joined Tessa on the porch as she unlocked and opened her front door. When she hesitated, he put a hand to the small of her back. "You all right?"

"Yes." She straightened and led them into the cozy, colorful great room. It looked warmer than it felt, and Genie went directly to the woodstove on the left and started laying a fire.

"No furnace?" Smith searched for ductwork.

"Just the stoves." Genie fed small hewn logs into the bright yellow blaze.

At the back, a rustic kitchen was surrounded by brick-red ceramic countertops. Plant-covered shelves flanked dun-colored couches and red-and-green overstuffed chairs. Several built-in bookshelves reached the ceiling around the outer walls.

Bair muscled the luggage inside as the gusty wind whirled white snow dust around his head. Genie pointed him toward the split-log staircase. "You guys are up there. I'll show you." With their two bags Bair followed her up.

Tessa rolled her bag to a room adjoining the great room on the main level. A scent of woodsmoke drew him to that doorway, and he hovered there while she lit another wood-burning stove. She looked up and saw him.

He smiled. "May I?"

"Come in. This was my parents' room. Now it's mine."

Spacious, yet homey, with a slanting board roof and windows all across the wall opposite the bed. A conglomeration of glass and copper hummingbird feeders partially obstructed the view of a dense grove of white-trunked aspen. An alder-wood drafting table sat in front of the center window, and he pictured Tessa working there with jewel-toned hummingbirds hovering just outside the glass.

She closed the stove and straightened, absorbing the warmth with outstretched hands. "It shouldn't take long."

"It's a well-designed house."

"I thought you'd like it. Mom was woodsy, not fussy, so it skews masculine."

"How much of it is you?"

She looked into his face. "Enough." She was holding herself together by a thread.

"Come here."

She buried herself in his arms. "I don't know why I thought I could do this."

He stroked her hair. "What's making you think you can't?"

"I just . . . maybe it's better not to know."

"You don't have to do anything you don't want to, Tess." What did it matter that they'd flown out there to settle the matter once and for all? She knew what she could handle and what she couldn't.

She pressed her face against his chest. "What if knowing is worse?"

"It almost never is." He raised her face. "But, Tess, it's far from certain we'll find anything."

She drew a calming breath and nodded. "I have to look. I know it." She stepped back, folding her arms and grasping her elbows. "I should tell Dr. Brenner I'm back—"

"Or not."

She searched his face. "What do you have against him?"

"I can't put my finger on it. Probably that he occupies so much of your thoughts."

"He's treated me for a long time."

"I'm not sure you need treating."

She sighed. "You haven't seen it, Smith."

"Actually, I have."

"Well, now I have coping skills. When Mom died, I didn't."

"He should recognize the skills you have and terminate the therapy."

"It's my call."

"Then make it."

She walked to the window and stared out. "It's not that easy."

Who was he to tell her what she should or shouldn't do? "I know it's not my business. Only . . ." He turned her from the window, caught her face, and looked hard into her eyes. "I want it to be."

"I can't replace Dr. Brenner with you. If I get through this, I have to find a way to cope on my own."

"No one copes alone. We were created to support and encourage each other. I want to do that for you."

" And what do I do for you, Smith?"

"Besides saving my life, you mean?"

"I didn't—"

"Yes, Tessa, you did. I don't know how long I'd have held on. I could not convince him to let me go. You did."

Her forehead puckered. "Is that it? You're trying to reciprocate?"

He spread his hands. "Reciprocate? What's gotten into you?"

"I don't know." She wrapped herself in her arms. "I can't understand why you're here."

He couldn't understand what was going on inside her head. From the moment she'd approached the house, she'd begun disintegrating. "What's the matter, Tess?"

She looked away. "You don't owe me."

Her gaze shot back looking bruised.

He raised her chin. "You said you'd fight for me, but now you're pushing me away. Why?"

"Because I'm not . . . I didn't . . ."

The thought rushed in. "It's guilt, isn't it. Guilt or blame or condemnation. That's why you expect to be disappointed."

She pressed her hands to her face. "It's overwhelming me. I can't sleep. I can't think without pieces of it pushing in."

"Let me help."

"I don't know how."

He slid her hands off her face and held them between his. "Start by believing I care."

She swallowed. "Okay."

He slid his fingers into her hair. "Now, believe I love you. I don't say it easily."

She closed her eyes.

"Look at me, Tess."

"You don't understand. I saw inside, and it's . . . wretched."

"I've been there, just as wretched." Did she think she was the only one? "And it was my own choices that made it so. This thing of yours . . . You're not responsible."

She opened her eyes. "Then why am I so afraid?"

He couldn't answer that, just drew her to his chest and held her. He pressed his face to her hair. "We're going to get through this." His head spun, and he swayed.

She looked up. "You're woozy."

"I feel a little . . ."

"It's the altitude."

"No. It was the thought that entered my mind."

"What thought?"

"How easy it was to say *we* were going to get through this. And I thought of the night we made our design and how we could do anything. We could get married."

She startled. "What?"

"Life can end in a moment, one thrust of a blade. What are we waiting for?"

"You're not over Danae." Her statement crushed his enthusiasm.

"I am, Tess."

"Seriously, Smith. You need to sit down. You're pale, and you do not need altitude sickness." She led him back to the great room where Genie sat with Bair, a large album on the table before them. Landscape photos by the look of it. Tessa's, no doubt.

Bair looked up. "Have you seen this?"

Smith shook his head. He'd hired her on reputation and memories. He dropped down next to Bair, who slid the book his way as Tessa went into the kitchen, looking fragile. What had induced him to spring that on her? He had not proposed to Danae when it would have been natural to do so, yet now he popped the question with no preparation or forethought?

Tessa returned with a glass of water and instructed him to drink it all. "You need to hydrate up here to keep your brain oxygenated."

"Thank you." She had an alarming capacity to bury her distress. Moments ago, it had overwhelmed them. Now she carried the glass back to the kitchen as though she hadn't just admitted a pervasive terror consumed her—or that his proposal might have scared her even more.

He paged through the collage of landscapes and labyrinths that showcased Tessa's talent. They'd been awesome that night, working Gaston's plan, and these photos showed even more what an asset she would be if he could bring her into the firm—he and Bair and Tessa.

Except she lived here. In her parents' house, with her parents' things. And it was nice, very nice, but was it healthy? She and her mother, and then Tessa by herself, living as though they hadn't lost each other. Would anything induce her to leave it, to stop immersing herself in the past?

A dish clattered in the kitchen, and Genie went to help. She was dark and dusky, with wide, flat hips and a generous but melancholy mouth. There was, overall, an edge to her that was not unattractive but might keep a man on his toes.

"Nice on the eyes," Bair murmured.

"Have you spoken to her?"

Bair shrugged.

"Well, trust me, verbalizing has its pitfalls." He glanced into the kitchen, where Tessa and Genie worked at supper.

"Put your foot in it again?"

"I mentioned marriage."

"In a theoretical sense?"

"In a suggestive sense."

Bair crowded him. "As in 'let's do it'?"

"Fairly close." Smith dropped his hands on his knees.

"You can't just bandy marriage about," Bair snapped in a low tone.

"I didn't say it lightly. Bad form and timing, but honestly I see a future with her."

"You've hardly seen a present."

"We had three years of preliminary friendship."

"Far from stellar for Tessa."

Smith frowned. "The end was bleak but the substance was there. You said it yourself: who carries a grudge for six years without substantial feelings behind it?"

"Sure this isn't about Danae coming, some knee-jerk reaction?"

"I haven't thought of her once. Seeing her, even kissing her—"

Bair expelled his breath.

"Let me finish. I think she was feeling out the possibilities, in case Edward doesn't work out. I think she wanted me to know she still has feelings. I didn't realize it at the time, but as soon as she'd gone, she was gone. I don't need or want anything from her."

"You told her you're in love with Tessa?"

He swallowed. "Not yet."

"You see?"

"I do see, Bair. Tessa means the world to me. I'll do anything for her." Saying it aloud created such a certainty he felt more alive than ever before. *This* he was meant for, not just to help or protect her, but to join himself to her, to love her in a way he could never properly vocalize and had no chance of making clear to Bair.

He got up and walked around the great room, studying framed drawings that must have been Tessa's childish rendering of chipmunks, birds, and trees. Even then, she had a skilled hand and an eye for detail, though frequently the subject was less elaborately rendered than the plants and branches around it, emphasizing the environment necessary for the animal's survival.

No matter what Bair or anyone thought, he was in love with her. He had never felt such purpose, and it had nothing to do with nearly dying. Or maybe it did. Maybe that experience clarified what mattered. Danae had given him the chance to boast of his success, and it had seemed insignificant. The need to impress her, gone. His proposal to Tess had sprung from something far more real.

Throughout the room, on the various shelves, pottery and glass sculptures erupted spontaneously from the foliage of so many plants the place seemed to have been overtaken by the mountain. He examined one elongated clay piece glazed in blues and purples, turned it over and saw *Vanessa* scratched into the base. Her mother's name, wasn't it?

"Look here." Bair motioned him over to the three-tiered cupboard, where Genie had directed him.

Smith joined them. The project models he'd created were

intricate, scaled representations and fine work in themselves, but Tessa's model labyrinths were art, each stone, each plant as real as if a garden had been shrunken to fit the base.

"Planning and development," Genie said. "Tessa does it over the winter unless she's consulting. She sees the labyrinths that way in her mind, as if she's flying over."

Bair replaced an intricate hedge garden on the shelf. "Has she, um, built them all? I mean . . . in a real location?"

"Not all."

Smith turned to see Tessa in the kitchen watching his reaction. "Very nice."

She ducked her chin. "We're ready to eat."

Smith set the labyrinth back on the shelf, and they gathered around the square pine table. Tessa's broiled chicken with rice and miniature carrots, cooked with sprigs of something she'd snipped off a plant in the window, made a disgrace of Bair's roast.

"This is excellent." Bair beat him to the compliment.

"Thanks." Tessa turned. "How's your head, Smith?"

"Never better."

"You need to take it easy. The doctor was clear."

"Didn't you know?" Genie's eyes developed a dark gleam. "All doctors are ogres."

"Genie had her gallbladder removed." Tessa sent her a glance. "Her recovery was a little like yours—heavy on the whine."

"Hey," he and Genie chorused while Bair chuckled.

Tessa laughed, and he might have believed it—except for the shadows behind her eyes.

CHAPTER

34

"I'll clean up." Genie sent her a meaningful glance. Balance was important to her, and when one of them cooked, the other washed up afterward. Just one of the quirks that indicated a need for order in her deceptively easygoing style.

"I'll, um, clear." Bair stood up and started stacking plates.

Tessa hoped they would make it to the sink, but left Bair and Genie to it when Smith tugged her to the couch. He stretched out and motioned her down beside him. The fire crackled. Her heart rushed. He'd said life could end abruptly; why waste the time they had? Because she needed answers. She could not dream until she had finished the nightmare once and for all. When she had, he might realize he didn't want her at all.

Bair's phone rang. It took him moments to wrestle it off his belt, then he brought it to Smith and mouthed, *Rumer Gaston*.

Smith took it. "Yes, hello." A pause, then, "Sorry, I can't get to my phone. It's on the property and I'm in Colorado recuperating. Doctor's orders." He winked.

Her fears of Rumer Gaston seemed like another life. He was not her nightmare monster, only an odious man with an over-inflated ego.

336 \ KRISTEN HEITZMANN

"That's generous," Smith said, "but I'm not sure I'm up to the stress of the tables."

"Gambling tables?" she whispered and Smith mouthed, *Black Hawk*.

Please don't let him demand it. She had to finish this.

"I'm sorry. It's just not possible." He rolled his eyes. "Yes, as soon as I get word that we're clear to proceed." He nodded. "The moment I know something. Good-bye." He handed the phone back to Bair, then rested his head back in the crook of his arm. "I could get used to this."

Tessa startled.

"What?"

"My dad used to say that. I just remembered him standing outside with his arms spread wide, snow falling in his face, hollering, 'I could get used to this!' " The image was heartbreakingly clear.

"Other memories are coming as well?"

"Maybe they've been trapped behind the other and as it corrodes they slip past."

Firelight danced on his lenses as his gray eyes settled on her. "The good memories might cushion the difficult one."

"Or make it that much harder." She swallowed the dread. "Maybe I blocked the happy memories so the guilt wouldn't crush me."

"You can't believe you're guilty. Nothing you could have done at that age makes you culpable."

She drew a ragged breath. "It feels like it, Smith."

"Apply logic."

"That from the man who just proposed marriage?"

He sighed. "That wasn't any decent sort of proposal."

"And now that you've applied logic?"

"I'd say it again." He looked surprisingly sincere. "More elegantly."

She shook her head. "How did we get into this mess?"

He threaded her fingers with his. "Think of it as a complicated path leading to a predetermined point at which something of value will be gained and brought back."

Her jaw fell slack. "You get it."

"Your explanation made perfect sense. If it's a labyrinth, no matter how difficult, the way in also leads out."

"So entering the memory will also provide a release."

"I hope so. I pray it will." Shifting more to his side, he settled her against his stomach, turning her so she could see his face. "I want this to work. I want you free to move forward, to let go of the fear and guilt. I meant what I said before about the Father's love. I see your yearning."

His words touched the ache. Maybe if she recovered tender memories of her dad, she might be able to accept a Father God. But for now—

A memory hit so hard it knocked her breath out. Her dad in his workshop.

"Back to bed, kitten. Does Mommy know you're up?"

Rubbing the silky blanket between her fingers, she reaches for his hug. He hears a noise outside. His face gets long and stern.

"Go inside, Tessie. Find Mommy and stay there."

"Tess?" Smith's fingers tightened on hers.

The whimper had escaped her throat. She pressed up from the couch. She had to see it, the workshop. She had come home to remember and the memory started there.

"Tess, where are you going?"

"Dad's workshop." She went to the closet and grabbed her fleece-lined woolen coat.

Smith snagged her dad's bomber jacket and hurried out behind her. The clouds had opened up on a clear, brittle sky. Pine needles crunched beneath her boots as she approached the small cabin behind the house. She felt for and found the key over one of the pine slats. Holding her breath, she opened the door and flipped on the light.

A low bed covered with a flannel quilt pressed against one wall. The workbench and cabinets filled the other half of the space. It smelled of wood and dust and motor oil. An airplane propeller hung on the far wall along with topographical maps and wind patterns.

Smith said, "Was your father a pilot?"

She moved to the center of the room and stared at the white propeller, chipped and wind blasted. When Smith cupped her shoulders, she was only slightly aware of him. "We made a delivery. The day we flew over the labyrinth. When we got back, Mom was upset."

"Angry?"

"Afraid. They argued, and I got upset. That's why I had my worry blanket." She turned and walked toward the door.

"Tess?"

She went out and stood for a moment staring at the house. Their voices came as hollow echoes.

"They left me no choice."

"And now they've left you no protection."

She turned toward the slope behind the workshop.

Smith spoke low. "Not now, Tess. Not in the dark."

"I have to see it at night."

"We don't even have a torch."

"We have a moon." She passed between the first two pines, climbing the slope.

The moon shone like a spotlight through the thin atmosphere, but clouds lurked higher up, and it was never a good idea to take off unprepared into the night. "Tessa." He considered running in and alerting the others, but Tessa had set off, and it would be all he could do to keep up.

The fingers of her right hand rubbed against her thumb. Her other hand curled up against her throat. If he wasn't close enough to gauge her height, he'd say it was a child creeping through the woods. Had she slipped into the memory so completely?

He didn't talk or try to stop her. He conserved his breath and followed as she moved like a waif through the woods. What kind of imprint dominated a child's mind so entirely, that this many years later, she was back in that moment? He thought he heard a whimper, though she didn't pause. She knew he was there if she needed him.

The only other sounds were crispy pine needles crunching beneath his shoes and the breath wheezing in his lungs. Long-needled branches redolent with pine sap pressed in and swung back like hinged doors. Tessa veered to the right when the slope flattened. A huge rocky outcropping loomed up against the starry sky.

She stared up and shuddered. If she tried to climb it, he'd stop her. No way they were scaling that in the dark. But she put a hand to the stone and moved around its base. Bending to see a small hollow at the base. With a cry, she pressed both hands to her head but kept walking, searching side to side until she stopped abruptly. The moment she sank to her knees, he was there.

"Was it here?" he breathed, tightening his arms around her. "Can you tell me what you saw?"

"Four men with bats. And my dad."

He winced.

"Another man over there." She barely stretched her finger to point. "He sees me!" Panic seized her.

"It's over, Tess. It happened a long time ago."

It wasn't over for her. She broke into deep, wracking sobs. He didn't try to comfort her with useless words, but as he held her he prayed hard that this would not break her.

The barrier collapsed. Into her mind with horror and debilitating grief came every blow, every kick. The blood, the cries, the brutality knotted her stomach. She jerked back, screaming. "No!" The word tore through her throat. "No!" With everything in her she wanted to stop what was happening, but it was too late. She had sat there frozen with horror, and every scream in every nightmare and the screams that now broke through the years of restraint and ripped her throat raw were all too late.

Pain and fury coursed her nerves, her veins, muscle tissue, bones. Terror and grief took her body like an invading army leaving carnage in its wake. Her screams punished the voice that had kept silent, ripping through her larynx until no vibration could wrench sound from any cord. She collapsed, aching in every place her daddy's bones had cracked and his flesh had been torn and crushed. She'd followed the path into her dad's suffering, but she'd been wrong. There was no way out.

Smith held Tessa, unresponsive, in his arms as the night deepened around them. Her screams had rent his composure until he shook almost as hard as she. Now, if not for her shallow breaths against his chest, he wouldn't know she was alive. Several times he tried to rouse her from her faint, if faint it was, thinking any moment she would awaken, but she seemed deaf to him.

He'd been so focused on her going up that he had not paid close attention to the way, and even if he had, could he retrace it? He did not want to get them lost by trying to navigate a strange mountain at night. But the time passing grew untenable, and the thought nagged that he should have let the professional handle it.

Would Dr. Brenner have made her remember it all somewhere safe, where he had control of the process? Smith frowned. He didn't know the first thing about psychiatry, but even if Dr. Brenner knew his business, the control he wielded over her seemed excessive. Wasn't a therapist's job to help a patient toward independence? Why, as she said, did she live with her psychiatrist on speed dial? Unless . . .

Smith faced the uncomfortable truth. She must be more fragile than he had wanted to believe. Fear assaulted him, fear that he had caused irreparable damage, pridefully believing he could do for her what no one else had. *Lord.*

He had honestly believed he had a part in this, that Tessa trusted him because God had entrusted her to him. His promise to protect her was not false bravado, but a divine conviction, he'd thought. Had he been wrong?

Before Danae's rejection, he'd believed himself capable, sufficient. He'd been astonished by his actual inadequacy. God had strengthened him through that rejection, prepared him, he'd thought, for this moment.

Tessa's faith looked nothing like his, but he recalled now how badly she had wanted to find that cross in the labyrinth. Maybe her insistence had not been to recover an artifact but to satisfy a spiritual hunger. She had pursued God assiduously, yet she'd seemed unable to receive the Father's love and forgive herself for the betrayal she'd remembered tonight. Maybe instead of the Father's love, he should have given her the cross, the blood of Jesus covering her guilt.

Lord, help and console and heal her.

Clouds closed in, diffusing the moonlight into a surreal white glow. Foamy pellets of snow dropped through the trees, and the gusty wind stuck rude fingers into his collar. He couldn't wait any longer. Gathering her up, he pressed up from his knees and started down. The slope was as good a compass as he would get, though it was growing slippery.

He sighed with relief when he reached the stone outcropping where she'd paused. Though he'd worked up a thin sweat inside his shirt, the cold sank into his bones as he assessed his direction. Unsure of the angle at which Tessa had approached the boulders, he tried again to rouse her. No response.

How long before the others noticed? They must have seen them getting coats and going out. Or had they been immersed at the sink that faced away from the door? He kicked himself for not retrieving his cell phone in Maryland. Tessa had been willing to go back for it, but he hadn't wanted her to. Now he wished he'd climbed back into that hole himself.

But wait. Tessa might have hers. He braced against a boulder and felt her pockets. Disappointed, he gathered himself and went on, straining to see through the darkened tree spires, trying not to slip. His chest throbbed with each draw of frigid, pine-and-snow-scented air. From somewhere to his right a chorus of yipping barks suggested coyotes on a kill. What else lurked in the dark woods with eyes nocturnally attuned and a taste for blood?

Wind gusted the dry pellets into his face, and in minutes larger flakes swirled around them. "God, help me," he whispered. What was it doing snowing in October?

A shout came from below. Bair. Too winded to holler back, Smith headed the direction from which it came. A second shout. Genie's voice. They were out together. With the continuous calls drawing him down, Smith drew near enough to answer.

Some distance farther, he saw the beams of their torches looking insipid. "Bair," he called again. One light swung up to meet him, then the other, effectively blinding him.

Bair hurried up. "What happened?"

"She remembered."

Genie came in closer. "Remembered what?"

"What happened to her father."

"The guy who ran off?"

Bair had been briefed, but Genie seemingly not. Smith considered the options, then said, "She witnessed his murder."

Genie gaped in the moonlight. "When?"

"She was almost six. But the memory was so real. This is some emotional shock, I imagine." As the adrenaline passed, he staggered.

"Let me." Bair handed Genie his torch.

When Smith transferred Tessa, his knees almost buckled. Genie steadied him with a hand, but his main concern was Bair's conveying Tessa the rest of the way down. *Let strength trump clumsiness*, he thought in the continuous silent dialogue he'd been holding with God.

Genie led the way back to the house. He had only been a little off course, might've landed at one of the houses farther down or to the right. Fatigue caught him from behind and sank its fangs, but they'd reached the back door swamped by golden light. Bair maneuvered Tessa inside. Genie followed. Smith gripped the jamb a moment, then closed the door behind them.

CHAPTER

35

Bair laid Tessa on the couch. Genie draped her with a soft green throw. Smith crouched beside her. "Tessa, can you hear me?"

Genie leaned in. "Wake up, Tessa. Wake up."

Bair pressed his fingers to her throat and consulted his watch. "Pulse is elevated. Maybe we should call that bloke with the goatee."

"No."

"Aren't you afraid—"

"Yes, Bair. I am. But I'm not sure her shrink is the best and only choice."

Genie rested her hands on her hips. "Tessa trusts Dr. Brenner. He's like a father to her."

Smith eyed her. "That doesn't strike you as strange?"

"He's her therapist."

Yes, but to what degree did a therapist insert himself into his client's life? "Just give her a while. Let her realize she's safe." Was she? Or was she trapped somewhere by the monster in her mind? "I don't know how long it's been since she's slept."

"If she were sleeping, we could wake her."

"There's no point going out in the storm." He slipped onto the

346 \ KRISTEN HEITZMANN

couch and nestled her head in his lap. "Give her until morning. Then we'll decide."

Genie frowned. "Are you sure?"

He wasn't sure of anything but did not want to give her up to anyone else when he'd promised they'd get through this together. "It's only a few more hours."

Bair nodded. "All right. Till morning."

When Bair and Genie had gone upstairs to their respective rooms, Smith stretched out alongside Tessa and held her tightly against his chest. He wanted her to know without doubt that he was there. "Hang on, Tess. Hang on." With his face immersed in her hair, he succumbed to sleep, opening his eyes only when the light of dawn came through the uncovered windows.

The landscape had been transformed by a thin layer of snow. Cottony gray clouds draped over the mountainside—more snow to come? He shifted. Tessa hadn't stirred or given any sign of waking.

Bair came down the stairs. "Has she . . ."

"Not yet."

"I'll brew some tea." He headed to the kitchen with which he'd seemingly grown familiar.

Genie came down, assessed for herself that Tessa had not awakened, and joined Bair in the kitchen. Smith got up from the couch, went upstairs to wash up and change clothes. Back downstairs, he took the offered mug and sipped. Bair had brewed the tea the British way, with the leaves loose in the boiling water. The agony of the leaves, that method was called, and produced a more robust effect—as human suffering brought out the deepest essence of an individual?

He rejoined Tessa. Was it arrogance to think he understood her situation better in the time he'd spent with her than the doctor who'd treated her for years? Or did he see with a fresh eye that something was off, even if he couldn't tell what?

He leaned closer, noting a mottling on her skin where the sleeve of her coat had slid up. She looked bruised, even though she hadn't fallen or hurt herself. All the while she'd screamed, her limbs had gone rigid, but she hadn't beaten her arms on the ground or him.

Genie joined him. "How'd she do that?"

"I don't know." He lifted the lower edge of her coat and shirt. Her side and back were bruised, as though she had absorbed her father's beating. Impossible. It must be a physical reaction to her extreme strain.

Genie frowned. "What happened out there last night?"

"Nothing that would have caused this."

Genie leaned close. "Tessa, can you hear me?"

Without opening her eyes, Tessa started softly keening.

Genie turned away. "I'm calling Dr. Brenner. We need to bring her in."

Smith didn't argue. Dr. Brenner might be necessary, but his own conviction had not lifted. He had promised he'd battle the monster to the death, and they were not clear of the labyrinth yet.

Daddy! The nightmare had never been so awful. She couldn't find him, and the labyrinth itself had turned against her. The walls were closing in, the path getting narrower, darker. It followed no pattern she'd ever seen. If this path led to the center—what would she find there?

The hedge tore at her and she beat it back with her arms and fists. *Daddy? Daddy, where are you?* The hedge grew too close, engulfing the path. She had to press sideways to keep moving. When she looked back, the walls had closed in behind her. If she stopped, the labyrinth would swallow her. *Daddy, please. Where are you?*

She pushed against the hedge with all her strength, but it wasn't enough. It had almost grown together. *Please. Please!*

She felt someone at her back, a strong arm pushing back the hedge, pressing her on. She tried to look but couldn't turn her head. She had to reach the center. Or be smothered in the hedge and die.

Smith buckled Tessa into the seat beside him in the Jeep Wagoneer. He cradled her head in the crook of his neck while Genie followed the directions Bair read off to the Cedar Grove care facility. Dr. Brenner had said he would meet them there, and though they had wakened him, he was waiting when they arrived. "Bring her through here," he directed Bair, who carried her limp in his arms.

They passed through the office bearing his name on the door to a smaller room with wall cabinets, a burgundy leather couch in the center, and a matching chair on casters. "Lay her down there."

Bair eased her onto the couch. Dr. Brenner pulled back an eyelid and shined a penlight into her eye. He examined the bruising on her arms and stomach and straightened. "How did she get these?"

Smith shook his head. "They appeared with no explanation."

The doctor pressed her mottled forearm, then lifted his finger. "There is an explanation, probably psychogenic bruising, or extreme distress bursting capillaries." He straightened. "There's no need for you all to wait. I'll be admitting her."

"No," Smith said. Bair and Genie had started back out, but he wasn't leaving. "I've brought her to you, but I'm not going anywhere."

"This is no time to argue."

"I promised her." He sensed the animosity the doctor masked, but he was not letting Tessa out of his sight. Their standoff lasted only moments before Tessa resumed keening.

"Close the door behind you." Dr. Brenner ordered Bair and Genie as he rolled the chair near the couch and sat down. "Tessa. Can you hear me?"

The soft wailing continued. Smith stood behind her, unwilling to surrender his post.

"I know you can hear my voice," Dr. Brenner said in a smooth, even tone. "Wherever you've gone, I will bring you back. I'm going to count. . . ."

Smith clenched his jaw and prayed. Dr. Brenner might think so, but he was not God. There was only one source of absolute power. *Help her, Lord. Find her, wherever she is. Be her strength, her protection, her champion.*

With a cry she burst through the smothering foliage into the center. The hedge formed a solid circular wall around a dim space. *Daddy?* She was alone, without even the one who had given that final thrust. She took a step toward something shining. A thin bronze cross holding the crucified Christ.

Another step. Tears streamed. She had thought she would find him, thought her daddy waited there if she could only reach him. "Daddy!" The scream tore out of her throat.

Peace, child.

It was not her daddy's voice. She wasn't sure it was a voice. But she knew it. Deep inside, deeper than she'd ever gone on any path, with any meditative intention, and still the response she found was, "Daddy?"

Reaching out, she touched the cross and sank to her knees.

"I didn't help him. I didn't make them stop. I didn't tell what I knew. I was afraid."

I know.

The sense of that knowing was deeper than any human knowledge. It went inside and knew all of her, every path she'd walked, every stumble, every fall, everything that had happened. It knew her yearning, knew her fear. *He* knew her need and touched it.

The joy that filled her had no edges. It would not cut and leave her bleeding. He would never abandon her.

Tessa's shriek had pierced more than his ears, but Smith remained still and silent. One wrong move and Dr. Brenner might eject him. Three different approaches had failed to bring her to consciousness. Once again the doctor checked her eyes. They were not rolled back, but whether she saw the light he shined there it was impossible to tell.

"Tessa. This is Dr. Brenner, and I'm—"

She opened her eyes. Smith fought a smile at the fact that she hadn't waited for his command, count, or instruction. She'd come back on her own, and he wanted to shout with triumph.

"Hello, Tessa." Dr. Brenner's smooth tone hardly expressed the relief he must feel. "Don't get up."

"How . . ." Her hoarse voice scraped through her throat.

"Smith brought you here."

She looked up and Smith reassured her with a smile. She lowered her gaze to the doctor, whose benign manner suddenly seemed forced.

"I understand you've been doing some work without me. That was dangerous, though perhaps . . . fruitful."

"I remembered something."

"And I'd like you to tell me about it."

She blinked, then nodded.

"With your permission, I'm going to use a voice recorder."

"Why?"

"So that I can refer to it as we continue to process the trauma."

Smith searched Tessa's face for discomfort, but it didn't seem to concern her. She trusted him, even after he'd sold her out to the sheriff. Given her limitations, that said so much.

Dr. Brenner fiddled with the handheld recorder he pulled from a drawer, then expelled an impatient breath. "It's not charged. Just a moment." He went to the outer office with the door closing behind him.

"Smith." Tessa moistened her lips with her tongue. "Can I have a drink of water?"

He located the cooler but, in circling the couch, bumped the open drawer. It tipped onto the floor. Tessa sat up while he knelt to gather the scattered contents.

"Stop."

He looked up at her surprisingly strident tone. "What?"

"That picture. Give it to me."

He handed over the snapshot she indicated.

"That's . . . that's Dr. Brenner." She pointed to the first of two men in front of a small aircraft. Her finger trembled. "And that's my dad." Her knuckles whitened. "He never said he knew my dad. All this time . . ."

The door opened. Occupied with the recorder, Dr. Brenner entered, then glimpsed her sitting up and frowned. "I didn't want you to get up."

"You knew my dad." She sprang to her feet. "You were part of it."

He saw the photo in her grip. "No, Tessa."

She shook. "Were you there with a bat? Did you murder him?"

He drew himself up. "I was not there. I was not part of it."

"You knew him! This is your picture with him."

"Please sit."

"How dare you keep that from me? You . . . you liar!"

"I never lied to you." Dr. Brenner's clipped words showed Tessa had scored a hit, and for once Smith didn't think she'd exaggerated. If he'd kept something this monumental from her, there had to be a reason.

She hissed through clenched teeth. "I told you everything you wanted to know—my dreams, my fears. I ached for my dad, and you never said anything!"

"If you will sit down . . ."

Smith caught her before she launched herself at the doctor. "Careful, Tess."

Dr. Brenner's glance flicked to him, then back. "I had nothing to do with his death, unless you count warning him."

"Warning him? About what? No, don't bother. Why should I believe anything you say?"

"I understand you're upset." Dr. Brenner took the photo from her fingers. "This isn't how I would have wanted you to find out."

"How exactly would you want it, since telling the truth was obviously out?"

"That isn't accurate. Telling you the truth before you had reached this point was out."

"Why?" Tears filled her eyes.

"Because I needed you to remember, to break the silence you'd imposed that night."

Still holding her waist, Smith caught her slackened weight. "You knew what I'd seen?"

He shook his head. "I knew you'd seen something. You were mute and catatonic. Your mother—"

She shook her head emphatically. "My mom was not part of this."

"Sit down, Tessa. Do you want the truth?"

Smith was prepared to take her out the moment she said no. When she nodded, he guided her over to the couch, sat beside her, and kept a firm arm around her shoulders. Though Dr. Brenner had regained some control of the situation, Smith would not give it over completely.

"Your mother and I agreed your mental health could not be sacrificed."

"To what?"

"To learning what you'd seen." His face grew stern. "I've waited a long time for the information you've kept inside."

"Why didn't—"

"I urged you more than once to trust me with it, but each time you refused to acknowledge the memory."

Smith expected her to argue, but Tessa slackened. She pressed her hands to her face. "It's my fault."

"That's not a productive direction."

"Mom died without knowing. She thought he'd left us because I was too scared to say what really happened."

"You chose that explanation, not your mother. *You* needed to believe he was out there somewhere."

Tessa groaned. "What do you want me to do?"

Dr. Brenner rolled his chair closer. "Tell me what you know."

36

Grief hit like a hammer beating her down with each throb of her heart. How could she say what she'd seen, what she had kept secret, pretending it hadn't happened? Dr. Brenner set the machine to record. "Before you tell me what you remembered last night, I want you to recall the first time you saw a labyrinth."

Confused, she looked into the face she had trusted with so many issues. "I've told you that already."

"There might be more now."

Now that she knew they were connected. The memory didn't start in the workshop; it started with that flight, the one she had carried inside her, that had driven her over and over again to make paths that would enlighten her. How stupid not to realize the connection.

She swallowed the painful wreck in her throat, closed her eyes, and expected to feel the rumble of the plane seat. Instead she was in her dad's Jeep. "I'm excited Dad's taking me in his plane. He has to make a delivery, but he wants the company of someone small and talkative." Had she remembered that part before? Mostly she'd recalled flying, seeing the labyrinth.

"What does he have to deliver?"

"I don't know. Someone at the airport gives him a box." Definitely new.

"How big a box?"

"Not very. Wider than a shoe box, but about that high."

"Are there words on the box like a commercial package?"

She frowned for a moment, then shook her head. "Just brown, I think. Maybe it's wrapped in brown paper."

"Go on."

"We're flying over the mountains, then down into a valley. I see roads and fields and horses like dots." She opened her eyes. "They might have been cows, but I wanted them to be horses."

He smiled, the little triangle of beard beneath his lower lip jutting sharply. "Do you want to lie down?"

She leaned into Smith. "No." She closed her eyes and drew a slow breath. "I see the labyrinth. Daddy tells me what it is, and it's . . . magical. I can't stop thinking about the curling path."

Smith's fingers rested gently on her shoulder. He must have been really worried to have brought her there to Dr. Brenner.

"Go on."

"We bounce down on the dirt road. Daddy says, 'Hold on, kitten.' " She felt the rumble of the gravel as they touched and bounced up, then touched again.

"Are you near the labyrinth?"

"I think so."

"Does he use it as a landmark?"

"I don't know." Tessa frowned. "I don't think it's there anymore. I've located all the documented labyrinths in the country."

"Stay with the memory, Tessa."

She swallowed. "Dad gave someone the box, and then we flew back home."

"Describe the person he gave it to."

"I don't remember."

"Try."

She glared. "I was five years old. I don't remember anyone but my dad."

Dr. Brenner's jaw twitched. "I want you to lie down."

She started to protest, but he said, "Please."

She looked at Smith, who reluctantly got off the couch but took up his guardianship behind her.

Dr. Brenner directed his gaze to Smith. "This might go better without distraction." His suggestion carried an uncharacteristic edge.

"I want him here."

Smith folded his arms and remained.

Dr. Brenner acquiesced. "Close your eyes. I'm going to relax you."

His declaration alone created a physical response, an autonomic softening of every muscle. She closed her eyes.

He spoke slowly. "Relax your forehead. Relax your face. Let your jaw hang slack."

Could she stop it?

"Relax your throat."

Her airway cleared.

"Relax your shoulders—the left, and the right."

The tendons and muscles softened.

"Relax your arms."

She couldn't lift them if she tried.

"Relax your diaphragm. Let your abdomen go slack. Your hips and pelvis are melting into the couch."

She was no longer aware of Smith's presence.

"Let your legs go limp. Relax your feet. Relax each toe."

She lay a moment absorbing the silence, then realized she wasn't alone in it. The warmth, the light she had encountered enclosed her once again. He was there. Not the dad she had lost, but the Father she'd found. *Help me.*

"Relax your face."

She let it go slack again.

"The plane has landed. Your father gives someone the box."

Daddy said to stay in the airplane, but she wants to ask about the labyrinth. She jumps down from the stair onto the pale gravel and skips over to her daddy, her white sandals kicking up the dust.

Daddy puts his hand on her head and pulls her to his leg. The man says something. She looks up.

With a cry, she flew up from the couch. "It's him. The man in my nightmare. The man I saw, that I remembered."

She had looked into his face. And that was why she'd believed it when he said he would find her. If he had found her daddy all the way up in the mountains, where would she ever hide?

"Tell me what he looks like."

She described him.

"Do you know him?"

She shook her head.

"Say it out loud."

"I don't . . . know."

"Would you know him if you saw him?"

"Yes."

"It's been a long time."

"I'd know him."

Dr. Brenner hesitated, then said, "Tell me what you saw last night."

So many years he had walked her through exercises to relax and reveal. It all came together now. She drew a breath and described her dad's brutal death. Smith's hand formed a protective cuff around the curve of her neck, but she didn't need protection. She was exposing the monster at last.

By the time the doctor turned off the recorder, Smith seethed under a thin veneer of civility. "Are we through?"

"*We* are through when Tessa says so. This has been a traumatic session—"

"You think?" Smith's hands fisted. He could hurt the man for dragging her through every gruesome detail.

"She might need to further process the emotions."

"What exactly does that mean? That you tell her what to think and how to feel?"

Dr. Brenner sat back in his chair. "I hear your hostility, Smith, but I'm unsure of its basis. Is it my treatment of Tessa that's making you antagonistic . . . or your own?"

"My . . . You've kept her helpless and dependent."

"I've kept her safe from her own mind."

"She's strong and capable."

"You don't know—"

"Stop. Please." Tessa looked from one to the other. "I just want to finish this." She focused on Dr. Brenner. "I gave you what you wanted; now tell me what happened to my dad. Why did they kill him?"

Dr. Brenner slow-blinked. "Another day would be better for that."

"No it wouldn't."

"Give yourself time to deal with this much."

She raised her chin. "Tell me what you know."

"I don't—"

"You said you warned him."

Dr. Brenner looked away. "If you're willing to spend the night here, and let Smith go home, we can—"

"No." Smith spoke for her. "She's coming with me."

Dr. Brenner pursed his lips. "Tessa?"

Smith held his breath. Did she have it in her to resist the man's power?

She sagged. "I'm going home."

Thank you, God.

Dr. Brenner's eyebrow twitched. "We'll talk tomorrow or the next day."

Smith took her arm and led her to the door, looked once over his shoulder at the doctor, then took her out. Bair and Genie stopped talking and stood up.

"Let's go," Smith said, before anyone asked another question. Something felt wrong, and the sooner they were out of there the better.

From his seat at the breakfast table, through his dark glasses, Donny saw her. He looked up and saw her outside the barred window, walking. He ground back his chair and rushed over, banging his hands against the glass. He wanted her to look, wanted her to see him, but he couldn't get to her, couldn't . . .

"Stop banging the glass, Donny," the attendant with pink hair said. "You'll get in trouble." Only part of her hair was pink. The other part was like straw, like the tall grasses in his field, and he had found it interesting, but he didn't care about that now. Tessa was out there.

"It's her. I have to talk to her. I have to tell her I want to go home."

The attendant gave his arm a little tug. "You can't talk to her. She can't hear you."

Because he'd been caught, trapped, taken away. He wasn't in a cage but in a room again and couldn't run and couldn't go outside at night and couldn't see the stars and feel the cool air on his face. "I have to tell her I want to go home."

"Why would you want to be back in that hole?"

"It's not a hole. It's a cistern and it's mine, and she said Dr. Brenner would help me, but I don't want help. I want to go home."

"Well, you have to stop banging the glass or someone's gonna get ticked."

Pink-haired Danielle didn't look at him. She looked around him, because she couldn't stand looking. He wanted Tessa, who looked and didn't scream—if he could only make her see him. He slapped his hands against the glass, shrieking when they came and pulled him away, pulled him where she couldn't see him as she went farther and farther away.

And then Dr. Brenner was there, his face stern and unhappy. "What are you doing, Donny?"

"It's her. It's Tessa. I want to see her. I want to talk to her."

"She can't talk to you now. You need to go back to your room."

"I want to tell her I have to go home."

"We'll talk about seeing her another time. Now you need to go to your room. I'll bring you a book. How would that be?"

Donny started to shake his head, then said, "What book?"

"A science book." Dr. Brenner nodded at the men who had grabbed hold, and they let go. "Would you prefer astronomy or geology?"

They were in the hall now, and he couldn't see Tessa at all. "I'd prefer them both and all my others."

"Well, I can't get the others, but I'll bring you the stars and the stones. How's that?"

He wanted Tessa, but he would take the books because Tessa was gone, but now he knew she was close. Somewhere close and he would find out where. Find her and make her take him home. He imagined sharing his place with Tessa. The thought made his stomach shrink in and his throat get tight and his hands get sticky and his whole body feel like it was lit on fire.

Dr. Brenner's phone rang, and Donny stared at it. His phone would have Tessa in it the way Smith's had. All he needed was Dr. Brenner's phone. But how to get it? No knife. Oh no, no. But somehow.

Dr. Brenner motioned him into the room without windows that felt like the cistern when the lights were off. He didn't have his well of nice pure water, but he had seven books already against one wall and soon two more.

"Excuse me." Dr. Brenner stepped into the hall and answered his phone. With the door closing between them, he said, "What took so long? Never mind. I thought you should know . . . she remembers everything."

CHAPTER

37

Genie plowed up the steep road, gunning it for the final curve, but even so the wheels spun and fishtailed to the edge and wedged. She put the vehicle in gear and turned the key. "That's as far as we can go."

Tessa climbed out of the car into the falling snow. She raised her face and stared up through the twirling flakes to the gray womb that birthed them. Each cold flake that landed on her cheeks melted into tears, but she didn't cry. Her sense of loss was deep and silent.

Had her dad—whose sweatshirt she cuddled up in—done something bad enough to get him killed, bad enough Dr. Brenner wouldn't tell her what? He must know. Or had he only guessed, or was he part of it? She didn't know what to think. If she believed he'd been protecting her mind, she would have to believe her mother knew also, that she had created an illusion of waiting for Dad's return, all the while knowing it impossible. Tessa closed her eyes.

"Why did Daddy go?"

Her mother's hand stroking her cheek. "Sometimes things happen."

"I want him to come back."

Sorrow in her face. "*I wish he would.*" Or had she said *could?*

Smith slid his arm around her waist. "Come on. Let's get inside."

She opened her eyes, her face wet with snow, her lashes clumped. A gust of wind stole her breath and her vision, but she tromped behind Bair and Genie up the final grade to her home that she didn't remember leaving.

Genie unlocked the house door and Roscoe squeezed out onto the porch to rub Tessa's legs. She picked him up, and he wrapped his paws around her neck, rubbing the sides of his mouth against her jaw and purring deep down in his throat. She carried him inside, then released him before he embarrassed himself.

Genie turned. "So are you all right?"

Was there any gauge by which she could say yes? "I need to call the marshal, ask him to look for Dad . . . for Dad's body. The least I can do is not leave him. . . ." Grief kicked her again as she imagined all the snows that had fallen over him.

"I'll do that," Smith said.

"Thanks, but I need to." She would not let him protect her from her responsibility as Dr. Brenner and her mother had. "Verbalizing it is important."

He nodded. "All right, but there's nothing anyone can do now with the snow."

"You're right." She sighed. "I'm sorry for falling apart."

"You're doing fine. Better than fine. You're stronger than people think."

"You mean Dr. Brenner?"

He cupped her shoulders. "If I was out of line, I apologize."

"But you don't think you were."

"I don't know what to think, Tess. It doesn't sit well."

Genie fed the fire, then shut the black metal door. "Are you going to tell us what happened?"

Smith turned to her. "She relayed her father's death, at length, to her therapist, and the less said about it now the better." He looked at Bair. "Maybe we could have some tea. We're all chilled."

As the men went to the kitchen, Tessa clasped herself in her arms and told Genie, "I know what happened, but I need to know why."

"Are you sure you want to?" Genie flicked her dark hair back.

"I have to." Tessa drew a ragged breath. "The monster's still out there."

"What is it with you and the doctor?" Bair spoke softly over the water running into the kettle.

"I hope I'm wrong. I really do. Maybe the man just has a God complex and needs to be integral in his patients' lives. I thought that until today, but learning he knew Tessa's dad cast a different light on things."

"She didn't tell you?"

"She didn't know. He kept it quiet all this time."

Frowning, Bair put the kettle on the stove. "That is odd."

"Plus, he wouldn't say how he knew him or what he knew about the murder unless I left her there overnight."

"Was it a mistake, taking her there?"

Smith looked at her sitting by the stove with Genie. "I don't know. I wish I did."

When the tea had brewed, they brought mugs to the girls and sat down to get their bearings. Wind worried the windows, packing the screens with snow, but the stove drove back the cold.

Tessa set her mug on the low walnut table. "I need to search what's here. Maybe there's a reason Mom kept Dad's things, besides making me believe he was still alive."

"Fair enough." Smith nodded. "Where do we start?"

"Dad's workshop. Mom boxed some things and stored them out there. I've never gone through them."

He touched the bruising on her wrist. "Does this hurt?"

"Not as much as it did."

Bair spread his hands. "What are we looking for? Some sort of record or . . ."

"I don't know." Tessa sighed. "But if Mom knew more than she said, I think it would be out there."

"Let's go." Genie stood up.

None of the coats from the closet fit Bair, but he pulled on a thick rain poncho while Smith replaced his loafers with waterproof boots. The shed wasn't that far, but the snow was getting deep and still coming down, and Tessa said the workshop would be cold until the space heater did its job.

They formed a grim parade to the little log shed he'd entered the night before. Tessa's jaunt up the mountain in search of answers had gutted her. He hoped this wouldn't do the same. They tromped inside, and while Bair started the heater, Tessa unlocked the cupboard. She handed Bair and Genie boxes from the shelves, then pulled one out for him.

As they transferred the weight of the box, he said, "Are you sure you're up to this?"

"I can't depend on anyone else to give me answers. I need them straight from my dad."

And she would need all the support she could get. "Would you all mind if we prayed first?" A heaviness had descended, and he felt disinclined to go into this unprepared. He bowed his head. "Lord, guide this search, we pray, and protect Tessa from what hurt the answers may bring. In your wisdom reveal what you would have her know. We make this prayer in the holy name of Jesus. Amen."

He sat on the bed and set the box beside him. Tessa sat next to him with her side just brushing his as he dug through memorabilia of several different sports, nothing at all about transporting illegal goods or anything else worth dying for. He refolded the box flaps, replaced it, and took another while Tessa scrutinized the contents of hers—cards and photographs mostly. She went slowly, examining each item, absorbing it. He set his new box on the bed but didn't dig in.

She looked up. "I wish I'd known these were out here. Mom must have stowed them because it was too painful." She lifted out a handful of letters. "It's early correspondence from their different colleges, cards from when they were first married."

Probably nothing to do with her dad's death there either.

She pulled out an envelope of pictures and thumbed through the images. "I'm in these."

Smith fit himself around her back to look over her shoulder at the pictures of a happy family. Her spine pressed against the tender spot in his chest, but it felt good to have her nestled there. That close, he felt it the moment she began to shake.

"What's wrong?" He stared at the photo she held, her dad, he presumed, with little Tess on his back, her mom with a hand against her willowy waist, and another man.

"It's him."

He took the photo from her unresisting hand. "This is the man you remember from the woods?"

She nodded. "He must have been a friend." The shaking increased. "I must have known him."

"You were awfully small."

"I would have recognized him." She drew a ragged breath. "Why can't I remember knowing him?"

Bair said, "I don't remember anyone my parents knew when I was five."

"That's not the same."

Smith stroked her arm. "If he was involved in your dad's murder, you probably never saw him again."

With trembling hands she searched the other photos in the batch and found two others that included the man from her nightmares. She looked on the backs for a name. "They must have known him well enough that he didn't need identifying."

Smith stroked her arm. "We'll give those to the marshal."

She looked through the remaining snapshots. No more of the unidentified man. Genie opened a new box and took out a large manila envelope. She raised the flap and peered in, then dropped it with a cry. Before Smith could get to it, Tessa snatched it up and drew out the eight-by-ten photograph. She screamed even after it fell from her hands.

As Bair grabbed the gruesome photo and shoved it back into the envelope, Smith caught the words written on the back. *Don't make me hurt Tessa.*

"Shh," he breathed into her neck, though he wanted to scream along with her. "Shh, dear heart." Who would send such a thing to the people it would hurt most? A monster. Tessa had been right to believe it. "I'm sorry. I'm so sorry."

Her spine straightened. "I want him," she rasped. "I want him found."

"We'll take it all to the authorities."

Sniffling, Tessa eased back and looked into his face. "Why didn't Mom do that?"

Genie said, "She was afraid for her child."

Tessa rubbed the tears from her face. "She obviously knew who she was dealing with, that they would kill without thinking twice, but she must have believed as long as I didn't remember, didn't say a word, we'd be safe. She kept me from remembering by helping me believe Dad was alive." She looked around. "All his things the way he'd left them, his clothes in the closet, as though he could come back and pick up where he'd left off."

Bair shook his head. "But Dr. Brenner —"

"He made me so afraid to recall the trauma without him that I denied it completely."

"Why would he do that?" Bair asked the million-dollar question.

She shook her head. "Protecting me, like Mom."

Maybe, Smith thought. *Maybe*.

CHAPTER

38

As soon as Dr. Brenner delivered the books, Donny added them to the stack. He would read them, but not now. Now he had to find Tessa, to make her come for him. He had trusted Dr. Brenner, but he should have stayed in his place and not left it.

Tessa would help him. He only had to get the phone, get the phone and get out. His heart raced at the thought. He pressed a hand to his chest. Dextrocardia with situs inversus it was called, having his heart on the opposite side of his chest, all his organs reversed from other people's.

Dr. Brenner had shown him the diagram. He had looked at anatomy books before but never realized it a mirror image. If he had held it up against him, the hearts would have matched. He had done that with Dr. Brenner's book, but the doctor had explained about the mirror image. Now he knew.

Part of him wanted to let Dr. Brenner teach him other things, but he couldn't go out at night, couldn't run and find food, find places, find books. They gave him books, then made him put them back. Except Dr. Brenner. He let the books he brought stay, but Donny couldn't stay. He twisted a crackle from his spine.

Everybody stared or looked away. Some of them screamed and

he screamed back. He had been lonely, so lonely, wanting someone to see him, but now he wanted to be invisible. Except to Tessa. He wanted her to look and not look away. He wanted it and he would have it. He was small and he was clever and he had found a way.

He had already undone the bolts. Now he let himself into the vent. He crawled with the stealth of a field mouse under the owl's stare, pulling himself on his stomach, his shoulders only narrow enough when he pressed them down where they shouldn't go. His body was a marvel of ill-design, but it served him now.

As he neared each vent he paused and listened. He knew how the halls went, and he had counted the vents before the turn that would take him where he needed to go. Slowly, slowly, quiet as a mouse, he pulled himself to the vent he wanted.

"Two million dollars and the recording goes away." Dr. Brenner's voice sounded odd and cold. "I assure you Tessa's description was very detailed. Time dims recall, except when a memory is trapped and unprocessed. Then it remains sharp as glass. My explanation follows Tessa's eyewitness account."

Moments of silence.

"It's only a matter of time before they locate the remains. Tessa doesn't know who you are." Dr. Brenner paused. "But I do."

Tessa startled when her phone rang. She had tucked it into her coat pocket but hadn't really expected anyone to call. She looked at the number, heart sinking. "It's Dr. Brenner."

Smith tensed. "Tell him nothing about this." He indicated the photos and the envelope that held the threat. Before, she wouldn't have thought twice about telling him everything, and that loss only added to the others. Had his fatherly affection been nothing but a ruse?

She raised the phone. "Hello?" Then, "Donny?"

"I knew I'd find you. I only had to get the phone and it was easy, so easy to take it off his desk when he wasn't looking."

Tessa pressed her hand to her forehead. "What are you talking about?"

"I miss the stars. I need the stars. And it's snowing, snowing and they wouldn't let me out, and they wouldn't let me see you, or the stars or the snow."

She knew how it was to be locked in there with no freedom and no control. "Did you tell Dr. Brenner what you want?"

"You. I'm telling you. I want to come where you are. I can't stay here."

"But, Donny—"

"They stare and scream. You said he would help, but he isn't helping. Only you can. Only you."

She looked at Smith, whose countenance told her his position. But it was her fault Donny was there, and if Dr. Brenner couldn't be trusted . . .

"You need to come. It's cold out here."

"What? Where are you?"

Donny breathed rapidly. "You can't tell."

"No, I won't tell."

Smith frowned.

"Outside the fence. A drain tunnel in the little valley."

She pictured him huddled somewhere, freezing. *Oh, good grief.* "Okay. Hang up, but keep the phone on in case I can't find you." She disconnected. "I need to get him."

"You can't be serious." Smith looked dumbfounded.

"I know how you feel."

"No, you don't. It wasn't your chest he plunged the knife in, but it could have been. It still could. Think, Tessa."

"He's already out and he's freezing and it's my fault he was taken there. I have to go."

"You can't just spring a lunatic from custody."

"He's no more lunatic than I was."

"You haven't aimed a knife for anyone's heart."

She looked into his face. "He could have killed you, Smith. But he let us go, knowing he'd lose everything. This is too much for him." She knew the feeling. "All he wants are the stars and the snow."

"Oh, is that all he wants? I've heard him speak your name, seen the gleam in his yellow eyes."

Her jaw dropped. "You're jealous of Donny?"

"I am not jealous. I'm trying to warn you. You could be in danger already. Do you really need more?"

Could she be? "Then someone who stabs first and talks later might come in handy."

Smith didn't appreciate the joke.

She took his hand. "Are you coming?"

"How do you expect to get through the snow?"

"Down is all right. Might be harder getting back, but Mom's old Wagoneer is practically a tank." Turning to Bair and Genie, she said, "Can you carry the boxes into the house? We won't be long." Their faces matched Smith's, an incredulous trio. They didn't understand how good it felt to do something for someone else and forget for just a little while what had been done to her.

He had made himself so small, smaller than ever before. Once he had the phone he had not turned back, not cared how the drain hurt, not allowed himself to hurt, only to get out. He shivered in his thin clothes and blinked through his dark glasses at the white, white, white.

The snow kept coming and it was cold. What if she didn't come? If she told them and they took him back. He shivered and shivered. He would run. He would run but he didn't have shoes only slippers and they were wet and his feet were so cold as he waited and waited. But then she was there!

He unfolded from the ball he had become and slipped out of the culvert as she came close enough to see him. Smith came right behind her, and for a minute he was afraid, but it was only Smith and no others, and he had to believe she hadn't told.

She looked worried. "Are you sure about this? It's not good that you left without Dr. Brenner's permission."

"He won't give permission. He wants me to stay with the people who stare, who stare and look away. He wants me to talk and talk to him, but he won't let me go outside. I had to go outside, but I'm cold, too cold."

"You're not dressed to be out here."

"They took my clothes. The attendants took them and I don't like them except the one with pink hair but she wouldn't let me see you and I tried to but they pulled me away. I got mad and Dr. Brenner put me in my room, but I can't stay there."

Smith scowled. "Did you hurt someone when you got mad?"

"No, no, no." He looked at Smith and wished he hadn't stabbed him, but Smith looked better now, all better.

"Come on." Tessa turned and started walking.

Smith motioned him to go next and closed in behind like a fox ready to pounce, but Donny followed Tessa—glad to see her, glad she hadn't told, glad to have even the cold air in his face. He sneezed. Maybe not the cold.

Smith didn't like the situation, but there it was. They reached the Jeep Wagoneer and got in, Tessa driving, and he keeping watch over Donny in the back. He'd been caught once unawares. It wouldn't happen again.

Tessa cranked up the heat until it blew like a furnace. She actually seemed cheerful, as though helping Donny had lifted her spirits. He looked at her sidelong, and his wound throbbed. She understood people's motivations, limitations, and needs. But really, what was she thinking taking charge of this miscreant?

A phone rang, and Smith looked at Tessa, then Donny. He held out his hand, and Donny gave him Dr. Brenner's phone. "Does he know you took this?"

Donny shook his head. "I was clever, very clever."

"Then he might be trying to locate it. The call is from Cedar Grove."

Tessa glanced back. "That was stealing, Donny. You'll get in trouble for it."

Smith pocketed the phone. "Do you understand *now* that you can't take things that aren't yours?"

Donny hugged himself. "I had to call."

"Well, you've made a habit of nicking things you shouldn't."

"Have to eat. And read. I have to read too."

A smile touched Tessa's lips. "We'll feed you. And you can read all the books I have. But you can't take them."

Donny turned aside and stared out the window. "I don't want them. I want *my* books."

Smith arched his eyebrows. "Those were actually someone else's."

Donny muttered under his breath. "My books. My place. Mine."

Tessa sighed. "We'll get it figured out. And forget what I said about the books. If you want some, you can have them."

Donny's face lit, and no wonder. Tessa's kindness might be the first he had known, at least for a long time. He was, after all, a malformed young man who had lived rather tragically to this point.

Smith glanced back and wondered if he might find something for Donny to do when this was all over.

Though the snowfall now was hardly more than fine confetti, so much had previously fallen that they could not even reach the spot Genie had managed before. Smith frowned. "Does it ever stop?"

"Eventually."

"No one thinks to plow?"

"We're low priority. Some of the neighbors have scoops on their trucks, but they'll wait until it's stopped."

Smith looked at Donny with his thin cotton scrub-style pants, T-shirt, and slippers. He pulled off the bomber jacket. "Put this on."

Swallowed up in the coat, Donny beamed. Smith climbed out and opened the back door. "Walk in the track I make." He stamped up the road in the boots he'd borrowed as Tessa made her way beside him, a light in her eyes he hadn't seen for some time. "What?"

She sent him a sidelong smile. "Thank you."

"For?"

She cast a glance over her shoulder at Donny walking delicately in the plowed path. Oh, well, if that was all it took to please her . . .

He was breathing hard by the time they reached the door, his chest throbbing once again. Bair let them in, absorbing with somewhat less than a grimace Donny's toothy mandible, malformed spine, sloping shoulders, and spindly limbs—though his pale, eerie eyes were hidden behind dark glasses.

At first, Smith thought they'd turned off the lights and lit the candles because of Donny's sensitive eyes, but Bair said, "The power's out."

"That happens when it storms." Tessa seemed unconcerned. "The stoves will keep us warm."

He hadn't imagined her in such rustic circumstances but should have. Donny shed the coat and began to reconnoiter, walking around the room, sniffing the plants and touching everything. Working hard to soften her revulsion, Genie watched him from the floor, where she sat cross-legged with the boxes from the shop around her. Donny was an odd and untimely complication, and yet he'd relieved Tessa's gloom and reminded them that—to greater or lesser degrees—everyone struggled.

When Donny reached the shelf with the tiny labyrinths, he went completely still. Tessa walked over there and Smith followed, unable to trust the bloke's harmlessness to the degree Tessa seemed to.

"It's your drawings," Donny whispered. "The lines in the circle."

Tessa nodded. "They're labyrinths."

He ran his finger tenderly over the models.

"It's how I plan what to do on real properties with real plants."

"There's one over my place in the grass," he whispered.

"A very old one. Some people built it for God."

Would Donny have a clue what she was saying? Depended on what books he'd read, Smith supposed.

"My cistern is right in the middle, but I never saw it until your picture showed me." Donny reached into his shirt and pulled out papers that turned out to be Tessa's drawings. Probably the ones that had disappeared from her desk when Donny broke in. He held them out to her, but she gently pressed them back.

"You can keep them."

Again that beatific glow. He slid them back against his skin, which Smith realized no longer smelled like the grave. Grooming must have occurred at Cedar Grove. They'd need to clothe him in something more than he had, though he was more Tessa's size than

Bair's or his own. Maybe she had some warm-ups or something. At some point, they would have to let people know where he was.

Donny didn't want to leave the labyrinths, so they left him there while Tessa went to feed the fire in her room and keep that side of the house warm. Genie must have gone upstairs, and Smith joined Bair, who stood watching Donny silently.

"You suppose God looked away on his begetting?" Bair murmured.

"Only so many times you can limit genetics before someone suffers."

Bair nodded. "Poor bloke."

"He's smitten with Tess."

Bair repeated with irony, "Poor bloke."

"You've recovered, from what I've seen around here." Smith cast him a knowing stare.

"Can't blame me for looking."

"Not just looking. I've actually heard dialogue."

"There've been serious matters to discuss. Tessa's, of course, but that's triggered some revelations from Genie, and . . ." He shrugged.

"What sort of revelations?"

"Things that one wouldn't learn on a first date, typically. We've shown our scars, and she's quite wonderful, actually."

"Well, good. Did you find anything more in the boxes?"

"Nothing blatant, but you know we wouldn't have known the photos mattered. Tessa's going to have to look for herself. We've made sure there are no more gruesome surprises, though."

"Thanks, Bair."

"Thank Genie. That threat infuriated her. She has no tolerance for cruelty and a rather creative penchant for retaliation." Bair beamed.

It obviously stoked Bair's natural attraction to rough sports and fiery women, though he sobered when Genie came down the stairs and walked past them to the pot heating on the great-room stove. With a raise of his brows, Bair went to join her.

Genie grabbed the spoon and potholder. "I thought for a while Tessa's little friend would start grazing on the plants. But I guess he's waiting for dinner after all."

Bair leaned in to sniff when she lifted the pot lid. "Smells good. What is it?"

"Eugenia's gypsy stew."

"Eugenia?"

"I was named for my grandmother." She turned her dusky eyes on him. "When she died I had it legally changed to Genie."

"Well." He flushed. "I'm honored to be in the know."

With the temperature rising on that side of the room, Smith went to sit with Tessa.

Surrounded by the boxes, Tessa went through her dad's things. Not constant, the grief rose and subsided as pictures or other items brought silent tears streaming, or a pang of loss, or a moment of keen remembrance. Emotions and memories held back by her silence found voice as she described them to Smith.

Last night, the pain of recall had driven her deeper into herself than any prayer walk, so deep she'd almost been lost. In that vacuum, she'd been found. Recognized. Cherished. It didn't matter who she was; it mattered who God was.

"Tessa."

She looked up.

Smith tucked a finger under her chin. "Acorn squash baked with butter and caramelized brown sugar."

Her breath got ragged. How could he make vegetables so sensuous? She brought her fingers to his beard-roughened cheek, keenly conscious of his manliness. "I've never seen you with whiskers."

"I was a bit hurried this morning."

"That can't have been this morning."

"Mind-boggling, isn't it. Come here."

Her drew her up onto the couch, caught her face between his hands and kissed her softly, deeply, drawing a response she'd never experienced. Had more than her memory been released? What she'd felt before had been a fledgling, idolizing love compared to this potent, mature exchange. She had been relationally stunted, but now . . .

She rested her forehead against his. "Was it last century Rumer Gaston had me so annoyed?"

"At least. The dark ages when I thought nothing mattered more than impressing him."

"It feels like time bent when I couldn't move forward anymore, bringing me back to the place I had to start over."

Smith nodded. "Time is a human construct. God works outside of it."

"Smith, I don't remember how I got down the mountain."

"Last night? I carried you."

"Against doctor's orders?"

"Quite against."

She put her hand to his chest. "Are you hurting?"

"Not from that. Just everything you've gone through."

"I'll be all right." She looked into his face. "I got to the center and found the Father, like you said."

His eyes lit. "That's brilliant."

"Now my spirit feels strong, though the rest is still shaky."

"Your spirit is God's province. I'll work on the rest."

"You already have. More than you know." She nestled close and sighed. "Do you really think Dr. Brenner is involved?"

Donny turned from the window where he'd been watching the storm. "Dr. Brenner talked about you."

She looked up. "What?"

"On his phone. He said you remembered, and he wants two million dollars to make it go away."

CHAPTER

39

Smith stared at Donny. "Are you sure?"

"I was at the vent. I heard him, but he didn't know it. He didn't know I was there."

"Donny." Smith got to his feet. "Could you tell who he was talking to? Did you hear a name?"

"He said, 'I know your name.' But he didn't say the name. I'm hungry." Donny walked over to the table. "It smells better here than there. I'll eat now."

Smith pulled Tessa up. "We need to get out of here."

"Look outside." She pointed to the blizzard-whitened window. They'd been shaken up like a snow globe, and the flakes flew wildly past. "It's almost dark. The wind is drifting the snow, and we won't get the car out."

"We can't stay here."

"If we can't get out, he can't get in."

Maybe. Probably. As the wind howled around the cabin, he nodded reluctantly. "As soon as it's clear, we'll go."

"What difference does it make? He'll find me. Wherever I go, he'll—"

"Don't. Fear is not productive."

"You sound like Dr.—" Her voice broke. "I can't believe he—" Tears sprang to her eyes.

"I'm sorry. I wanted to be wrong." Anger burned inside with a cold, steady flame. He felt equal parts avenger and protector, but was he truly either? "We'll stop them." Somehow, God willing, they would end this.

While Tessa helped Genie serve the meal, Smith took Bair aside and told him what Donny had heard.

"Sure he's not making it up?"

"How would he know about blackmail?"

"Depends what books he's read."

"I don't think so."

Bair frowned. "We can keep watch in shifts."

Smith nodded. "Tessa doesn't think anyone can get through until the storm stops, but I'll bunk Donny on the couch. He's pretty aware, I'd guess. I'm staying in Tessa's room, and I need you and Genie to know—"

"You don't have to say it."

"Thanks, Bair. I'm glad you're here."

Bair fitted his shoulder with a hammy grip. "I've got you covered, mate."

Tessa turned at her bedroom door, expecting to say good night, but Smith pressed in. "I'm staying with you."

"No, Smith."

"I'm not suggesting anything untoward." He arched his brows. "I'd like to, but what I want right now is to keep you safe."

"Then you won't be." She drew herself up. "You're an architect, not a bodyguard."

"I'd like to think I'm not wholly ineffective."

"You're already injured."

"Donny caught me by surprise. This time I'll be watching."

She shook her head. "I saw you die once."

"As you see, I didn't quite."

A flicker of desperation caught her. "Nothing's going to happen."

"We'll be ready just in case." He went over and drew the wooden blinds, tipping the slats so he could see out, but all except the glow of the stove and two candles was blocked from outside. He went into the bathroom, checked the window lock, and closed those blinds completely.

Tessa leaned in the doorway. "No one could fit through that."

"Donny could."

"Well, he's already inside."

"Another reason I'm staying in here."

She didn't need reminding of Donny's frightening penchant for invading her room, but she doubted she'd close her eyes for one moment with Smith beside her. "The thing is, I'm—"

"Attracted?" The corner of his mouth pulled.

She paced. "Suddenly you're . . . all . . . manly and irresistible."

"Irresistible, hmm?" He snagged her, pulled her up by the elbows and kissed her.

"That's not helping."

"Believe me, it is." He brought a hunger to the next kiss that all but left her gasping.

"Smith." She pressed her palm to his sternum. "I'm telling you my arrested development is accelerating like Bair on a straight road."

"And I'm telling you, it's all right." He was laughing. "I promise." He grabbed her up again. "More than all right. I'm ecstatic."

"Ecstatic? This is a terrible time. I should be thinking of—"

"What, Tess? The fact that you feel this is fantastic. After years overshadowed by fear and guilt, don't you think it's time to live and love as the woman you are?"

She hadn't thought of it that way. She didn't want that monster to have one more day of her life, but as long as he was out there . . . "I have to finish this."

"I know." He sobered. "Which is why I'm in here. I'll sleep on the floor."

She released a slow breath. "You can't. It gets frigid and you're barely over pneumonia." Now that her mind had cleared, she wanted him close. Dr. Brenner had betrayed her to the very real flesh-and-blood man who had murdered her dad and now knew that she'd spoken.

Smith pulled her close. Still sentiently aware of his masculinity, she felt like Eve with her eyes suddenly opened. Exactly how had Eve offered that fruit?

"I'll wash up upstairs." His gaze sharpened. "Let me back in when I knock."

She changed into her mother's flannel pajamas, brushed her hair, her teeth, washed her face, and stared into the mirror. Why had this happened? What had her daddy done?

Smith came back dressed in navy lounge pants and a white T-shirt. Even in college she'd never seen him so informal. He smelled of shaving cream and toothpaste, his hair stood up around his cowlick, and he slow-blinked at her through his glasses. She wanted to slip them off and feel his freshly shaved skin. His mouth had never looked so expressive, so sensual. Her heart thumped.

"Come here."

She went to him.

"I will guard your body with my own. You're safe with me."

"I can't really say the same."

He lowered his mouth and kissed her, burying his hands in her hair. She felt the rush and pull of his heart beneath her palm and yearned for him with an aching intensity.

"Get into bed."

She pulled aside the covers and got in. He tucked them around her, then went to the closet and pulled out a spare blanket that he wrapped around himself like a cape, blew out one candle, then the next. Her eyes were riveted as he pulled out the drafting table chair and sat down.

"What are you doing?"

"Don't worry. I mastered desk sleeping at Cornell."

"You'll be miserable. There's room here."

"I'd intended that, but it's . . . better this way."

"Smith."

"Go to sleep. Believe me, I will. I'm bushed."

She stared at him in the glow from the stove that glinted off his teeth and the glasses he laid on the table. Then he turned the chair around, folded his arms, and rested his head. He was right. The only way she'd sleep was if he stayed there. She rolled to her side and murmured, "Good night."

"Night, Tess."

She said "I love you" into her pillow and closed her eyes. Physical and emotional fatigue slipped in like goblins and dragged her down. Tomorrow they'd have to dig out, decide what to do about Donny and go to the marshal, then find someplace to hide until this was over. She couldn't think of that now. The breath seeped through her lips. Tomorrow.

"Open your eyes." The voice was low, but she knew it. "Don't make a sound."

A chill spread down her spine. She looked up over her shoulder at the face she dreaded—aged but unchanged in menace. He stared back from across the room. By Smith. She shot up, gripping the covers against her, though they'd be no protection from the gun he held.

Smith's head was down. He hadn't moved. "What did you do to him?"

"I injected him with thiopental. I'd intended it for you, but now you'll have to come willingly."

"How did you get in?"

"I lifted the key from Ryan years ago. You remember when."

Her throat constricted. Her hands felt like damp clay. All these years he'd had a key. That was almost more frightening than his being there now. "Who are you?"

"Don't you know Uncle Ev?"

Evan Bly. The name came like a gunshot.

"Why won't you leave me alone?"

"I have. All this time, Tessa. All you had to do was keep your mouth shut." The glint of his eyes narrowed in the glow of the coals. "Now get up."

She trembled, unable to leave the bed, as though he were still a nightmare that she had only to resist.

"Here's how this looks in the morning." His voice grew shockingly cold. "A house full of bloody corpses, or one troubled girl dead on the mountain. Your choice."

Tears stung. Though he'd obviously rather not leave carnage for the investigators, she had no doubt he would kill them all to silence her. She pushed aside the covers and got up.

He motioned her out of the bedroom to the side door into the mudroom. "Put on the coat."

It was her dad's old parka. She pulled it on, choking back the sobs in her throat.

"Boots."

She prayed no one would hear him and surprise a bullet that

would start the massacre. She slipped into her rubber-soled boots, her hands shaking with the ties she tugged over the leather upper. She reached automatically for gloves.

"Good," he murmured.

She straightened.

"After you." He nodded toward the door.

It was unlocked still from his ingress. He had not entered through the front past Donny, and she was glad for that. She had to believe they'd be safe. He had no reason to kill anyone who hadn't seen him.

She sank knee-deep into the drifted snow. How had she thought it would keep him out? Being an October storm, the temperature was not cruel, but it was cold enough to make her shiver. Or was that fear?

She tramped past the workshop, up the slope where she'd taken Smith the night before. A troubling thought entered. Smith had heard everything she told Dr. Brenner, and Dr. Brenner knew it. But this one might not.

"Why did you kill my dad?"

"I didn't."

"You ordered it." The fact that his hands had not drawn her dad's blood did not mean they would not draw hers.

"Ryan made a very bad choice." Evan ducked under a branch, casting the powdery snow into the night air, still and windless. "He betrayed me."

The gibbous moon shone with intensity in the bitter, clear sky, reflecting off the newly fallen snow like daylight. Wending between the gangly pines, she kicked her way up the powdered slope. She reached the granite boulders heaped up like a pile of giant skulls with shadowy indentations forming sockets and mouths.

She started past, but he said, "No. Climb."

She turned, confused.

"Up the rocks."

So he didn't mean to shoot her. He'd called her a troubled girl. Her breath caught jaggedly. He would make her fall. What should she do? He might not want to shoot her, but he'd pull the trigger if she forced him. She started up the crevice between the lowest boulders, gripping the snowy stone with her gloved hands, and suddenly remembered holding his. He had reached for her hand and she'd taken it, letting him walk her down the mountain after what he'd done to her dad. It sickened her.

She reached for a handhold and jolted at the cry behind her.

Donny had sprung out of the craggy shadows and knocked Evan Bly to the ground. He must have lost the gun in the snow, because he flailed with Donny's hands around his neck. In only moments, he flung Donny aside, but Bair rushed up from behind and used his fists like iron demolition balls. Uncle Ev lay limp and bloody in the virgin snow.

"Have you something to tie him?" Bair gasped, rubbing his knuckles.

She scrambled to the ground, knelt, and all but ripped the laces from her boots. Bair rolled Evan over, oblivious to the face pressed into the snow, and bound his hands with both laces. They all three stood over him, breathing hard; then Donny dropped to his knees, thrust his hands into the drifts, and brought out the gun.

Tessa looked from one to the other, eyes shining with tears. "How—"

"Donny heard voices and saw you go out the door and up the mountain." Bair rolled Evan to his back. "He tried to wake Smith, but—"

"The monster doped him."

Bair nodded. "So he came to get me and we took a parallel route. Good thing the snow muted our steps. That one's silent as a wolf." He nodded toward Donny, who flashed his mouthful of teeth. "But I'm, well, you know."

She rushed at him, hugged his broad chest, and clung while he patted her back with the mitts that had driven consciousness far from Evan Bly's brain. "All right, Tessa. All right."

She let go and hugged Donny after Bair relieved him of the gun. "Thank you."

"I didn't hurt him."

She laughed. "You were perfect."

Bair studied the gun's mechanism and set the safety. "I'll wait here while you call the authorities."

Tessa nodded, elation rising as she and Donny hurried down the slope.

Smith groaned. His head spun; his stomach roiled. Lead infused his limbs. Had he relapsed?

"Smith."

He dragged his eyelids up his blurry eyeballs. "Wha . . ."

"Can you hear me?" Tessa's hand was icy on the back of his neck.

He dragged his head up from his arms, groping for his glasses.

"Here." She put them in his hand. "Don't fight it. You've been drugged. I just wanted you to know Bair's on the mountain with Dad's killer."

He jolted up in the chair.

She gripped his shoulder. "It's all right. He's bound and Bair has his gun. We called the marshal."

"We?"

"I called. But Donny's the one we need to thank. He heard the monster taking me up the mountain."

Smith groaned again. "Coffee."

"Do you mean tea?"

"I mean wretched, black, inky coffee. My head's a carnival ride."

"Don't try to get up. I'll be right back."

He pressed both palms to the drafting table and hung his head like a bowling ball from his aching neck. Tessa. On the mountain. With the monster and his gun. His breath came in shallow bursts. He warped in and out of consciousness until Tessa came back with a mug of coffee. He blew the steam and slurped it hot into his mouth, little by little getting it into his reluctant stomach, though he'd have preferred to infuse it directly into his veins and avoid the tastebuds.

He reached over and gripped her wrist. "Are you all right?"

She nodded. "I wouldn't be if you hadn't been here."

He must be fuzzier than he realized. "I did nothing."

"If he hadn't drugged you, it would have been me. He'd have carried me out and Donny wouldn't have heard our voices."

Smith swallowed. "So he meant to kill you."

She nodded. "And make it look like suicide."

"A drug screen . . ."

"Maybe he'd have left the needle next to me so it looked like I put myself to sleep in the place I'd watched my dad die. Or maybe so I'd freeze to death before I woke. I don't know."

"He really is a monster."

She nodded. "But we have him."

"Bair . . ."

"Will need some ice for his knuckles."

Smith's mouth pulled up. "Thank God he was here."

"And Donny. And you."

He drained the last of the coffee. "Tessa—"

Donny pressed through the door. "He's here."

"The marshal?"

He shook his malformed head. "Dr. Brenner."

"Where?" Tessa's gaze shot to the window, where dawn brightened the spaces between the wooden slats.

"He's coming to the door."

Smith gripped her arm. "You can't trust him." He blinked the bleariness from his eyes.

"I know." She turned. "Donny. Go very quietly upstairs and tell Genie what's happening. Stay there with her."

As Donny retreated, Smith said, "What are you doing? We might need him." Especially if he couldn't shake the dopey effects of the drug.

"I don't want Genie taken by surprise."

"We can slip out the side."

She shook her head. "I'm facing him, Smith. The marshal's on his way, but right now I want answers."

The knock came on the door. Smith groaned. "Help me up." He gripped her shoulders and pulled himself to a wobbly stance. Together they went out to the great room. He leaned against the wall beside the window as she pulled the door open only as wide as she.

"What are you doing here?" Tessa's tone was as cold as he'd ever heard it.

Dr. Brenner squared his shoulders. "We need to talk."

"You said I wasn't ready."

"That was yesterday."

"And it's barely today." She squinted out at the blushing sky.

"Let us in, Tessa. Now."

A man in a suit stepped away from the wall. "Ms. Young. Special Agent Tyson. FBI."

CHAPTER

40

Staring at the badge he offered, Tessa felt Smith move in behind her as she pulled the door open. Dr. Brenner looked up, then back to her as he crossed the threshold. She closed the door behind them and folded her arms. "What is this?"

Agent Tyson took a quick survey of the room. "You could be in danger."

She expelled a short laugh. "Oh, really?"

"Please sit down, Ms. Young, Mr. . . ."

"Chandler. Smith Chandler." He managed not to slur, but looked as though he needed to sit.

They dropped down together on the couch. Across from them, the gray-haired agent's stomach formed a bowl beneath his jacket when he took a seat, though the rest of him was lanky. Dr. Brenner took the other red chair, crossed his leg, and folded his hands over his knee in a position she'd seen so many times.

"Dr. Brenner told me you remembered what you witnessed." The agent spoke with a pushed-air kind of voice that sounded as though he'd lost half his vocal cords.

She didn't understand. Dr. Brenner had blackmailed the FBI?

"I'd like to hear it from you."

She looked from one to the other. "I saw my dad killed."

"I'm sorry for your loss, Ms. Young. But I've waited a long time for you to remember that."

Almost the same words Dr. Brenner had used. She frowned. "What do you mean?"

The agent took a photo from his jacket pocket and laid it on the table. "Evan Bly. We believe he sold technological secrets sensitive to the Federal Government."

She looked at the picture, a somewhat younger version of the man who wanted her dead. "What does that have to do with my dad?"

"Ryan Young transported the prototypes. He claimed ignorance of the contents, said he was doing a favor for a friend. Nonetheless, he would have been implicated if he had not agreed to assist us in exposing Mr. Bly."

The betrayal that cost him his life.

"We fitted the last delivery with a tracking device to lead us to Bly's contact. The device must have been discovered, because the package could not be traced past the point of your father's delivery. Dr. Brenner said you were also an eyewitness to that delivery."

"I was five years old."

He dipped his head. "It's not much by itself. But if we locate your father's remains and you can describe what happened that night, that's a solid case."

"I don't understand. You knew he killed my dad?"

"Your father disappeared after assisting a sting. There were suspicions."

"Didn't you assume it was Bly?"

"He was interrogated as a person of interest. He gave nothing up. I wanted you to identify him in a lineup, but your mother refused. Dr. Brenner concurred. They said you were too deeply traumatized." The agent glanced at Dr. Brenner. "I know now that your mother received a threat. She believed you were in mortal danger."

Dr. Brenner nodded. "She showed me a photograph—"

"I have it." Tessa repressed a shudder.

Dr. Brenner's tone softened. "When your mother passed, I brought you to Cedar Grove. I hoped to help you access the memory in a safe environment and put all this to rest. But you had encased it in an entire mythology and denied there had been a trauma."

She swallowed the lump of tears in her throat. That denial had given Evan Bly years of freedom.

"The threat is real, Ms. Young. Now that you've remembered, you could be in danger."

She turned to Dr. Brenner. "Because you told him?"

He looked startled.

Smith roused. "You set her up, just like her dad. Used her as bait."

Dr. Brenner frowned. "I wanted to keep her safely in the center. You refused."

"That's no excuse."

"I tried to make myself the target, but Bly didn't show, and now I'm afraid he'll go for Tessa."

"He did." Her voice cracked.

A siren penetrated the morning, the marshal coming at last.

"Did?" The agent straightened.

"Bair's holding him on the mountain, where he intended to kill me."

Agent Tyson sprang up. "Why didn't you say so?"

"I didn't know who to trust."

Dr. Brenner gave her a grim appraisal. The siren died, and a minute later the marshal banged on the door. The officers of the law exchanged credentials, and Special Agent Tyson took jurisdiction.

Marshal Filby didn't object. Younger than her by three years, he'd held the office only a year since obtaining his criminal justice degree.

Tessa went to the closet for a coat. "I'll show you where they are."

Alone with Dr. Brenner, Smith glowered.

"You don't look good, Smith. Is there something—"

"He doped me."

"A barbiturate?"

"Whatever it was, it knocked me out." Smith rubbed his face, still barely able to focus. "He meant it for Tessa, so he could take her out where her dad died and leave her to freeze or push her to her death, an apparent suicide."

The doctor paled. "I thought I had provoked him into coming after me. The FBI staked out my property all night. When he didn't make his move, we rushed here, or as near rushing as we could on these roads."

"Too late." Smith pressed his palms to his eyes.

"It must be a zero-elimination barbiturate and you're in the half-life still." Dr. Brenner checked his eyes, his pulse. Noticing Donny's pillow and blanket, he said, "You slept here last night, to keep watch?"

Smith did not correct his misconception. "Not a very good watch."

"A fast-acting drug such as thiopental would have given you no chance to react."

Smith closed his eyes. When he opened them again, Tessa and Dr. Brenner were talking.

Dr. Brenner stood at the window looking out. "I knew them both. We trained and served together as volunteer firemen two years before you were born. After that Ryan said he had too much to lose, my practice was taking off, and Bly went his own way."

Bair had come in and stood behind Tessa's chair. Genie was stirring what might be oatmeal on the kitchen stove, so the power had come back on. There was no sign of Donny.

"Your dad and I stayed in touch. He bought his plane and I went to see it. That's the picture you saw."

"But what about Bly?" Tessa stood up and crossed to the window. "Couldn't you tell he was evil?"

"Ryan never suspected. He thought the best of everyone." He turned. "I had caught Bly in a lie several times, and it struck me that there had been little need for prevarication. He'd simply done it. That's always a flag."

"So what happened?"

"Bly showed up again and commissioned your dad to make some deliveries. Sensitive material he didn't want trusted to the mail carriers."

"And Dad did it?"

"He had no reason not to, Evan Bly being an old and charismatic friend. Agent Tyson's information stunned him."

"And he went to you."

Dr. Brenner looked back out the window. "He asked if I thought it possible. I told him yes, and he should watch his back." He gathered himself and faced her. "I'm sorry I didn't do more."

Tessa gulped back tears. "What more could you have done?"

"I've asked that so many times."

She sniffed. "I'm sorry I called you a liar."

He pulled a grim smile. "Understandable. It doesn't help that Smith has a poor opinion."

"He didn't know."

"No, I didn't." Smith pulled up to sit, clearing his head with a shake.

"In one sense you were right." Dr. Brenner folded his arms. "I did grow overprotective and overly fond of Tessa. But I'd promised her mother."

"Promised her what?" Tessa's voice rasped.

"Not to give up until you were whole."

Tears glistened in Tessa's eyes. "That took both of you. And God."

"That's a powerful support system," Dr. Brenner said. "I suggest you hold on to it."

"Does that mean you're not through with me?"

"I hope not." He rested a hand on her shoulder. "But I have an issue to deal with that you won't be happy about."

Tessa looked into his face. "Your missing phone?"

"How did you . . ." He cocked his head. "He's here, isn't he?"

"Upstairs."

"That little weasel. How did he get out?"

"I don't know. He just called for pickup."

"And you brought the person who stabbed Smith into your home?" He turned. "Smith?"

"She's hard to resist."

Tessa planted her hands on her hips. "He isn't dangerous."

Dr. Brenner frowned. "While I have concluded that he acted in self-defense, having only a limited grasp of his actions, I have not determined whether he would repeat them."

"He saved my life." She raised her chin. "He jumped a man with a gun to protect me; then Bair did the heavy work."

"There's a lot he doesn't know, Tessa."

"But have you known anyone who wants to learn things the way he does?"

"Yes, actually. A young lady who pored over everything she could find about labyrinths. Are you still going to build this last one?"

She nodded. "I signed a contract. And the architect in charge is big on integrity."

Smith got to his feet, found them functional. He got the phone he'd left on the counter, brought it to Dr. Brenner. The look on the man's face was priceless.

"I suppose we'll address the concept of personal property next."

Bair grinned. "Should I bring him down?"

"Definitely."

Tessa turned. "Has he told you his story?"

"Some. I've gleaned more. His mother gave birth and rejected him. The midwife took him in but kept him hidden. I don't know her name. He calls her Nursey. She left him a document naming him, though: Donny Griswold."

"Birth certificate?"

"That's my guess."

Smith frowned. "Did he say why she left him in the cistern?"

"There was an incident, one at least, in which people broke into his room to torment him. I think she feared she'd be unable to prevent it happening again."

"But why keep him hidden?" Tessa looked pained.

Smith spread his hands. "There's a paucity of charity in this world."

Dr. Brenner nodded. "Ignorance and fear."

She sighed. "What now?"

"He hasn't had any controls or expectations since she put him in the cistern. He developed his own code, but while the midwife seems to have instilled a fear of punishment, he has no clear boundaries." Dr. Brenner looked up. "Well, Donny. What have you to say for yourself?"

Donny stopped partway down the staircase. "I only borrowed

the phone. It had Tessa in it and I had to call her but no one let me call when I saw her and I had to."

"And sneaking out of a locked facility? How did you manage that?"

Donny only grinned.

Genie said, "Would anyone like some oatmeal?"

"Yes." Donny came down the rest of the way. "And Coke."

CHAPTER

41

Just days after the storm, the snow had completely melted and it was warm as Indian summer. Standing between Smith and Genie at the cemetery, Tessa stared at the coffin that held her dad's remains. He was truly gone, not waiting, lost in the labyrinth, anymore.

Her grief would heal with time—now that the monster had been arrested and charged. She would have to testify, but the case against him was solid for conviction. Twenty years too late, but in terms of eternity she shouldn't worry that Evan Bly's punishment would not last long enough. Her challenge was to forgive, so the rest of her life was not contaminated by his evil as her other years had been.

Smith circled her waist as the presiding minister concluded the prayers. Surprisingly dry-eyed, she looked up at him with all the gratefulness and love she felt. Donny, in dark glasses and hooded poncho, came over and hugged her. Since her embrace on the mountain, he'd taken every chance to make up for the dearth of human contact.

"You're sad."

"I'm okay, Donny."

When Dr. Brenner approached, her throat tightened at the

satisfaction she saw in his eyes. He'd given her time when the waiting must have been so frustrating. She took his hands. "Thank you for helping me all these years."

He squeezed hers. "It wasn't a favor, Tessa. I wanted justice, but more than that I wanted you to find peace. Ryan was my friend, your mother adamant in her hopes for your recovery, but you were the one who made it matter."

She bit her lip. "I need to ask you something."

"Ask."

"The private scholarship that took me through Cornell."

His jaw twitched.

"Was it you?"

"I'm not married and I've done very well in my practice, not to mention the numerous hours I've billed you."

Now the tears came. "I don't know how to thank you."

"It was my pleasure."

"When I'm back in Maryland, can I keep a phone appointment once in a while to talk about Dad—or complain about Smith?"

He smiled. "Call after hours so I won't have to charge." He spread his arms and gave her a brief hug. Then he turned to Smith. "Look after her."

"I intend to." Smith extended his hand, and they shook.

Dr. Brenner turned. "Ready to go, Donny?"

"To your house, right? Not that other place—not Cedar Grove and the locked doors."

"Cedar Grove for some of the time, and my house at night. For now."

"And lots of books."

"All the books you want."

Tessa watched them walking to the silver BMW, Dr. Brenner and his new project. Her heart swelled. Bair cupped Genie's elbow as they turned from the gravesite; then their hands slipped together as they started for the car. Tessa glanced at Smith, who gave her a knowing smile.

The minister came to her. "May Christ's peace be yours."

She nodded, throat tight. "It is."

⌐⌐⌐

Patches of snow remained on the mountainside above Tessa's house, but the sun shone warmly as Smith reached down to stroke Roscoe, sunning on the porch where neighbors had left flowers and candles and notes.

Tessa stopped and stared at the outpouring of support. "How did they know?"

"It's a small community," Genie said. "Word gets around." She slipped an arm around Tessa's shoulders. "I don't think you realize how many friends you have."

Smith could only imagine what it meant to her now.

Tessa stooped and picked up a hand-scribbled note tucked into a small potted ivy. Smith looked over her shoulder as she murmured, " 'Sorry about your dad. He was a good guy.' " It was signed Lyle Donner. She looked down at the roof and bare backyard of her downhill neighbor. "It would have taken quite an effort for him to bring this plant up."

In the sunshine next to her cat, she read one card after another. Smith sat next to her, resting his forearms on his knees. After a while, Bair came out and handed him the cell phone. Smith read the number and frowned, then raised it to his ear. "Yes?"

"Um, Smith?"

"What is it, Danae?"

"I've been trying to reach you. Do you still not have your phone?"

"That's right."

"I wish you'd get it. It's really awkward going through Bair."

He moved his hand to Tessa's knee. She had grown still, though she tried to look as if she wasn't listening.

"What is it you needed?"

"I was hoping we could talk."

He looked into the azure sky. "I don't think so. I'm seeing someone else."

"Really." Her voice held distinct disappointment. "Because Ed and I, well, it's over and—"

"I'm sorry. I know you had big hopes." It surprised him that he did feel sorry for her.

"Is it serious, this new thing?"

"I hope to marry her."

Tessa looked up. He slid his arm around her shoulders.

"That's . . . awfully fast, isn't it?" A hint of petulance colored her tone.

"I've known her for years."

"While we were together? Did I meet her?"

"Just the other day. In the trailer."

"The landscaper?"

"Landscape architect. We went to school together. She's brilliant."

"Smith, I . . . I should be happy for you. But I have to say I'm confused. The other day—"

"I should have told you then. It wasn't fair to either of you."

"It's just that you always seemed reticent about marriage. Rushing into it now could be reactionary."

"No, believe me, it's not." He looked into Tessa's face. "It's the most carefully thought out thing I've ever considered."

"Well. Knowing how diligently you consider everything, I guess that's saying a lot."

"It's saying everything I have to say—except good-bye."

"So that's it?"

"Good-bye, Danae." He hung up and lifted Tessa's chin. "I'm sorry you had to hear that. I don't think she'll call again, but if she does, I promise—"

Tessa stretched up and kissed him. Where was the girl who took everything so personally?

He brought her hand to his lips. "I want so much to put a ring on this finger."

"Because . . ."

"It would mean you're mine."

She rested her head against his shoulder. "I think it's—"

"Smith. Tessa," Bair burst out. "Come see this."

"What is it?" Smith helped her up, and they hurried inside to the TV in the corner.

"Rumer Gaston," Bair said. "Indicted for tax fraud."

"What the blazes?" Smith expelled a breath.

The anchor spoke with a photo behind her of Gaston shaking hands with celebrities inside his opulent lobby. "Casino mogul Rumer Gaston has been indicted for tax fraud. . . ." The newscast showed several casinos, hotels, and properties, but made no mention of a home being built. Had Gaston kept it secret from investigators?

Bair raised his brows when Smith speed-dialed the cell phone. "What are you doing?"

"Seeing where we stand." He moved off to the side.

Wrapping herself in her arms, Tessa couldn't help wondering if she would not finish the labyrinth after all. Surprisingly, she still wanted to re-create that prayer path—as a pilgrimage to the Father.

Smith hung up and rejoined them. "I spoke with his house counsel."

"You mean your dad?" Tessa asked.

"One of the partners, Zachary Brandenburg. He said Gaston signed title over to Petra before charges were filed."

"Is that legal?" Bair asked.

"He dotted his i's and crossed his t's. The property belongs to Petra."

Tessa stared. "He didn't do it for her sake. He must think he'll slip these charges and get it back."

"Will he?" Genie joined them.

"Mr. Brandenburg is not Gaston's criminal counsel, but he has the inside track on the financial picture and thinks there's no chance. The IRS was swindled. There's a whiff of laundering as well."

"So . . ." She looked from Smith to Bair. "Are we building for Petra?"

"That's my next call."

Tessa reached for the phone. "Let me do it."

He keyed the number and handed the phone over.

When Petra answered, Tessa said, "Petra, this is Tessa Young. I just heard about Mr. Gaston, and—"

"Please don't pretend you're sorry. You and I both know he got exactly what he deserves."

Tessa cleared her throat. "I was wondering about you. The lawyer said Mr. Gaston signed over the property."

"You still want to build your labyrinth?"

"We didn't know whether you'd want to pursue it now, or—"

"You know what? Take it."

Tessa's breath stopped. "What?"

"I'll send you the title."

She fell speechless. "Are you . . . Petra, are you serious?"

"I never wanted that godforsaken place anyway. You can take it or it can rot."

Her whole being trembled. "I'll take it." She looked up at Smith, whose expression had gone from concerned to baffled.

Take what? he mouthed.

She gave Petra her mailing address, then asked her again if she was sure.

"You stuck your neck out for me. You know how often that happens in my world? It doesn't. I don't know why you want that old ruin, but it's yours."

"Thank you, Petra. I hope you find what you're looking for too." Tessa closed the phone. "If Gaston weasels out of this indictment, he won't find Petra or the property waiting."

Smith expelled his breath. "She's giving you the land."

Tessa nodded. "Too isolated for her, I think."

Smith's throat worked. "Then I guess we're still building."

She searched his face. "I want to build the labyrinth, Smith, but I don't have money for anything like the house you designed."

Smith drew himself up. "Yes, well, my spoon is shiny enough for that much."

"Are you saying you want to build your house on my land?"

"Our house on your land." He raised her chin. "I still haven't done this right. I don't have the ring or anything. But I'm asking you to marry me."

Genie raised her brows and breathed, "Whoa."

Tessa's breath grew shallow with emotion. "Would we keep our design?"

Smith laughed. "It's more our design than Gaston and Petra's."

"We could do without the mirrors."

"No, we can't."

"And the Roman bath."

"I'm especially attached to the bath, but I'd prefer it in blue Spanish tile."

She shook her head. "Is it possible?"

"It's more than possible. By this time next year, we could be living there. If"—he took her in his arms—"all those questions meant yes."

"We could open the labyrinth for people who need the path?"

"Anything you want."

Bair cleared his throat. "I think I'll just take this." He plucked the phone from Tessa's hand. "And go where it's not quite so . . ." He and Genie slipped away.

Tessa tipped her face up. "You know when I said I'd rather be anywhere than on a date with you?"

"I remember it clearly."

"I was lying."

He smiled. "I know."

She shoved his chest. "Arrogant."

He caught her hand and held it against his chest. "Here's where you say yes."

CHAPTER

42

Tessa straightened in the sun-drenched morning and looked across the thriving labyrinth as he approached. After seven months, he could tell it still caught her by surprise to realize he was there, loving her. But he didn't mind. She might never take it for granted, and that was a good thing.

She had decided against the gate, but the boxwood stood waist-high around her—separate plants that would grow together until they were indistinguishable. He hoped for that same thing between him and the woman he took in his arms. "I scheduled the final inspection for tomorrow."

Her eyes shone. "It'll take a little longer out here."

"We have time." He drenched his hands with her hair. "Are you busy?"

"Not really, why?"

"There's a Roman bath inside, filled with hot, scented water. I'd like to share it with my wife."

She looked into his face. "I love those words."

He smiled. "I love you." He couldn't get enough of her, the days they spent honing each other's art, arguing the best ways to do things, the evenings they spent sharing hopes and dreams.

The times he cherished her with soul and body. Oh yes, life was beautiful.

Hooking her with his arm, he led her toward the house. "I hope I don't have it too hot. I'd hate to boil my egg."

She shoved his side, and he tossed back his head and laughed.

ACKNOWLEDGMENTS

Thanks to all the people who were part of this book:

Jessica Lovitt for the characters Smith and Tessa,
the labyrinth motif, and much, much more.

Steve Meredith for architectural expertise.

Kelly McMullen for on-site setting stomping—
glad you got your sandal back from the sea.

Karen and David Mohler
for Maryland history, prayer, and friendship.

Tommy Courtney, Maryland waterman,
for fish straight from the net and great stories.

Tom Gandolfo for "paucity."

David Ladd for encouragement and insight.

Karen Schurrer, editor, for services over and above.

My husband, Jim, my daughter, Jessie, and my mom, Jane,
for proofing and loving me through it all.

Anxious to solve a long-kept family mystery, Lance Michelli sets off for an old Sonoma villa. But diving into past secrets may jeopardize both his life and the life of the villa's beautiful owner.

Secrets

When Lance Michelli returns home with Rese Barrett, the revelation of his family's secrets sends him on yet another quest. As he uncovers truths that could change everything forever, Lance finds himself caught between two women he loves.

Unforgotten

Sofie Michelli hopes to make a new start, but then a phone call from New York causes an emotional whirl wind. How can she even begin to handle the problems now haunting her?

Echoes

When a young woman stumbles out of the Hanalei Mountains with no previous memories, Cameron Pierce agrees to find out what happened to her. But knowing the truth will cost more than they ever expected.

Freefall

When Jill Runyan reenters Morgan Spencer's life, the news she brings will either set him free or bring him to his knees. Either way, his life is going to change forever.

The Still of Night

Still believing in fairy tales and miracles, Alessi Moore pulls into the tiny town of Charity. But its beauty hides a lurking darkness—and not all is as it seems.

Halos